MW00614854

Redeeming the Outlaw

Cross Family Saga, Volume 2

Jodi Basye

Published by Jodi Basye, 2022.

REDEEMING THE OUTLAW

First edition. June 30, 2022.

Copyright © 2022 Jodi Basye.

ISBN: 978-1-7374125-8-8

Written by Jodi Basye.

For my parents. If it wasn't for your unwavering love and support, I wouldn't be living this dream. Your belief in me ignited my passion for writing as a youth, and you have been fanning the flames ever since. Thank you for everything you have done to make this book possible.

Chapter 1

Southwest Colorado, 1899

Matthias Noble rode out of the tall ponderosa pines into an open meadow and blinked against the bright sun of late spring. The harmonic tinkling of water over rocks drew his attention and enticed him to locate the source. It had been a coon's age since he'd tasted water fresh from a spring.

He dismounted, leaving the reins of his sorrel gelding, Copper, to dangle in a ground tie, knowing the well-trained horse would stay. The source of the musical sound appeared to be crystal clear water cascading from a crack in the curious yellow rock formation at the base of the cliffside. It never ceased to amaze him the vast array of countryside the southwest boasted.

He'd spent the past four years of his life in the young states and hadn't seen the same thing twice. He'd seen snowy peaks, jagged red rocks, rolling hills of sagebrush, and even a great expanse of white sandy desert he'd crossed when he'd first arrived in Colorado. It seemed he'd wandered the entire earth, judging by the variety of scenery he'd seen.

Yet, his time in Colorado had been anything but enjoyable. Maybe this gurgling mountain spring was a sign things were looking up. His parched throat ached for the fresh, icy-cold water. He crouched in front of the water source and cupped his hand for a refreshing drink.

The immediate stench of rotting eggs filled his nose a split second before scorching hot water singed the palm of his hand. He fell back from his crouched position, and gripped his fist tight, pressing it against his mouth.

What in the crooked sky had just happened? He stretched out his stinging fingers to inspect the damage. His palm was blotchy red from the hot water, but no actual damage had been done.

A mountain spring with hot, smelly water? *That figured.* His lot in life had been one cruel blow after another. God had a mighty twisted sense of humor.

Copper nickered, and a huff of air warmed the back of his neck before the horse nudged Matthias's hat, knocking it off his head.

"Lay off, ya imp." He picked it up and crammed it back on before standing.

Hot water from a mountain spring. He'd heard talk of the healing waters in this area. Legend said there was such a pool on the San Juan River's edge right in Pagosa Springs. Thirty years prior, the Utes and Navajo had battled for ownership of the priceless wonder.

He might see the famed pools yet. He'd been told there was plenty of work in southwest Colorado as ranches sprang up and railroads brought commerce to the area. Maybe this time, he'd find a place to settle. Not his own place, but a quiet life cowboying for one of the big ranches could be just what he was looking for. A way to live out his second chance in peace.

So far, he hadn't had much luck finding the fresh start he'd been offered when he'd left his outlaw life behind. No matter how low Matthias tried to lie, trouble seemed to follow. He was beginning to believe that there was nothing else for him.

The trickle of hot water appeared to increase as it flowed west, growing in depth and width as it followed the base of the mountains. Matthias picked up Copper's reins and tossed them over the gelding's neck.

"Come on. Let's see where this water's heading." He followed the water on foot, and Copper trailed behind him, munching the short spring grass as they moved along.

Rounding the base of the cliffs, the water flowed into a small pool shaded by an overhang. He crouched down and grazed tentative fingertips over the surface of the water. It was hot, but not boiling here. Actually, it wasn't unlike the hot baths he paid good coin for whenever he chanced to stop in a town.

The day was warm, but in the cool shade of the rocky outcropping, a bath sounded mighty tempting. The water smelled faintly of spoiled eggs, but by what he'd heard about these springs, it might be worth stopping to soothe his sore muscles from the days of riding since he'd left Chama.

He sat down and pulled off his boots, rolling his pant legs up. His skin prickled in the heat as he slid his feet into the water, but within seconds, the sensation of ants chomping at his toes simmered into tingling pleasure.

He sighed with relief. This may not be a bad place to make camp for the night. Reluctantly pulling his feet back out of the water, he unbuckled the gun-belt at his waist and dropped it to rest on top of his boots. He unsaddled Copper and hobbled him in the meadow, where there was plenty of grass to graze, then gingerly made his way back to the pool barefoot.

The report of a rifle rang out close by, and Matthias hit the dirt, but the sound was too far off to have been aimed at him, he supposed. He grabbed for his gun-belt and buckled it over his union suit and scrambled for his saddle to retrieve his rifle from its scabbard.

Voices carried up from the valley below. Matthias scrambled to the edge of the slope that swept down from the meadow he and Copper occupied. Two men hunkered down behind some trees on the edge of the valley. About twenty head of cattle shifted restlessly, spooked by the gunfire. Matthias scanned the area, looking for the rustlers who must be after the herd.

There. One of the thieves moved in on the men guarding their livestock. The cowboys wouldn't see him from where they were crouching.

Do something. Matthias's stomach clenched. He gripped the rifle tight, pressing his cheek against the stock. He'd had enough of outlaws to fill two lifetimes. His blood boiled like the water from the spring. He refused to be party to this kind of lawlessness any longer and wouldn't stand by to watch innocent men killed or have their livelihood stolen from them.

His grip on the rifle tightened. Was this the right thing to do? He'd sworn he'd never kill again. But wasn't protecting two lives enough to outweigh the balance of taking one?

Lifting the peep-site of his Savage, he took careful aim at the rustler creeping up behind the cowboys with his pistol drawn. Acid boiled in Matthias's gut as he released half of a breath and squeezed the trigger.

Chapter 2

Elaine shifted forward and arched her back, leaning from side to side. The Pullman car was the most comfortable option available on this train, but after days of travel, she'd grown weary of the constant jerking and jostling.

Mrs. Cross was sound asleep in the seat next to Elaine, her head pillowed on her coat against the window. This was Elaine's chance to stretch her legs and be free of her chaperon.

Of course, it was only appropriate to have a traveling companion. Mrs. Cross was pleasant, though sometimes brash, but Elaine felt smothered with the attention.

For months, she had been under constant scrutiny. It only made her more nervous, more on edge. What if the woman noticed there was something different about her? Although Mrs. Cross had acted as housekeeper for the Bradford family all of Elaine's life, she had always kept reserved distance, just as Grandmama had taught her.

Nothing about being sent to her wayward sister Jo's new homestead was in keeping with what Grandmama had instilled in her. Elaine's plans were coming unwound like a great ball of thread, and Elaine was grasping at the slippery ends, trying to wind it all back up.

She shifted carefully, lifting her dress so as not to drag it across Mrs. Cross's skirts and wake her. Slowly, she side-stepped into the aisle and allowed her body to adjust to the swaying motion of the narrow-gauge rail. Keeping her balance with a gloved hand on the seat-back beside her, she made her way to the back of the car. When she reached the back door of the car, she gripped the doorknob, closing her eyes.

Taking a slow breath in, she tried to settle her roiling stomach. She hated the five steps it took to cross the frightening chasm that had to be traversed every time she made her way to the dining car.

She'd learned on her first day not to look down at the tracks, or to the landscape sweeping by. The key to surviving the gut-wrenching fear was to hold her head high, keep her eyes straight forward, and never look down.

She crossed the narrow, swaying platform between cars and rushed inside the dining car. Leaning back against the door and closing her eyes, she composed herself.

A sudden thump against her back knocked her forward as the door behind her was pushed open. The heel of her shoe slipped on the polished wooden floor, and she fell back. A hand caught her by the elbow, steadying her from behind.

"Pardon me, ma'am. I am quite the oaf." A voice like polished silver spoke over her shoulder.

Elaine turned to find her assailant, and subsequent rescuer, was a handsome man in a gray, tailored suit.

"No sir, it was my mistake. I shouldn't have been blocking the door, Mr.—?"

"Dashel, Frank Dashel. And you are?" His brilliant white teeth lent him a winning smile that was contagious.

"It's a pleasure to meet you, Mr. Dashel. I'm Elaine Bradford. Miss Elaine Bradford." Elaine took his offered hand and gave a light squeeze of her fingertips.

The train car swayed and tipped as it had been doing all day, winding its way through the mountain passes. Elaine teetered again, and Mr. Dashel reclaimed her elbow, steadying her once more.

"May I repay your gracious forgiveness with a cup of coffee?" Frank waved a hand of invitation toward a small table in the corner. "Or are you perhaps meeting someone here?"

Elaine hesitated, but the car was well lit, and she could find no reason she shouldn't accept his kind offer. In fact, turning it down could seem ill-mannered. She nodded and led the way to the table, pausing for him to push in her chair.

He retrieved a tray with two cups of coffee, a silver pitcher of cream, and a bowl of sugar from the man behind the counter. Mr. Dashel was quite the gentleman. Perhaps things wouldn't be quite as uncivilized in Colorado as she feared. Could this be the answer she was praying for?

"Tell me, Miss Bradford, what brings you to southern Colorado?" Mr. Dashel took his seat and poured the coffee.

Elaine's stomach clenched. Maybe accepting an offer of friendship hadn't been the best idea. What could she say? *I disgraced my family and was banished to live with my stray sister.*

No, that certainly wouldn't do. She added a spoonful of sugar to her cup and stirred it three times. Each revolution of the swirling liquid eased her anxiety, and she painted on a pleasant expression.

"My sister and her husband are expecting their first child. I came out from Dodge City, along with my brother-in-law's mother, to help during my sister's confinement." Elaine lifted the porcelain cup to her lips, pleased with her answer.

There, that sounded quite respectable.

"Has your sister been in the area long, then?" Mr. Dashel stirred a heaping teaspoon of sugar into his coffee.

"No. In fact, they've only just moved to the area a few months past. They purchased a sheep ranch near Pagosa Springs."

It was quite nice to have an enjoyable conversation with someone who didn't know the turmoil of her last several months. Perhaps this move would provide her the distance from her mistake she needed for a clean slate.

"That's quite the Christian thing for you to do for your sister." Frank sipped his coffee and cleared his throat, adding another spoonful of sugar.

Elaine quite agreed with his reaction to the coffee. She had never acquired a taste for the drink, and this brew held a bitter edge. She much preferred tea, but expressing such would be ill mannered when he had just purchased her a cup.

"I must say, this coffee is nothing compared to the superior brew I've grown accustomed to in Philadelphia." Frank straightened his tie and tugged the bottom of his vest.

So, he was indeed a man of substance and intended her to know it. But after Jacob Sinclair, Elaine couldn't afford to be swept away by a handsome face and heavy pocketbook. The last thing she needed was another scandal.

"I do mean it though," Frank leaned forward, his soft brown eyes looking concerned. "It's evident you are a lady, and to travel all this way, to act as a nursemaid on a small homestead? Why it's going to be downright primitive conditions, I'm sure. You are an angel of blessing, I dare say."

Elaine couldn't claim any such thing. Truth be told, she hadn't any choice in the matter. After being discovered in the embrace of a man who promptly cast her aside like unwanted refuse, rumors had flooded their social circle. Elaine's parents had decided it was best for her to go live with her sister, Jo.

The whole thing had been a murky haze. She'd known living with her sister would be a challenge, but had she underestimated what their actual living conditions would be? Jo and Gideon had purchased an already established homestead. Surely it wouldn't be entirely primitive, would it?

"I am bound for Durango, myself," Frank continued. "The place is booming, I hear, and I'm moving there to establish a law practice." Frank took another tentative sip of his coffee, grimacing. "Please know, if there is ever anything you need, you may certainly send word." He gave her a genuine smile that calmed her nerves a bit. "Durango is a good sixty miles from Pagosa, but I do hope I could be of some service."

"Thank you, Mr. Dashel." The kind offer warmed Elaine's chilled nerves.

Maybe there would be some civilization in her future after all.

"Please, call me Frank." He rested a hand over hers and patted it before pulling it away.

She didn't think he had meant the gesture as anything untoward, but the touch sent an uncomfortable prick of unease through her gloved hand.

Here was a man that was everything she had always hoped to gain in a husband. Well-mannered, well-endowed, and nearly radiating sophistication. Undoubtedly, someone like Frank could offer her the gentile life she needed to feel safe.

Yet she wondered if she would always feel so uneasy at the touch of a man. She feared that allowing herself to be manipulated into disgrace had ruined her ability to trust a man ever again. It had just been a kiss, but they'd been caught in a passionate embrace by the biggest loudmouth busybody in Dodge City. And for all the hardship and punishment Elaine had been through since, she might as well have hung a red lantern above the barn door where they had been found.

Her only goal had been to find safety and security, but she had trusted the wrong man. If she could find a husband like Frank—a gentleman that would provide a life in town—she would be safe from the kind of situations that would send her into a panic.

It was of the utmost importance she hide her condition. Only Grandmama had ever known the truth, and it was with her instruction she'd kept her embarrassing antics hidden thus far. But if she couldn't bring herself to trust again, how would she ever find a husband and the protection she needed?

Chapter 3

The outlaw in Matthias's sights dropped like a stone, and the weight of what he'd done landed in his gut. Remorse warred with relief. Silence followed the report of his rifle for the space of three heartbeats before the onslaught of shouting and gunfire commenced between the men below.

With no one sneaking up behind them now, the ranchers had the upper ground, having plenty of tree cover.

The cowboys' horses spooked and reared but, hobbled as they were, they hadn't been able to go far. The cows, though, bolted for the path of least resistance, tearing off down the valley, bent for leather.

Matthias scooted back from his position and went for his horse. He couldn't stomach any more killing, but the defending cowboys seemed to have the battle well in hand. He'd round up the cows and, when all the dust had settled, he'd drive them back where they belonged.

Dressing quickly, he pulled on his britches and boots, and caught his horse. He saddled Copper in haste before swinging up and heading in the direction the cows had gone.

He found the cattle at a creek, stopped for a drink, and rode a wide arc around and behind them, driving them slowly back up the narrow valley. It was ironic. The only experience he had with driving cattle was the bit of rustling he'd done himself with the Blake Gang.

When he'd pushed the cows back where they belonged, he approached the cowhands cautiously, not wanting to startle them after such a tense gun battle.

He hollered out to announce himself as he approached. "Hallo there!"

The men turned to see where the voice had come from, and Matthias raised his hands wide to show he meant no harm. The two exchanged wary looks, but seeing their herd returned to them, they allowed him to continue, hands hovering over their firearms.

"Just came to see that you two were alright and not in any need of further assistance." Matthias spoke, keeping his hands outstretched.

The younger of the two narrowed his eyes on Matthias and cast a sidelong glance at his companion. He nodded slowly, and a relieved smile stretched across his face. "So, it was you who laid down yonder fella a-sneakin' up on us. Was it?"

"It was." Matthias lowered his hands.

"Much obliged to you, sir." The cowboy scratched at the stubble on his pointed chin.

"Well, I don't see how I could just let'm sneak up on you from behind like that. Didn't seem decent." Matthias lifted his shoulder in a half-hearted shrug.

To be thanked for taking a man's life didn't feel right, but he supposed he had saved these men, so maybe it was an exception.

"Name's Shane McBride. This here is my hired hand, Hank Sutton," the man continued, speaking for both cowboys.

"Ki—" Matthias cleared his throat. "Matthias Noble."

Using his given name still didn't come naturally after years of going by *Kit* during his time with the Blake Gang. But if this was his chance to start over, he'd best leave the name Kit far behind him, along with the rest of his past.

"Where you boys taking yer herd?" He didn't know much about cattle, but this seemed too small a lot to be grazing through the territory.

The shorter, beefy man scowled at Matthias in suspicion. "What's it to you?"

"Back off, Hank, the gentleman here has been a great help to us. He's only being friendly." Shane smiled. "We're headed to Chama to sell."

"So far?" It surprised Matthias the distance they were taking the cows to sell.

Hank glowered at him under heavy black brows.

"The cattle market in these parts just ain't what it should be right now. They'll fetch a better price in Chama." Shane crossed his arms and narrowed his eyes at Matthias. "And what is it you're doing out here on your own? This trail isn't traveled much these days."

"Wanderin' I reckon." Matthias shrugged, "Looking for work."

"That so?" Shane rubbed his unshaven stubble and nodded. "You know, my father's ranch is just west of Pagosa. We could use a man like you."

The dull ache in Matthias's chest eased a bit. Things might turn around for him after all. This could be just the opportunity he needed.

"We need to keep pushing these cows, but you can head on straight to our ranch. The Lazy M. My pa will put you to work."

"Reckon we ought to deal with this first?" Matthias jerked his chin at the man laid out under a cedar tree.

Matthias's throat was thick, and he had to choke the words out."Hadn't I oughta ride into Pagosa first and tell the sheriff about all this?"

"Oh, don't you worry about that," Shane answered. "My father will be needing another hand as soon as possible, especially without Hank and I around. We've been needing some extra protection at the ranch to deal with the varmints that've been encroaching on our land. It was my cattle being lifted, anyway. We'll take care of this fella with the sheriff before we move on."

Matthias breathed a sigh of relief. The less he had to deal with the law, the better. He may not have been well-known for his past escapades, but the Blake Gang was, and Matthias didn't need to heap any more misery on his own path.

"Much obliged, sir." Matthias nodded, eager to be on his way.

Shane withdrew a piece of paper from his saddlebag and scribbled something. "Take this to my father. Darby McBride is his name. This is a letter of introduction."

"Pardon the question, but how can you be sure he'll hire me?" Matthias hated to doubt, but this chance seemed too good to be true. He'd spent months looking for an opportunity like this.

Shane looked up at the ridge Matthias had shot from. "A man with your skills would be mighty useful in these parts." He took a bite of a chaw of tobacco and spoke around the wad in his mouth. "Its wild country, and our cattle need protecting. I think you'll be just the man for the job. Besides, I owe ya a debt for stopping those rustlers."

The tension in Matthias's shoulders eased. This was the kind of work he needed. He didn't hold out hope of a chance at a ranch of his own after everything he'd done, but if he could hide away and live out his days in solitude, that would be enough for him.

Chapter 4

E laine's bones jarred with every bump of the wagon as it dropped over ruts in the road. The train seats had been luxurious compared to the wooden plank she now sat on in the back of a freight wagon. Bags of grain, bundles of oily scented wool, and burlap sacks of dusty potatoes filled the box of the wagon, leaving a small space behind the driver's bench for Elaine and Mrs. Cross to sit on.

She clenched her intertwined fingers and pressed her lips together so tight they ached. The handsome Frank Dashel was right. This type of life would never work. In fact, it directly opposed what she needed.

Not that she'd been raised in high society. But her mother's family had immigrated from England when her mother was a young girl. Grandmama, who had lived with Elaine's family until her death when Elaine was eight, and Mother had brought Elaine up with the manners and refinement of a well-born lady.

Her younger sister, Jo, had been dreadfully inept at adopting any culture, rather, taking after her father like some ordinary farmhand. But Elaine embraced every bit of sophistication available on a cattle ranch in Kansas. They may not have had a butler or lady's maid, but with Mrs. Cross acting as housekeeper, they were able to maintain a level of protection from the harsh conditions some poor farmers endured.

So how, then, with all the efforts and coaching Grandmama had instilled in her, had she ended up being hauled like a bag of grain to some barely civilized corner of backcountry-Colorado? There wasn't even a train station yet for heaven's sake.

The mule-skinner, Fred, cracked the whip and yelled something unintelligible to the mules. Did he have to shout so loud? The beast's ears were nearly a foot long. Surely they could hear a mouse in the grass, much less Fred's booming voice.

"Isn't this exciting, dear?" Mrs. Cross grinned broadly and patted Elaine on the knee as she took in the mountain scenery around them.

"Quite." Elaine bit the tip of her tongue to keep back her true, ungracious opinion.

Mrs. Cross gave her a crooked smirk. Having been a part of their household for Elaine's entire life, the housekeeper would recognize Elaine's clipped tone.

She checked her snappishness. It was only natural for Mrs. Cross to be excited. Elaine couldn't fault her for that. Mrs. Cross had lived the past four years with little to no word from her son, and now she would be living with him and his new wife. A mother's love knew no boundaries.

On the train, Gideon's mother had said she wouldn't care if they were bound to live in a mountain lion's den. She would have her son back, and that was all that mattered.

"In a cavern, in a canyon, excavating for a mine ..." Fred fairly gargled the words of the song in between sips from a large brown jug braced on the back of his forearm.

Amber liquid drizzled down the man's chin, and Elaine turned away, pressing a hand against her waist, tapping her middle finger against the cameo pendant hidden in the waist of her skirt. *Tap, tap, tap.* The compulsions were increasing with every mile from home. This uncouth slob of a man was only making things worse.

"These mountains are breathtaking, aren't they?" Mrs. Cross continued, undeterred by Elaine's tension or Fred's yodeling serenade.

"I suppose they are." Elaine forced a conversational tone past the tightness in her throat.

She couldn't find any appeal in the wild land that surrounded them. All she could see was an untamed wilderness where she would be forever lost to society and stability.

The wagon jerked side to side in a motion that rattled Elaine's teeth. The trail was getting even rougher if that was possible. Little flecks of mud flew up from the wagon wheels, and Elaine leaned against her companion's shoulder, hoping her traveling frock wouldn't stain.

A clump of mud landed on her skirt, and Elaine's heart rate increased. She reached down to brush it away, but hesitated. Who knew how long it would be before her gloves could be laundered? She tightened her fist to resist tapping the cameo again, tapping her toe instead. *Tap, tap, tap.*

She had to be extra cautious to be discrete, traveling in such close quarters with Mrs. Cross. Grandmama's warning to Elaine echoed in her mind, at war with the urgent aching in her fingers.

"Hold on to yer hats, ladies. Might get a bit bumpy back thar," Fred yammered over his shoulder.

It had been bumpy since they left the train station in Lumberton. Did he think they hadn't noticed?

"Dwelt a miner, forty-niner, and his daughter, Clementine." At the peak of his off-tune warbling, the wagon slammed to a stop, then jerked to the side, tipping hard.

The sound of wood snapping heralded the fate of the wheel. Elaine flew overboard, landing face-first in a puddle of thick, sloppy mud. Her screech reverberated off the walls of the high cliff next to them. She pushed herself up onto all fours, and spat out a mouthful of foul, gritty muck.

"Ya lost yer hat, there ma'am. Tole ya to hang on to it." Fred chortled and clambered down from the wagon, now tilted at a precarious angle.

Elaine's arms shook as she rocked back on her heels and swiped her mud-stained, calfskin gloves across her eyes. Reddish brown clay marred her gloves. *No, no, no, this can't be happening.* Rocking back and forth, she wrapped her arms tightly around her.

The prickling sensation rushed over her, and she sucked in shallow breaths, trying to gain focus. She was going to ruin everything before they even reached their destination. As if this whole move to Colorado hadn't been humiliating enough, Mrs. Cross was finally going to witness the truth of Elaine's condition and put together the pieces she surely had noticed over the years.

"Oh my heavens, dear, but you are a sight." The older woman climbed down from the wagon and leaned down to lift Elaine.

A look of sympathy settled on Mrs. Cross's face. "Let's get you cleaned up." She produced a handkerchief and retrieved a flask of water from the wagon box.

"Thank you, Mrs. Cross." Elaine's voice came in a thready whisper.

"Why don't we dispense with the need for formality, dear? You're a grown woman now, and I reckon this trip has taken a turn that veers far from propriety. You should call me Mary."

Elaine bobbed her head in a jerky motion, grateful to have Mrs. Cross—Mary—with her on this perilous journey.

"Did I ever tell you about the time I had to travel cross country on horseback with a total stranger?" Mary's amiable tone was comforting.

Elaine shook her head, trying hard to focus on Mary's words and not the gritty mud itching at her scalp.

"Why, that was when I'd first met my Charlie." Mary poured water onto the handkerchief and scrubbed a patch of mud from Elaine's forehead.

Elaine had never heard the story. In fact, she wasn't sure she had ever thought of Mary having a life before becoming a housekeeper for the Bradford family. The realization shamed Elaine. Had she allowed herself to become so consumed with her own worries, as to become entirely self-centered?

"It was my fault, I suppose," Mary continued. "We had to flee across the prairie like that because of my bravado and lack of good sense. But I wouldn't have changed the outcome for the world." Mary's eyes brightened, and she shrugged.

"I wouldn't be a wastin' that water if I were you." Fred interrupted their conversation, tucking his thumbs under the straps of his overalls, and wobbled slightly. "We're not goin' nowhere in a hurry. Dad-gum if that axle ain't busted in two," he slurred to himself, observing the wreckage.

Elaine held a muddy, gloved hand above her eyes to shade her view of the sun. It was on its downward descent now, possibly mid to late afternoon. Precisely how much longer were they going to be out here?

She pressed her hand over her stomach and tapped her middle finger. *Tap, tap, tap.* The rut the wagon had fallen into must've been three-feet deep. The wheel tilted at an odd angle, quite wrong for its purpose. A jagged piece of wood stuck out, one end buried in the mud and the other jutting out of the center of the wheel, pointed to the sky.

Mary stepped away and was speaking to Fred, presumably about their prospects for a timely repair. Thank heavens for the need of a chaperone. Elaine couldn't imagine what she would do if she were alone in this situation.

"Well, there's nothing he can do about the wheel," Mary explained while Fred walked crookedly over to a tall tree, carrying his large ceramic jug.

He collapsed to the ground, leaning his head back against the trunk, and pulled his hat down over his eyes.

"What—What is he doing!?" Could they be stranded here over night? How could they even survive such a scenario?

"The axle broke. He says there's nothing to do but wait for help to come by." Mary's even tone rose in pitch ever so slightly.

The hint of unease in the steady woman made Elaine's elevated heartbeat pick up pace to hummingbird speeds. She peeled off the gloves that seemed to be drying two sizes too small and pressed a hand over her tight corset, wishing she could rip it off too.

She couldn't breathe. The air was thin and fleeting, and she couldn't get enough to fill her lungs. She drew short, rapid gasps, and her chest ached as she stumbled back against the wagon.

"Here now, child, sit down." Mary placed a hand under Elaine's elbow and guided her to a seated position, leaning against one of the good wheels.

Elaine pressed her forehead into her knees and gripped her skirt tightly in each palm. If it wasn't for the barrier of her skirt fabric, she'd have bloody, half-moon cuts in her palms from her fingernails.

A soft thud-thud-thudding registered somewhere in her hearing. Hoof-beats. Someone was coming. Elaine didn't wait to find out who.

"Mary, hide!" she whispered fiercely as she scrambled under the wagon, wedging herself under the lowest point of the wreckage where the wagon box lay against the ground.

Elaine tugged at Mary's skirts, but the woman seemed determined to be scalped or kidnapped. She didn't hide but rather stepped away from Elaine's grasping of her hem.

The hoof-beats stopped dangerously close, and four white-socked horse hooves and a pair of worn, leather boots appeared next to Mary's skirt. This man could be any kind of dangerous outlaw.

Her fingers dug into the grass as she clawed and gripped for something to hold on to. It wasn't until the cool, wet sensation of mud pressed against her palms that she remembered she wasn't wearing gloves. Spots floated in front of her eyes. She reasoned with herself that not being clean was the least of her worries right now. Mary was going to be murdered, and Elaine would either be discovered next or be left to the wolves.

"Elaine, come out here, you silly heart." Mary's soft voice rose above the rushing of blood in Elaine's ears.

Confident and calm again, Mary's tone was steadying. Elaine didn't want to face whatever threat beset them next, but she also couldn't lie here in the mud any longer. Mary reached a hand under the wagon, and Elaine grasped it, still shaking. Hesitantly, she scooted and wriggled her way out from under the wagon.

Frantic heartbeat slowing down now, she opened her eyes. She was still staring at the dusty boots from before. She tentatively raised her eyes, and found a man wearing a pair of chaps, a dust-coated bib-front shirt, and a gray cowboy hat. Under the hat, edges of dark hair framed a tan face that would be handsome if it weren't frowning intently at her like she was a lunatic.

Breath slowing, and heartbeat finding a steadier rhythm now, Elaine drew herself up, held her head high, and did her best to return the man's intent gaze. He looked at Mary, an eyebrow raised, and the corner of his mouth turned up. The nerve of the man. What possessed him to look at her like that? He didn't even know her.

She placed her hands on her hips, and the grit of drying mud clinging to the fabric under her fingers reminded her of what a dreadful mess she was. Heat blazed in her face, and a self-conscious hand reached up to pat ineptly at her hair.

Having lost her hat when she fell from the wagon-bed, her hair was stringing down from her chignon in long, mud-streaked tendrils. The tightening sensation prickling at her skin indicated her face must still be caked with drying mud as well. Add that to the scene she'd created by hiding under the wagon, and she fumed with frustration and embarrassment. She wanted nothing more than to climb back under the wagon until the man left.

He'd certainly witnessed her at her worst. Elaine prayed he could help them on their way and that he had no intentions of sharing their destination. If he told this story around Pagosa Springs, people would talk, and she knew all too well what the result of that would be.

Chapter 5

Matthias blinked, unsure of what to say. These people clearly needed his help, but what had he gotten himself into? The young woman standing in front of him looked like she'd been dragged behind the wagon she just crawled out from under.

"My name is Mary Cross, and this here is Miss Elaine Bradford." The older woman reached out a hand confidently. An uncommon gesture for a woman, but he appreciated her forthrightness.

He shook it and looked over at her traveling companion. "Ma'am." Matthias tugged at the brim of his hat.

She blinked at him quickly, her eyes darting around as though looking for danger. Strange one, this girl. He turned back to Mary, who seemed much more reasonable of the two.

"You say you were traveling as passengers on this freight wagon? Where precisely is the driver?"

"Asleep under yonder tree." She nodded toward the large cottonwood against the hillside.

"How long have you been here?" Matthias glanced back at the driver. How could the man be so careless as to leave the women unattended along the road?

"Not long." Mary shrugged in dismissal of their plight.

"Is he ill?" Matthias walked over to the man under the tree, and the women followed close behind.

"Only on account of that brown jug there." Mary gestured to the whisky next to the man.

Matthias kicked the ceramic jug away from the man and nudged him roughly with the toe of his boot. The man stirred but didn't rouse. Matthias booted him again, just firmly enough to tip him over. This time the lout grumbled and squinted up at Matthias.

"May I help you?" the muleskinner asked in a mock-formal tone and grinned broadly up at Matthias, showing a wide gap in his front teeth.

Well, at least he was a friendly drunk. Matthias sighed and scrubbed a hand over his face in resignation. Clearly the man would be no help, but at least he might not be a hindrance.

"Get up, man. There's work to be done." Matthias picked up the jug, walked back to the wagon, and pitched it into the box. After sixteen years of living with a drunk for a father, Matthias had no patience or tolerance for the stuff.

"Where are you headed, ma'am? Pagosa Springs?" Matthias walked back to the wagon and kneeled down beside the broken axle to assess the damage.

"Yes sir, we were meant to take the stage, but the man at the station said the daily coach hadn't been seen in two days."

A twinge in Matthias's belly told him the fate of that stagecoach. He knew all too well the dangers of traveling the wilderness by coach or freight wagon. He had, in fact, been the cause of such perils in company with Kane Blake. It surprised him this man had no one riding shotgun. Stagecoaches and freight wagons were prime targets for robbery.

Matthias stood and flipped open the snap of his gun belt, scanning the area. Likely, the men who had robbed the stage had long since moved on to another area and another stage line. But just the same, best to be on his guard. The younger woman's eyes widened at his action, and she stepped instinctively closer to him, her own eyes trained on the road.

"How long will we be here?" An unexpected bell-tone voice came from the muddy mess at his elbow.

He couldn't help but focus on the little wrinkle in her forehead and wide, doe-like eyes filled with panic. She was like a deer, braced to run at the smallest noise.

"Sun's getting low, and this axle's clean busted in two. We best be makin' camp." He scanned the area for the best place to set up.

"Camp." Miss Bradford repeated the word slowly, not as a question. Just one word.

He answered anyway. "Yes, ma'am. That spot there'll do. Against the cliff so I can keep watch." He pointed to the grove of cedars.

She blinked up at him with wide, golden-brown eyes. "Camp?"

Now it was a question. But what was so hard to understand? She knew English. She'd just spoken to him in a full sentence a moment ago. Maybe she was a little soft in the head after all.

"We—we can't camp here. We have to get to town. Have you lost your mind?" The foggy haze she'd seemed to float in a moment before lifted, and suddenly her words flowed like water. She most definitely spoke English.

She planted her hands firmly on her hips, and her chin jutted out the way his grandmother's used to do whenever she'd been asserting her authority. He couldn't stop the quirk of a half-smile that tugged at his lips. He recognized the gesture as one of covering her unease and not one of actual condescension.

"Well, ma'am, Pagosa Springs is another fifteen miles, and this repair'll take hours. Ain't no way we could make it down the trail in the dark. Our only option is to make camp and get y'all safely into town tomorrow."

"But what about wolves or—or bears or Indians? Is this Navajo territory or Apache?" She frantically looked around the open park, pressing a hand against her stomach.

The resemblance to his grandmother stopped at the commanding mask she'd donned in the face of fear. His grandmother had been short and round, with white curls pinned into little swirls all over her head. This young woman was tall and willowy, with rich brown hair swept into what must have been a loose knot before whatever misfortune had pulled wild strips of it out to hang freely down, framing her mud-streaked face. He curled his fingers into a fist to keep from reaching out and tucking a strand behind her ear.

"I don't think we'll have any difficulty with varmints or natives here. They're farther south and have no cause to take issue with us." He hoped his calm tone would temper her anxious spirit.

A warbling serenade preceded the muleskinner, who had finally roused from his siesta and was making his way back to the wagon. "Skip to ma'lou ma darlin'."

With a surprisingly agile skip and a hop, the man grinned and bowed elaborately as he approached. "Frederick T. Franklin. Will you be purchasing fare to join our party?"

Mrs. Cross rubbed a finger under her nose, attempting to hide her amusement. Matthias struggled between mirth and irritation.

"Matthias Noble, and no, I don't wish to purchase a fare. However, I believe you and the women here might benefit from some help."

Elaine's forehead scrunched, and she looked at him like a puzzle she couldn't quite put together. Something about this mud-caked girl intrigued him. Even under all the earth and twigs, she had the air of a lady.

He had no business noticing her in that way. He needed to keep his focus where it belonged. Find honest work and a place to lay his head at night. That's all he could ask for.

Chapter 6

The sky took on a pink hue as evening drew near. Elaine rubbed her arms to ward off the chill of evening. Sunset wasn't far off. She laid out her handkerchief on a fallen cottonwood tree and sat down on it, waiting for Matthias to return.

After hiding the mysterious brown jug from Fred and practically pouring a pot of coffee down his throat, Matthias had mounted his horse and disappeared around a bend in the trail. He'd said he was going to hunt up some grub, but Elaine would rather have eaten a cold biscuit if it meant keeping him close by.

Though she didn't know for certain he was trustworthy, she supposed if he weren't, he wouldn't have stopped to help. She glanced over at Fred, who was hobbling the mules. She supposed he might offer some protection now he was sober, but she would feel better having another man around.

Despite her fears of being caught out on the trail after dark, fatigue weighed heavily on her shoulders and she longed to find somewhere to lie down. Mary hadn't seemed the least addled by this whole escapade. She was snoring peacefully under a tree across the campsite. Elaine ached for that kind of peaceful somnolence.

She was always tired. Hadn't slept well since she was a girl. Not really. There was no time for rest with so many worries to entertain.

A few months ago, she had been all-consumed by the need to find a life with position and security. A wealthy husband and a fine house were what was important to her—had to be important to her.

Alas, it had dashed her hope to pieces when the suitor she thought God brought to her turned out to be a snake. Since then, her nights were filled with worry about whether she would ever find a man with a suitable position.

When Jo had returned after abandoning them and getting into who knows what kind of trouble, their parents welcomed her with open arms. Elaine had made one mistake, and they had cast her aside—banishing her to this uncivilized back-country.

Something fell to the dirt beside her with a thud. Her heart leaped into her throat, choking back her scream and causing it to come out in a panicked squeak as she ducked instinctively.

"Supper." Matthias's voice came from behind her. She peeked an eye open. Four lifeless birds rested in a pile of feathers at her feet. Her heart slowed its hammering, and she released the painful breath she'd gasped.

"You are a jumpy thing, ain't ya?" Matthias lowered his brows at her, a muscle twitching in his right cheek.

"You scared the daylights out of me." Elaine pressed a hand over her chest, willing her breathing to slow.

Matthias walked to the back of the wagon and filled a tin pan from the water barrel. Returning with it, he held it out toward her. "Thought you might like to wash up." He shrugged one shoulder.

"Fred said we couldn't waste the water, not knowing how long we'd be stranded here." Gratitude rushed through her at the thought of washing away the grime that clung to her.

"Well, we'll be outta here by mid-day tomorrow, I reckon, and the San Juan River ain't terribly far from here if we need more.

Elaine dipped her hands into the water and submerged her face. Relishing the indulgent sensation of clean water on her skin, she scrubbed away the dried mud. It was a kind gesture to have come from a man who had the perpetual expression of an angry hawk. The twin lines of concern or frustration, she wasn't sure which, seemed to have permanent residence between his dark brows.

A stubborn clump of mud clung to Elaine's skin, matting her hair to the side of her face. She scrubbed vigorously, grimacing at the sharp pull of the tiny hairs at her temple that refused to release their hold of the mud.

Matthias stood, petting one of the tall mules, and gestured to the wagon as he explained his idea of how to go about mending the broken axle. The men walked to the wagon, and Matthias looked to the horizon where pink and orange streaks painted the deepening blue sky.

His clothes, like her own, were now mud caked from lying under the wagon earlier to inspect the damage. Even without the mud he'd gained, she'd noticed the layer of fine, dull dust that coated his clothes and hat, though his narrow face was clean.

How long had this man been riding around the wilderness without a proper bed and a bath? The hired hands on her father's ranch all had a similar dress and disposition, but the dusty cowboys had never piqued her interest. She'd had her eyes set on the finer things of life.

Matthias rolled up his shirtsleeves, baring muscular forearms, and lifted the wheel out of the mud. His arm bore a thick white scar, and she couldn't help but notice the stark difference between this man and the kind she'd always had her sights set on.

She tried to picture Frank Dashel streaked with mud, repairing a broken wagon axle. An unladylike snort fizzled through her nose at the idea of Frank, in his morning coat, doing the same. He'd be no help at all.

Elaine eyed the birds on the ground beside her. She swallowed against the bitter taste in her mouth and smoothed her skirt over her knees. The absence of her gloves left her feeling exposed.

Was he going to expect her to do something with them? She couldn't even make tea. The mere thought of what needed to be done to make the lifeless creatures into something edible sent a shiver down her spine.

"Mind pluckin' those birds for supper? We're fixin' to lose the light," Matthias called across the wagon bed as he rolled the large wheel out of the mud and laid it out on dry ground.

Elaine looked over her shoulder. Had Mary woken up? No, the Mary-shaped bundle under the tree only shifted and rolled over. Elaine had a feeling the woman was well aware of the request and was intentionally leaving the job to Elaine.

It was unlike her to rest during the day. In all of Elaine's upbringing, Mary had worked tirelessly. Something told Elaine this ill-timed nap was intentional. Some method of forcing Elaine out of her cocoon. What Mary didn't understand was Elaine's aversion to getting her hands dirty had nothing to do with snooty behavior and everything to do with avoiding the panic that would overtake her if she did.

She stared down at the birds, frozen. Her chest tingled with every sluggish heartbeat. She stood and backed away from the fire, nearly running, and dropped to Mary's side.

"Mary," Elaine whispered. "Mary, please."

Mary rolled over and blinked. "What is it, child?"

"I can't do this. I can't. It's too much."

Mary sat up and looked back toward Matthias and Fred working beside the wagon.

"He wants me to pluck them, but I can't. I just can't." Elaine's voice shook, and she stopped herself, pressing her lips together.

Something passed through Mary's eyes, a kind of understanding, and she quickly rose to her feet. "Come on, then." She nodded toward the fire. "I'll take care of the birds. Why don't you go rummage through my carpetbag? I believe there are some wrapped biscuits that will go along nicely."

A wave of relief washed over Elaine, and she gripped Mary's hand, squeezing.

"Thank you," she whispered before rushing off to find Mary's bag.

By the time they had eaten their supper, darkness had filled the little valley. The cloudy Milky Way and thousands of white pin-pricks blanketed the black canvas overhead. The sky here in Colorado didn't seem as big as it had on the flat Kansas prairie. But something made the stars feel closer, like she could reach up and touch the glittering lights.

After supper, Matthias ensured Mary and Elaine the wagon was steady and they would be safe to sleep in the wagon box. Mary bade the party good night and rustled around, making a bed for them. Elaine held back, mesmerized by the night sky.

"There is no light in earth or heaven but the cold light of stars; and the first watch of night is given to the red planet Mars." Matthias's husky tone was so quiet Elaine almost missed it.

She looked up at the man beside her in astonishment.

"S'pose I best not leave the watch up to Mars tonight." The flicker of firelight glowed on the quirk of his lips before the shadows of the night whisked the moment away. "Get yourself tucked away safe in yonder wagon-bed with Mary now, and I'll keep watch tonight." He tugged at the brim of his dusty hat and retrieved his rifle from his belongings before climbing the hill to a better vantage point.

Elaine wrapped herself in her traveling cloak and curled up with her head pillowed on a bag of lamb's wool. For once, it wouldn't be *worry* keeping her awake, but the peculiar contradiction of a dusty cowboy who quoted Longfellow in the moonlight that would rob her of sleep tonight.

Chapter 7

Jo pressed a fist against the dull ache in her lower back. Being on her feet for long periods of time had become excruciating these past few weeks. Surely the extra weight she carried now would cause her bones to crumble soon.

When Elaine and Mary hadn't shown up in Pagosa Springs on the stage yesterday, Jo and Gideon had stayed overnight at the Patrick Hotel, and the lumpy mattress had done her back pain no great favors.

They'd been standing in front of the station, waiting on the stage for what felt like an hour. Finally, Gideon had gone inside to find out what the hold-up might be. It was bad enough she didn't know what to expect when her sister arrived, but to add so much time, waiting, was just about more than she could handle.

If she were honest, though, Jo knew exactly what to expect from Elaine. She would be straight-backed and aloof as always and most certainly would be unimpressed by the underdeveloped territory.

She could imagine the prim way Elaine would step down from her wagon to grace the street with her step and the pinched expression she'd adopt at the faint aroma of eggs that continually hung in the air here from the natural hot springs.

Yet again, Jo wondered just what Pa and Ma had in mind when they said that Elaine would come out with Mary to help with the new baby. Elaine hadn't done a day's work in her life. How would she be of any help?

Jo swayed side to side, shifting her weight from one leg to the other. She wasn't sure if the habit had developed by trying to find some relief for her back or from some instinct to rock the child growing in her belly.

A door opened behind her, and Gideon's baritone could be heard from inside. It soothed her nerves. She wasn't given to nervousness often, but she'd rather put a pack saddle on a wild mustang and take a ride than entertain Elaine's bitter disdain as a house guest over the next several months.

Gideon had been encouraging about it, though he had his own cause for nerves. Having his ma moving in with them as well was uncomfortable enough. After leaving her and his younger brother, Jimmy, with little to no word about his whereabouts for over three years, he was as fractious about this change as she was.

Gideon wanted his ma to come stay with them, but he was still plagued with guilt over leaving the way he did. But even with the uneasy circumstances, Gideon was Jo's anchor, and she was his sail. Standing together, they could tackle anything.

"Will you go sit down?" Gideon waved a hand in grand invitation to the wooden bench against the building. "Please?" He softened the request with a smile.

The stiff wooden bench didn't look any more appealing than standing here on the boardwalk.

"I can't sit." Jo shrugged off his suggestion. "What'd they say?"

"Seems the stage hasn't come for three days. Could've been bandits." Gideon looked down and scuffed the toe of his boots on the rough planks of wood.

Being tactful didn't always come naturally to the big mountain man, but with Jo's tarnished past, he generally avoided the subject all together.

"But what does that mean about today's stage?" Jo leaned forward on the porch-rail, stretching her back. Gideon placed firm hands on her back and rubbed in a soothing, circular motion with his thumbs.

"Well, when a stage isn't available, there is a freight wagon that will carry passengers here. But the freight wagon was due to come in last night and didn't."

"We're going." Jo stood straight and gripped Gideon's arm as a wave of dizziness washed over her.

"*We're* not going anywhere. You, my dear, should go back to the hotel and get some rest." Gideon's brows drew together, and he looked down at her with pleading brown eyes. "Let me take the wagon and go look for them."

"I'm fine." Jo waved her fingers as if she could shoo away his concern. "I can't let you go on your own, Gideon, not when there may be trouble."

"You aren't well, Jo—"

"You aren't going alone." Jo attempted to prop her hands on her hips, but her round belly prevented her from doing so.

Her hands slipped off, making her pregnancy that much more obvious and her argument that much more difficult to maintain.

Gideon's lips twitched under his bushy brown beard with the obvious attempt to hide his laughter. Jo tried crossing her arms, but the bulk of her belly prevented that too. She snorted on her own laughter and grabbed the fringe of Gideon's buckskin jacket instead, pulling him down, nose to nose.

"Clay is back at the homestead, and I don't want you going alone." She yanked on the leather, giving his lips a long, tingling kiss. All the tension in his posture softened, and he spread his hands across her lower back, holding both of them steady.

Jo pushed him upright, and he stumbled back. "I'm going, and that's final."

Gideon raised his hands in surrender, and shrugged. "Yes, ma'am. But when you're bouncing around on that bench seat for an extra twenty miles today instead of sipping tea on a plush couch at the hotel, you remember that I tried to stop you."

The gritty scraping of wheels in gravel and the rumble of hooves pulled Jo's attention back to the street.

A team of tall black mules pulled a long freight wagon up directly in front of the stage station. A toothless man in sagging overalls and a slouch hat, stood from his bench and waved grandly to the women in the back of the wagon.

"Pagosa Springs, my ladies." The man gave a courtly bow with a flourish from his perch and plopped back down, pulling a brown jug from under the bench-seat.

Mary lit out of the wagon with the grace of someone half her age and squeezed Jo's hands, turning her back to the wagon.

"Just look at you." She pulled back to get a full view of Jo and her swollen belly.

Wiping a tear from her face, she kissed Jo on the cheek and threw her arms around Gideon's chest. Her blonde hair was pinned up under a straw hat that was a bit disheveled from travel. Jo hoped their trip hadn't been too troublesome.

She turned back to the wagon with a slow, fortifying breath, ready to face the scorn of her elder sister. But rather than a lacy parasol, yards of taffeta, and a smug expression, in front of her stood a muddy, bedraggled woman with slumped shoulders.

"Elaine?"

Fool. Of course, it was Elaine. The same dark brown locks framed the angular face of perfection Jo had always feared she couldn't live up to. The same dark lashes fluttered over downcast eyes. What on earth had happened here?

At her name, Elaine met Jo's eyes, and a pink shadow flushed her cheeks. Elaine could even blush pretty. Jo looked like a tomato when embarrassed.

"What happened to you?" Jo choked back a giggle.

Pretty, pink blush or no, the girl looked like she'd been dragged through the mud behind the wagon for half the trip.

In true Elaine fashion, she rallied, standing straight and elongating her neck. "I should ask the same." Elaine cocked an eyebrow in challenge.

Jo let a smile broaden across her lips and rested a hand on her stomach. As much as she loved to get Elaine's goat, it wouldn't do to start things off on bad footing.

"Let's get you home. You look like you could use a bath." Jo tried to soften her words with a smile, but Elaine's lips tightened, and a muscle locked in her jaw.

For Pete's sake, could Jo say nothing right? She looked at Mary, who was beaming at Gideon's side.

"Would you mind sharing the tale of your adventure?" Jo jerked her head in Elaine's direction. "Your traveling companion doesn't seem to have much to say."

"Oh, it is quite the story, I assure you." Mary chuckled. "We had some wagon trouble, and Miss Elaine fell head-first over the side, into the mud." She pressed her lips tightly together and schooled her expression into one of appropriate gravity.

How Jo wished she'd been there to see such a sight. She'd never even seen a speck of dirt under her sister's fingernails.

"We thought we'd be stranded for sure. But a nice young man happened upon us on the trail and saved our bacon." Mary glanced over her shoulder at the muleskinner settling his payment with the stage manager, and lowered her voice. "Our driver wasn't much to be desired."

"Well then, where is your rescuer? I'd like to shake his hand." Gideon looked around the crowd gathered to receive their shipments.

Mary scanned the street. Standing on tiptoes, she pointed to a man on the other side of the mules. "There he is, in the gray hat."

Jo squinted against the midday sun. The man walked around the mules, and Jo's heart stopped. She'd know that chiseled jaw anywhere. Kit.

Her heart hammered in her chest, and Gideon stiffened next to her. He must've recognized the former outlaw as well. At least, she *hoped* Kit's outlaw days were behind him. If he'd truly stopped to help and not taken advantage of the opportunity of a broken-down freight wagon, maybe he had indeed put his days with the Blake Gang behind him.

What should she do? Should she acknowledge him? She had hoped to leave all reminders of her past life behind her, and she was certain Kit had intended the same.

"Mr. Noble!" Mary called over the din of conversation between them. "Mr. Noble, over here."

Lord love you, Mary, stop calling. Jo wanted to clap a hand over Mary's mouth and drag the two women out of there.

"Gideon, Jo, this is Matthias Noble. Our hero and escort back to civilization." Mary beamed from Kit—or Matthias, rather—to Gideon.

Gideon reached out a hand, and Matthias blinked rapidly. He looked quickly from Gideon to Jo, his blue eyes as wild as a hunted hare.

Gripping Gideon's hand, he nodded to Jo and choked out, "Ma'am," before looking down at his boots.

Matthias, not Kit. When they parted company last year, Matthias had said he would leave the false, outlaw nickname, Kit, behind, and go back to his given name, Matthias.

"Thank you for helping our stranded family." Gideon returned Matthias's nod and stepped back.

"Your family?" Matthias's brows rose to meet his hat.

"That's right. This here's my ma, and Elaine is my wife's sister." Wrapping an arm behind Jo's back, Gideon pulled her to his side.

It had taken some convincing to talk Gideon into allowing Kit, or Matthias, to go free after his involvement with the Blake Gang and Jo's kidnapping. After what Jo had been through, only the fact that Matthias had set her free had kept Gideon from leaving Matthias's body lying in the dust right next to Kane and the others.

"My pleasure." Matthias cleared his throat and darted a quick glance at Elaine. "Well then, I best be going now."

Touching the brim of his hat first to Mary, and then Elaine, Matthias spun on his spurs and worked his way back through the knot of people. Mounting his horse, he turned back, looking both desperate to be off and reluctant to go.

Jo breathed out a sigh of relief. One she hoped Mary and Elaine wouldn't notice. She was grateful that he'd left before any awkward explanations became necessary. Was he just passing through, or did he intend to stay in town? If he meant to settle down in the area, would they be able to continue on as if they didn't share a secret past?

For now, she would leave those old ghosts to lie.

Chapter 8

Matthias rode down into a sprawling valley edged by sloping hillsides clustered with oak brush. Ahead, a tall iron gate towered over the dusty wagon track that led to a large, one-story ranch house. Barbed wire fences stretched out from the gate in either direction, framing a pasture scattered with black cattle.

Matthias allowed himself to hope he could find a place here. This sure would be a peaceful place to put down roots. Finding steady work in a beautiful setting like this would be more than he could ever wish for. He ought not to hold out hope, though.

Would his chance to settle down be compromised by the presence of Jo and that mountain man she married? He'd not counted on his past catching up to him here. When he had parted ways with Jo and Gideon, it had been a few hundred miles east, and he'd never bargained on seeing them again.

He and Jo had come to an understanding during their time in the gang, but after Jo's kidnapping, that big, buckskin-clad husband of hers had looked like he was a hair's breadth from murdering Matthias. It was only for Jo's sake Gideon had let Matthias go. Would Gideon change his mind now about giving Matthias a second chance?

He rode down the winding wagon track toward the ranch house. Two dogs rounded the barn and ran toward him at full speed, snarling and barking. They stopped a hundred yards in front of the house—forming a rather effective barrier. Copper stopped short, his back legs sliding in the dirt, and reared, backing away rapidly.

A sharp whistle and a gruff voice split the commotion. "Shut up, dogs."

The dogs winced and dropped to their bellies with a whine and a groan. "Who're you?"

An elderly man with steel gray hair and a wiry frame spoke around a large cigar as he stood sentinel on the porch with a shotgun braced in his hands.

Matthias hesitated. Would the man's welcome be as friendly as Shane had ensured him?

"Are you Darby McBride?"

The man nodded and gripped his gun tighter. "I am."

"Matthias Noble, sir. Your son sent me." He reached back and pulled the paper from his saddlebag, waving it in the spring breeze.

He rode forward, and Copper trotted between the dogs in light, high steps, shying from one to the other. Matthias knew how he felt. Straightening his back and pushing aside his usual unease with people, he side-passed up to the wide front porch and handed the note over. Darby scrunched his face and held the paper to the light as he read.

He looked down at Matthias from the porch, nodding his head. "It seems my son thinks you'll be a good hand."

"I'm a hard worker, sir. I may not have much experience with cattle, but I learn quickly."

"You won't need much know-how for what you'll be doing." McBride folded the paper and nodded toward the barn. "You can settle your horse and turn him out in the corral. Come to the house when you're through, and we'll talk business."

Matthias nodded his appreciation and rode out to the large barn. He tied Copper to the hitching post and stepped inside to look for a curry comb. They'd been weeks on the move, and his companion was looking a bit worse for the wear. He could barely keep himself fed, much less afford a curry comb and hoof pick.

He brushed down Copper until his red coat shone in the late-afternoon sun and took the extra time to clean his hooves. It was time for a trim and new shoes for the gelding. Taking this job was the right thing to do. At least now, he could take better care of his horse. He led Copper into the corral and gave him a friendly smack on the hindquarters, sending him to trot away, shaking his mane.

Back at the house, he rapped on the door, waiting to meet his future.

A stiff, stern-looking woman answered. "Yes?"

"Excuse me, ma'am." Matthias removed his hat. "Mr. McBride asked me to come to the house when I was done with seeing to my horse."

She frowned slightly and looked over his shoulder toward the barn before stepping to the side to allow him entry. "Follow me."

Inside, the house smelled of frying meat and strong coffee. Matthias took a long breath in and savored the aroma of food. Sure, there was a touch of acrid char in the air, too, but

Matthias hadn't eaten a full meal in two weeks. He wasn't in any kind of way to be picky.

The housekeeper led him to a dining room where Darby McBride sat at a large table.

"Sit." He pointed the tip of his knife to a chair at the table.

Matthias complied, anxious to share a meal and find out the kind of man he was going to be working for. "Much obliged for the supper, sir, and for the job."

"You'll earn yer keep, that's certain." McBride forked several small steaks from the platter and piled them up on a plate along with what appeared to be the charred remains of fried potatoes. "Help yerself."

He sat in a seat across the table from Matthias, straightening out a stiff leg that must give the man some grief. Matthias dished himself steak and potatoes, and the woman who answered the door poured him a cup of coffee.

"This is Mrs. Patton. She's cook and housekeeper here at the Lazy M. Though I don't reckon after today, you'll have much chance to know her."

Matthias gave Mrs. Patton a polite nod and bent over his plate to eat.

"You'll join the other cowboys in the bunkhouse tonight. That's where you'll eat and sleep from here on out."

Matthias cut a piece of the steak and took a grateful bite. His stomach juices roared to life at the prospect of a hearty meal. He savored the rich flavor of the steak, but disappointment settled in his belly when he began to chew. Despite his anticipation of a good meal, the meat was tough as the sole of an old boot. The bite wedged in his throat as he tried to swallow.

Several minutes passed in silence as they ate, but Matthias felt McBride's penetrating gaze. The uncomfortable scrutiny itched up the back of his neck.

Matthias couldn't take the uncomfortable silence any longer. "So, what exactly is it I'll be doing for you, Mr. McBride? Your son didn't rightly say. Only that a man like me would be helpful."

McBride stabbed a bit of steak with his fork and chewed forcefully. "What I need from you is varmint control." The old man's gruff voice rasped.

"Varmints, yes. Now that you mention it, Shane said something along those lines, after all."

The old man continued, speaking around a bite of steak. "We're overrun with animals taking over our territory, and my cows are suffering for it."

"I see. Wolves, cats, and the like?" Matthias had finally swallowed the wad of sinew-laced meat and thought it might be best to attempt the potatoes instead.

"Oh, there's plenty a'rascals to be run off or killed. That's for right certain." McBride pushed his plate away and pulled a cigar from his breast pocket.

Matthias attempted to stab a piece of blackened potato. It jumped from under his fork and shot across the table. Mr. McBride's gnarled hand slapped down on the potato and leaned forward, narrowing one eye. He flicked the potato over to Matthias and settled back in his chair again.

"You up fer the job, then?" McBride scratched the tip of a match against the rough wood of his chair and lit the cigar, drawing puffs of air until the tobacco inside crackled like a campfire.

"I reckon I'd be happy to take any work I can get." Truly, Matthias would be happy enough just to be free from the cigar smoke that wasn't mixing well with the acrid taste of burned potato.

The scent brought him to his childhood and the cigars Pa smoked. It was an unwelcome memory he'd rather do without.

"Well then, eat yer supper and find yerself a spot in the bunkhouse. Shane should be home tonight, and he'll set you straight with what needs done in the morning." The old man leaned forward, grimacing as he stood and settled his weight on the stiff leg. "We'll see if you're worth your salt come morning."

Was Matthias worth his salt? Jo seemed to think so and had made sure he had this second chance. But Pa had never thought Matthias was worth anything, and in the end, Kane Blake would've shot him in the back had Jo not killed Kane first. If Pa and Kane didn't think he was worth anything, what made him think Jo knew any better ?

Chapter 9

Elaine clenched her teeth to keep them from clattering together as the wagon jolted over the bumpy ruts of dried mud. This being her second full day of wagon travel, she was thoroughly unimpressed with this homestead life so far.

The clear blue Colorado sky was deceptive, suggesting sunshine and warmth, but yielding a spring breeze that nipped at her cheeks and ears. She wished she hadn't already donned her spring toque hat. Though piled high with green velvet, it sat perched uselessly atop her head and did nothing to shield her from the cooler Colorado weather.

The wagon hit a hard bump and Elaine gripped the edge of the wagon bench with one hand, rubbing a thumb rhythmically over the brooch with the other. She would not allow herself to go overboard again. What a humiliation that had been.

Her backside must be bruised by now, with all the bumping around she'd endured these past few days. It wasn't like her family had driven around in a parasol-topped runabout or handsome cab, but the buckboard she was accustomed to at least boasted a lighter suspension and cushioned seats.

This contraption Gideon was driving was hardly more than a hand-built hay wagon with a rough bench seat facing backwards behind the driver's seat as the freight wagon had. Wooden barrels filled the rest of the wagon, and Elaine felt trapped.

Gideon turned the team of mules up a new trail, following a creek bottom. The mountains on either side seemed to grow taller and more immediate, pushing in closer until she could almost reach out and touch the cliff-side. The air thickened with a cool, damp earth smell overlaid with pine resin.

The trail pinched down to a point between the creek on their left side and the rock wall on the right. Her heart raced as she realized if anything blocked their path, they had nowhere to go. Pressing her hand flat against the hidden cameo pendant, her eyes followed the rock wall up, up, and up.

"Look there!" Mary pointed to the overhang they had just passed under.

A bighorn sheep stood proudly on the rocky mountainside. Elaine gasped. There seemed to be much less air to breathe in these mountains. That animal could've jumped right down on top of them, dashing them to bits with its tiny cloven hooves. If an animal that size could be right overhead and go unnoticed, what else could lurk unseen in this forest, ready to strike?

Her breath quickened as the narrow trail closed in tighter. Gloved fingertips brushed her lips, and she turned on the wooden bench to look up to the driver's seat.

Jo leaned against Gideon's side, resting her head against his shoulder. The trip had been nearly silent, a wall of tension jutting up between the passengers and their escorts. Elaine had never got on well with her younger sister. Jo had been wild and unpredictable since childhood. The girl had been headed for trouble with all due haste from the time she could walk.

Nothing about their childhood had been the same, aside from the parents and home they shared on their father's Kansas cattle ranch. Even the girls' parental preference had differed. Elaine preferred the company of Mother while Jo had shadowed their father, Pa as Jo so stubbornly insisted on calling him, all around the ranch. As soon as Jo was old enough to tag along with Gideon, whose father had been a wrangler on the ranch, they had forever lost Jo to the hay-barn, the millpond, and the hayfields. Anywhere Gideon went, Jo followed, dirty bare feet leaving a cloud of dust in her wake.

Now, Jo had followed Gideon to the wild Rocky Mountains, and somehow, Elaine had been dragged along with them.

"How much farther is it?" Elaine did her best to keep the shaky tone out of her voice.

"Not far." Jo spoke over her shoulder, "We'll stop up here for water and be home before dark."

It already seemed to be growing dark as far as Elaine could tell. In this tight ravine, the sun was completely out of sight. The trail widened, and Gideon pulled the mules to a stop near the creek. A small waterfall tumbled down from boulders taller than Elaine was. The swirling water had cut out the bank, digging out a deeper pool before finding its way back down the creek bed.

Elaine stood and stretched. Though eager to reach the end of this journey, she was grateful for the reprieve from the wooden bench seat.

Gideon rolled the empty barrels down two planks he'd propped against the back of the wagon and over to the water's edge. "Toss me that pail, will you, Elaine?" Gideon pointed to the wagon.

Elaine located a wooden bucket under her seat. She'd recoiled at the thought of touching the dusty thing. She carefully lifted the hem of her skirt and stepped down from the wagon, holding the bucket away from herself. Gideon raised an eyebrow and took the bucket with a smirk. Only then did Elaine recall the state of her dress, which was still mud-stained from her tumble from the muleskinner's wagon.

"This is as good a place as any to wash yer things." Gideon nodded to the creek. "Just do it downstream from here. No use contaminating our drinking water with your muddy petticoats." His laugh boomed and echoed off the cliffs.

"Here?" Elaine looked around. "You want me to disrobe in the open air?" Elaine's eyes widened as she took in the terrain's wildness.

"Oh, for Pete's sake, Elaine." Jo took Elaine by the elbow to the other side of the wagon. "Get yourself a fresh dress from your trunk and come stand here."

Jo pulled a quilt down from the wagon and draped it over the high bench seat on one side, holding up the other side to make a screen of privacy.

Elaine stared at her sister. The idea of undressing outdoors with a man ten feet away seemed positively ludicrous. Jo began tapping her foot. Clearly, they were serious.

"No need to waste the extra water supply to wash these things at home when we got plenty of it right here. It may not be hot water, but I reckon it'll do the job."

Elaine retrieved a dress that, if not suited for travel, would at least not be too frivolous for the short distance they had left. Hiding behind the quilt, she removed her gloves to unfasten her layers of clothes. Cool air, stirred up by the small falls, rushed over her, exaggerating the exposure of her bare skin.

"Pass them to me, deary, and I'll get'em started." Mary took the bundle of soiled clothes from her.

Elaine let out a small sigh of relief. Even if she was on the edge of the wilderness, at least she had Mary to offer a little piece of normalcy. Living alone with the uncivilized antics of Jo and Gideon would've been much more daunting without Mary by her side.

She lifted the new skirt to step into, and a shout carried down the canyon. On a rocky outcropping farther up the trail, a figure with dark braids held a rifle balanced across his shoulders as he shouted something unintelligible. He sat atop a white horse blanketed in brown spots.

A scream ripped from Elaine's throat, and she yanked the quilt from Jo, ducking low and trembling. Was this a hostile or a bandit? Had he seen her in her small clothes? What if he killed them all to steal the mules? What if he killed the others and took her prisoner? Exposed as she was, who knows what kind of savage ideas he might have.

"Land's sake, Elaine, ya nearly split my eardrum." Jo scowled at Elaine, wiggling a fingertip against her ear.

The man rode down the hillside toward them. She was well-covered in the quilt but might as well have been naked as the day she was born, exposed as she was.

"Who—who is that?" Elaine gripped Jo's arm tight and hid behind her.

Jo sighed, and Gideon chuckled.

"That, dear sister, is Clay Anderson. He came out here with us when we moved from Pike's Peak."

Elaine's chest tightened, and spots swam in her vision. Was she going to faint? She hadn't had a fainting spell since she started carrying the cameo brooch. Giving her an object to focus on had helped her to not allow herself to be overcome with panic. Wrapped in nothing but a quilt, and without her good luck token, she was without help.

The man approached, grinning broadly. His cheekbones were broad as they were high, and his coloring was even darker than Gideon's sun-bronzed skin. He wore a broad-brimmed hat with a large feather sticking in the band and a linen shirt and vest. But he wore the buckskin leggings and tall moccasins like the natives she'd seen back in Kansas.

Elaine gripped the quilt tighter around her, trying to smother the tingling sensation that swept up her back and neck. She inched her way behind Jo, using her sister as a shield. Even if this Clay character was friendly, Elaine was completely indisposed. She dropped her eyes to the ground, willing herself to become invisible.

"I see you found our long-lost relatives!" Clay called to Gideon as he approached.

Who was he calling a relative? She didn't even know this man.

"That we did." Gideon's voice strained as he rotated the barrel around on its circular base toward the wagon. "Sure will be nice to have someone to cook who can do more than boil coffee and burn the biscuits."

Jo picked up an acorn from the roadside and threw it at Gideon. It bounced off Gideon's hat, and he laughed heartily. Had he truly just said that about his own wife? The nerve of him! Elaine gaped in shock, but Jo joined in the laughter as if she hadn't been insulted.

"Our prayers have been answered." Clay looked up to the sky. "Thank you, Father, for looking kindly on our starving souls."

Another acorn bounced off of Clay's back as he walked over to help Gideon with the barrel.

Jo turned back to Elaine and Mary, who had returned with Elaine's wet garments.

"I'd have let them starve if I hadn't needed the food. Gideon's elk stew and hard tack is tolerable at best, and if it were up to Clay, we'd be living on pemmican." Jo wore an amiable smile.

Elaine had never understood Jo and Gideon's odd dynamic. Why on earth would Jo choose to attach herself to such a rough, unmannered character? Not only did she tolerate his brutishness, but she also seemed to find it appealing.

Nothing about the way her sister lived made the least bit of sense. How long would Elaine have to live in such a rough manner before she could find someone more civilized to take her in? Any length of time would be too long.

Chapter 10

Matthias reined his gelding to the edge of the cliff and dismounted. The sheer drop opened the close forest into a vast landscape of mountains and valleys blanketed with dark green evergreens and the brighter spring green of aspens and oak brush. A tapestry worthy of a king. Being in such beauty always humbled him. He was so small and inconsequential in such a vast wilderness.

Pa would box his ears for taking the time to appreciate the magnificent scenery. "You're soft," Pa would say between blows, "weak." And maybe Pa had been right.

It was a side of Matthias he could never show to anyone. He slipped his hand into the pocket of his trousers and grazed a thumb over the etching in the metal.

"No son of mine." The words echoed in his mind with the memory of being tossed out of the house to sleep in the snow.

It hadn't been so bad that time, Matthias told himself. He'd only had to sleep outside for two nights before Pa let him come back to the house.

He pulled the harmonica from his pocket and glanced back toward ranch headquarters. No one would hear him at this distance. He'd asked McBride if he could ride out and get a lay of the land while the cowboys were gathering cows. It was clear he wasn't hired on as a cowhand, but precisely what they had hired him to do was still uncertain. A hired gun, he supposed. Wolves and bears would definitely be a concern in this territory.

Bringing the harmonica to his lips, he released a breath and poured all his uncertainty into the box, transforming the emotions into a clear harmony that carried out on the breeze. He'd first heard the tune "Lone Prairie" when the gang had stopped at a saloon in Colorado Springs. This may not be a prairie, but the sentiment seemed to fit. He was alone in a vast wilderness and would have to keep it that way.

The image of a slender brunette caked in mud came to mind, and the song faded from his lips. As strange and bedraggled as Miss Bradford had been, her beauty had been impossible to miss. Those golden eyes had haunted him since the first night he'd come upon the stranded freight wagon.

He wondered if he'd ever see her again. His heart ached for just another glimpse. *Fool.* He couldn't allow himself to hold a woman in his thoughts, much less in his arms—ever.

This job—this opportunity—was the only thing he could look forward to. Three meals and a place to lay his head was far more than someone like him could ever wish for. He'd be grateful for the work and shut the door to hope before it had time to work its way any closer to his heart.

He brought the harmonica back to his lips and finished the song. The last notes carried out, whispering through the trees the things he could never say out loud.

When the music faded and the sun settled behind the distant peaks, Matthias tucked the harmonica back into his pocket and mounted Copper. "Let's go home, boy." He rocked forward in the saddle and turned his gelding's nose downhill.

Back to the ranch, Matthias pushed open the door to the bunkhouse that would be his home for the foreseeable future. A haze of smoke hovered in the air like a low-lying cloud bank. He stifled the groan that rose in his throat. The hired hands crowded around a round table, playing cards and drinking whiskey.

Silence fell as he entered. The sound of his boots against the wood plank floor echoed in the cabin.

A burly man with a bushy red beard and a lazy eye leaned back in his chair, leveling a glare at Matthias. "Who are you?" His gruff voice was as abrasive as his appearance.

Matthias stiffened. This was going to be no warm welcome. Had he imagined it would be? He'd endured endless months of mockery and rough talk from the other outlaws in the Blake Gang. This would be no different.

Would he ever find a quiet life without trouble? He would either have to maintain his distance and focus on the job, hoping they would leave him be, or fall in line and join in the crass talk and drinking so he would be accepted.

Pulling in a fortifying breath, he answered, "Matthias Noble." He injected as much confidence and authority as he could muster into his tone.

"Didn't you hear?" A lanky cowboy leaned against a bunk, rolling a cigarette. "McBride hired himself another hired gun. He's a real outlaw, from what I hear."

A boulder the size of Texas landed in Matthias's gut. *Outlaw?* Did they know? How could they know?

"That so?" An older man with an iron-gray mustache drooped over his mouth spoke before tossing back the amber liquid in his glass.

The air stirred behind him as the door to the cabin opened again, admitting two more men. A wiry blond man with a jagged scar over his left eye, and the man he'd met with Shane McBride earlier, walked in. Both assessed Matthias with narrowed eyes.

"Jasper, Hank, this here's McBride's new gunman." The man with the lazy eye spoke from across the table, gesturing to Matthias.

"We've met." Hank glowered.

"So, this is him." Jasper stiffened. "And what makes you think you're up to the job?"

"I reckon I just need the work. Your boss was kind enough to remedy that." If Matthias kept his words few, maybe he could avoid much confrontation.

Jasper pursed his lips and nodded. "Well, I s'pose we'll see if you're up to the task tomorrow. Hank and I have been out scouting this evening. Tomorrow, we'll go on a little hunting expedition."

"I'll be ready." Matthias gave a quick nod and jerked his chin toward an empty bunk. "That one taken?"

No one answered, and Matthias took the lack of response as an affirmative. They hadn't said no, had they? He dropped his saddlebags on the foot of the wooden bunk.

The uncomfortable itch of eyes on his back skittered over him. He smoothed out his bedroll and sat down, pulling off his boots.

"What's the matter there, little fella? You homesick already?" A mocking tone carried across the room, followed by raucous laughter.

Matthias stifled a bitter laugh. What these men didn't know was Matthias hadn't been homesick in the ten years he'd been gone, and no insults they could hurl his way could sink into the scarred, leathery hide he'd developed by Pa's abuse. They could jab and poke fun at him all they wanted. Matthias needed this job, and no amount of harassing was going to scare him off.

Chapter 11

With every mile passed after leaving Pagosa Springs, Elaine's stomach tightened more and tension ached in her arms. Just how far from town was this homestead? If Pagosa Springs could have even been called a town. It was little more than a few buildings along a smelly river surrounded by wild, unsettled mountains.

Regardless of her anxious spirit, though, Elaine needed to be grateful for this. At least she wasn't enduring the gossip and speculative glances around their circle in Dodge City.

Maybe a small ranch in Colorado wouldn't be so bad. Elaine had been raised on a cattle ranch in Kansas, after all. Even on the ranch, they had a spacious, if not elaborate, home. A hand water pump in the kitchen, a bathtub, and even gas lights.

Mary had taken care of everything around the house. It stood to reason, things might not be so different from what Elaine had known before. In addition, Gideon and Jo had purchased an active sheep ranch rather than building up from the ground this spring. Certainly there would be more comfortable accommodations than the average homesteader's soddie.

The wagon crested the hilltop after an arduous climb, and the homestead came into full view. The tentative hope building in Elaine's heart shriveled like an uneaten piece of fruit. This was no ranch.

The house was hardly more than a shack. Elaine's fretful gaze darted around the clearing. A small cabin, hardly large enough for two rooms, stood to one side of the open area, and a barn stood on the edge of a fence crowded with bleating sheep. Was this it? This couldn't possibly be all of it. Perhaps this was just a shepherd's cabin, and the ranch boasted a larger home behind some trees.

She gripped her skirt in tight fists and prayed for strength to survive what was coming.

"Home, sweet home," Gideon announced, and Elaine swayed in her seat.

"This—this is your home?" Elaine's voice shook, betraying her shock.

"It's our home now." Jo's voice was as short as ever.

Her sister had never learned the art of adding melody to her tone. Pa called it "matter of fact" and "honest," but Elaine knew it to be ill-mannered and uncouth.

She bit back the questions battering her mind. She would see soon enough where they would all stay. Surely, they had some sort of accommodations planned out, knowing Mary and Elaine would join them for the foreseeable future.

She dismounted the wagon and followed her sister's pregnant waddle to the little cabin. It was a log house, packed with mud and straw between the logs. It surprised Elaine to find the space felt larger on the inside than it looked, though nothing like the ranch house she had hoped for.

The kitchen area and what she supposed could be called a parlor shared an open space divided by a roughhewn dining table. The entire area was no bigger than their dining room back home. There was a cot draped in a colorful blanket by the wood stove, and two doorways, covered only by blankets, must be bedrooms.

An elderly woman with dark skin slept in a rocking chair by the stove. Elaine blinked, confused. Who was this woman? Did she live here? How could they possibly fit more people in this little cabin out in the woods?

"Welcome home, ladies." Jo's voice bubbled with excitement. "Isn't it something? Two bedrooms. Two. Can you believe it?"

Elaine watched her sister with a jealous fascination, as she always had. Jo had the freedom to relish every bit of life and find adventure in it, while Elaine spent her life stifled and terrified.

Though she'd never admit it to her little sister, she'd always envied that. Jo's free-spirited way was something Elaine could never experience herself.

"When we purchased this place from the shepherding family who lived here before us, it was only a one-room cabin. Gideon and Clay got straight to work, adding the extra rooms.

We've only just finished with them." Jo rattled on about what a blessing this all was, and Elaine lost herself in her questions that filled the room.

How could Jo consider this primitive life to be a blessing when she'd known far greater comfort back home in Kansas? Who were these other people? Where would everyone sleep?

The journey here had been troublesome enough. Being pulled from the habits and routines that protected her from having an episode had been frightening and strenuous. But she had hoped when they reached the homestead she could once again establish those routines and quiet the compulsions that battered her daily.

Seeing the state of their living conditions now, Elaine could no longer fool herself into believing anything would be familiar. She tapped the space where Grandmama's pendant should be. It wasn't there, and its absence left her even more unsettled.

She hadn't pinned it back when she'd changed her dress at the creek. Her hand shook with the need for relief from the driving compulsion. She dropped her hand to her side, hiding it behind her skirt, and closing her fist. One time, two, and three. The sleeping woman stirred and roused. Jo walked to the woman's side and placed a hand on her shoulder.

"This is Florence, Clay's grandmother," Jo continued, unaware of Elaine's distress.

The older woman patted Jo's hand on her shoulder and smiled up at her.

"Clay and Florence have been close friends of Gideon's since he came to Colorado." She bent down and spoke directly to the older woman. "Florence, this is my sister, Elaine, and Gideon's mother, Mary."

Florence's dark eyes locked on Elaine's in an unsettling stare. "You are home."

Elaine bristled. She was not home. As a matter of fact, she couldn't imagine being farther from what home should be.

"You can set your things in here, ladies." Jo waved to the bedroom on the right. "You'll sleep in there. Florence prefers to sleep by the stove, so it's just the two of you in here. Clay will sleep in the barn, and Gideon and I—well, we have the other bedroom." Jo's pressed lips did nothing to hide her smile, and Elaine turned away, blushing.

Her younger sister and Gideon's close bond had always fascinated Elaine. The fact they found each other after three years of separation was nothing short of miraculous. Truthfully, it wasn't fair. Her sister had abandoned family and duty, doing heaven knows what, only to find her happy ending, even so.

Elaine would never have that kind of love. She couldn't afford the luxury of chasing wild abandon. She needed to find a man with wealth. Someone who could offer her a household staff who could handle the unsettling things that could send her spiraling. The less she had to engage in household duties and chores, the better her chances of hiding her affliction.

She followed her sister and Mary into the bedroom. The clicking of her boot heels on the wood floors of the main room fell into a solid thumping. She froze, staring down at her feet. A dirt floor? *No. It couldn't possibly be.* She gripped her skirt at her sides and swayed.

"We haven't been able to add the wood floors to this bedroom yet," Jo explained. "We got the room dried in, but it's lambing season, and the men have been working sunup to sundown just to care for the animals. We've hard-packed the floors best we could. We're lucky the ground here is such stiff clay. With a little water and hard packing, the dirt hardened up nicely." Jo offered Elaine an apologetic smile.

Elaine continued into the small bedroom, her eyes trained on the reddish-brown clay under her feet. How was she going to endure this? It was impossible. She must write to Mother immediately and insist on coming home. The tickling sensation under her skin prickled to life, sending waves of unease up her arms.

"Isn't this just lovely?" Mary's voice was full of enthusiasm.

Elaine pulled her gaze from the dirt floor to take in the rest of the room. It was small, just enough space for the two cots and a small table between. She chided herself for a lack of gratitude.

Despite the dirt floor and the logs packed with dried mud and straw, it was clear her sister had made the room as comfortable as possible. She set her carpet bag down and sat on the neatly made bed, running her fingers over the cool, clean quilt.

Maybe writing to Mother would be hasty. Elaine should do her best to endure things here while the rumors settled at home. Who knew, even though Frank Dashel wasn't staying in town, maybe there would be other civilized men like him in the area. She might yet have hope to marry someone with better circumstances.

Surely Jo and Gideon couldn't spend all their time up here in the high country. They must make trips to town for church and supplies often enough. She would bide her time for now. Heaven knew how she would get through her days here, but she would find connections in town. She must.

Chapter 12

Gideon hung the last piece of harness on a nail with a heavy sigh. Nothing more to do here. Clay had already insisted on brushing down and watering the mules so Gideon could spend time with Ma, but he wasn't so sure he was ready for that yet.

Ma had shown nothing but forgiveness and understanding when they visited Kansas earlier this year, despite Gideon's long absence and lack of word sent back home. Though heartbroken to hear about Pa being committed to an asylum, she insisted she was just happy to have her son back. Still, it hadn't been easy for them to find a way forward.

With Jo's encouragement over the past several months, Gideon was learning to forgive himself for what had happened to Pa. But the bur of guilt still rubbed him raw. Less for being responsible for Pa leaving, but more for not sending word home when he found Pa.

Hiding away in the mountains had been the coward's way out. Despite Ma's forgiveness, there would be consequences to his selfishness.

Clay plopped a hand on Gideon's shoulder, jarring him out of his ruminating. "Go," his younger friend insisted. "It won't keep well with time."

Gideon nodded and straightened his shoulders. "Alright, I'm goin'."

He found Ma in the house, already fussing about the kitchen. There was a pot of something bubbling on the cookstove. The sweet fragrance of onions and herbs mingled with the heartier aroma of roasted meat. It smelled far better than anything he'd made since leaving home.

"Land's sake, Ma," Gideon spoke with wonder, "how do you do that?"

Ma looked up from the biscuit dough she was gently folding. "How do I do what?" She shrugged and smiled.

Gideon looked around the kitchen and shook his head. He couldn't form the words to describe the gift she had to turn a few simple ingredients into a feast. Or a barely constructed cabin into a warm and comfortable home. In the time it had taken Gideon and Clay to unhitch the wagon and unload supplies, Ma had rebuilt Gideon's childhood.

Not that having Jo didn't make this place a home. Her presence had healed him and given him a sense of purpose—of hope. But she wasn't exactly the homemaker most women set their intentions to become.

That didn't matter to him. Her free spirit and adventurous ways had been what had captivated his heart since childhood.

Neither of them could cook much beyond beans and hardtack or a simple stew. Whatever Ma was concocting on the stove now filled the cabin with the sensation of home. Gideon pinched off a piece of biscuit dough, and Ma slapped his hand.

"You stay out of that." Ma's tone was stern as ever, but a playful smile lingered on her lips. "You were always one for the biscuit dough."

"And you never wanted me to have any." Gideon leaned against the counter and savored the dough.

"If I had let you and Jimmy have as much dough as you wanted, we wouldn't have had any biscuits to our supper." Ma shrugged.

A pang of regret pinched in Gideon's chest at the mention of his younger brother. "How is he?"

Jimmy had been old enough to take care of himself and Ma when Gideon left. But when Jo and Gideon had returned to visit their families in Kansas, Jimmy had taken a job in Topeka, planting wheat. Gideon suspected Jimmy's absence during their visit had more to do with avoiding Gideon than with any need for work.

Ma's eyes tightened at the corners, and she pursed her lips in thought. "Jimmy is, well—" Ma hesitated. "He's a restless soul, like your Pa, I suppose." A sad smile crossed Ma's face, and Gideon's heart clenched. "Maybe all my men are. Though I never expected you would have been."

The biscuit dough formed a heavy lump in Gideon's belly. The pensive line between Ma's brows told him she didn't mean the barb, may not have even realized she'd said it, but there it was—the pieces of her heart all scattered in front of him.

He'd been a big part of that. He'd been young and irrational when he'd left to find Pa, yet he couldn't regret going. Even finding Pa in the condition he had, at least he *had* found him. Still, he should never have allowed the shock and guilt of finding Pa so changed to keep him from being there for the rest of his family.

"Ma." Gideon struggled with what to say—how to rebuild the relationship he had fractured. "I know—"

"Gideon!" Jo called from outside.

There was a tone of agitation in her voice, and Gideon ran out the door. She was on the ground in the middle of the sheep pen, her green skirt piled around her as if she were part of the landscape.

She sat hunched over, her back to him, the copper-colored waves of her hair glinting in the sun. It wasn't quite near her time yet, or so she said, but his worry over her condition was an ever-present, gripping pressure in his chest. He jumped the fence and flew to her side, dropping beside her. If anything happened to her—he couldn't bring himself to finish the thought. She looked up at him, not with pain but pleading in her eyes.

"He was all alone." She moved the corner of her shawl to reveal a fuzzy white nose peeking out from the layers of homespun. "I think his mama's kicked him off, but I don't know which ewe it is."

Gideon's breath rushed from him with relief. Jo wasn't in any danger. The haze of fear dissipated as he settled next to his wife and tucked the tiny lamb back into its cocoon of warmth.

He scanned the sheep fold for any sign of a ewe that had recently given birth. One ewe stood to the side, nuzzling and cleaning a newly born, shaky-legged lamb. So, that was the way of it. This little one was a twin, and the mama had only accepted one of them, kicking the other off.

It happened from time to time. The farm journal the former owner of the homestead, Hector Sanchez, had left behind, mentioned situations such as this. He scooped the baby from Jo's lap and carried it back to its mother across the pen. It may not work, but he had to try.

He neared the ewe, shuffling on his knees now, and placed the newborn lamb at her feet. She sniffed it and stomped her foot, turning and nudging it further away. Gideon sighed and looked back to Jo, who was struggling to get back to her feet. He repressed the chuckle that bubbled under his ribs at the sight of Jo stalled like a turtle on its back.

"Hold on, Love. I'm coming," Gideon called and scooped up the infant lamb.

He hurried over to Jo's side to help her up with his free hand. "Looks like we'll have to find another ewe to graft this little one to."

Jo's eyes glistened, and she took the lamb from him, tucking it back into the folds of her shawl. "Well then, we'll just have to see what we can do for the poor thing." She looked up at Gideon and leaned into his side.

He wrapped an arm around her and pressed a kiss to the top of her head. Peace filled him at the fresh, herbal scent of pine that lingered in her hair, and he breathed out a sigh of relief. Despite the mistakes he'd made over the past few years, God had blessed Gideon beyond anything he could have hoped for when He brought Jo back into his life. He needed to trust God to help him rebuild his relationship with Ma and Jimmy, too.

Chapter 13

Matthias followed Jasper and Hank as they navigated a narrow game trail that weaved through a thick clump of oak brush at the base of a steep hill. Despite the rocky start last night, the men had been friendly enough this morning. After a quick breakfast of cold biscuits and a slice of ham, the three of them had saddled up their mounts and headed out on their hunting expedition while the cowboys stayed back to brand cattle.

Jasper led the way, urging his horse up a rocky slope that led up to the next bench of the mountain. They reached the top, rocks tumbling down the embankment behind them, and stopped in an aspen stand, sheltered by quaking green leaves that scattered the light. The edge of the trees bordered a steep slope overlooking thousands of acres of hills, valleys, grassy parks, and rocky cliffs.

Jasper reached into his saddle and pulled out a chaw of tobacco. He jerked off a bite and offered it to Matthias.

"Thanks, no." Matthias shook his head, hoping he wouldn't sound like he was putting on airs.

He should have just accepted, but after sixteen years of choking on the thick, sweet scent of Pa's cigar smoke,

Matthias couldn't stomach the smell of tobacco, much less the taste.

"Suit yerself." Jasper shrugged and put the leathery stick back in his saddlebag.

Matthias reached into his own bag and took a bite of jerky instead.

Hank took a long drink from his canteen and eyed Matthias's rifle scabbard. Jutting his bushy, black chin toward the gun, he said, "So, Noble, what you shootin' there? I never got a good look at yer piece t'other day, but by what I saw, you're a crack shot."

A prickle of unease itched the back of Matthias's neck, and he glanced over to Jasper. Did he know too? As he saw it, killing that rustler had been an unfortunate necessity in order to save Shane and Hank's lives. It was something he wished he hadn't needed to do, but he couldn't have just sat there and watched as they were ambushed.

Despite the justification of it, though, he'd rather not have any rumors spreading about what he'd done. He needed to lie low, keep his head down, and keep out of trouble.

He rolled his shoulder in an uncomfortable shrug. "Oh, that wasn't nothin'. You were in a bind, and I helped. That's all."

Jasper and Hank exchanged a look.

Matthias's pulse quickened, and he cleared his throat, veering the conversation in a safer direction. "But to answer your question, the gun's a Savage. Bought it off a feller in Colorado Springs."

In truth, he'd robbed it off a stagecoach near Colorado Springs, but he couldn't well admit that, now could he?

These men may have been acting friendlier this morning, but he could never let it slip he was an outlaw. That was a part of himself he would keep locked up tight along with all the other things better left unsaid and forgotten from his past.

"Seen any sign yet?" Hank asked Jasper, his eyes scanning the aspen trees that surrounded them.

Matthias took a bite of the jerky and chewed thoughtfully. He hadn't asked many questions this morning, not wanting to sound ignorant. But he still wasn't sure what it was they were hunting. He'd best be straight about it. Better to look foolish than to be of no use.

"What exactly are we looking for? Mr. McBride wasn't too specific about what we're after," Matthais asked before taking a sip from his canteen.

Jasper's lips twitched as he gave Hank a knowing look and rode over to one of the larger aspen trees. Matthias followed. He scanned the ground for scat but found none.

Jasper patted the tree next to him. Black scars from its growth marked the white bark, as was always the case with aspen. Yet, something was different about this tree. Upon closer inspection, this tree had more scarring than most. Down the length of the tree were markings—letters and symbols, all with differing degrees of aging. The last marking was new. The cuts in the tree were green, not black. Whatever these markings were, this last one was fresh.

"What exactly is this?" Matthias asked, rocking back in his saddle and rubbing his jaw.

"Filthy Mutton busters," Jasper spoke the words through gritted teeth and spat on the ground, wiping a sleeve across his mouth.

"Sheep herders, you mean?" Matthias asked, riding closer to the tree to inspect the markings. They seemed to be a sort of record, marked at different times. Each carving had aged differently, showing the passage of time.

Jasper nodded and exchanged another look with Hank before turning his horse to the north, riding without another word. That was odd. Weren't they supposed to be looking for tracks? Wolf or coyote sign?

Matthias followed Jasper and Hank up another steep embankment. Copper lunged up the sharp angle, and a popping sound thudded beneath Matthias before the saddle slipped free. He slid backwards, tumbling down the hill, and landed hard on a stob sticking out of the ground. He groaned and rolled off, pain shooting down into his hip.

He blinked up to find Copper, who stood at the top of the ridge, saddle dangling from the back cinch, looking down at Matthias as if questioning why he hadn't made it up the hill yet. Matthias pushed himself up to his knees.

He stood, sucking in a breath from the knife sensation in his hip, and climbed the hill, grasping at tree roots and rocks to make his ascent. By the time he reached the top, breathing heavily, Jasper and Hank were riding back in his direction.

He unhooked the back cinch and set the saddle up on a rock, inspecting his rigging. Sure enough, the leather latigo that bound the cinch to his saddle had cracked through and broke at the D ring.

"What's the problem?" Hank muttered through his bushy beard.

Matthias took Copper by the reins. "Broken latigo," he answered, though the problem was plain to see.

Jasper swore, and looked between Matthias's saddle and the game trail the two men must have been following into the trees.

"Can you mend it?" he asked. His impatience was clear by the tapping of his finger against his thigh.

"I'll manage," Matthias assured him. "You go on ahead without me. I'll catch up."

Jasper glanced back at the trail again and nodded. "Make it quick," he added, before turning back to retrace their path.

Matthias dropped to his knees next to the saddle, wincing at his aching hip. He had to find a solution right quick. If Jasper and Hank didn't think he could keep up, they might tell McBride Matthias wasn't a good hand. He couldn't let that happen.

He rolled the saddle over to remove the leather strap, revealing a large paw print in the damp soil at the base of the rock. It was nearly as large as his hand. A shiver rushed over the back of his neck.

So, there were wolves in this country, after all. He hoped he'd be the first to find the wolf and prove his worth to the other men.

He pulled out the roll of canvas containing his leather tools and set to work. Stretching the latigo out on the ground, he cut off the section that had failed him. There was just enough length to work with, but he needed to buy new leather with his first week's pay. This strip was on its last leg, and he wouldn't have enough left to repair if it broke again.

The old strings were still good. He could use them again, so he cut a new hole and tied the saddle maker's knot he'd learned from his grandfather as a boy, securing the cinch and latigo back on the D ring. As he raised the saddle to set it on Copper's back, a gunshot cracked in the distance, splitting the air and echoing off the cliff side above him. *Wolves?*

Matthias tugged hard on the new latigo and buckled the cinch. He wiggled the saddle to check that it held sturdy. When it did, he stepped up into the stirrup and tested the new latigo against his weight. It held. He urged Copper into a trot, shifting in the saddle to check again that he wouldn't have any more trouble.

The repair held, but the trail was too tight with trees for him to pick up much speed. It seemed an interminable amount of time before the trees opened enough to urge Copper into a run. The space between trees widened as he approached an open park.

He broke into the clearing to find a man dressed in a poncho and wide-brimmed hat, kneeling in front of an oddly shaped wagon—a shepherd's wagon, he realized. The man was shaking with his hands beside his ears. Another man, dressed similarly to the first, lay sprawled out in the grass, a dark red patch soaking his poncho.

Matthias jerked his eyes from the dead man back to Jasper and Hank, who held pistols trained on the other shepherd.

Matthias turned his head, avoiding the gruesome sight, dread clouding his thoughts. What had happened here? He opened them again and scanned the area. The field was scattered with sheep—all dead—every one. Blood stained their shaggy white wool in dark red patches on their necks and heads.

There hadn't been but one gunshot. What—

He glanced down at the club carved from a rifle stock he'd seen strapped to Hank's scabbard earlier. Bile rose in Matthias's throat, and he choked back the exclamation of horror he would have uttered. The club dripped slow rivulets of red down his horse's side, painting the white hair with streaks of crimson.

Matthias had heard of feuding between cattle ranchers and sheepherders before, but this was beyond anything he'd imagined. Hank shifted and trained his pistol on Matthias. He checked the repulsion that burned in his belly and schooled his expression into stoicism.

Jasper cast a casual, yet curious glance at Matthias and the memory of Kane Blake's cavalier demeanor flashed in his mind. He knew men like these. If Matthias showed any sign of weakness now, he would be lying among the dandelions with the sheep before he raised a finger in defiance.

"You alright, then?" Jasper nodded to Matthias's saddle.

He cleared the stomach acid from his throat as noiselessly as he could and adopted an unruffled tone. "Right as rain."

Jasper eyed Matthias, evaluating. When apparently satisfied with Matthias's benign mask, Jasper turned back to the shepherd. "You mutton busters have had warning enough. Had yonder fella not reached for his rifle, I wouldn't have had to kill him. He didn't have to die. You remember that."

The shepherd exclaimed something in another language. Matthias didn't know the language, but interpreted it as a string of intertwined cursing and pleading. A muscle bulged in Jasper's jaw and Hank's horse edged closer to the man.

"Easy there, Hank. We need this fella to send a message for us." Jasper turned back to the kneeling man again. "Savvy English?"

The man nodded slowly, and Jasper continued, "You tell Jon Ibarra to keep his filthy bags of wool off our grazing range." He wiped a bead of sweat from his brow. "And if Ibarra tells anyone about this, his pretty daughter will look like yonder ewes there when we're done."

The man's dark face blanched at this, turning the color of pewter. But he nodded solemnly. With that heinous threat lingering in the air between them, Jasper turned his horse and headed back the way they'd come. Hank reined in behind Matthias, trapping him between them. There was nowhere to go—no way to run. So, Matthias rode silently back to the Lazy M, cold sweat trickling down his spine.

Chapter 14

Elaine yawned and rubbed sleep from her eyes as she pushed past the heavy quilt hung from the bedroom doorway. An oil lamp gleamed from the dining table, filling the open room with a warm glow. The sun wasn't even up yet. Why had Mary woken her so early?

"Morning, hun." Mary held an apron out to her.

Elaine accepted the garment with wary hesitation.

"Put that on, and we'll get started. Gideon is already out doing chores. He'll be hungry when he comes in."

"Get started with what exactly?" Elaine asked as she cinched her apron strings tight around her waist and tied them securely in front of her so the knot pressed against the brooch pinned in her skirt.

Mary wiped the flour from her hands onto her own apron and braced them on her hips. "Breakfast. I know you've always had me around to cook and clean. So, it's reasonable you'd expect things would go on the same as they had been in Kansas, but things are different on a homestead. Everyone needs to help out."

Elaine's stomach quivered. This was all wrong. She knew nothing about cooking. Working with her hands went against everything Grandmama taught her to avoid.

"We'll start simple today. The most basic thing needed around here is sustenance. A good, strong cup of coffee and a hot meal will fuel a hard-working man for his day's labor. Farming and homesteading are hard work. Unless you want to go help your sister in the sheepfold, this is what you can do." Mary quirked an eyebrow and smoothed the back of her gentle hand over Elaine's cheek.

Elaine nodded and raised her head, chin up.

"We'll start by making coffee." Mary showed Elaine a handle on the back of the stove. "This here is the damper. Any time you open the stove, you'll want to pull this so you don't fill the house with smoke. Go ahead and do that now." She gestured to the handle.

Elaine reached out tentatively, afraid of being burned, but it wasn't hot. She pulled, and it slid free with the grating sound of sliding metal.

"Now, see this bundle of split wood? Gideon splits smaller kindling for us to use for cooking. You'll learn how much wood to use depending on how hot you need the stove." She took out a bundle of wood and opened the top of the stove.

"In the warmer months of the year, we won't need a fire all day, so it will dwindle down to coals between meals. When you need to cook something, just stack the wood in like this."

She fed the pieces of wood into the fire and stacked them in a crisscrossing pyramid over the hot coals in the bottom. Then she slid the lid back over the top of the open hole. "Now, open the front like this"—she turned a different handle in a clockwise motion—"to allow air in. Then close the back damper again. Don't forget that part or you're likely to cause a chimney fire."

Elaine swallowed hard. "What—what if I make a mistake? What if I burn the house down?"

"Don't worry. I'm here to help, and you'll do this so many times a day, it will all become habit in no time." She flashed a smile over her shoulder as she pulled down a wooden box with a crank on the top. "Now, scoop up some of those coffee beans there and add them to this here grinder and turn the handle until it's all ground up."

The powerful scent of coffee filled the kitchen as she turned the crank. She had never enjoyed the smell of coffee brewing and somehow it seemed even stronger now. She sighed, longing for a cup of tea. Why was everyone out here so fond of coffee?

"I think it's done." Elaine opened the box and peered inside. Ground bits of coffee scattered all over the counter and dusted her hands. She wiped frantically at the granules that clung to her bare skin. She'd never needed her gloves indoors before. Her pulse raced, and she sucked in a gulp of air, wiping the grittiness of the coffee onto her apron.

"Now, fill the pot with water from the barrel with the hand pump outside." Mary spoke with her back turned, unaware of Elaine's discomfort.

Turning to hand Elaine the water pot, her keen eyes traveled over Elaine, who was still desperately trying to remove the sensation of the coarse granules from her skin.

"You can wash your hands while you are out there." Mary gave Elaine a pointed look.

"Thank you," Elaine whispered and rushed outside with the pot.

She cycled the pump handle, letting the cold water run over her hands, and scrubbed feverishly.

The sensation of ants crawling over her skin eased with the cleansing of the water. She looked down at her apron and realized she couldn't dry her hands on it. It was covered in coffee as well. Instead, she shook off the droplets of water and surveyed the little farm as she allowed the morning breeze to dry her hands.

The air was crisp and sharp against her damp skin, and a dusky hue of pink light blanketed the quiet homestead. Darkness began to give way with a faint yellow glow on the horizon. Wilderness surrounded her as far as her eyes could see. No houses, no neighboring ranches, just endless miles of trees blanketing hills and valleys below.

How had she ended up so far from civilization? How would she ever find the life she desperately needed? She reached under her apron, careful to avoid the coffee grounds, and pressed a hand against the hollow ache in her stomach. This endless sea of wildland was going to swallow her whole.

Chapter 15

Jo moved through the quaking aspen trees as quietly as a woman large as a grizzly bear could. A spring breeze floated up behind her, cooling the back of her neck and ruffling the fine hairs loosened from her braid. The sensation eased her headache some, and she stopped to enjoy it for a moment before coming to her senses.

If the wind was tickling the nape of her neck, that meant her scent would carry straight to the clearing she meant to watch over. She'd never bring home supper if she couldn't get into a better position. Not long ago, she would have crouched in some low brush to conceal herself. Now, though, she feared she'd never be able to stand again if she tried to crouch down like that.

She ambled around the edge of the clearing until she found an outcropping of large rocks she could hide behind. She closed her eyes and relished the breeze as it whispered over her face. That was better. She had a clear vantage point, and the wind wouldn't give her away. She swung the rifle strap from her shoulder and brought the long gun down in front of her to rest on the tall rock.

Retrieving the curious box Clay had given her from the leather pouch strapped over her shoulder, she propped her arms on the rock and closed her eyes. She lost herself in the sounds of the forest. The rustle of leaves and the distant chatter of birds filled her senses until all her concerns over Elaine, Mary, and her upcoming delivery faded from her mind. In this moment, it was just her and the forest. Aside from the contentment of being curled against Gideon, warm in their bed, it was these moments in the wilderness she was most at peace.

Fully immersing herself in the stillness of the surrounding woods, she took hold of the box in one hand and its lid, attached on one end with a nail, in the other. She slid the lid over the emptiness of the box and a squeak echoed from the contact. A thrill bubbled up inside her. *It worked—amazingly well*. She moved the lid in short, sweeping motions, sending out a pattern of clucks that mimicked a turkey hen. *Boc-boc-boc-boc*—the box echoed across the clearing and into the trees on the other side.

She waited, listening for a response. *Boc-boc-boc*—she worked the lid again. *Nothing*. Sighing, she arched her back as the dull ache deepened from standing in one place too long. It looked like maybe it would be beans for their supper again tonight. She wasn't patient enough for this on a good day, but it was becoming clear her hunting days were coming to a close, at least until she wasn't growing a tiny human inside her.

She slipped the turkey call into the bag and a trilling gobble erupted from the trees. Jo jumped, and the little nugget responded to her sudden motion with a solid kick to her ribs. She stifled a groan and picked up the rifle, resisting any more sudden movements and scanning the trees for the tom who had answered her call.

Jo's heart beat faster as she watched and waited. She slowed her breathing, though her heart rate was less cooperative. With each heavy thump of her racing pulse, the pressure built in her chest until the pounding in her head nearly overcame her. She braced her elbows on the rock in front of her, balancing the gun, and stretched out her fingers, opening and closing her fist. Trying to work out the stiffness building in her joints the past few weeks.

Grateful as she was God had blessed them with a child, she would much prefer the pregnancy that had overtaken her body would be over so she could snuggle this little nugget and regain the strength and vibrancy she had lost.

She blinked away the tired haze from her eyes, and her focus cleared on the strutting array of colorful feathers fanned behind the puffed brown chest of her prize. *Thank you, Lord.*

She shifted her position and situated herself behind the iron sights of the rifle, aiming carefully to not waste any meat. She squeezed the trigger just as Gideon had taught her. The tom dropped, and Jo released the breath she held. Her surge of gratitude for the food this turkey would provide mingled with a prickle of sadness at the loss of life that was necessary. The juxtaposing balance of survival had become so much stronger now that she carried another life inside her. She blinked away the ridiculous feeling. She'd be mighty grateful when she had her body and her emotions back in check again.

She slung the rifle over her shoulder and pushed away from the rock, stiffly moving to the place where the turkey lay. She lowered gingerly to pick up the bird, and even that slight bending of her knees rebuilt the pressure in her head like curds being squeezed from whey.

She gripped the turkey by its feet and stood straight again. Her vision dimmed with spots floating at the edges, and she wavered, dizziness swirling in her heavy head. She blinked rapidly, trying to regain clear sight. *Lord, don't let me fall out here.*

Gideon had been scouting grazing territory with Clay this morning, and Jo had told no one where she was going. If she didn't return, would anyone find her?

Perhaps she should sit down before the collapse was involuntary. She wavered back to the rocks and found one she could rest on without being too low to the ground. She braced her hand against her chest and breathed slowly, willing her heart to find a gentler rhythm.

A rushing sound echoed in her ears, reminiscent of the great waterfall she and Gideon had encountered on their move to their homestead. Gideon had insisted on wading out into the frigid pool of snowmelt at the bottom of the falls and taking a bath.

Despite the unnerving sensation, she relaxed at the memory. She would be alright. Surely God wouldn't have brought them through all their perils, only to take her to glory now. There was still so much life ahead of them, and she was determined to live it to the fullest.

The clouds moved across the sky, and sunshine warmed the clearing. She rolled her shoulders back and raised her chest in a deep, sighing breath. When the pounding in her chest and the rushing in her ears subsided, she pushed up and waited for the stars to clear from her view.

She would not let herself faint out here in the grass like some damsel in distress. The shadows cleared from the edges of her vision, and she breathed a sigh of relief. She worked her way back through the trees, singing the lines of her favorite hymn to herself as she returned home.

Brightly doth His Spirit shine, into this poor heart of mine;
Where He leads, I cannot fall; trusting Jesus, that is all.

Chapter 16

Matthias hadn't been able to eat supper after they returned to the ranch. The beans and hard tack had stuck in his throat, and he'd pushed his food around his plate, hoping to maintain an appearance of unconcern. He'd wrapped two biscuits in his bandanna and tucked them away. He couldn't stay here. He would have to leave tonight. Maybe once he put some miles between himself and this place, he could stomach a few bites.

Darkness shrouded him as he paced the tree line behind the main house, working up the courage to tell McBride he wouldn't stay on and be party to the ruthlessness he'd seen that morning. It was a new moon, and the crisp night air surrounded him with inky black.

His frantic thoughts were too rapid to follow. He was lucky to be alive right now. If he'd shown any hesitation up there on the range, Jasper and Hank would've left him in that bloody field with the sheep. He gave a mirthless chuckle in the dark. He wasn't sure if he was lucky to be alive, if this was the life he was left with.

He'd sworn he was through with lawlessness—had moved from job to job seeking a place he could settle in and put his past behind. Now, here he was, working with men just as cruel as Kane Blake had been.

The difference was, when Kane had lured him into the life of an outlaw, he'd been young, lost, and naïve. He'd no notion the band of fortune hunters he'd joined up with found their gold by robbing stagecoaches and trains. By the time he'd realized what Blake and his gang were up to, he was trapped.

It had been a massive mistake to trust the cavalier stranger then, and yet another mistake trusting the McBrides in this new venture. He wouldn't be a victim to intimidation any longer. Darby McBride could take his so-called honest work and go hang. He certainly wouldn't stick around to be caught when the law caught wind of what they'd been up to.

He smoothed a hand over his hair and straightened his hat back onto his head. They would have to settle this like men. Stalking around the side of the house to confront Shane and his father, he passed a window, and tense voices trailed out of the open crack.

"I'm not all together certain this one's going to work out, Pa." Shane's voice didn't hold the smooth tone Matthias had heard from him when they'd just met. Rather, it quavered with tension.

"What are you talking about?" Darby McBride asked. "He stuck around, didn't he? Didn't interfere with Jasper and Hank, and he didn't run off. Not everyone is as weak stomached as you are."

"No"—Shane stammered—"no, he didn't. But Jasper's not convinced he'll stick it out."

"A man that can ride away from a scene like that and sit down to his supper is a harder man than you give him credit for."

"I don't think he's as hard as he'd like us to think," Shane continued.

"He shot that rancher without hesitation, didn't he?" Darby's voice dripped with condescension.

"But Pa." Shane's voice sounded like a child about to be taken to the woodshed, but he pressed on. "He thought he was shooting rustlers, then."

Darby's laugh rasped. "Well, that's a fact, but it's also why I reckon he'll fall into line. Any man willing to shoot first and ask questions later like that won't be touchy over a bunch of lousy sheep." McBride's voice held a confidence in Matthias that sank into the pit of his stomach.

Rancher? The man he shot for stealing the McBride's cattle had been the owner? That would mean the real rustlers were the McBrides. An icy wave of nausea washed over Matthias, and he leaned back against the house, his head thumping against the weathered logs. He was a fool. Would he never be free of the villainy that seemed to hound him wherever he went?

That man had been an honest rancher trying to get his own cattle back, and Matthias had killed him for it. Maybe McBride was right, maybe a killer was just who Matthias was now—all he'd ever be.

He squeezed his eyes shut. Thoughts of the first night he had crossed that line swam behind his lids. Thunder rolling outside their Missouri farmhouse, the scent of varnished wood crackling in the open woodstove, Pa swearing, Mama crying. Maybe Matthias had scarred his soul enough that night there could be no turning back.

"I don't know, Pa. I don't reckon we should trust him."

"Let it ride, Shane. If he's still here in the morning, you know he's solid." McBride paused, and the sickening scent of cigar smoke rolled through the open window. "If not, track him down and kill him. Nobody's gonna miss a drifter like him, anyway."

Matthias bent forward with his hands on his knees, breathing heavy. He would never escape his demons, would he?

"Now that Ibarra has been dealt with, we need to weed out the rest." McBride's gritty voice spoke up again. "Who's got the Sanchez place now?"

"Someone named Cross, I think. Bought the place and took over the flock," Shane answered. "Should we deal with them too?"

"Hmm ..." McBride hummed the hesitation.

Cross. Why did that name sound so familiar? He didn't know anyone in this area except—Jo. The hairs prickled on the back of his neck. Jo's man. Gideon *Cross* was his name, wasn't it?

McBride continued, "Not yet. Not so soon after yesterday's warning to Ibarra."

"So, what do you want us to do?"

"Discourage them in their new endeavors. New settlers won't have the stomach for the extra hardship. Make it clear this isn't where they want to be. If they turn out to be stubborn about it, we'll deal with it after we're certain there's no recourse for what happened today."

Matthias balled his hand into a fist and pressed it to his forehead. What now? Had he ought to light out of here tonight and warn Gideon? If he did, Shane, Jasper, and Hank would likely be on his heels in no time. *They'd track him down.*

McBride's words came back to Matthias, and the image of Hank's club dripping blood haunted him. Even if they didn't find him right off, Matthias had killed an innocent man, and the McBrides knew about it. They'd been ranching in this area for years. It was likely the sheriff would side with McBride. Once the law found out what he'd done, it would be Matthias in the hangman's rope. There was no going back to mend the things he'd done. Maybe an outlaw was all he would ever be.

He pushed away from the wall and set his hat back on straight. He may be beyond rehabilitation himself, but by the looks of things back in town, Jo had found her fresh start. Matthias couldn't stand by and watch their life destroyed. He had to warn them and hightail it out of the territory before the McBrides could hunt him down.

Chapter 17

E laine tucked her feet up under her and turned the thin page with anticipation. Reading Esther always gave her a sense of reading some adventure novel, full of danger and intrigue. She held her breath as Esther entered the king's throne room unannounced. Oh, how Elaine longed to be brave like Esther was, much like her own sister, as a matter of fact.

The needle of jealousy, always present regarding her sister, pricked her heart. Jo was bold and unruffled by social expectations in a way that infuriated Elaine. Why couldn't she have that same freedom? Why was she bound by these unwanted thoughts and fears?

Jo's free spirit leaned dangerously near recklessness, and judging by the scar on her face, she had clearly gotten herself into a mess of trouble when she ran from home. But somehow, she was still happy despite the scar and her lack of social standing.

That Jo, nor her parents, had told Elaine what happened to Jo or where she disappeared to for three years, left an uneasy feeling in Elaine's bones. It certainly did nothing to assuage the feeling she was on the outside of this family looking in. If Jo didn't trust Elaine with the truth of her past, how could Elaine trust her sister with her own secret?

She ran her finger down the page of her Bible to find her place. Just then, a motion outside the bedroom window caught Elaine's eye. She rose from her comfortable perch to see what was outside. In this rugged territory, it could be anything from wild savages to a grizzly bear, and that uncertainty kept Elaine on constant, exhausting alert.

She pulled the curtain aside to find the danger was only her sister. Jo was strutting through the barnyard, as much as a woman near her confinement could, draped in what must be Gideon's buckskin tunic.

She was singing something while casually swinging a giant dead bird in her right hand. Elaine pulled back from the window in revulsion and checked her earlier jealousy. No matter how adventurous Jo seemed, she was also embarrassingly uncivilized.

The front door opened, and Elaine ducked behind the blanket that acted as a door for her and Mary's room.

"Elaine?" Jo called far louder than necessary for the small cabin.

Elaine held her breath and squeezed her eyes tight. *Go away. Oh, please go away.* She wasn't sure what Jo would want from her, but it wouldn't be good.

She pressed herself flat against the wall and eyed the narrow bed. Could she sneak onto the cot and feign sleep? Maybe claim a headache? Before she could cross the room, Jo's head popped through the doorway.

"There you are." Jo quirked an eyebrow in a way that unsettled Elaine's stomach. "Put your apron on. We're having turkey for supper."

Supper. Elaine took a breath and warily stepped out of her corner. Perhaps she would only have to help Mary prepare the meal. She'd helped with breakfast this morning, and it hadn't been quite as distressing as her attempt to make coffee.

She'd mixed a cornmeal batter and fried johnny cakes on the wood stove. It had been intimidating, but with Mary patiently walking her through the steps, she'd managed alright. She put her Bible on the small table between the beds and took a deep breath, fortifying herself for another round of domestic duties.

When she entered the kitchen though, Jo was waiting at the front door.

"Well, come on then," she said, impatiently rolling her eyes.

"Come where?" Elaine asked warily, tempted to back into the bedroom. "I thought I would help Mary with supper."

Mary nodded to Elaine and tipped her head toward Jo. "That you will, but first we need something to cook. Go on, Elaine. Jo will show you what to do."

"Grab your apron," Jo said.

Why would she need an apron if they're going outside? And why did they need to go outside to get supper ready? She shot a glance to Mary, who nodded encouragingly and handed her an apron. She put it on and smoothed a hand over her stomach before following her sister outside.

Out front, there was a large pot steaming over a fire and a table made from wooden crates turned on end with a slab of wood on top. The dead turkey Elaine had seen her sister carrying lay on the table, its head lolling over the edge.

Elaine stopped in her tracks. "No," she said to herself but must've spoken aloud because Jo turned around and put a steadying hand on Elaine's arm before she could bolt back to the house.

"Yes," Jo said firmly and tugged at Elaine's sleeve. "You're going to learn how to properly dress out a bird."

"I can't." Elaine shook her head violently.

"You have no choice." Jo squeezed Elaine's hand and smiled patiently. "Elaine, you never know what obstacles lay in your future. You certainly can't expect to live the rest of your life in a parlor somewhere with someone to bring you tea."

Little did Jo know that was precisely what Elaine planned. She had no choice. It was the only way to protect herself from a fate like their great-grandmother, Vivian Forsythe. Her neurosis and resulting incarceration had been a closely guarded secret, but Grandmama Helen told Elaine as a warning.

It hadn't taken long for Grandmama to recognize Elaine had the same affliction as Great-grandmother Vivian and would suffer the same fate—imprisoned in an asylum—if she didn't keep herself from the situations that would send her into a fit. Situations just like this.

Elaine's eyes stung, and she pulled her hand from her sister's grasp, clutching the fabric of her skirt. She shook her head. "I can't."

"You must," Jo insisted. "I know it may seem harsh to you, but this is a harsh world." She raised a scarred eyebrow, and Elaine cringed. "These kinds of skills may help you survive one day. Besides, living up here on the mountain and building up a homestead is something that takes hard work. We all eat here, sleep here, and keep warm by the same fire. It takes all of us to make sure we have food to fill our bellies, wood to heat our stove, and wool to clothe us." Irritation laced Jo's tone. "We don't live in Philadelphia or London, Elaine. This is the west. You don't have the luxury of cooks, butlers, and lady's maids."

Elaine shook her head and held her hands up, palms out, in a defensive gesture. Jo took one of Elaine's hands and pulled her closer to the carcass on the table. Her hand shook, and she breathed steadily to stop the tremor.

It wasn't that Jo was unfeeling. She did not know of Elaine's infirmity. No one truly did, aside from Grandmama.

Elaine had to keep her secret safe, even from Jo. There was no way her strong, willful sister would understand Elaine's condition. They had never shared a close relationship, and for all Elaine knew, Jo would send her away just to be rid of her.

"Now, see here, we have our boiling water and this fire. First, we'll remove the head and dip him in the boiling water, then scrape away the feathers." Jo's matter-of-fact tone did nothing to subdue the waves of nausea threatening to overtake Elaine.

The thought of touching the bloody thing with her bare hands, much less pulling slimy wet feathers from its skin sent prickles up her arms.

"And then we burn off the pin feathers over the flame."

Heat flooded Elaine's body as her heart raced. The words of her rebuttal dried up in her throat, and the parched feeling only exaggerated the sensation of being trapped in a furnace.

Breath escaped her, and her lungs hardened. She had to try. She had no excuse not to. She pressed her hands against the rough board and lifted her chin, setting her jaw.

Jo braced the turkey's head between two nails in the tabletop and placed one of Elaine's hands on the soft feathers of the bird's body. The colorful feathers were smooth, cool, and oddly comforting. Then, Jo put the hatchet in Elaine's right hand and the weight of it might as well have been a boulder. She couldn't lift it.

Jo sighed but her tone softened. "Alright, I'll do it this time. But you'll have to learn, eventually."

She took Elaine's place at the table and raised the small axe. Panic surged through Elaine's veins again as Jo brought it down with a thunk.

The turkey's head dropped to the ground and blood sprayed the front of Elaine's apron. Elaine stumbled backward and rocked her head. Elaine ran to the nearest bush and dropped to her knees, heaving until her stomach was empty and aching.

She wrapped her arms around herself and moaned as the pulsing panic surged through her veins. A hand smoothed over her back, and Jo's round belly peeked into Elaine's periphery.

"I told you," Elaine said in a shaky voice, and retrieved a clean handkerchief from her pocket to wipe her mouth. "I ... *can't.*"

"Oh," Jo whispered, her ever sassy voice having lost its tone of strength.

Elaine sighed and stood straight, untying the apron and folding it so the blood stayed inside. Though she might play the prim, wilted flower, the lines of concern creasing the corners of Jo's eyes said her sister was realizing Elaine's antics were more than just aloof feminine sensibility. She handed the soiled garment to her sister and walked back to the house on shaky legs.

Her mask was off now, at least where Jo was concerned. The question was, what would Jo do with the knowledge that her sister was mentally infirm?

Chapter 18

Elaine threaded the large eye of the yarn needle and pulled some excess through. Today's chore was helping with Mary and Florence as they darned socks and mended clothes.

After her episode with the turkey, she did her best not to garner any additional scrutiny. She stayed as close by Mary's side as she could, avoiding her sister and learning domestic tasks like mending clothes and cooking meals, though she hadn't shown much promise. She found some chores were easier than others, particularly sewing, and volunteered for those duties as often as possible. Mary seemed to understand Elaine's struggle on some level and never called attention to her avoidance of the messier jobs.

Elaine never would have considered a task like darning to be an art form, but there was a satisfactory effect in weaving tattered ends of yarn that soothed her frayed nerves.

Florence retrieved a sock from the basket and handed it to Elaine. When Elaine had arrived at the homestead, her new Ute acquaintances had frightened her. But she had since grown accustomed to their presence.

Clay had quickly proven himself to be an animated, if not somewhat mischievous, character. His grandmother said very little but was a constant presence of peace on this back-woods homestead.

She took the sock from Florence and surveyed the damage. It had three holes in the top. Florence picked lengths of blue and yellow threads. The colors contrasted garishly with the light color of the sock, and Elaine blinked in confusion. Florence picked up the other sock, which had similar flaws.

"We make beautiful." Florence's dulcet tone was unwavering and sure, despite Elaine's misgivings about the choice of color.

She picked the same yellow and blue thread for her sock and held it up to the light that gleamed through the window. Elaine followed Florence's stitches as her needle poked up through the material in seemingly random places around the first hole. After about five stitches, Florence pulled the thread tight, and the hole closed together in a sunburst of yellow thread.

Elaine gasped at the result and followed her steps. Next, Florence took the blue thread and weaved over the other holes with triangular shapes under the sun. In the end, both socks boasted geometrical versions of sun and mountains and the result was, in fact, quite beautiful.

Florence nodded and patted Elaine's hand. Flashing a somewhat toothless smile, she then closed her eyes as she basked in the sun shining through the window.

A flurry of chickens squawked and scattered in the door-yard, and the large white dog that guarded the sheep barked menacingly. Elaine's heart skipped. She jumped up and crossed to the kitchen window to see what had caused the commotion.

A man dismounted from his horse and spoke with Gideon, his back turned to the house. There was something vaguely familiar about the man's build, but, of course, she knew no one here in Colorado aside from Jo, Gideon, and the Andersons.

Elaine pressed her lips together and tapped at the pendant in her waistband. Gideon gestured to the house, and her stomach clenched. Should she escape to her room until the visitor was gone? This was just some cowboy—not anyone she needed to become acquainted with.

She checked her instinct to flee. Regardless of who this man was, hiding from visitors would only call more attention to her eccentricities. She smoothed her skirt and patted down any flyaway hairs loosened during the day's activities.

When she looked back through the window, Gideon and the other man were approaching the door. Her heart seized in her chest. It was Mr. Noble. The man who had stopped to help when they were stranded.

What was he doing here? When Mary had introduced them in Pagosa Springs, it didn't appear Jo and Gideon knew him. She straightened and gripped the edge of the countertop, frozen. This was the last thing she needed. Someone else who had seen her at her worst.

Upon her first encounter with Mr. Noble, Elaine had been hiding under a wagon, covered in mud, in the throes of panic. Her stomach tightened into a knot. The more people who witnessed her moments of excitement, the more likely she would be locked away like Great-grandmother Forsythe.

The men entered the cabin, and Elaine darted a glance around the room, looking for an escape. She couldn't duck into her room, as Gideon's imposing bulk was directly in her path. She tapped nervously at her waistband. *One, two, three.* Then intertwined her fingers to stop the tapping.

There was no help for it. She must pull herself together and convince Mr. Noble she was nothing more than a proper young woman who had been momentarily overcome by her circumstances that day. Perhaps if she wore the mask well, he wouldn't think her an invalid.

Gideon pulled a chair out and gestured to Mr. Noble to take a seat.

"Where's Jo?" he asked, turning to Mary and Elaine.

"I believe she's checking the lambs," Mary answered. "I'll fetch her. Elaine, why don't you boil some coffee?"

The knot between Elaine's shoulders eased some. Bless Mary, she had volunteered to find Jo, so Elaine wouldn't have to muck about through the sheep fold. Coffee was a simple task so long as she could keep from making a mess of the grounds this time.

She added beans to the box of the grinder and turned the crank. *One, two, three. One, two, three.* This time, when she finished grinding, she tapped the box carefully on the counter to let the coffee granules settle before opening it. Then she spooned the grounds carefully onto the square of cheesecloth and tied it securely.

When she set the pot over the hot side of the stove, nothing happened. The pop and sizzle that should rattle the thin metal was absent. Huffing in frustration, she lightly tapped the stove top. It was cool. The fire needed to be stoked.

She darted a glance over her shoulder, but the men were paying no mind to her bustling around the kitchen. Sucking in a fortifying breath, she pulled open the knob on the back of the stove as she'd seen Mary do, then retrieved a handful of the split kindling from the wood box. With one hand, she opened the lid on the top of the cookstove and, with the other, she dropped in the kindling.

When she pulled her hand back, it brushed the edge of the stove top, leaving a long streak of black soot smeared across the back of her skin. She dropped the stove lid into place with a clatter and both men turned to look her direction. She pasted on a weak smile and turned her back.

Her heart raced as she frantically looked for a cloth to wipe her hand. She found a dry towel, but that only brushed off the loose bits. The long black line stayed stubbornly put. She soaked the cloth in water and scrubbed madly at the mark, fighting, and failing, to slow her panicked breaths. Her eyes prickled and stung as she scrubbed futilely.

Mary's gentle hand reached over her shoulder and rested over hers to still her frantic motions. She handed Elaine a bar of soap and squeezed her shoulder in a side hug without saying a word. Elaine washed the black stain from her skin while Mary opened the stove and arranged the wood correctly.

Elaine whispered a prayer of thanksgiving for Mary's kindness, but Mary could only cover so much. And at that, how much would Mary hide for Elaine before she realized this was something more than just an aversion to getting her hands dirty? This wilderness homestead of her sister's was going to be Elaine's undoing. She had to find a way to engage in whatever society Pagosa Springs offered. If she didn't find

a husband who could offer her a life away from these challenges soon, her secret would be exposed, and she would risk
being locked away.

Chapter 19

Matthias smoothed the denim of his britches over his knees and braced his elbows on the table, pressing his folded hands against his forehead. How was he going to explain all this? It was dangerous enough to come here and warn these people of McBride's questionable ranching practices. But knowing who Matthias was, and his past crimes, would they believe he hadn't been involved?

Yet again, Matthias wrestled with whether he'd made the right decision to sit idly by on the mountain while Jasper antagonized that shepherd. The gunmen had left the man alive, which was a small comfort, but if they had planned to kill him, too, would Matthias have had the nerve to try to stop them? He wasn't so sure, and the fact he couldn't say spoiled in his gut like sour milk.

Who was he to act so high and mighty now—as if he hadn't been party to these kinds of dealings before? Matthias was no better than Jasper and Hank, and Jo knew it well. What would she think of all this after the second chance she'd given him?

He shouldn't have come. Yet, he couldn't stand by and do nothing. Not when he knew McBride's plans for them and had seen his brutality firsthand.

The front door of the cabin opened, and Jo sidled into the room. When their eyes met, Jo froze, her hand on the swell of her belly and eyes wide. He stuffed down his own reaction of shock, once again, at the sight of her. He wasn't sure he would ever grow accustomed to the scar that ran down the length of her face. She'd always been a beautiful woman, though, and whatever had happened to her after she'd broken ties with the Blake Gang hadn't diminished the bright spark in those green eyes of hers.

Matthias stood, and after a moment of silence while Jo gathered her jaw from the floor, she gestured to his chair. "Kit—er—Matthias, please, sit down."

Matthias waited for Jo to lower herself into a chair before taking his own seat.

A look of frustration crossed her face, and she pressed her hands on the table to stand again. "I should have offered coffee. I'm not much of a hostess, I'm afraid."

Gideon rested a hand on her arm to stop her. "Sit. Elaine is making coffee."

Matthias followed Jo's look to the wood stove where the intriguing brunette was drying her hands on a kitchen towel. He was glad for the opportunity to see she had found her family and safety. She was such a stark contrast from her sister. Where Jo was wild and fierce, Miss Elaine seemed delicate, like she might shatter at a touch.

"What brings you here?" Jo's voice pulled him back to the matter at hand, and the sour feeling in his gut churned.

"Mr. Noble here says he came with a warning of sorts." Gideon's grizzly bear voice did nothing to ease Matthias's nerves.

It was clear the man didn't trust him, and why would he? The only interaction they'd had, Gideon was rescuing Jo, who was being held hostage by the gang Matthias was a part of. Granted, he had helped Jo escape, and they'd parted ways on civil terms, but he couldn't blame Gideon if there was a lack of trust.

Elaine poured coffee, and Mary set a plate of soda bread in front of him. Matthias's stomach rumbled at the familiar treat his grandmother used to make. He broke off a bite, and his senses filled with the mild sweetness and spice of caraway and currant. It settled his roiling stomach.

He took a slow breath and pushed his plate away. It was best to get down to the matter at hand.

"It's a long story, but not a pleasant one, so I'd best get on with it." Matthias straightened in his chair and braced his elbows on the table. "I took up a job as a hired hand for Darby McBride. But I've come to see he is a dangerous man, and I'm afraid you all may not be safe." He paused and glanced between Jo and Gideon, letting the information sink in.

Jo and Gideon exchanged looks of confusion. Jo spoke up first. "McBride ... he owns the ranch just this side of the Piedra River, doesn't he?"

Matthias nodded. "Last week, I was passing through the territory looking for work. I happened across a skirmish between some ranchers and cattle rustlers. I—I intervened. And when all the dust settled, Shane McBride was so grateful for my help, he offered me a job on the spot."

Matthias couldn't believe he was about to tell these folks what he'd done. But there was no help for it. They needed to know the truth, and seeing as they already knew his outlaw past, he might as well level with them.

He cleared his throat and continued. "They said they had all the cowboys they needed, but needed another man for protection. I supposed it was wolves and mountain lions and the like. But it wasn't." He pressed his forehead against his folded hands. "It's not predators they're after. It's sheep—says they're eating up all his grazing territory. Yesterday, his men wiped out one man's entire flock."

"Wiped them out?" Gideon asked. "You mean they killed the sheep?"

"Every last one."

Gideon leaned back in his chair and crossed his arms. He leveled a dark glare in Matthias's direction. "You were party to this?"

"No, sir." Matthias straightened. "I'd fallen behind, and when I caught up to them, the deed was done. They'd slaughtered the flock and killed one shepherd when I got there. They left the other man alive to send a message."

A soft thump sounded beside him as Elaine dropped into an open chair, and shocked silence filled the cabin.

"I'm sure sorry to have been there. I reckon I ought to have done something right then."

"Hogwash," Jo spoke up first. "You know as well as I do, you'd be lying there dead with the sheep had you a said a word against those men."

Matthias let out the breath that had been pent up inside him. He hadn't realized how much he needed someone to understand. But of course, Jo would. They knew the pull of being caught between crimes they didn't want a part of and the knowledge of what would happen to them if they didn't comply.

He pulled his plate back in front of him and took another bite, then sipped his coffee. "When we got back to the ranch, I overheard a conversation between McBride and his son. I'm sorry to tell you this, but you're next on their list."

Matthias looked over his shoulder at the window that looked out on the sheepfold. "I don't reckon he'll show up and kill all your sheep out right. After yesterday's havoc, he means to lie low. But they do mean to run you out of here. You can depend on it."

"We need to go to the sheriff." Gideon reached out and covered Jo's hand with his own.

Jo grew still and looked from Gideon to Matthias. Tension crackled through the air between the three of them.

"I suppose we should." Jo's voice was flat and distant. "Do you think it's safe?" She darted an almost imperceptible glance in her sister's direction.

"No." Matthias surprised even himself when he spoke up.

Gideon looked up sharply at Matthias, his free hand balling into a fist.

"Beg your pardon, Gideon, but Jo shouldn't have any part of going to the law. Not ... in her condition." Matthias darted a glance at Miss Elaine and Mrs. Cross.

He wasn't sure how much they would know of Jo's involvement with the Blake Gang, but she certainly didn't deserve to take the risk of getting involved with the law if the truth came out.

"I can take care of myself," Jo quipped.

The corner of Gideon's mouth twitched in a grimace or a grin. Matthias wasn't sure which.

"He's right, Jo. *You* best keep out of this, at least as far as the sheriff is concerned," Gideon said and turned back to Matthias. "But someone has to come forward about it. They'll need a witness."

"I can't. Gideon, forgive me, but there's more to this than you know." Matthias was acutely aware of Elaine's intense eyes on him. "I'd just as soon not talk about it here, though."

"You should write to your brother, Gideon. Maybe Jimmy could help." Mary spoke up for the first time from where she leaned against the counter.

"Jimmy has his own life, Ma," Gideon snapped. "He doesn't want to see me, and I can't say I blame him. Now's certainly not the time to bring him into this mess."

"Maybe it's not Jimmy who's the one avoiding his brother." Mary crossed her arms and gave Gideon a look that outmatched the burly mountain man in terms of intimidation.

Matthias shifted in his seat. "I reckon I owe you an explanation why I'm not so keen as to go meet with yonder sheriff, but might we step outside? I'd best be on my way soon. McBride's men will come for me, and I ought to get as far from here as I can before they hunt me down." He stood and retrieved his hat. "I'm much obliged for the coffee and soda bread."

Matthias nodded both to Mary and to Elaine, who sat frozen and pale, her fingers intertwined in her lap. When they stepped outside, Matthias put his hat back on and squinted against the bright sun.

"So, now what more is there you didn't want to say in front of the women, son?" Gideon crossed his arms, waiting for the rest of the story.

Matthias chuckled at the word *son*. He was likely only a year younger than Gideon, but had always been mistaken for much younger than his age. If only he were as innocent as his features made him appear.

"The rustler I killed last week?"

"Yes?" Gideon's jaw tightened as if he already suspected the answer.

"He wasn't." He sighed and braced his hands on the hitching post in front of the house.

"He wasn't what?" Gideon asked, his eyes narrowing.

"The man I killed wasn't the rustler, after all. Shane McBride and one of his men had stolen the cattle and the man—he was just trying to get his cattle back." The words tumbled out of him in a rush, and he hung his head. "I didn't know. Honestly, I didn't."

All his energy was spent with the release of the truth he'd been so tempted to hold back. Speaking the words aloud twisted his stomach, and he squeezed his eyes shut, hoping he wouldn't be sick.

"Lord, help you." Gideon whispered and looked up at the sky and closed his eyes.

Matthias's chest tightened. Would the Lord help him? Not likely after all the wrong he'd done.

"You see, I can't go to the sheriff. McBride knows what I did. As soon as an accusation comes against him, he'll tell the sheriff what happened to those men, and I'll hang." Matthias had known it, but speaking the words aloud cut deep.

"Well, you'd best sleep on it. I wouldn't high-tail it just yet. McBride won't suspect you've come here. Any man with a lick of self-preservation would've left the county right off and not have come to warn us. Why don't you take your bedroll there and find a corner of the barn to sleep in tonight? Have some supper and a good night's rest, and we can talk more in the morning."

Matthias wanted to argue but weariness tugged at him. A safe place to lay his head was mighty tempting. His shoulders sagged with his sigh and he reached out a hand to Gideon.

"Mighty obliged." Matthias would take Gideon up on the offer of respite, but he would leave at first light and ride far, far away from here, before stopping again.

Chapter 20

Elaine's arms tingled with nervous energy as she carried the bowl of mashed potatoes to the table. Why did Gideon have to ask Mr. Noble to stay? That was a silly, selfish thought. Of course they should ask him to stay. By the sound of it, the man had come out of his way to warn them when he could have been riding as fast as he could out of the county. Noble seemed quite the appropriate name for a man who would do something like that.

The story he told about the shepherds had left her with an undercurrent of panic humming in her veins all afternoon. There was an ample amount of danger up here on the mountain without adding a murderous neighbor to Elaine's list of worries.

Her hands shook as she reached out to set the bowl on the table, and the spoon clattered against the ceramic. Mr. Noble's hand brushed hers as he steadied the dish, coming to her rescue, yet again. Heat radiated through her fingers at the sudden contact, and she flexed and fisted her hand to the count of three. He glanced down, catching her movement, and she tucked her hand behind her apron.

"Thank you, Mr. Noble." Elaine said.

"Please, Miss Bradford, call me Matthias."

His manners were far more refined than any cowboy she'd ever been around. Ever the mystery, this man was.

"Alright, Matthias. Please call me Elaine, then." She bobbed her head and pressed her lips together.

"Why don't you sit there, Matthias?" Jo pointed to the seat next to Elaine.

Why was it her sister always had the uncanny instinct to make things as uncomfortable as possible for Elaine? She chewed the inside of her cheek and pasted on a practiced smile as everyone gathered at the table.

Being seated so close to him was only going to put her under more scrutiny. He had already seen her at her worst upon their first meeting. What if he noticed other odd things about her?

Now that Jo had witnessed her panic over the turkey, it would only be a matter of time before people saw the truth behind her aloof demeanor. The longer she was here, in such close quarters and in such constant danger, the more her carefully painted mask cracked, chipping away bit by bit.

She straightened her shoulders and raised her chin. She was being paranoid and needed to collect herself. It didn't matter what this drifting cowboy thought. He would be gone in the morning. It was Jo and Gideon she must convince she wasn't feeble-minded.

When everyone was settled at the table, Gideon took Jo's hand as he did every night, and bowed his head. Matthias stiffened next to Elaine as Gideon began the blessing. After the prayer, Jo picked up the plate of sliced turkey and passed it to Elaine.

Gideon turned to Matthias. "So, tell us what you know about the McBrides."

"From what I saw"—Matthias took a slice of turkey and passed the plate to Elaine—"he's got a crew of cowboys who mind the herd and tend to the work around the ranch."

"But ..." Despite his casual posture, Gideon's shoulders were tight with tension.

"But then he has hired guns. I think just the two men, now. I was the third," Matthias continued.

"And what made you take a job like that? I thought you wanted a clean slate." Gideon lowered an eyebrow.

Matthias stiffened again, and sat up straight. Gooseflesh skittered up Elaine's arm as it brushed against Matthias's sleeve.

A clean slate from what?

"I did—I do." Matthias braced his wrists on the edge of the table and closed his fists tight, breathing out a hard exhale. "You must believe me."

"Of course we do." Jo nodded and widened her eyes at her husband in some matrimonial communication.

"I didn't know that's what the job was. Not really. I'd no notion what they were up to."

"Like murdering men and slaughtering hundreds of sheep?" Clay spoke up, dishing up a spoonful of potatoes onto his grandmother's plate. "That had to be a bit of a surprise."

"You could say that." Matthias's mouth quirked in a wry grin.

Elaine's heart fluttered, and she couldn't help the bouncing of her knee under the table. Matthias glanced down at her leg and up to her face for a moment before blinking rapidly and focusing his attention back on the men.

"Well, I reckon we'd best be on our guard. We'll keep a gun by the door." Jo turned to Mary. "Which do you think you are most comfortable shooting, Mary?" She spoke around a bite.

Her sister's lack of manners was the least of Elaine's concern now. Jo was asking which gun to keep by the door with no more concern than what they should have for breakfast in the morning.

"Anything is fine." Mary shrugged but turned to Florence. "You think you can handle the .22 pistol if you need to?"

Elaine goggled as the elderly woman nodded slowly. "I shoot the bad men," Florence agreed, a dauntless expression on the woman's dark features.

Even Florence? The woman could barely cross the room—how was it she was braver than Elaine in this situation? All of them were treating this like it was only a minor inconvenience.

"Far as I know, you folks will have some time to get ready. They'll be wanting to keep things quiet until they see Mr. Ibarra will not involve the law."

"Well, I suppose we ought to get on with the shearing within the next few days then and get ready to move the sheep." Gideon looked over at Clay. Why don't you ride out tomorrow with the maps Hector left for us and plan out a route to the high country?"

A note of alarm vibrated through Elaine like a plucked harp string.

"Have you all lost your minds?" Elaine's shriek escaped before she could contain it.

Everyone stopped and stared with mingled expressions of confusion, consternation, and, for Clay, amusement.

"We should be packing up to leave this place, and all you can think of is shearing sheep?"

"Maybe," Gideon continued, as if Elaine hadn't spoken at all. "Just maybe, if we move the flock up higher, McBride won't bother us. There's an unwritten rule around here. If shepherds keep to the high country during the summer, cattlemen will tolerate them."

Matthias wiped his mouth on a napkin. "I'm afraid I wouldn't count on it, Gideon, but I hope that's the case for your sake."

Elaine wrapped her arms tight around her waist and clenched her teeth. The fears and worries she'd groomed herself to avoid all these years had come crashing down on her and she had no way out. She was in an impossibly unsafe situation and there would be no surviving, not unless she could contrive a way to find a husband of substance who could protect her from all of this.

Chapter 21

Matthias reined Copper up next to Gideon's paint gelding as the road descended the long hill leading into Pagosa Springs. Gideon had offered to escort him to town, both for protection and support.

There had been no sign of McBride's men on the road today, but Matthias was grateful to have Gideon along if there had been any trouble. Matthias chuckled bitterly to himself.

The protection may prove meaningless once he reached the sheriff's office. Matthias may well be headed straight for the gallows. Today, he would finally come face to face with the consequences of his actions.

The hill leveled out as they approached town, and a trail led into the trees off to the left. He could run. He could turn his horse's head into the pinion and oak brush and be gone from sight before Gideon could blink. He'd done it before—run from the consequences of his actions.

The sky seemed to darken with the shadow of Matthias's past. He'd run from home at seventeen, escaping the law and the immediate repercussions of what he'd done. But he hadn't escaped the ever-present guilt that haunted him.

That curse had led him straight into the path of Kane Blake and years of being a consort to his ruthless marauding of Colorado's front range. Matthias had been given freedom and a second chance when the gang's reign of terror had ended with the death of its leader and every other gang member—everyone except him.

He should have been lying there in the desert alongside Kane and the others, but Jo and Gideon had shown mercy because Matthias had set Jo free. Were the scales balanced by that one redeeming act, though? Hardly.

He'd been party to more stagecoach robberies than he could remember, many of which came with a loss of life when a robbery would turn into a gunfight. When he met with the sheriff today and confessed to the most recent men he'd killed, he could hang—and *should*.

Enough was enough. Even if no one found out about his life in Missouri or his past deeds, an innocent man's life had been taken. He'd never paid the debt for all the lives he'd harmed over the years. It was time to settle his account and pay the price.

His stomach rolled as they drew closer to town. At least his sacrifice today would do some good. If he could convince the sheriff what Darby McBride had done, and what he planned to do—if he could stop a man like that and protect the Cross family—it would be worth it.

He clenched the reins tighter in his hand, crushing the finger threaded between the leather straps. He would not turn left. He would stay the course. Jo and Gideon needed protection, and the Ibarra family deserved justice.

As they rode down the dusty street, the faint scent of egg wafted up from the hot springs on the river's edge below, adding to the unsettled pit in his stomach.

Gideon stopped in front of what must be the sheriff's office. They both dismounted and hitched their geldings out front.

Gideon clapped Matthias on the shoulder. "It will be alright, Matthias. Have faith."

Faith in what? Faith in the God who his grandmother prayed to—to the God who gave him to a father who beat him and his mother? To the God who allowed men like Kane Blake and Darby McBride the freedom to steal and kill and harm innocent people?

"I have no faith anymore." Matthias shook his head and turned to face his fate as they walked up the porch steps. The hollow sound of his boots on the wooden planks echoed his own emptiness.

Matthias wasn't sure what he'd been expecting, but the young man with a tin badge behind the large wooden desk wasn't it.

He looked up from the wanted poster in his hand. "Can I help you, gentlemen?"

"I'm looking for the sheriff." Matthias removed his hat and curled the edge of the felt brim in his hand.

The man laid the paper down and reached out to shake their hands. "Jack Barlow. I'm the sheriff here in Archuleta County. How can I help you?"

The sheriff was a well-dressed man, no more than the age of thirty, with neatly combed hair and a dark, manicured mustache. He was a pleasant-looking fellow, though Matthias had never had much reason to trust a lawman. In Matthias's experience, those in authority abused it.

Gideon took a step back, giving Matthias the floor.

Matthias swallowed. "My name is Matthias Noble. I'm new to these parts." His voice wavered. *Weakling.* He clenched his fists at his side, determined to push through the fear. "This here is Gideon Cross. He purchased a homestead and flock of sheep west of here a few months back. I recently came to the area looking for work. A local rancher by the name of Darby McBride hired me."

Sheriff Barlow nodded and gestured to the two empty chairs in front of the desk. He took his own seat and leaned back in his chair. Matthias and Gideon followed suit, and Matthias gripped the arms of the chair until his knuckles lost their color.

"I know I'm a newcomer and likely out of my depth in telling you the character of a man I've just met. But Darby McBride is a scoundrel, sir. Now, I'm no innocent man, which you'll find by the end of my tale, but he and his son are building a cattle empire on a foundation of theft, murder, and destruction."

Barlow's eyebrows lifted, but he kept silent.

"As I was traveling through the territory, south of here, I happened across an ambush—cattle rustlers. From my vantage point, I watched as two men snuck up on some cowboys and their herd." Matthias faltered, his voice shaky and weak. "It appeared the men were bent on mischief. They approached through the trees, weapons drawn, and the cowboys had no idea what was coming. I couldn't bear to stand by and witness as two men were killed." Matthias swallowed.

His heart hammered wildly in his chest. Whether he'd come to terms with his fate or not, he wasn't ready to die. Wasn't ready to hang. Sweat beaded on his lip, and he wiped it away, sending a glance over to Gideon, who nodded solemnly, his eyes full of pity.

"I shot one of the rustlers and helped to recover the scattered cattle." The pain of his admission cut deep again. Would it ever stop hurting?

Sheriff Barlow sat straight. A calculating, suspicious gleam in his eyes.

"The cowboys turned out to be Shane McBride and one of their cow hands. Hank Sutton. Shane offered me a job on the spot. Said they needed help with varmint control. I reckoned wolves or bears had been harassing their herd, and as I was looking for a job, I gladly accepted the offer."

"Alright." The young sheriff smoothed a thumb under his mustache. "And what brings you here today, then?"

"The McBrides are bent on clearing the area of shepherds and sheep farmers. He claims they're decimating the grazing ground the cows need."

"I've heard as much from most every cattle rancher I've met between here and Texas." The sheriff picked up a cup of coffee from the desk and swirled its contents, relaxing again.

"I reckon not every cattle rancher you've met slaughter entire flocks of sheep and murder shepherds, though."

Barlow jerked up, and the coffee splashed on his vest, eyes wide.

"I quickly found I was a hired gun, not for predator control, but as brute force to terrorize the sheep ranchers in the area and push them out. His men attacked Jon Ibarra's shepherds and killed every sheep. I wasn't there, mind, I'd fallen behind and caught up to them after the fact."

"I've heard nothing of it."

Matthias gritted his teeth at the man's ignorance. Lawmen had an uncanny knack at assuming they knew all the comings and goings of their jurisdiction. As an outlaw, Matthias knew better. Menacing threats and fear mongering went a long way to secure the silence of victims.

"Well, you wouldn't, now would you?" he snapped. "McBride's men left one shepherd alive with the message they were to get out of the territory before the same retribution came down on Ibarra's family. In my experience, a threat like that, especially to a man with a family to protect, will ensure compliance."

Gideon stiffened next to Matthias, and a faint rumble emanated from the man. He had a family of his own to protect. But something told Matthias Gideon Cross wasn't one who would run. He would fight for what was right, but the fear for the safety of his wife and those under his protection must be a heavy burden.

"I overheard McBride's plans, and Gideon here is next on their list."

The sheriff bunched his lips in contemplation. "So, you're sure this wasn't just a skirmish between rivals? A fight that got out of control?"

"No, sir. This was butchery."

"I see. Well, I thank you for bringing this to my attention." He drummed his fingers on the desktop, as if unsure how to proceed.

Could Matthias leave things at that? It seemed enough information to set an investigation in motion. Maybe he could disappear quietly now without divulging the rest of the tale and be free to find work somewhere else, somewhere far from here. He swallowed against the thickness in his throat. No. He wouldn't run this time. It was time he faced the music, somber a tune as it was.

"There's more." Matthias pushed on. All shakiness had left his voice now. "Those men I killed were not cattle rustlers. Shane McBride stole those cows, and the man I killed was the rancher attempting to get his animals back." He shifted uncomfortably in his chair. The hollow ache in his chest deepened.

Sheriff Barlow didn't move—didn't react. He remained in his seat, his elbows braced on the desk and fingers steepled. Moments ticked by, and Matthias's breathing faded to shallow, meaningless wisps of air. Finally, Barlow looked up and met Matthias's eyes, dead on.

"Why come to me with this? Why not hightail it out of the county the moment you found out?"

Good question. "I couldn't stand by and let that kind of treachery continue. Gideon Cross here is a ... friend"—he hoped—"and I wanted to make sure he and his family were safe. I also want to see justice done for those who Darby McBride has hurt. If that means I pay the price for what I've done, so be it."

Sheriff Barlow's eyes widened. "It's a mighty courageous thing you've done here, sir."

Matthias raised one shoulder in a shrug but kept his eyes trained on the floor. This stranger knew nothing about him. He wasn't courageous. That was why Pa had been so hard on him all those years. He hadn't been able to abide a son who was so soft—so weak.

"Matthias—can I call you that?"

"Yes, sir."

"Good." He turned to Gideon. "And Gideon, correct? I have a proposition for you both, and I'd just as soon move past the formalities. You can call me Jack."

"A proposition?" Matthias's stomach flopped like a fish, and he pulled his eyes from the floor to look over at Gideon. What could that mean?

"Can you show me on a map where you killed those men?"

"I reckon so," Matthias said.

Jack stood and crossed the room, rummaging through several dusty, rolled-up maps. He chose one and stretched it out across the desk. Matthias scanned the map of the area and pointed out roughly where he'd first encountered Shane McBride.

"Alright then, that's good," Jack said, rolling the map back up. "It's still within my jurisdiction."

"I'll level with you two. You're not the only ones new to the area. I just stepped into this job a few months back. I've had my suspicions about the Lazy M—even have caught wind of some rumors, but I have no evidence to go off of. No actual witnesses. Everyone seems too scared to speak up. I need someone who I can rely on to help me bring this scoundrel down."

Relief warred with panic, and Matthias stuttered, "I can't go back there. I left after the Ibarra's sheep massacre. They'll already be hunting for me. They'd never trust me to sign back on."

"Well, that's a shame, but I do believe you're right. It likely wouldn't be safe now." He turned to Gideon. "Do you trust this man?"

"I do," Gideon answered so quickly Matthias was dumbstruck.

"Enough to keep him on as a ranch hand or shepherd? If they hired him as a gunman for McBride, I reckon he must be an asset in case things get dicey up there."

Understanding dawned on Gideon's face. "Yes, he would."

Matthias jerked his glance back and forth between the men. What was happening? Why wasn't Jack putting Matthias in irons right now?

"I got report of what happened by the man's brother. I'll need to speak to the families first, but if they're agreeable with my plan, I'd like you to stick around the area while we try to gather evidence. How I see it, McBride's men were in the wrong that day."

"No—I—"

"I know you made a grave error in judgment, one I hope you won't make in the future. But you wouldn't have gone to Gideon or come today if you weren't remorseful. Shane McBride stole those cattle, and it was an honest misunderstanding. If the family of the man you killed sees it that way, I won't arrest you. This is how you're going to make it right."

Chapter 22

Elaine plunged the soiled shirt into the cold water of the creek Gideon had nicknamed Cross Creek that flowed behind the house. It was too small of a tributary to warrant its own name according to any of the maps he'd seen, so Cross Creek it had become.

She shook her head at her brother-in-law's bold confidence. No decorum with that man. He was as gentle as a buffalo, but he had the heart of a lion.

She rubbed the fabric against itself, dislodging the dirt embedded into the fibers. This was a job she found she didn't mind. The satisfaction of releasing the filth and watching it float down the creek was settling to her nerves.

She wished she could do the job in a cauldron of hot water rather than on a creek bank. But the water supply they collected in barrels on the way up from town was preserved for drinking water and cleaning dishes. Nonetheless, cleaning clothes was a chore that felt good. Washing away the mess rather than getting her hands dirty.

She dipped the shirt again and rubbed the bar of soap against the fabric. Something nudged the back of her arm, and a wet nose grazed the back of her neck. She squeaked, startled.

Soft black and white fur filled her vision as Scout, the border collie pup Gideon and Clay had been training to work the sheep, nuzzled her neck and face.

"Get off of me, you imp," Elaine scolded and pushed the dog away from her face. "Down. No."

The furry creature lay down on the flat rock she used as a laundry table, fluffy tail wagging back and forth, sweeping up dust.

Elaine huffed and scowled at Scout. "Filthy creature."

It was hard to be angry at the shaggy dog, but she couldn't get past how filthy it must be, always rolling around in the dirt. Much less its wet nose and tongue.

She knelt back down onto the cloth she used to keep her dress clean and dipped water from the creek to wash the slobber from her face and neck. "Why do you insist on pestering me everywhere I go?"

"Can't blame him for being fond of you." A voice spoke from behind her, and her heart hammered against the confines of her chest.

Elaine whipped around to find Matthias standing at the edge of the clearing, cowboy hat silhouetted against the midday sun. She pressed a hand against her chest and sighed.

"You scared me." She gasped.

"My apologies, ma'am." Matthias touched the brim of his hat and her ire melted away. "Don't mind Scout here. He'll protect you if you let him stick around."

"I thought those great white beasts in the field were the protectors." Elaine stood and wiped a handkerchief across her neck to dry the creek water.

"Ah, those are the Great Pyrenees." Matthias stepped forward, and Scout ran to his side, tail wagging wildly. "The Pyrenees are fierce protectors alright, but they stay out in the fields to guard the sheep. Scout here is meant to learn to herd the animals. He may just be a little one, but I reckon he'd warn you were there to be any danger about."

"I hadn't thought of it that way." Elaine shielded her eyes from the sun.

Matthias moved to the side where she could see him clearly. She knelt back down and scrubbed the shirt against the washboard.

"Can I help?" he asked, kneeling beside her. "Go on now, Scout." Matthias shooed the dog away before it could lick her again.

Elaine nodded to the last item that needed scrubbing. Matthias picked it up and soaked it in the creek. Something fluttered inside Elaine. She'd had no occasion to talk to Matthias outside of mealtimes since their encounter on the trail when they had first met.

The memory of hiding in the mud under the wagon came to mind, and she flushed. She had made an absolute fool of herself that day. She could only hope to keep her nerves at bay around him in the future.

"We weren't expecting you back until this evening." She scrubbed at a stubborn spot on the garment against the washboard.

Matthias quirked a wry grin. "Oh, Gideon was all-fired to get back here. Soon as there was enough light to travel, we were on the road again this morning."

"How did your talk with the sheriff go? Is he going to do something about Mr. McBride?"

Matthias frowned and shrugged. "I s'pose it went alright. I'll be staying on for a time while I help Sherriff Barlow with some things. It was mighty kind of Gideon to offer me the work, and I'd like to help if I can, in case McBride's men come looking for trouble."

Elaine's stomach fluttered. He was staying?

"How are you liking your new home?" Matthias asked as he took the washboard she offered him.

Was that what it was? Home? Her chest tightened at the thought.

"It's fine, I suppose. Though it isn't what I'd ever expected for myself." She pressed her lips together.

Perhaps she shouldn't say so much, though she supposed it was likely clear to anyone who cared to notice she was out of place here

"Where do you hail from, then?" Elaine changed the subject quickly.

He cleared his throat. "I was born in Missouri, but I've spent the last several years here in Colorado."

Elaine wrung the shirt tight and placed it back in the basket with the other washed items. "Do you have family back in Missouri?"

A tremor of discomfort crossed his face. "No. Not anymore."

A tense silence stretched out between them like a piano wire, and Elaine's stomach tightened. She focused on the playful melody of water trickling over rocks in the creek, letting the musicality of it soothe her. Had she said something wrong?

He plunged the fabric he held into the creek to rinse it, then wrung it so tightly she thought the fabric might tear. But the tight lines around his eyes told her it wasn't anger that hummed through him, but deep sadness.

Elaine's heart ached for him. It was clearly a painful subject. So many people lost loved ones as they traveled west. She shouldn't have prodded him.

"Thank you for your help, Matthias. I should get these back to the house and hang them on the line." She reached for the basket.

Matthias blinked rapidly and the lines of his face smoothed as he snapped out of whatever dark place he'd disappeared to.

"I'll carry it for you." He stood and took the basket from her.

She peeked at him from under her straw hat as they walked back to the house. Matthias's gentle presence soothed her nerves. He certainly didn't seem to hold her ridiculous antics from their first meeting against her. Perhaps they could find a place of amity with each other. It would be nice to have a friend while she was here–someone who didn't think of her as spoiled or prim.

Chapter 23

Elaine shivered against the morning chill and tightened the scarf over her ears and hair, knotting it under her chin. She had learned springtime in the mountains was far colder than Kansas had been. The weather could be warm and welcoming one day, but a chill could seep in over the homestead overnight, freezing puddles and leaving a thin layer of frost over the ground.

She longed for home. At least back in Kansas, if the day was dreary and cold, she had no cause to venture out of doors. Here, there was no escaping the work that needed done, no matter the cold or mud. At least this morning, the colder temperature had frozen the puddles that routinely plagued her, soaking her skirt hems in muddy water.

She rested a hand on the stick that acted as latch to the chicken house door. This just might be her least favorite chore.

It was yet another job she could not do with her gloves on. She'd found if she wore her gloves to feed the chickens and gather eggs, the fine dust from the grain and little pin feathers clung to the soft fabric and left a gritty sensation against her skin—not to mention the off-putting smell that seemed to embed itself in every fiber. At least if she used her bare hands, she could scrub them after without the necessity of washing and drying gloves.

The pail of grain in her hand rattled with her nerves as she entered the henhouse. She shut the door behind her so no birds could escape, and coughed against the dust, blinking to clear her vision in the dark building.

She couldn't see why they couldn't just let the creatures run about outdoors, but Jo insisted they had too many predators here in the mountains, and the chickens must remain cooped until the men could build a proper, fenced-in yard.

When her eyes adjusted to the dim light offered by cracks between the boards, she looked about the room. The clucking and shifting of feathery bodies increased as Elaine took one ginger step forward. The birds stared intently at her, waiting for her to make her move. One hen, roosted near her face, leveled a beady, menacing eye at her and blinked.

Elaine covered her mouth with a handkerchief and inhaled against the cloth. Tucking it back in her pocket, she held the breath, and stepped to the middle of the coop to pour the grain into the feed trough. The rooster crowed loudly as if a general leading his troops, and they all flew in for the attack. Feathers and talons flying, the birds descended toward the feed, heedless of the hapless victim in their midst.

Elaine screeched, batting away the foul creatures and using the bucket as a shield. She couldn't do this anymore. It was too much.

She extricated herself from the melee and crossed to the wall lined with nesting boxes frantically to fill her pail with eggs while the chickens were occupied with their feed.

It took time to gather the eggs each morning as she searched the boxes for the colors she needed to gather in threes. Three white eggs, three brown, three white, three brown. In the end, she was left with a single white egg. She hesitated. She should take the egg, but her compulsion wouldn't allow it. That egg would just have to wait until tomorrow.

She rushed outside, and her feet slipped on the wet ice. She landed hard, breaking through the frozen exterior of the puddle. A shower of eggs rained down over her like giant, slimy balls of hail, soaking her hair in sticky egg yolk and her skirt with cold muddy water.

A loud laugh carried from the barn, where Clay leaned against the door jamb, helpless with mirth. Anger coursed through her as she rolled onto hands and knees, dripping with the raw eggs and the fowl stench of mud laced with chicken excrement.

As she sat back on her heels, a hand pressed under her elbow, lifting her up. Standing, she pushed at the scarf that had gone askew, covering her eyes and obstructing her vision.

"Here." Matthias's voice registered as he untied the knot under her chin and peeled away the sticky fabric.

"Thank you." Elaine managed a thready whisper as she fumbled in her pocket for her handkerchief and wiped her face with a shaky hand.

"May I?" Matthias took the cloth and wiped at the smudges she couldn't see. "Are you alright, Miss Elaine?"

Elaine shook her head. She had no words. What could she say? No. She most certainly was not alright. None of this was. While she was grateful for his help, it seemed such a small comfort to the anxiousness screaming inside her.

Why was she here? She needed to find a way out. A place where she could keep herself separated from such unpredictability. All she would find here would be spinsterhood or marriage to some backward mountain man. Both options would lead to living the rest of her life on a filthy, uncivilized homestead—more of this. Daily obstacles and a constant battle to maintain an air of composure and keep her neurosis hidden.

She could not stay here much longer. At the first opportunity to find a more suitable situation, she would have to take it.

MATTHIAS ARCHED HIS back and stretched to ease the ache there from the long day of shearing sheep. It had been a messy affair, and he was covered from fingertips to shoulders in the lanolin that exuded from the sheep's skin into the fleece.

Shearing had required all parties to pitch in. While the men sheared, Jo and Elaine had skirted and washed the wool, laying it out on large racks to dry in the sun. When it was dry, the wool would be carded and sorted.

He lifted the heavy cast iron cauldron from the hook it hung from above the fire and poured the fresh hot water into the washtub. Elaine stepped up with a look of panicked relief.

He smiled at the disheveled mess she was—so unlike the prim lady he knew her to be. Soft brown tendrils had come loose from the bondage of her pins and dangled around her face, and dark curls clung to her neck. Whether with sweat or oil, he wasn't sure. Even she hadn't been excluded from the day's labors.

Elaine was so unlike her sister. Where Jo was tenacious, her sister was refined, always striving for an air of composure. While he'd cared for Jo in their time with the Blake gang, it was Elaine he found himself more familiar with. She reminded him so much of his grandmother.

He knelt next to the washtub and dipped his hands in the hot water. It soothed his fingers that had grown cramped and stiff from holding the sheers for so long. Next to him, Elaine scrubbed her hands and arms vigorously with the lye soap.

She had kept a stout chin through the whole ordeal today, though the messy job had clearly been uncomfortable for her. Gathering and washing the fetid wool as the men sheared couldn't have been easy for her despite her efforts to maintain an unruffled disposition.

She pushed back a wayward strand of hair with her wrist. Even on her face, her skin glistened with lanolin oil. She scrubbed the back of one hand in circles—one, two, three, then turned her hand and scrubbed her palm in the same succession of circles before rinsing. Then started the same pattern over on the opposite hand—three circles, rinse, turn, three more circles.

Her motions were so precise, so calculated. When she moved her ministrations to her arms, she rubbed the soap up her forearms, again, with the circles. Something deep in Matthias's chest ached to watch her with her brows knitted together, lips pressed tight as she worked. He wasn't sure what plagued her, but it was becoming clear it was more than just uppity properness.

Focused as she was, she didn't even notice him next to her, and rather than breaking her concentration to ask for the soap, Matthias pushed back from the tub and stood to wait. Across the dooryard, Gideon and Jo stood side by side at the sheepfold fence, surveying the day's efforts.

Gideon leaned down and spoke to Jo, running his hand along her lower back and securing it on her hip, pulling her closer to his side. Freshly shorn sheep moved about the pen, bleating and bustling around one another. A rooster chased a hen across the yard, and the evening breeze carried the scent of salt pork and fried potatoes with onions down from the house.

This wasn't just a ranch, it was a home. Maybe that was the difference. Although Gideon hadn't built this place from the ground up himself, it was most definitely a *home*. Matthias had been without a home for so long, he'd forgotten what it felt like. The warmth that wrapped itself around you and lifted your spirits, the comforting scents and peaceful notion it garnered was healing to a weary soul.

His own home hadn't been that way as a child, but his grandparents' had. This place had the same sense to it. What was it that made a house a home, or a ranch a homestead? McBride's place was nothing like this one. It had been cold and stiff, even the food had been unpalatable. Matthias supposed Pa's love of strong drink over love for his family had been what made their house such a cold, miserable place to live.

Gideon turned Jo toward himself and kissed her thoroughly. The back of Matthias's neck burned, and he glanced down. He turned away, his eyes finding Elaine instead.

Elaine stood from the washtub and looked out at Jo and Gideon as she dried her face and neck with a clean cloth. Something in her expression pained him. It had been patently clear since his arrival here there was a tension between the sisters. But what Matthias witnessed now wasn't a sister looking at this display of affection with disapproval, but with a deep longing.

Elaine pressed a hand over her flat stomach. One finger tapping. Of course, she would want to find a husband for herself as well—a husband and a child of her own. From what he'd gathered, Elaine was the elder of the two. It must pain her to see her younger sister so well-matched.

Matthias rubbed a hand against the dull, empty ache in his own chest. He would never have that—a family or a homestead of his own. He scoffed and dug a toe into the dirt.

Who did he think he was fooling—thinking himself above the men at the McBride ranch? The Lazy M may have been a harsh place full of rough men, but maybe a ranch like that was where he belonged. He was a murderer and a thief, after all.

He'd best guard himself and not let this happy family tempt him into wishing for a life he couldn't have. He ought not to stay here any longer than was necessary. He'd brought trouble with him when he'd tried to settle into a new life. And now, he'd dragged it right to the Cross family's doorstep. As soon as Sheriff Barlow released him, he'd best move on from here and take the turmoil with him.

Chapter 24

Elaine pulled her shawl down from the hook by the door and draped it around her shoulders, crossing the ends and tucking them into her skirt the way Mary had shown her. She would need her hands free if she were to traipse around in the dark with supper and coffee.

She wiped her clammy hands on her apron and picked up Matthias's plate and cup. How could he stand to spend the entire night outside alone? Even the thought of venturing out into the dark to bring him his supper had her knees weak and shaky.

Her eyes lingered on the lantern burning on the stove. "How am I supposed to manage all this and a lantern?" Elaine fortified her voice with disdain to cover her fear.

Her sister opened the door to let her out. "It's a full moon out tonight. It will be easy for you to find your way."

Elaine elevated her chin but worried her cheek between her teeth. She wouldn't give Jo the satisfaction of seeing Elaine's turmoil. Her younger sister had seemed more insistent than ever lately on turning Elaine into some wild mountain woman like herself. Didn't she understand Elaine couldn't stay—*wouldn't stay*?

Though she dreaded the conversation, she would have to make Jo see Elaine had no intentions of living this life. She was destined for finer things. Well, if not destined, she was certainly desperate.

She stepped outside, and the glow of moonlight did, in fact, light her path as Jo said it would. But that did nothing to assuage her apprehension. She could just make out the silhouette of Matthias's cowboy hat atop the hill behind the barn.

Although she could see the path well, she had to force herself to take each step. Her heart raced, and the fork clattered against the tin plate in her hand. Who knew what could be behind the oak brush that edged the path up the hill? Only knowing Matthias was on night watch above her calmed her nerves enough to keep her moving. The sooner she reached him, the safer she would be.

An insect buzzed in the grass beside her, and she jumped, spilling some of the coffee. It burned her thumb, and she shrieked, gritting her teeth against the pain. This was too much.

How could she be expected to live like this—stumbling around in the dark with any manner of creatures lying in wait to attack? Not to mention dangerous, sheep-killing cowboys bent on mayhem. Tears welled in frustration from the burn and the futility of her circumstances.

Suddenly, a form loomed up out of the dark, and she opened her mouth to scream.

"Shhh," the form spoke and moved closer. "It's just me." Matthias chuckled, and Elaine's shoulders sagged with relief.

She sniffed and lifted her chin, determined not to appear like a foolish child. "What are you doing, popping up out of nowhere like that?"

"You screamed. I came to see if you were alright." Matthias's exasperated expression brought Elaine's indignation down a few notches.

"Oh." She dropped her eyes to the path. "Something startled me, and I burned myself with your coffee." She lifted the cup. "I'm sorry. It's only half of what I set out with."

"Never mind that." Matthias took the tin cup and set it down on the ground.

He held her hand between his and held it up, inspecting her thumb in the moonlight. His rough, work-worn hands grazed over her skin like a pair of leather gloves. Not supple like calf skin, but smooth and hardened like the buckskin her house mates seemed so fond of.

"Come with me, and we'll get that taken care of." Matthias tipped his hat toward the spot she'd seen him sitting.

Elaine wanted to protest. She just wanted to go back to the house. What good could he do with a burn out here? But he kept hold of her hand and picked the coffee up, leading her up the short trail to his perch on the hillside. When they reached the top, he guided her to a log.

"Sit here," he said as he rummaged in a saddlebag, retrieving a canteen.

He crouched in front of her and held her hand away from her dress, trickling cool water over the burn. It soothed the scalded skin, and she released a shaky sigh.

"Better?"

She hadn't noticed before how rich and smooth his voice was. It was as soothing to her nerves as the water was to her thumb. His hand encircled her wrist, gliding over her skin. A tingling rush of shivers crept up her arm at his touch.

"Better," she echoed, her voice a whisper.

Matthias shifted and sat next to her on the log, still cradling her hand in his. Propriety demanded she retrieve her hand and return to the house immediately. But propriety also would demand she not be out here wandering around in the woods in the first place.

She wasn't sure she was ready to make the trek through the dark back to the house just yet. It was comforting to have company. Just for a minute.

She shuddered a weary breath. Societal expectations had no business or bearing in the backcountry. She could see that now. The lack of decorum here had been exhausting these past few weeks. It had been her security for years, boundaries that kept her protected from her own infirmities. Yet, here she found herself, for the first time since leaving home, feeling safe. Protected not by bonds of appropriateness, but by the presence of this dusty cowboy.

"What has you so scared?" Matthias asked, his eyes searching her face for answers.

"Tonight?" Elaine hesitated. She should be careful with her answer, but she was tired. Tired of pretending to be okay.

"All the time."

Elaine sighed. "I'm afraid of everything. This place. Wild animals, smelly sheep, deranged birds that fly at my head every time I enter the coop, the dirt and filth on every surface—I don't know how all of you can stand it."

Matthias's smile held sympathy. "Can't you see the beauty in it all?"

"Beauty?" Elaine raised an eyebrow.

He stroked a thumb over hers absently and stared out into the dark. "Look at the moon. Have you ever seen such a peaceful sight—the way the moonlight casts its silvery glow over the whole valley?"

Elaine shook her head. "I see no *silvery glow*. It's dark and dangerous. Who knows what is lurking out there?"

"It's serene." Matthias bumped his shoulder against hers. "The stillness rests on the wilderness like a blanket, hushing all the clamor and noise of civilization."

A light breath of night air skated across the back of her neck, and she shivered, pulling her wrap tighter. He picked up his duster folded next to him and draped it around her shoulders. The heavy weight of the leather steadied her and quieted her unease.

Something fell from the pocket and tumbled over the toe of her boot. It was a harmonica. Matthias stiffened next to her as she picked it up.

She handed it to him and asked, "Do you play?"

Matthias ducked his chin. Even in the flat light, a darker hue shaded his cheeks. He rubbed the harmonica on his sleeve, absentmindedly polishing the metal exterior of the instrument.

"It keeps me company when I'm alone."

"Will you play it for me?"

"Ach." He shook his head. "It's not but a frivolous time waster." Matthias's words were dark and gruff, and she recognized they weren't his own. No doubt he was repeating something he'd been told many times before.

Her heart squeezed in her chest to hear the undertone of shame in his voice. She knew the feeling of bondage someone else's words could cause. Her grandmother's warnings echoed constantly in her mind. Even well-meant, they informed her actions, and at times, even stirred up her fear.

"Music calms me when I'm anxious," Elaine encouraged. "Just one tune? Perhaps it can bolster me for my walk back to the house."

Twin lines of frustration formed between his brows, and confusion warred on his face.

She rested a hand on his wrist. "Please?"

He looked over, and his eyes held hers for a long moment. Whether he was deciding if he could trust her or only seeking her understanding, she wasn't sure. But the depth of feeling there was fathomless and so dark she feared she might drown in the abyss.

Slowly, he brought the harmonica to his lips and a clear, sweet tone carried into the night. She'd never heard such a hauntingly beautiful sound. The notes of his song floated and filled the air with ribbons of harmony intertwining and dancing on the evening breeze.

She had expected he might appease her request with a quick ditty—some camp tune that would only last a few bars. Instead, he lost himself in music that seemed to pour from his soul and played until every last bit of her unease had melted away and puddled at her feet.

When the last note lingered in the air, he seemed to come back from wherever he'd been and looked down at her with a shy uncertainty.

She blinked away the trance she'd fallen into. "That was incredible."

"Nah, it's just a way to pass the quiet hours." Matthias offered a half smile that seemed almost painful. "You'd best get back to the house before someone worries."

He held out a hand to help her up from her seat on the log, surprising Elaine at how easily her hand found its home in his. She regretted the loss, both of his touch and the warmth of his leather duster as she removed it and a cold rush of air swept in its place, leaving her chilled.

She resisted the inclination to step closer to him and seek his warmth.

"Thank you kindly for the meal," Matthias said as he picked up the dish. "I'll be sure to bring the plate back in the morning."

"Oh dear, I've hindered you from eating, and now your supper is cold." Elaine chewed the inside of her cheek and looked down.

"I reckon I'd rather the company to a warm supper." His smile was genuine now, and the tips of Elaine's ears burned, despite the evening chill. "Good night, Elaine." He inclined his head and his voice slid over her, sending a tingling rush down to her toes.

"Good night," Elaine whispered, and turned back down the path to the house with easy steps, and no fear of the darkness nipped at her heels.

Chapter 25

M atthias sat up on his cot in the barn, scrubbing a hand over his face to clear the haze clouding his eyes from a lack of sleep. It was still dark in the barn, though the pink glow of early light filtered through the cracks between the rough boards.

He'd lain awake for some time now. Although Clay had relieved his night watch duty and Matthias had returned to the barn, sleep had evaded him. After Elaine had gone back to the cabin last night, he'd been haunted by their shared moment of vulnerability.

He hadn't played music in front of anyone since before he'd left his home back in Missouri. The exposure had left him open and raw.

He should have kept his guard up. Played some simple tune any cowboy would know. But, as always, when he opened his heart to the music, the flood of emotion came pouring out with it. Revealing his weakness—the fragility Pa could not abide.

But Elaine hadn't seemed repelled by it. On the contrary. It appeared to soothe her fear. He wasn't sure what it was Elaine struggled with, but it was becoming clear something troubled *her*. She was almost brittle.

Being able to ease her discomfort last night had awoken something inside him. A desire to help. With all the wrong he'd done and the problems he'd brought to these kind folks, he wanted to do some good before he left. Even if it was this small thing.

After the scene with the chickens the other morning, and Elaine's comment about deranged birds last night, he'd been mulling over a plan that might ease her discomfort with the messy chore.

He retrieved his pile of clothes from the end of his cot and dressed quickly. He should be sleeping now, so he wouldn't be needed for a few hours. If Gideon approved of Matthias's plan, he should have the work done before breakfast.

He found Gideon at the water barrels, filling buckets of water from the attached hand pump.

"Morning, Gideon. Need a hand?" Matthias reached for the bucket and carried it to the cauldron used to heat bath water for the women.

"What are you doing up so early?" Gideon asked as he filled another bucket.

"Couldn't sleep," Matthias answered honestly. "I have a notion of something I'd like to work on, if you don't mind. Something to help Miss Bradford."

Gideon raised a bushy eyebrow. "Elaine?"

"Yes, sir." Matthias busied himself with pumping another bucket of water.

He didn't want to say too much. Miss Elaine seemed to try to hide her struggles, whatever they were, and Matthias didn't want to draw attention.

"If you're aiming to court her—"

"No, sir," Matthias answered quickly. The last thing he needed was Gideon worried about the women. "I've no such intentions."

Heat flooded Matthias's chest, boiling up his collar and into his face. He turned quickly to haul the bucket.

"It's only, well, after the trouble she had the other morning with the chickens, I thought she might could use a little help. That's all." He shrugged.

"Alright, then. What is it?" Gideon crouched by the cauldron that hung from a chain on a tripod and struck a match, setting the pile of kindling ablaze.

After speaking with Gideon, Matthias gathered his tools and supplies and set out for the henhouse.

It wouldn't do her any good to take over the chore for her. She needed the skills this homestead life would teach her if she was going to survive this harsh world. Likely, the only reason Jo had survived her time with the Blake Gang was because she had skills that were useful to the men. Well, that and the fact the woman was as tough as boot leather after a rainstorm. In these parts, it wasn't likely Elaine would find a gentile life on some banker's arm.

He nailed leather straps to the top of a slat of wood on the outside wall of the coop and cut the ends of the board, exposing the nesting boxes built against the wall. He repeated the process with the board above that backed the other row of boxes. After rigging a similar latch to the sides of another board he had cut at the bottom of the wall, he went inside and used a few spare boards to create a trough attached to the lower board.

Mrs. Cross rang the bell for breakfast just as Matthias hammered in the last nail. An antsy bubbling filled his belly. He couldn't wait to show Elaine what he'd done.

ELAINE SMOOTHED HER napkin between her fingers over and over and over to calm her nerves and gain the courage to speak. She didn't know where she was going or how, but she couldn't stay here much longer. That had become quite clear.

Though Matthias's music had soothed her nerves last night, that wasn't enough to sustain her. She had to find a more controlled situation—where she wouldn't have to endure the constant triggering of her anxious distress.

She would announce her plan today and start making inquiries immediately upon their next trip to town. Perhaps Mary would teach her more about sewing and she could find placement as a seamstress?

She couldn't act as a schoolteacher or nanny. Grandmama had warned her about the unpredictability of babies, and working with small children wouldn't be any better than the chickens, as sticky and slimy as they always seemed to be.

The scraping of forks against plates signaled the meal's end. She needed to act quickly before she lost the nerve. She squeezed the napkin tight before stretching it out across her plate and cleared her throat to speak.

"I have something I need to share with you all." Mary's firm voice spoke up next to Elaine. "I'm going to be leaving for a short time."

Elaine's jaw dropped in what she was sure was a highly unattractive gape. All the bravado she had built up in herself dissipated.

"I need to go see my Charlie."

Silence filled the room, and the clatter of Gideon's fork, dropped against his plate, echoed in the void.

What was Elaine missing here? She thought Gideon's father was deceased all these years. Hadn't he left for the silver rush when the boys were youths, never to be heard from again?

Gideon and Jo exchanged a charged look, and Clay stared down at his plate.

Florence was the only one who seemed pleased. "Good. You help him. Bring him home."

Elaine bit back the flurry of questions on her tongue. By the pained lines around Gideon's eyes, this was a family secret with deep, painful roots.

"Ma, I—I know you want your husband back, but he's not there. His mind is gone." Gideon scrubbed a hand over his face. "If you want to go see him, I completely understand. I reckon it's been too long since I've been to check in on him. But he's beyond help. I tried. Tried living with him, helping him. He was a danger to himself and me. Otherwise, I'd never have taken him to an asylum." He leaned back in his chair—his shoulders pulled low.

Gideon had put his own father in an asylum. Shock reverberated through Elaine's core—shattering any hope she had that Jo and Gideon might understand if they found out about her.

"I've been in contact," Mary said, laying her napkin across her plate and threading her fingers together, wrists braced against the table's edge. "After you came to Kansas and told me where he was, I wrote him. I'd no notion whether he'd receive my letter, but there was so much between us left to be said." Mary's wavering tone blanketed the room. "I received a letter back from a worker at the hospital. Her name is Essie, and from what I gather, she's been caring for Charlie for the past year—taken special care of him." Mary looked up from her knotted fingers. "She said he's improved."

Something shimmered across Gideon's expression. Whether hope, guilt, or some odd mixture of the two, Elaine wasn't sure.

"I wouldn't get my hopes up, Ma." Gideon sighed. "Don't mistake me, I'm glad you're going. It will do you some good to see him. As a matter of fact, I wish I could go with you. But with everything going on right now"—Gideon looked down to Jo, beside him—"I reckon I ought to stay."

"It's no trouble. I sought out the train schedule when we were in town last. I'll leave on the stage Monday next. You have Elaine's help. She's shown a lot of promise these past few weeks, and I know you all will be fine." Mary squeezed Elaine's hand and smiled. "Jo isn't yet too near her confinement. I should have plenty of time to see Charlie and be home before the baby arrives."

Elaine gawked at Mary. She expected Elaine to carry on in her stead? She could barely boil coffee without disaster. This couldn't be happening.

Could she leave anyway? Gideon and Jo had done just fine without them before, hadn't they? Elaine tapped the cameo brooch at her waist, torn between self-preservation and virtue. She couldn't leave now. Not with Jo's time growing near and Matthias and Clay leaving soon to take the sheep up the mountain. Elaine would have to stay—at least until Mary returned.

Elaine raised her chin and returned Mary's smile. "I'm happy for you, Mary," she said before standing and clearing the dishes from the table.

"I'll wash the dishes, Elaine. Why don't you see to the chickens?" Mary said.

Elaine bit her tongue. She wanted to cry, to run away, to beg Mary to deal with the diabolical birds. But she must maintain an air of normalcy.

"Miss Elaine, may I show you something?" Matthias rose from the table, a sheepish grin quirking one side of his lips. "At the hen house, that is."

Elaine blinked. What on earth could this be about? She glanced at Gideon, who nodded encouragement.

"Alright, then." Elaine wrapped her shawl around her shoulders, and Matthias donned his hat, retrieving the pail of grain Mary had set out by the door.

Outside, they fell into step, walking together toward the coop.

"What is this all about?" Elaine gave Matthias a sidelong look, noting a brightness to Matthias's blue eyes that hadn't been there for the past few weeks.

He cleared his throat. "Well, I know you have little love for doing the chicken chores, and I hate to see your discomfort."

Was that color tinting his cheeks? She should be embarrassed she had garnered his attention with her struggle over the chore, but Matthias's own self-consciousness was disarming.

"So, you're planning to tend the chickens for me, then?" It surprised her a cowboy-turned-shepherd would lower himself to such a task, but that didn't matter. Relief washed over her.

"Well, no. I won't be doing that." Matthias stopped in front of the coop and turned.

She looked up at him, feeling as though someone had drawn a darning needle between her brows. If he would not help her, why was he here?

"Here," he said, taking her hand and leading her to the side of the building.

He turned two latches on either side of the wall and lifted the board, which opened on hinges like a window.

Elaine blinked. With the board lifted, she had access to the nesting boxes from *outside* the coop. She jerked her astonished gaze between the new contraption and the man who made it possible.

Matthias closed the shutter and opened another at the bottom of the wall. This one opened in the opposite direction, like a flour bin. He took the grain bucket and poured its contents into the new feeder, and closed the latches again.

"Now you only need open the big door to reach in and pour a pail of water, but that can be set up within arms-reach so you don't need to go inside every day.

A giddy laugh bubbled up in Elaine's chest, and she gripped Matthias's sleeve, stopping herself just before she embarrassed herself by bobbing up to kiss him on the cheek.

Never. She had never received a gift so thoughtful or so tailored to her needs. Had he realized just how much this meant to her? He couldn't possibly.

Though staying on the homestead until Mary returned was not Elaine's first choice, this gift would at least ease her struggles while she remained.

"Thank you, Matthias. Thank you ever so much." She blinked back the moisture gathering on her lashes.

She turned away quickly lest he notice her tears and think her soft-headed. To anyone else, this was a thoughtful convenience. But to Elaine, it was everything.

Chapter 26

Mary clutched the worn handles of her bag as the train swayed and rattled down the tracks. They would arrive in Pueblo soon, and she would finally see Charlie. *Her Charlie.*

Needle pricks of both excitement and trepidation stitched through her legs. She was sure if she could just deboard here, she could reach Pueblo long before the train did. Her longing to see her husband would carry her on swift wings to his side.

Twelve years. It had been twelve years since she had seen him—kissed his lips or held his hand. Their time had been cut far too short when he had left Kansas, never to return.

The memory of their last morning together haunted her. She hadn't wanted him to go. It hadn't mattered to her they had never started a ranch or a homestead of their own. She had been quite content to live in their little soddie on the Bradford ranch for the rest of their days.

But Charlie had always been a dreamer. Had always wanted them to have a home of their own. So, when young Gideon had come home, bubbling with excitement and news of a renewed silver rush in Colorado, Charlie had become determined to replenish the savings he had exchanged for her safety so many years prior.

"Just a few months, Love," Charlie had whispered into the waves of her loose hair that covered the pillow between them in the predawn light. "I've no plans to seek a great fortune. Only enough to see you in the home and life you deserve."

A few months was all it was supposed to be. But she never saw him again. He hadn't wanted to tell the boys he was leaving, afraid Gideon would insist on coming along. Jimmy was still young, and Charlie knew Mary would need Gideon by her side while he was gone, so Charlie slipped out before sunrise.

Not telling the boys had been a mistake.

Mary leaned her head back against the seat and rolled her head to look out the window. Blinded to the scenery speeding past, all she could see was the hurt the in the eyes of her sons when she told them their pa was gone.

Gideon had taken the blame all on himself and no amount of comforting or explaining would assuage his guilt when the months passed with no word from his pa.

So, when Jimmy turned seventeen and Gideon announced he was leaving to find Charlie, Mary knew there was no stopping him. Stubborn as an ox, that one. Always had been.

Mary opened her reticule and pulled out the worn leather journal Gideon had given to her when he returned to Kansas earlier this year with Jo and an astounding cache of silver.

The journal told a heartbreaking story of a man missing his family but determined to give them a better life. How he found the silver he sought, only to slip slowly into some kind of twisted state of reasoning, paranoia, confusion, until eventually the words on the page held no sense at all.

Mary's shoulders heaved. She hadn't needed a better life. She had only needed him.

The Bradfords had been kind employers and had supplied them a home of their own on the ranch. Yet, Charlie wanted more for her than a life as someone else's housekeeper and cook. Even though she'd rather have worked her fingers to the bone in a factory if it had meant keeping him home.

No sense in grieving over it now, though. What was done was done, and Mary was now the determined one. She would have her husband back, no matter what it took.

JO SHUFFLED TO THE corner of her bedroom and squatted slowly, leaning slightly back to pick up her moccasins. Even that slight effort made the pressure in her head build and her vision dim. *Drat.*

She eyed her bed with suspicion. If she sat down there to put on her shoes, she might never get back up. It had taken her far longer than it should have to rise this morning.

She waddled to the kitchen table and sat in a sturdy wooden chair, praying it wouldn't shatter into splinters under her bulk. Trying not to lean forward more than necessary, she slipped her foot into the supple leather and tugged. Nothing.

That was odd. The moccasins had felt tight with the swelling in her feet these past few weeks, but she had at least been able to put them on.

Grimacing, she tried the other foot. No luck there either. She pressed her lips together and sighed. She would just have to go out and check the horses barefoot this morning. Sliding the moccasins under the chair, she pressed her hands flat on the table and pressed hard, heaving her weight into a semi-stable standing position.

Glancing around the room to make sure the other women were occupied, Jo slipped out the front door—hoping to bring no attention to herself.

Outside, she drank in the cool mountain air. The cabin had felt so stuffy these past few days. She could hardly catch her breath. Maybe some time outdoors was what she needed. She curled her toes around the short grass under her feet.

She just wasn't used to being so sedentary, that was all. After Florence's recent pronouncement that Jo stop riding, Gideon had been fussing over her like a mama hen and had kept Jo captive around the place. She needed freedom, movement.

Enjoying the tickle of grass under her feet, Jo walked out to the corral where the horses were. Shadow noticed her approach and trotted to meet her at the fence, nickering and throwing his head. He was just as restless as Jo was.

Jo stroked his nose and fed him a lump of sugar from the leather pouch she wore across her chest. Sarge and Jack noticed Jo and came closer as well, but the new mule, Clarice, hung back, still a little unsure.

"Well, then, I'll just have to come to you," Jo said, lifting the board that acted as a latch to the corral.

"What do you think you're doing, woman?" Gideon's low voice rumbled over her shoulder.

Jo cringed but whipped around, donning the most innocent countenance she could muster. "What are you talking about? Am I so frail I can't even come out to see the horses now?"

Gideon looked pointedly down at Jo's feet, raising an eyebrow in question.

"Yes?" Jo braced her hands behind her back and leveled a glare at him.

"You ought not to be out here with nothing on your feet." Gideon tried to buffalo her, but she would stand her ground. Barefoot or not.

"Gideon Cross, you have known me my whole life, and you know I've never been in the habit of wearing shoes if I could help it. Well, at least not until Florence gave me my first pair of moccasins."

Narrowing his eyes, Gideon placed a hand over hers, lowering it and closing the latch to the gate. "And if you get stepped on, then what? You don't need any other complications right now."

"Complications?" Jo snapped. "Is that what you see our child as?" Jo looked at her belly defensively and placed a hand over the swell.

Gideon scrubbed a hand over his face and growled something that sounded suspiciously like *stubborn woman* under his breath. "You know that's not what I meant. Don't you even try to distract me with a fight."

Jo fought to keep her lips from curling into a smile. He'd caught her.

"You don't need an injury right now. Besides, those things are looking more swollen by the day. I'm afraid if a horse stepped on one of them right now, it would burst." All playful banter aside, genuine worry registered on Gideon's face now. "Is that why you're out here barefoot? Are your feet too big for your moccasins?"

She turned her back to Gideon and huffed, running a toe through the soft dirt. "I must have gotten them damp last night, and they dried a bit snug. That's all."

"Josephina." Gideon drew the syllables of her name out the way her ma used to. "Let's go back to the house and have a word with Florence about this." He reached down and laced his fingers through hers, tugging her to follow him.

Jo's shoulders sagged with submission. Florence had acted as midwife for Jo, far as they were from town. It was both a blessing and a curse to have someone who knew so much living with them. While Florence had an endless knowledge of remedies and the wisdom of her eighty years, it often ruffled Jo's feathers to be given orders. Florence would abide no argument when she made up her mind.

Gideon escorted Jo into the house and pulled a chair up in front of Florence. The older woman straightened and looked Jo over with a critical eye, her gaze stopping at Jo's bare feet.

"She can't wear her moccasins any longer." Gideon spoke, standing behind her and resting his hands on her shoulders.

Florence motioned to the bedroom. "You lay down."

She held out a hand, and Gideon assisted her to stand. Jo obeyed the woman, going to her bedroom and lying down on the soft quilt.

When Florence settled onto a low stool next to the bed, she shooed Gideon out the door. "Go now. Find nettle. Make tea."

Gideon made no hesitation, but went about her bidding. Thanks to Florence's stores, they had a supply of dried herbs in glass jars in the cellar. The lid of each jar was covered in oilcloth with the name of the plant it contained written in charcoal.

Florence turned back to Jo, brushing a cool hand over Jo's brow. "Head hurt." It was a statement, not a question, yet she paused for confirmation.

Jo nodded, then winced at the motion.

Florence's frown deepened, and she lifted Jo's hand, looking it over. "Skin tight." She sighed. "I see many times."

With no more explanation, she bowed her gray head, her hand resting on Jo's, and spoke a litany of words in her native tongue. She was praying. Jo had seen it often, but she hadn't been the subject of its fervency since Jo had arrived at Florence and Clay's cabin, wet, cold, and broken last year.

After a few moments, Florence raised her head and gave Jo a sympathetic smile.

"Jo stay in bed." She drew up the knitted blanket at the foot of the bed and covered Jo's legs, sealing her in.

No. Jo dropped her head back against the pillow, inducing a wave of dizziness. Surely Florence didn't mean for Jo to stay in bed. How could she? There was too much to do. It was time to plant a garden, and the men would take the sheep up the mountain soon. With Mary gone, it simply wasn't possible.

Just then, Gideon knocked on the doorjamb before entering with a steaming cup. Florence patted Jo's hip and pulled it toward herself. Jo understood the woman's intention and rolled onto her side. Turning back to Gideon, Florence took the cup and offered it to Jo. "Drink."

She looked from Jo to Gideon, her gaze landing on Gideon in the end. "No work. Jo stay down."

Jo huffed and took a sip of the slightly bitter tea. Swallowing with it, her pride. Though she had no notion how they would get by, this child would be worth the sacrifice of her freedom.

Chapter 27

Elaine wiped her brow with the back of her wrist and recoiled at the sweat soaking her skin. She might as well have been Shadrach standing before the fiery furnace, the way the heat blazed from the cookstove and radiated over her.

The front damper of the stove had to be fully opened in order for the oven to make enough heat to bake, but the need to stand over the stove and stir the boiling pot of soup while the fire was roaring like an inferno was causing her to drip perspiration in the most unappealing way.

She couldn't take it any longer. Setting her spoon on a plate on the table, Elaine fled outside to escape the heat. She turned and leaned back against the hitching post, closing her eyes and drinking in the crisp mountain air in greedy gulps, relishing the sensation of the breeze skating over her damp skin.

She wiped her hands on her apron, too tired to even allow herself to fret over the flour and cornmeal transferred to her fingers by the action.

"Fine evening, isn't it?" A voice spoke behind her, and she whipped around, heart pounding.

Matthias leaned forward in the saddle and rested his forearm against the saddle horn, grinning. His sleeves were rolled to the elbow, exposing the raised white scar that stood out in stark contrast to the olive skin and dark hair on his arms. Even at a distance, she could see the thick webbing of the scar tissue.

"Miss Elaine?" Matthias asked, confused by her trance.

She jerked her eyes away. Where were her manners, staring like that?

"Me? Oh"—Elaine straightened and lifted her chin against the weariness that weighed on her—"just enjoying the breeze. The house gets awfully hot when I bake anything."

Matthias grinned amiably. "It's a mighty pleasant day," he agreed, his eyes traveling beyond the house to the horizon. "I'd better get on about my chores. I'm looking forward to supper, and I wouldn't want to be late."

Supper. Elaine flew into the house, heedless of the man she'd abandoned. The acrid stench of scorched food lingered in the air. What was burning? Was it the soup or the cornbread?

She stirred the soup pot and large black flakes floated to the top of the broth. She groaned. How could she burn something that was essentially liquid? She'd chosen to make soup so she wouldn't risk ruining another meal.

Elaine had charred the lamb chops last night, and the flapjacks this morning, and served moldy cheese with stale bread for lunch. Tears stung her eyes, though she didn't know if it was from frustration or the smoky atmosphere.

After several minutes of frantic searching, she found her oven mitts on the wood stack outside the front door and slid the soup pot to the cooler side of the stove—careful to keep her face away from the exposed flames when she moved the pot from the opening.

She set the stove lid back in its place with a metallic clunk and opened the oven door to check the cornbread. An overwhelming wave of heat and smoke rolled over her and she choked and sputtered.

Covering her face with her apron, she removed the cast-iron skillet and deposited it on top of the stove.

"Everything okay out there?" Jo called from the bedroom.

Elaine gritted her teeth. "Just fine."

She poked at the blackened edges of the cornbread. Only one side of the pan had burned—the side that had been closest to the firebox. The other half of the pan was mysteriously unmarred. Elaine huffed and reached for a knife. Maybe she could salvage enough slices from the unburned side of the pan?

When she cut the cornbread down the middle of the skillet, it met with no resistance. That didn't seem right. She lifted the knife, and gloopy cornmeal mush clung to it, a few globs dropping back into the pan. She'd somehow burned one half of the pan while the other half remained raw.

She sagged onto a chair by the table and buried her face in her hands. If she couldn't do these minor tasks given her, what good was she to anyone?

There was no help for it now, though. All she could do was press on. Jo was under strict orders to remain abed. The men all had work of their own, and while Florence was a sweet presence and welcome company, she could not share the load and spent much of her time sleeping in her rocker.

It was up to Elaine to pick up the slack, whether or not she felt herself capable. She must press on.

The voices of the men increased in volume as they approached the house. Elaine quickly stood and brushed back the flighty strands of hair that hung down about her face and finished setting the table while the men washed up.

Then she lifted out the floating flakes of black char from the soup with the ladle and arranged the slices of charred cornbread on a platter.

She dished up two plates for Gideon and Jo and handed them to him with an apologetic shrug. He offered his thanks but eyed her offering as a man facing the gallows. Resignation to a fate he couldn't avoid.

Gideon took the plates to the bedroom to share supper with Jo, and Elaine joined Clay, Matthias, and Florence at the table. While Clay asked the blessing over the food, Elaine sent up a silent prayer of her own that the food would be at the least edible.

Clay and Matthias exchanged looks of foreboding.

"I'm sorry," Elaine burst out, covering her face with her hands. "It's awful, I know, but I'm doing the best I can." She swallowed back the sob that rose in her throat.

"Oh, it's not all that bad, Miss Elaine." Matthias took a bite of cornbread. "The char adds a smoky—campfire flavor. Reminds me of eating corn dodgers on the trail."

"Mhmm." Clay nodded enthusiastically before drinking down his entire cup of milk.

Florence tapped the hard bread with a crooked finger. It made a hollow, scratchy sound and her eyes widened.

"Oh dear, you cannot eat that, can you?" Elaine knotted her fingers together in her lap.

Florence smiled a nearly toothless grin and crumbled the hard cornbread into her bowl of soup and stirred it in. She nodded and took a bite. It must not have had much time to soften because she struggled to speak around the bite of hard cornbread wedged in her mouth. "Good."

The lump in Elaine's throat gave way, but instead of a sob, a laugh bubbled out. Matthias stared at her, stunned, and covered his mouth with a napkin, smothering his amusement. Clay had no such qualms. He bellowed out a hearty laugh that shook the rafters. They all laughed until tears streamed from their eyes, and Elaine's sides ached.

She wasn't sure she had ever laughed like that, not even as a girl. And for a few moments, she had no driving compulsion to tap or fidget. For the second time in only a matter of a week, she had found relief. First with music and then with laughter. Was it possible to find, if not freedom, at least an occasional reprieve from the hysteric restlessness that had plagued her for years?

She wiped away the tears streaking down her face and locked eyes with Matthias across the table from her. He was the common factor in her moments of stillness. Could it be that a dusty cowboy was the answer?

Chapter 28

Gideon tested the maul's weight in his hand, finding its balance before swinging it up and over his head to cleave through the round of wood in one solid strike. He'd been restless all night. Something didn't feel right, though he couldn't put his finger on it.

Chopping wood always gave him an outlet for his frustration, a lightning rod to absorb the tension running through him when he was troubled.

The morning held a quiet that settled a chill into his bones. Even for early morning, it was too still. Ominous. He hadn't slept most of the night. The uncertainty of what could happen once they moved the sheep up the mountain weighed heavily on him.

Would Clay and Matthias run into the same trouble the Ibarra family's shepherds had? For that matter, had he made the right choice vouching for Matthias and bringing him on as a hired hand? Or was Matthias just a wolf in sheep's clothing?

Gideon checked himself. He shouldn't even think such a thing. Matthias had been nothing but helpful. But the fact was, though, Gideon had helped a man walk free who killed a rancher just trying to get his cattle back. Gideon prayed it had been the right thing to do.

Matthias wasn't loyal to McBride or he wouldn't have agreed to go to the sheriff about what he'd done, but Matthias had lived as an outlaw for years. What if he was incapable of reforming, and Gideon had not only helped him walk free but invited him into his home to break bread with his family?

Sighing, Gideon swung the maul one last time, sticking it firmly into the chopping block, and gathered up the split pieces of wood heaped to the side. He carried them to the front of the house and added them to the stack.

Gathering up the smallest pieces, he filled the metal bucket Elaine would use for the day's cooking. The sound of thundering hooves carried from the upper trail, and Gideon turned to see Clay riding toward the house at a full gallop.

"Gideon!" Clay shouted, and Gideon ducked inside to gather his rifle and knife from the house.

He stepped outside to meet Clay. "What is it? Are McBride's men coming?"

Clay shook his head. "No, but I think they've been here already.

His words dropped in Gideon's gut like a ball of ice—chilling him to the core.

Jo came shuffling out of the house, clutching a pistol and the ends of the quilt wrapped around her. Wisps of her strawberry blonde hair that had escaped her braid stood out wildly in all directions. She looked fierce as ever, despite the swelling in her face and hands.

"You go back to bed." Gideon spoke through clenched teeth.

He regretted his words immediately. It wasn't that she couldn't help. In fact, in any other circumstance, she would be the first one he'd want by his side. But right now, she was in no condition for a fight.

He braced his rifle over his shoulder and moved to her side, kissing the top of her head to gentle his abrupt command.

"I will *not* go to bed until I hear what's happened." She tightened her grip on the quilt and pistol.

"I know, I'm sorry." Gideon offered her a half smile, then turned to Clay. "What is it? What's happened?"

Clay looked from Gideon to Jo. "We're losing sheep."

"Lost, as in, wandering off?" Gideon hoped it was that simple.

"Dead. The dogs, too."

Ice traveled through Gideon's veins. "All of the dogs?"

Clay shook his head. "Scout's been staying at the house with Matthias, but the Pyrenees—they're gone.

"McBride?" Gideon gripped the rifle stock.

"Can't be sure. Found the dogs and four dead ewes this morning. But I was on watch all night. No one came or went. There's no blood—no sign of injury."

Jo clutched Gideon's elbow with her free hand.

He turned to her. "We'll go check things out. It's likely they've gotten into some weed they shouldn't have. You go on inside."

Jo bristled.

"Please? I can't risk anything happening to you or our child."

Fire flickered in Jo's eyes, but her shoulders sagged with reluctant acceptance.

"I'm sorry," he whispered quietly before kissing her. "I just want to keep you and the babe safe."

Jo pressed her lips in a tight smile. "You be careful." She looked up at Clay, still mounted. "You too."

"Yes, ma'am," Clay answered and turned his horse toward the barn.

After saddling Sarge and informing Matthias he would need to keep watch at the house, Gideon and Clay rode out to the upper grazing pasture. Clay led Gideon to the edge of the flock. Tight lines formed at the corners of Clay's eyes as he pointed with his chin to where the ewes lay dead in the grass.

He dropped to his knees next to one, checking her over for sign of injury. Lambs tottered about, bleating for their mothers, and Gideon's stomach twisted. They would need to graft these lambs to other ewes. But was it too late for that?

If the ewes wouldn't mother on the orphan lambs, they would need to bring them to the barn to be bottle fed. Yet another new challenge Gideon would have to face. Not for the first time, he questioned the sense of buying a sheep flock. What had he been thinking? He was entirely unknowledgeable about this kind of ranching.

He checked one of the dead ewes over for injury. There was no sign of violence. While that knowledge eased his fear, it did nothing to pacify the gnawing ache in his stomach. How could this have happened?

Hector Sanchez had chosen this area to build his homestead because of the easy access to snow melt that provided water for the animals and the abundant grazing, where there were very few harmful plants.

"Let's scan the area for something amiss. Then we need to move these sheep back to the sheep fold as soon as possible in case they're eating something here they shouldn't."

Gideon and Clay hobbled their horses and separated to search the area, looking for anything that could have harmed the sheep.

"What about water?" Clay asked as he crouched down to inspect a plant with shiny, dark green leaves.

Gideon rubbed the back of his neck. "With spring runoff, it's not likely they'd be out of water, but I reckon you're right. We ought to check."

Gideon hiked over to the base of the rocky hill where a narrow trickle of run-off steadily fed into a small pond the sheep used for water. Just as it should be, there was plenty of water to be had.

He searched for anything that stood out as unusual greenery in the area. All he could find were mountain grasses and dandelions. Nothing that seemed out of the ordinary.

He huffed and crossed the clearing back to Sarge to retrieve the journal left to him by Sanchez. Turning to the back section of pages, he scanned the drawings of harmful plants for anything recognizable.

Something struck a nerve. He jerked his focus around the clearing. One plant from the journal looked familiar. Where had he seen it?

He stomped around the grazing site like a bull on a rampage. Sheep shuffled and scattered this way and that.

God help me. Where is it?

Frustration clouded his vision until he could hardly tell one plant from another. The toe of his boot slammed into a rock in his path and he tripped, flying headlong to the edge of the pond. Pebbles dug into the heels of his hands, and he trenched his fingers through the gravel and dirt.

He swallowed back the roar of anger building pressure in his chest. He wasn't a sheep farmer. He didn't know a thing about sheep. How had he even ended up here?

Scrambling up into a kneeling position, Gideon brushed off his hands. He rocked back to sit on his heels, and pressed his hands against his thighs, looking out across the reflective surface of the water. His eyes grazed a plant in the pool. *There it was.*

He knew he'd seen it somewhere.

Floating in the water were several long-stemmed plants, their dark green, fern-like leaves and white flower clusters limp and wilted in the water. He found a stick and swept the plants out of the pond.

"I think I have something," Gideon shouted to Clay, who was venturing farther down the hill in his own search.

Clay jogged up the slope to join Gideon. "What is it?"

"I'm not certain, but I know I've seen something like this." Gideon dried his hands on his shirt and flipped through the pages of the journal. He located the drawing. "Hemlock." His voice faltered on the word. "Have you seen this plant growing around here? I know I haven't."

Clay shook his head in response, scanning the area again.

"McBride." Gideon spat the name. "They've poisoned the water."

Chapter 29

Matthias rapped on the cabin door and stepped back, tightening his fist at his side as he waited for Elaine to answer. His heart pounded in time with every blow of the hammer Clay was using to repair the shepherd's wagon by the barn. Something about being near Elaine sent his nerves singing like the strings of a violin. Waiting on her appearance plucked the strand and anticipation reverberated through him.

The door opened, and Elaine's tawny eyes blinked with surprise. "Matthias, can I help you?"

Matthias cleared his throat. "Actually, I hoped I could be of some help to you. Would you be able to come with me for a few hours?"

Elaine pressed a hand to her stomach. "Come with you? Why—What could you need me for?" A shadow of uncertainty crossed her delicate features.

"Well, to be frank, I intend to teach you to shoot a gun."

"To shoot—what? Why would you want to do that? I am not my sister, Matthias. I have no desire to go gallivanting around the woods shooting turkeys."

Matthias stifled the laugh that hummed in his throat. He recognized Elaine's brusque demeanor at times was simply a tactic to cover her fears.

"Clay and I will leave tomorrow to take the sheep to higher ground. Without the dogs around, there will need to be two of us. It will be weeks before we return. Jo is confined to her bed, and if Gideon were to be called away for any reason, you would be here alone."

She drew up straight and gripped the doorjamb.

"I don't wish to frighten you, but there are real dangers here. You need to be able to defend yourself and the other women if trouble was to come."

"But I can't—"

"Go." Florence's voice spoke from inside the cabin.

Elaine whipped around to stare at the woman. "I can't," she told Florence forcefully.

Florence stood from her rocker with some effort, and shuffled to cross the room, her colorful skirt sweeping the floor. "Jo sleeps. I watch her. You go."

Elaine turned back to Matthias hesitantly.

"Gideon agrees with me. This is a necessity." He removed her shawl from a hook by the door and wrapped it around her shoulders.

"I can't," she repeated, her voice a shaky whisper. She took a small step forward, then backed up again.

"You must," Matthias said as he grazed his fingers down her forearm and took her hand into his. "Come."

He would accept no argument. He had to know that she, that they, would be safe. He tugged gently on their connection, and she followed reluctantly.

When they reached the barn, Matthias retrieved a rope and scooped a few double handfuls of grain into a leather pouch. He inclined his head for her to follow him and led her to the corral fence.

"You know how to ride, yes?" he asked.

She was raised on a ranch, after all, even if she preferred the confines of the house.

"Yes."

"Astride or side saddle?" Matthias opened the corral gate and motioned her in the pen.

"Side saddle, of course." Elaine looked truly perplexed he would even ask the question.

"But you may not always have that luxury. Some day you might need to run, either for help or from danger, and not have someone else to saddle a horse for you."

Fear tightened the corners of her eyes as he spoke.

"When I get back from tending the sheep, I'll make sure you know how to saddle and bridle a horse properly. But for now, I'd like to know you could ride in any circumstance. Can you whistle?" He turned to face her.

She shook her head. Matthias let out a ringing tone. Copper lifted his head across the corral and meandered in their direction.

Elaine's brow crinkled, and she pursed her lips. Nothing but air escaped.

Matthias tucked a finger under her chin and lifted it slightly. "Like this."

He formed his own lips into the correct shape, eyes focused on her mouth as she attempted to mimic him. Her soft, pink lips opened like flower petals to morning dew, and he suddenly had the desire to swoop down like a bee after nectar.

He pulled back and cleared his throat. This was not the time, and he had no right to even entertain such a notion.

"Keep practicing." He nodded to Copper, who had joined them and was nudging at the pouch slung at Matthias's hip. Matthias took out a handful of grain. "Horses often respond to a whistle, especially if they've come to expect a reward."

Jo's dapple grey, Shadow, and Gideon's paint, Sarge, followed Copper across the corral. Matthias took Elaine's hand and poured a trickle of grain into her palm.

"Now, hold out your hand." He moved behind her and lifted her arm so her handful of grain was outstretched.

He whistled again, and the other two horses trotted the remaining distance. Elaine tensed in front of him and he resisted the urge to tuck her against himself—to shield her.

Shadow reached out and nibbled the grain from Elaine's hand.

"See? Easy as pie." Matthias told her. "Now, just follow my movements." He scratched Copper behind the ear and patted the gelding's neck near his head.

"Some horses aren't very cooperative with taking a bit until you get them back to the barn. You're best off to halter them here and then take them back to the barn to saddle and bridle. This is what you're going to do." He took the long coil of rope and folded it in half.

Elaine followed his lead with the rope he handed her as he showed her where to tie the first four knots and how to run the end of the rope back through, double-knotting and adjusting each. She was a quick student and had no trouble grasping the steps as they gathered the excess rope at the noseband, tied a chin knot, then slipped it over their horses' heads and passed the poll end through the throatlatch loop.

They repeated the entire process over until the steps came easier, and she could make the halter without help.

He took the end of the rope and showed her one more step that ran the rope from one side to the other in a rein loop. "Now, we mount."

Elaine's eyes flew wide and stared at him like he had three heads. "Bareback? Like a—" Her eyes darted to Clay, still working on the wagon by the barn. "An Indian?"

Matthias chuckled and took hold of Shadow's bridle. "Exactly. There is much we can learn from our darker skinned friends. They survived thousands of years with none of the things we often think are necessities now. You need to be able to ride at any given moment."

"You know there's a reason more than just stubbornness your sister wears buckskin leggings rather than dresses. It's far more practical in a case like this."

Elaine frowned down at her long skirt. "I will not degrade myself to the level of wearing men's clothing, Matthias Noble."

His full name on her lips sent his heart strings humming.

"I'll respect that. But if you mean to survive when you're in danger, you'll need to not be tangled in skirts." He frowned and rubbed a hand over his chin as he contemplated. "Forgive me, but I'm going to suggest something you'll likely find highly improper. Please don't slap me."

A muscle in Elaine's cheek jumped as humor tugged at the corner of her lips. "I can't make any promises." Her smile spread into full bloom.

He leaned back and inspected her dress. Is that skirt a separate piece or is it all"—he waved a hand, gesturing up and down her attire—"one piece?"

"It's a separate skirt." She ran a hand over the garment, trailing a finger at the waist to indicate the separation.

Matthias nodded. "If you find yourself in need of riding, or running through the brush and trees, set decency aside and gird up your loins."

She blinked. "What?"

"I've seen you read the Bible in the evening. Have you read how the Israelites girded up their loins when they went into battle?"

She raised an eyebrow at him with pointed curiosity.

"Oh, I've read it too. Don't be shocked. My grandmother made sure I read the Bible every evening whenever I was with her. May not be on the best terms with God these days, but I know a few things about it."

She pressed her lips together and nodded.

"So, about the girding. Have you read that part?" he asked, brushing past the pensive stare she was giving him.

"I have." Elaine nodded.

"And do you know what that meant?"

She shook her head.

"Reach down in front and take hold of the back of your skirt. Draw it up"—he cleared his throat and turned away, rubbing the back of his neck—"between your legs and tuck it into the waist of your skirt."

The intake of her breath was audible behind him.

"Go on and try it," he said, focusing his attention on the horses.

"Alright."

"Good. Now, do you have a pair of britches instead of a dress?" Matthias scratched Copper's head, waiting.

"I do." Surprise rang through her voice.

Carefully, he turned around. "Are you decent?" he asked, keeping his eyes trained on the ground.

"I believe so."

Sunlight glittered on something in the grass, and Matthias bent to pick it up. It was a cameo brooch, the gilded edges worn from age. "Is this yours?" he asked, and held it out to her.

Something like panic shadowed her face, and she took the pin, clutching it in her hand. "Yes. Thank you." She turned away and fumbled at the waist of her makeshift britches, pinning the cameo back in place.

What an odd place to keep a memento like that pinned. Most women wore such things on their lapel. Whatever the reason, it seemed she preferred not to discuss it.

"What now?" Elaine urged the conversation away from the brooch.

"Now you learn how to swing up on a horse." He led Copper a few feet away, gripped the reins and the horse's mane, and swung up onto the horse's bare back with ease.

Patting Copper on the neck, he turned back to Elaine. "Your turn."

Elaine's jaw dropped open like an opera singer on the final note. "Are you daft?" Elaine flinched after she spoke, and shook her head. "I can't do that."

Matthias swung a leg over Copper's back and dropped to the ground.

"You can and you will." He came to her side and took her hand, searching her golden eyes for understanding. "Let me help you."

He had to help her. She was so innocent—one last thing in his world that hadn't been tainted or tarnished. She was like a beautiful piece of artwork, exquisite and priceless yet delicate. He pushed away the thought of how easily that vulnerability could be tainted. He would do whatever it took to protect her.

"Will you let me help you?" Matthias asked, hating how choked his voice sounded.

She nodded.

He placed her hands in position on Shadow's neck, then put his hands around her waist guiding her into position.

Chapter 30

They spent a significant part of the afternoon practicing mounting a horse with no saddle. He boosted her up for several attempts, allowing her to get the feel for the motion, and pausing occasionally for her to tuck her skirt back into place.

After many failed attempts, Elaine was bedraggled and pink to the ears with effort and exhaustion. Matthias was certain she'd never looked more beautiful.

"You have it now," Matthias stepped back. "Kick up."

He balled his fists at his side, resisting the urge to lift her. It wouldn't do any good to do the work for her. She had to have the confidence she could do it herself.

She turned sideways along Shadow's neck, backed up, and swung her leg over the gelding's back, pulling against his silvery mane and wiggling to heave herself up.

"You did it!" Matthias thought his heart might just burst from his chest at the elated smile that lit her face like sunshine.

He resisted the urge to pull her back down and embrace her, patting her knee instead. She breathed out a satisfied smile, relaxing, and he rested a hand on her knee.

"Now, riding bareback is difficult in the beginning, but it is a necessary skill. Stay on, and let's ride out yonder."

They rode to the edge of the tree line slowly, allowing Elaine to get a feel riding without a saddle. When they reached their destination, Matthias helped Elaine down and they left the horses to graze.

"Now, you need to learn to shoot." Matthias pulled the pistol from his holster and checked the cylinders.

Elaine took a step back and shook her head. "I don't think I can do this." Her voice wavered, and she pressed a hand against her stomach like she might be sick.

"Of course you can. Look what you've done already today."

She straightened her shoulders and raised her chin. He recognized the fierce determination he'd seen the first day he'd met her. She seemed so fragile at times, but there was an underlying perseverance in her that belied her delicate nature.

Matthias handed her the pistol. "First rule. No matter what, never point this at something or someone unless you're prepared to kill."

A pale shadow crossed her face, and she pressed her lips together, nodding.

He moved behind her and slipped the gun into her hands. "Hold it like this." He spoke over her shoulder and wrapped his grasp around hers, molding her fingers into the correct position. "Plant your feet. Now, hold the gun tight." He raised her shaky arms with his. "I'll keep you steady this time. Line the sights up on that big tree knot there. You see it?"

He loosened his hold on the gun long enough to point out a large, gnarled knot on an aspen tree.

Elaine's nod brushed the wisps of her loose hair against his cheek, and he had to steady himself, hoping she couldn't feel his heart pounding.

"Breath in and out," he whispered behind her ear, and the swell of her breath pressed against his chest. "Again, but this time only breathe halfway out and hold it. Line your sights up on the knot and slowly squeeze the trigger. Go ahead now, and I'll support you." He wrapped his hands around hers again.

She breathed deeply, paused, and fired the gun. A tree branch to the left of their target shattered.

"Not bad. Not bad at all." He turned her to face him and shock mingled with disappointment filled her eyes.

"It's loud." She blinked, eyes wide. "And I missed." She chewed the inside of one cheek, turning to stare at the broken branch.

He shook his head. "Have you ever shot a gun before?"

"Certainly not." A smile tugged at her lips.

"Then I reckon you did just fine. Now you'll try again, this time without me."

He moved to the side and coached her through the steps again, this time keeping his arms crossed against his chest to resist the urge to reach out and help. She braced herself, breathed slowly, and fired. The percussion jarred her, and she tipped over backwards, landing on her back.

Matthias ran to her and dropped to his knees. She lay sprawled in the short spring grass, sucking in gasps of air. He took the gun from her and holstered it before scooping her up and cradling her in his arms.

She groaned.

"Knock the wind out of you?" he asked, brushing the hair out of her eyes.

She nodded. "It's much harder when you're not there to hold me up." She beamed then, and leaned against his chest, shaking with laughter.

Matthias's heart squeezed at her bravery even when things were hard or uncomfortable for her.

"You'll do just fine without me." The words caught in his throat, coming out tight and constricted.

Her smile faltered. "I—I don't want you to leave."

He ran a thumb over her trembling lip. Everything in him wanted to pull her closer, and kiss her—pour any strength he had into her—give her all of himself, all his love and protection. But he shouldn't let thoughts like that take hold.

Even with his desire to protect her, she'd be much better off without him. Despite his attempts to stay on the straight and narrow, evil nipped at his heels no matter where he turned. He could give her a few skills that could help keep her safe, but that needed to be the end of their connection. Despite his growing feelings for her.

He searched her face, open and vulnerable, and cleared his throat. "You'll be just fine without me."

"I'm afraid." She ran her fingers over his as he cradled her face and pressed her cheek into his palm.

He closed his eyes and fought the desire to crush her to himself and promise his protection. Instead, he slid his fingers into the soft, brown hair at her temple and brushed his lips against her brow in a kiss.

She clung to his arms and pressed her forehead against his chest. Minutes passed and he held her there, nestled against him. Just when he thought he could never let go, Scout pushed between them, nuzzling them both with his wet nose.

Elaine squeaked, batting the dog away, and Matthias helped her up. She looked up, with eyes so trusting and open, stepping closer. He braced his hands on her waist and leaned back far enough to see her face clearly and drink in the beauty he didn't deserve to be so close to.

How could he ever merit a woman like this?

She rose on her toes and kissed him, so light and soft he barely felt her lips against his. No, he didn't deserve her, but he would do everything in his power to earn her favor.

Chapter 31

A jingle of harness in the drive rattled Elaine's nerves, and she jerked open the oven door, heedless of the blast of hot air that pelted her face. Matthias was leaving, and if she didn't hurry, she would miss her chance to say goodbye. She slid the sheet of biscuits on top of the wood stove and tapped the top of one dark brown biscuit. It was as hard and hollow as a gourd. But at least it wasn't black this time.

She had to hurry. Matthias had said goodbye last night and told her he would see her in a few weeks, when they would replenish their supplies. He hadn't wanted her to wake so early, but she wanted to send him off with breakfast. And if she was honest, she couldn't bear to wake knowing he was gone. He had become her safe harbor here in this wilderness, and she wasn't prepared to face it all without his reassuring presence.

She stacked the hard tack biscuits onto a clean towel three at a time, added a wrapped packet of ham and then some sheep's milk cheese from the pantry. Then she said a prayer for his welfare as she tied the bundle closed.

She wrapped her shawl around her shoulders and stepped out into the frosty morning air. Worried he might leave before she could catch him, she hadn't taken the time to dress properly or even put on shoes.

Matthias was tying Copper to the back of the wagon. She ran out into the flat, dusk light, clutching the bundle to her chest to meet him. The frosty ground was cold and harsh against her bare feet, and the sharp sensation of cold rocks and dirt against her skin sent waves of irritation through her.

What had she been thinking? Jo had made running around outside barefoot look so easy. She hesitated, wanting to run back to the house, but torn.

"Wait," she called to Matthias, cringing against a sharp stone that stabbed into the arch of her foot.

Before she could regain her balance, Matthias was beside her, a hand under her elbow, steadying her.

"What are you doing out here without your shoes?" He wrapped his arms around her and lifted her over to a grassy patch, away from the rocks.

The prickle of cold grass underneath her was better than the rocks, but still more than she thought she could handle.

"I made you breakfast." She fought the grimace of discomfort tugging at her mouth and held out the bundle of food.

"Thank you." He peeked in the cloth, and a genuine smile stretched his lips.

With her cooking, the statement would have been half-hearted from anyone else, but she knew with Matthias it was genuine gratitude.

"Fresh-baked biscuits? I don't deserve such a treasure." He wrapped his free hand behind her back, and she stepped forward, tucking herself against his chest.

"I don't want you to go," she murmured into the silk scarf tied around his neck and felt the pressure of a kiss against the top of her head.

A rumble of tiny hooves and small bleats of sheep carried from the hillside ahead where Gideon and Clay were already moving the flock. Glimpses of curly white wool moved through the low brush. Scout darted back and forth, keeping the stragglers moving. Matthias would bring up the rear, moving slower in the wagon containing all their supplies for the next month.

"You don't need me." He pulled back and smiled.

She had grown so accustomed to having him here. His music calmed her, and his thoughtful gestures eased her struggles. He had become her ally and protector.

"I'm afraid."

He smoothed his hands over her shoulders and pushed her back to look into her eyes. "You're far stronger than you know." He hooked a knuckle under her chin and lifted her mouth to his.

He kissed her, soft and slow, sending a shiver down to her bare toes, smoothing out the painful prickles there. She sighed when he pulled away, gripping his shirt sleeves. Matthias cast a glance toward the disappearing flock.

"I need to go. But it will only be for a few weeks or a maybe a month." He stepped back, and Elaine straightened herself.

She should at least pretend to be as strong as he thought she was.

"You keep that pistol I gave you handy. If you need help, take Shadow. He knows you now. But don't worry. Gideon will be back tomorrow, and if McBride intends on mayhem, it won't be *you* they're after."

Her heart chilled at the thought of what Matthias and Clay might face. "What about you?"

Matthias shrugged. "There will be the two of us, and I've dealt with my share of outlaws. Don't you worry."

She shivered, and he wrapped her shawl tighter around her.

"I'll be back soon." He squeezed her hand and kissed it before mounting the wagon bench.

With a slap of the reins, Matthias set off. Elaine watched until the rounded top of the shepherd's wagon disappeared over the last hill. She pressed a hand to her stomach, remembering belatedly she was still in her dressing gown and didn't have the brooch to fall back on. Her hand shook with the absence of her talisman, and the antsy prickles of apprehension needled her arms and up her neck.

She gripped the fabric of her dressing gown. Was Matthias simply another object to focus her anxiety on? Would she be as lost without him as she was without Grandmama's pin?

Chapter 32

Mary clutched the handle of her carpetbag with mingled trepidation and elation as she approached the imposing brick building. She wasn't sure which emotion was stronger, but the result on her nerves showed in the white of her knuckles.

Should she be here? What if Charlie wasn't the man she remembered? She had thought him dead for years until Gideon had come back to Kansas bearing the leather-bound truth in the form of a journal. If he wasn't her Charlie anymore, would she be forced to leave him behind and grieve his loss once more?

She eyed a bench in the front courtyard. Perhaps she could sit a moment and collect her thoughts. Though the iron seat offered no comfort once she sat down, she wasn't sure she could stand again. She was frozen—immobile.

Gideon had warned her this trip wouldn't be easy. Though he paid the staff extra with Charlie's silver for more attentive care, he said the building and grounds were dilapidated and morose. By the look of things, he was right.

No one walked the grounds for fresh air; no cheerful flowers greeted her in the courtyard. Had it not been for the wagon tracks in the dusty drive, she might have thought the place uninhabited.

Although it was only late spring, a dry heat blanketed the grounds. Pueblo was far warmer than the mountain homestead she'd just come from. She swallowed convulsively and found her throat as parched as the brittle grass under her feet.

The climate reminded her of her and Charlie's flight for safety across the short-grass prairie when they first met. Had they come through the Pueblo area? It was possible, though she didn't think so. Perhaps farther east?

"Excuse me, ma'am," a delicate voice spoke, snapping Mary out of her reminiscence.

She blinked against the bright sun to find the silhouette of a young woman with a plain skirt and white blouse.

"Can I help you? Are you here to see someone?" the young woman asked, and Mary stood, reaching out to shake her hand.

She hesitated, looking at Mary's hand uncertainly, and bobbed in a polite curtsy instead.

"Yes, please," Mary continued to cover the uncomfortable moment. "My name is Mary Cross, and I'm here to see my husband."

A light flickered to life in the woman's eyes, and the strained expression vanished. "Oh, Mrs. Cross. I'm Essie. Essie Sayer. We corresponded about your husband."

Essie was a waif of a girl, just over five feet tall, perhaps, and so thin she appeared almost transparent. Despite her warmth after the introduction, something in her eyes seemed distant. Like part of her was somewhere else.

"Come." She turned and motioned to the double front doors of the asylum.

Mary stepped forward. She'd come this far. She'd be a fool to turn around and go back now.

"Have you been here before?" Essie asked, clasping her hands behind her and lifting her face to the sun as they walked forward.

"No, I haven't." Mary's hands were slippery on the handle of her bag, and she took it in turns to wipe them on her skirt as they mounted the steps.

"How exciting. We—we almost never see family come." She opened the door and gestured Mary in first.

"Thank you, Miss Sayer." Mary's voice shook as she crossed the threshold and was met by the unpleasant, medicinal malodor of the facility.

"Oh, do call me Essie." She beamed. "I sit with Charlie often. He is a dear, sweet man."

Hope bubbled up inside Mary's chest. Maybe Charlie wasn't as unwell as she had feared. Maybe the extra care Gideon had provided for had helped him improve.

"Although, I must say I haven't ever been able to pin down just where Charlie is from. He slips in and out of an accent at times. Irish I think. It comes so naturally to him I can't determine if it's real or not. Isn't that strange?"

Mary laughed, though her heart wrenched with a homesick desire she hadn't expected for days long ago when she first met him. "Actually, no, it makes perfect sense." The release of laughter did much to balm her shaky spirit. "He was a bit of an ... actor once. He used the accent to put people at ease."

Essie blinked for a moment and bubbled with laughter. "Well, that must be it. Because even though it's my intention to provide comfort, he does much to lift my own spirits."

Mary followed Essie to the front desk, her steps feeling lighter than they had before.

"This is Mrs. Charlie Cross," Essie told a severe-looking woman with her gray hair pulled into a tight bun. "She's here to visit her husband."

Mary retrieved the letter of introduction Gideon had written from her bag and handed it to the woman at the desk. She read the letter and looked Mary over from head to toe as if she could judge the woman's identity by sight alone.

"Sign these," the stern woman told Mary as she pushed a stack of papers. Mary scanned the documents, not minding too much about what they said. At this moment, nothing could stop her from seeing Charlie. Even if it meant admitting herself to this place.

When she signed and returned the documents, the woman eyed Essie and flipped the page of a schedule book in front of her. "Essie, would you like to escort Mrs. Cross to the men's building? Dr. Busey is making his rounds there now."

"Of course I would." Essie's voice hummed with excitement.

Essie turned and nearly bumped into a woman wandering the foyer. "Oh, excuse me, Polly."

The woman shied away, hunching her shoulders and covering her head as though fearing an attack.

A lightning bolt of shock reverberated through Mary when the woman dropped her hands. The woman had cropped red hair, and a scar ran the length of her face, precisely where Jo's scar was. Mary braced herself against the desk with one hand, heart hamming against her ribs as Essie comforted the patient. The woman behind the desk took control and escorted the shaking woman down the hall. Essie turned back to Mary.

"Shall we?" Essie had gone a little pale while helping the woman and seemed shaky, herself.

Mary swallowed. "What happened to her?"

Essie shook her head. "Sad case, that one. She was attacked by some man in a brothel. I know some folks shun the women forced to work in such places, but no one deserves that kind of cruelty."

Mary shook off the darkness that settled over her. She would find out more later. For now, she was here to see Charlie. They followed a long hall to a door that opened into another dry courtyard. A cracked sidewalk led them to another building where a brass placard affixed to a stone column by the door read *Men's Ward*.

Essie rang a doorbell and waited. A burly man in a white uniform opened the door.

She straightened as tall as a woman her size could and adopted an air of authority. "Ms. Slavin sent me to reunite Mrs. Cross with her husband."

The man narrowed his eyes at both women. "The men are in the sunroom. Dr. Busey and Nurse Walton are there now."

Essie squeezed Mary's hand. "Come." She radiated energy and tugged Mary's hand, turning down yet another long hallway. "Now, don't be too discouraged when he doesn't recognize you. Even Mr. Gideon has to spend some time sitting with him before he sees a glimpse of familiarity."

They turned into a solarium lined with glass windows all around. The sunlight was a welcome change from the dimly lit corridor. Men sat in rickety chairs, here and there, about the large room.

Essie took hold of Mary's sleeve. "There he is." She pointed to a man who sat close to the windows.

That wasn't him. Couldn't be him. She stepped forward hesitantly. A heaviness settled into her core and slowed her steps. *Ten years.* Had time changed her as much? Aged and frail for a man in his early fifties, his hands lay limply on a quilt folded over his lap. The vibrant, charismatic man she once knew was gone—wrapped in papery skin and an empty expression.

She stopped and swayed on her feet, wishing she could go back to a time when she didn't know what had become of him.

Essie crossed to Charlie's side and knelt beside him, touching his shoulder. "Charlie, someone is here to see you."

Little moved behind the dull eyes as he looked at Essie. She stood and patted his shoulder, gesturing for Mary to join her. Charlie's lifeless eyes fell on Mary and snapped to life.

"Charlie, this is—"

"Mary." His voice cracked and shattered Mary to her core.

FIRE CRACKLED AND POPPED in front of Matthias as he lay on his bedroll, propped up on one elbow. A haze of clouds hid the moon, smothering the world around him in darkness. Only Clay's face was visible in the flickering light.

"You're awful quiet tonight." Clay raised an eyebrow at Matthias across the flames.

"No sense in talking when there's nothing to say." Matthias rolled onto his back, stretching a hand under his head.

A rock dug into his back, and he sat up.

"I think there's much to talk about." Clay tossed a pinecone into the fire, and it erupted in a quick burst of flame.

"Like what?" Matthias shouldn't have asked, but if he hadn't, Clay would have just continued pestering him. Better to get it all out in the open.

"Oh, I don't know. How about Jo's sister?"

Matthias stiffened and glowered at Clay. "What about her?"

Heat rose up the back of Matthias's neck that had nothing to do with the campfire.

"She is interesting, isn't she?" Clay pushed black hair away from his eyes. "Nothing like Jo."

She sure wasn't. Wasn't like any woman Matthias had ever known. It was what he found so captivating about her.

"No, I reckon she's not."

"I think she won't last long in this country. Seems to me she might be a bit more suited to town." Clay paused, gauging Matthias's response, and tossed another pinecone in the air. "Unless she found a good man, that is."

Had it been so obvious? Matthias had tried hard to not make a spectacle of his attraction to Elaine. But she'd stricken him so completely blind to all else.

"I'm going up yonder to look around." Matthias avoided the subject and picked up his rifle, standing. "Without those dogs around, we ought to be on the lookout for predators."

"Alright. You go and keep us safe. I'll sit here and keep the fire warm." Clay grinned amiably.

Matthias climbed the hill above camp to gain a better view. In the meadow below, the sheep slept, curled up in little woolly shapes nestled in the grass.

Matthias sat on the rocks and braced his forearms on his knees. He looked down at the empty spot beside him, remembering the night Elaine brought him supper. That had been the beginning, hadn't it? The night she'd reached in and taken hold of his heart. He'd had no hope after that. He was besotted.

Look at him—leaving camp to avoid talking about her, only for his thoughts to be consumed with her, regardless. He heaved a breath against the impossible weight, crushing his chest.

Clay was right. This life didn't suit her. She was suited to be a fine lady in a grand house. Not elbows deep in wool and smudged with ash from a cook stove. Could he ever be enough for her? He hoped with everything in his being, he could.

How could she stay with a bandit like him? Living the life of an outlaw on the run? He wasn't worthy of her. That, he knew. And yet she seemed as enamored as he was.

Matthias reached into his pocket and pulled out his harmonica. He brushed the instrument against his lips, and memories of the previous week lingered in his mind. The way she clung to him in the afternoon sunshine, the caress of her fingertips along his jaw.

A branch cracked in the dark, and Matthias froze, searching the black night in vain for the source of the sound. Was it a bear?

He had heard a bear's step had an uncanny similarity to that of a man as they shuffled through the forest. Oak brush rustled below him. Matthias raised his rifle to take aim at the disturbance.

The metallic cycling of a lever action rifle behind him rose the hairs on the back of his neck, and Matthias prayed to a God he wasn't sure existed. For mercy. For another chance.

Chapter 33

Matthias's stomach turned to stone as a chill skated over the back of his neck.

"So, you didn't skip town after all." Jasper spoke behind Matthias. "Reckon you should've."

McBride's hired thugs. Likely only Hank and Jasper, unless Darby had found a replacement for Matthias already. But where was Hank?

In one quick motion, Matthias dropped the harmonica and grabbed his rifle as he dove forward and rolled down the steep hill. He braced his body around the rifle as best as he could and prayed he'd tumble into the oak brush before Jasper could get a shot off.

He slid to a stop at the base of the hill and froze. Nothing but the grating of footsteps and whispered curses came from above him. He drew a steadying breath and checked his rifle. No damage he could see. He cycled the lever and crouched, scooting through the brush as quietly as he could back toward camp. He had to get to Clay before the other men did. He doubted they'd leave any witnesses this time.

Heart hammering against his rib cage, Matthias reached the end of the brush thicket and peered out to the flickering firelight where Clay sat carving on a piece of wood.

Should Matthias call out? *No.* He wasn't sure why they weren't shooting yet, but he didn't want to call attention to his position. Hank and Jasper were likely waiting to see what Matthias would do before they made their move.

He picked up a rock and chucked it toward Clay's feet. *Miss.* Clay glanced at the spot the rock had landed in the grass beside him but returned to his whittling. Matthias threw a second rock and bounced it off the toe of Clay's moccasin. Scout sat bolt upright and growled.

Matthias clenched his teeth, willing Clay to not make a scene. Clay stiffened and put a hand on the dog. Scout was turning out to be a good herding animal, but he wasn't the livestock guardian the Great Pyrenees had been. He'd be no help against such brutal men.

Clay feigned an itch on his hip and reached down, scratching himself before sliding a hand down to the bow on the ground beside him. He scanned the brush where Matthias was, and Matthias moved forward—just far enough Clay might see him in the campfire light.

Matthias motioned to the hillside where Jasper and Hank had been. They were gone now, but maybe Clay could get a glimpse of them.

Now that Clay was on his guard, Matthias pushed back through the oak brush and headed for a better vantage point on the flock. He couldn't let Gideon down. These sheep were all the Cross family had as a means of income. If they lost their sheep, who knows where the family would scatter to? Elaine could be lost to him forever.

Sheep shuffled in the distance, restless. Matthias picked up his pace to a run. A sickening thunk cut a sheep's cry short. Matthias slid to a stop, swallowing the bile in his throat. Reaching the edge of the clearing, he raised his rifle and took aim at Hank's back as he raised the club again.

Something dropped across Matthias's vision and all the air was forced from his lungs as he was jerked off his feet. A lariat crushed his chest as a horse dragged him through the brush and trees. His body twisted and tumbled, his face scraping through rocks, pine needles, bushes and sticks. He choked on a mouthful of dirt but had no breath to cough it up. Rope burns dug deep into his hands as he gripped the rope to steady himself.

A gunshot cracked in the distance, and the horse came to a stop. Jasper swore and whipped his horse around, dropping the rope. Matthias covered his head as the horse ran nearly over the top of him as Jasper raced back toward the campfire.

He gasped for air, straining against the tight constriction. With raw fingertips, he grabbed the rope and wrenched it loose from his chest. Air burned a pathway through his lungs again. He crawled to his hands and knees and coughed. Fiery pain shot through his sides from what must be bruised ribs. He blinked against the grit in his eyes. Another shot rang out in the night.

Clay. Matthias pushed up onto his feet and ran, blocking out the stabbing pain in his side, the pressure in his lungs, and the muddy smear blurring his vision. None of it mattered. Clay was facing those demons alone.

More shots rang out. Oak brush pelted Matthias's face and tangled in his chaps as he ran. He covered his eyes with an arm and barreled through like a buffalo in a cornfield.

Reaching the edge of the clearing, he stopped, heart pounding against his bruised ribs.

He couldn't see Hank, but Jasper was shooting into the trees, still mounted on his horse.

Matthias reached for his pistol. His holster was empty. He must have lost it when Jasper dragged him through the woods. Regardless of being unarmed, he had to do something.

He ran out of the thicket of scrub brush, boosted off of a large rock in the ground, and leapt at Jasper. The horse shied, but Matthias made his target. He slammed into Jasper, knocking him out of the saddle. Both men tumbled to the ground, grappling with one another.

Jasper got the upper hand and straddled Matthias. He wrapped his hands around Matthias's throat and the crushing force caused stars to float in Matthias's vision. He struggled and kicked, his sight fading to darkness.

He clawed and scrambled at the surrounding ground. His hand found a rock, and he slammed it into Jasper's head. Jasper collapsed on top of him.

Relief and dread surged as the memory assaulted Matthias. He pushed away the guilt and forced himself back into the moment. No time for old ghosts now. He shuffled out from under Jasper's weight and rolled the man over.

Jasper's eyes popped open, and an evil grin spread across his face before he fired the pistol Matthias hadn't seen him holding. The blow of the bullet knocked Matthias back, but the pain didn't immediately register. He grabbed Jasper's wrist, wrestling for the gun.

A swish split the air, followed by a thud behind him, and Matthias spun around to see Hank on his knees, blinking in confusion. Red bloomed on his shirt, and he dropped his club, an arrow protruding from his chest.

Clay emerged from the trees—nocking another arrow and training it on Jasper.

Jasper threw his pistol aside and whimpered, hands in the air. "Don't kill me, please, don't kill me."

Matthias retrieved Jasper's pistol and pressed it against his chest. His finger itched to pull the trigger. Hank and Jasper were the sort that would only cause more harm and bloodshed.

"What now?" Clay asked Matthias, unmoving from the full draw of his bow.

Matthias lowered the pistol and turned his back to Jasper. "We can't shoot an unarmed man."

Clay glanced down at the wet patch spreading across Matthias's shirt. "You need a doctor."

Matthias looked down, having nearly forgotten the injury. He pulled a bandana from his pocket and pressed it against the bullet hole. The pressure brought the wound's discomfort to the surface. Searing pain laced the raw edges of flesh surrounding the deep ache in his shoulder. He wavered to his feet and nausea restricted his throat.

"You need a doctor," Clay repeated himself. "But I can't just leave these sheep with no dogs to protect them.

"Let him go." Matthias forced the words out. It wasn't what he wanted to do, but it was their only option.

Clay lowered his bow.

"Take your partner and be gone," Matthias told Jasper. "If you come near this family or the flock again, it will be the end of you."

Chapter 34

Gideon heaved the sack of buckwheat over his shoulder and deposited it in the wagon bed. The general mercantile hadn't had lima beans, but the dry goods store might.

Jo had been increasingly uncomfortable these past few days and fractious as a broody hen. He didn't like being gone from her so close to her time, but he had a suspicion the errand he'd been sent on—finding buckwheat, lima beans—was as much to get him out of the house as it was because Florence said Jo needed the items.

Not that he didn't want to help. He would do anything to ease Jo's discomfort and ensure her safety. But leaving for an overnight trip to town didn't feel like a reasonable way to keep her safe.

Logic told him all would be well. With Matthias, Clay, and the sheep gone, there would be no reason for McBride to attack the homestead or harm the women. If there was any risk, it should only be the sheep. And Jo wasn't due to deliver for a few more weeks.

He pushed open the door to the dry goods store, and a bell rang overhead. The stout, middle-aged woman who owned the shop bustled through a back door with several bolts of fabric braced against her chest. Her stack teetered precariously, and Gideon crossed the shop quickly, taking some of the material.

"Oh, thank you kindly." The woman set the fabric down on the counter.

Gideon added his to the stack and nodded. While he'd learned to let go of his old demons, three years of living alone in the mountains had left him still a bit stifled in conversing with strangers.

"Can I help you find something today, sir?" the woman asked, straightening her apron.

"Lima beans?" Gideon raised a shoulder.

It seemed such an odd request. Gideon wasn't sure he'd ever even eaten a Lima bean.

"Lima Beans?" The look on the shopkeeper's face said she quite agreed with Gideon's assessment.

"It's for my wife. She's with child and not feeling well?" It came out as a question, and Gideon chuckled at himself. He must sound like a fool. "We have a Ute woman who lives with us, and she wanted me to fetch buckwheat and lima beans."

"Ah, yes." Surprisingly, the woman seemed to understand. "I had some trouble with my own little ones. My midwife also insisted on having me eat buckwheat porridge and drink some kind of tea, though I can't rightly say what was in it."

Gideon was relieved to know he hadn't just only been sent to town to get him out of the house.

"And do you have them, then, Mrs.—" Gideon faltered, realizing too late he didn't know her name.

"Harris, dear. And you are?" Mrs. Harris turned to scan the shelves to her left, lined with canned food items before finding one and pulling it down.

"Gideon Cross."

The woman dropped the can and spun around, eyes sharp as a hawk. "Cross." She whispered the name to herself.

Gideon bent to pick up the can of Lima beans she had dropped. "Are you alright, Mrs. Harris?"

"Are you the man who spoke up for a new fella in the area? The one who shot my brother-in-law?"

Gideon's heart seized in his chest. "I reckon I am." Gideon spoke the words, low and quiet. The way Jo would speak to a wild mustang she was training. Words spun rapidly through his mind. What could he say? What should he do?

"If your brother-in-law died while attempting to retrieve his stolen cattle, then yes. I spoke up for the man."

Mrs. Harris's face may as well have been carved from stone. Gideon set the can on the counter.

"We are awfully sorry for your family's loss, ma'am. Matthias, he's mighty sore about what happened. He never meant to harm an innocent man. By what he saw, it looked as though your brother-in-law was the one about to do the rustling. He couldn't bear to stand by and watch."

"Is he still around? Is he going to help us catch the man who stole the cows in the first place?"

"He is, and yes, he's committed to helping however he can." Gideon rubbed the back of his neck. "We both want to help your family, but we're still not sure yet how we can do that. If McBride's men find Matthias to still be in the area, they'll be gunning for him. But once Sheriff Barlow finds more evidence, Matthias will testify." Gideon ducked his head. "Thank you for being so kind as to allow Matthias to make this right rather than hang. He's a good man. Truly he is."

Mrs. Harris nodded, placing her hands flat against the countertop, tapping one finger against the glass. "Times have been awful hard these past weeks, Mr. Cross. My Jarred is looking after his brother's farm as well now. My sister-in-law, nieces, and nephews are living with us." She sighed. "I'll not say it's been easy to accept things as they are. But the killing and thieving around here must stop, and if this is the only way to see that happen, so be it."

The back door opened, and a young boy entered, perhaps seven years old. "Auntie June, the stage is here and there's some crates for you. Do you want me to hitch the wagon?"

A heavy weight settled in Gideon's stomach. This boy had been left fatherless, just as he and Jimmy had been at a young age. Was Gideon wrong to protect Matthias the way he was?

No. Mrs. Harris was right. It was best to cut the head off the snake. The only way to do that was to stop Darby McBride.

Mrs. Harris pinched her lips between her teeth. "No dear, that new mule we bought isn't safe around children. I'd best lock up here and do it myself." She smoothed a weary hand over her nephew's head and stepped toward the front door.

"I'll pick your crates up for you," Gideon offered. "I've already got a wagon hitched, and I'd be happy to help."

Mrs. Harris looked up at Gideon. "You'd do that?"

"Of course, I would."

Her shoulders sagged with relief. "I'd be much obliged if you would."

At the stage station, Gideon handed the stage driver a note from Mrs. Harris giving Gideon permission to pick up her shipment, then scanned the paper tags tied to the crates and boxes being unloaded from the stage and stacked in the street.

"Thank you kindly for the ride, sir." A familiar voice carried through the press of passengers, kindling Gideon's curiosity.

"Much obliged for you riding shotgun, son." The stage driver turned to shake hands with the man who had just climbed down from the stage with the last piece of baggage. "It's been mighty nerve wracking these past few weeks without someone by my side."

"Happy to help. I couldn't leave a man in need."

Gideon blinked in a dazed stupor. Sure enough, the lanky cowboy speaking to the stage driver was—

"Jimmy?" Gideon barely choked out his brother's name.

Jimmy spun on his heel, green eyes snapping wide under a grey felt hat. "Hey, big brother. How did you know I was here?"

"I didn't." Gideon blinked. "What are you doing here? I thought you were planting wheat."

"Heard you needed help. That's what brothers do, isn't it?" Jimmy's cheek twitched with something that wasn't quite a smile.

"Ma sent for you?" Gideon gripped the edge of the wagon bed beside him.

With everything they had going on right now, he wasn't sure he was also ready to face the distance that had grown between him and his brother. "How did you plan to find our place?"

"Well, Ma said ya'll live far enough from town that it might be hard to get reliable word out to you. So, she sent a map." Jimmy pulled a piece of paper from his vest pocket. "I reckoned on buying a horse and heading out in the morning."

Gideon grunted. He wasn't sure how he felt about Ma stepping in like this, but with all that had happened, he was grateful to have another man around.

"Well, load up then. I need to get these supplies back to the dry goods store and then we'll head back home. Jo won't be riding for some time. You can use her gelding, Shadow, for the time being." Gideon climbed onto the bench seat of the wagon and waited while Jimmy gathered a leather saddlebag from the stack of luggage and his rifle down from the driver's bench of the stagecoach.

Jimmy tossed the saddlebags into the bed of the wagon and mounted the seat next to Gideon. The bench groaned under the two men's weight, and Gideon blew out a heavy breath. The seat may hold their bulk, but the burden the last four years of separation added might make the entire wagon buckle.

Chapter 35

"Gee," Gideon called out to Jack and Clarice as he tugged the reins and urged the mules onto the trail that led to the homestead.

Miles had passed without a word between him and Jimmy, and the unspoken friction between them threatened to cause a fire if someone didn't speak up. Growing up, Jimmy had been a sickly thing, unable to run and play with Gideon without straining for breath. Over the years, his health had improved, but they'd never been as close as brothers should be.

Now, with Gideon's four-year abandonment of Ma and Jimmy, things weren't likely to have improved with time. Now that Jimmy was here, Gideon wanted to make things right.

He scratched the thick growth of beard covering his jaw. "So, how was the wheat planting?"

Jimmy tipped his hat up with one finger and leaned back on the bench. "Well enough, I reckon, though I had to leave before I'd seen things through. When I got Ma's telegram that you needed my help, I asked for my wages and headed this way."

Gideon heaved a breath that stretched his shoulders tight against the buckskin tunic he wore. Was Jimmy suggesting it was Gideon's fault Jimmy didn't finish out his time with the wheat farming?

"I didn't ask you to do that." Gideon's stomach tightened.

Jimmy leaned forward, bracing his elbows on his knees. "Well, I was happy to come all the same, brother. Especially being it was Ma asking. I'll always be there for her."

"Ha," Gideon shouted to the mules, encouraging them around a deep rut in the road.

"What brought you out this way?" Jimmy pulled a strip of jerky from his saddlebag. "Last I heard, before Ma's latest letter, you settled up near Pikes Peak."

"It was time for a change. Hadn't proved up that homestead yet, and Jo and I wanted to have a fresh start." Gideon hunched his shoulders and flicked Clarice's rein. "Step up."

"Ma said you both had been through the wringer these past few years. You didn't have to go through all that with Pa on your own, you know." Jimmy took a bite of the jerky and chewed solemnly.

Gideon rubbed the back of his neck. "I couldn't bring myself to tell you and Ma about him. I took it on myself for Pa leaving in the first place and—" He shrugged and abandoned the sentence. "I just saw it as my fault, and I couldn't face you. That's all."

Jimmy clapped Gideon on the shoulder. "I hope you've put that behind you. Ma and I never saw it that way."

Gideon closed his eyes and released a heavy breath, and the tension in his back abated. Without warning, the wagon shifted and slammed to one side, coming to an abrupt halt. Jimmy slid into Gideon, and the bag of jerky tumbled into the dirt.

"What in the Sam Hill—" Gideon anchored the rein and climbed down from the tilted wagon.

One wheel was wedged into a crack in the road. He gritted his teeth and hammered a fist on the wagon bed. They didn't have time for this kind of setback. He needed to get back to Jo. What if something went wrong while he was gone?

Jimmy whistled. "Well, that's a pickle."

Gideon bit back a sharp retort and leaned into the side of the wagon bed. Nothing moved. "It's wedged in there tight. We need a pry bar."

Jimmy scanned the surrounding trees. "Maybe we can use a limb."

"That won't be strong enough." Gideon groused. "It'll just break. Maybe we oughta unhitch these mules and ride back to the house. Jo's nearing her time, and I don't much like the idea of being gone so long."

"How far is it?" Jimmy asked, shading his eyes and peering up the trail.

"It's a fair piece. Five miles or so." Gideon reached up to take the reins.

"I hate to disagree with you, Gideon, but I don't think we should. At least not without trying a few things first."

"We don't have time to be fussing around with this. I need to get home to check on my wife."

Jimmy's cheek twitched, and he blew a long breath through his nose. "Hear me out, big brother. If we ride back to the house for a pry bar, and she's had the baby, what then? It'll be days before you'll be able to get back down here. If she hasn't had the baby, then you'd be leaving even closer to her time. That's worse, right?"

Gideon huffed. Jimmy was right, of course. Gideon needed to stop letting worry over Jo cloud his judgement. He just couldn't abide any more delays. He needed to get back home.

"Alright then." He yielded. "Let's see what we can do about it now."

After a few minutes of searching the immediate area, the two men collected rocks in varying sizes and shapes.

"I'll lean into the wagon to take some weight off that wheel. You slam one of them big rocks against the base of the wheel. Might just be we'll make a little headway," Jimmy said, stacking the rocks next to the wheel. "Then we can wedge rocks underneath it so it doesn't fall back in. What d'ya think?"

Gideon lifted his hat and ran his fingers through his hair. "Alright then. Let's try it."

Jimmy pushed his back against the wagon bed, and Gideon hit the wheel hard. The jarring blow reverberated through his arms, but the wheel moved a bit, and he jammed a small rock under the wheel.

Jimmy let the wagon down and took a breath. "I think we gained a little ground there."

A little of the pressure in Gideon's chest lessened.

"Let's give it another go then." Jimmy leaned back again, and the wagon bed shifted.

Gideon gave the base of the wheel another hammering blow with the large rock and the wheel popped free of the rut.

"Hold it." Gideon rammed a shoulder into the wood and kicked the pile of rocks into the rut.

They eased the wagon down onto the rocks and Gideon stood straight, stretching his back.

"I'm glad you came, little brother," Gideon said as he led the mules forward, guiding them away from the deep crack in the ground. "I'm sorry I didn't ask you myself. To be honest, I was afraid you wouldn't want to come."

Jimmy lifted one shoulder. "I'll always be here for you. Family is the most important thing there is."

Gideon's eyes burned, and he scrubbed his face with one hand. For years, he'd resigned himself to living alone in the Rocky Mountains. Aside from his friendship with the Andersons, it had been endless days of solitude that leached the strength from his bones and left him hollow. Now, here he was, with a wife, a child on the way, a sister-in-law, his mother and brother moving to Colorado to be together again. A family.

He would never feel that emptiness again. He would do whatever it took to keep this family together and build a legacy here that would provide a close family bond and heritage for generations to come.

Chapter 36

Elaine set down the crate full of straw Florence had sent her for and checked the time on the mantle clock again. Five minutes. Jo's pains were five minutes apart now. Heaven help her, Elaine was going to act as midwife.

She brushed and picked violently at the bits of straw clinging to her. This was too much. She may have learned to boil coffee and darn socks, but this was far beyond her capabilities.

She wasn't even sure what delivering a baby would entail, but she knew she wasn't equipped for this. Jo gave up a deep groan, and Elaine spun around. Jo was the toughest woman she'd ever known. Since childhood she'd seen her younger sister use that blasted stubborn streak to push past pain and injury with a mask of calm.

But this was different. The low moan turned into a choked half-sob, and Elaine crossed the room to her sister's side. Jo was standing now, something Florence had insisted against for the past few weeks. However, this afternoon, Jo's discomfort had become more intense, and her pains more frequent, and the elderly woman had allowed Jo to get up and walk about the room.

"Not stop it," Florence had said, shaking her head. "Child come now."

Elaine had thought she knew fear before, but now, knowing what was ahead, all her fretfulness over simple things seemed childish and inconsequential.

Her chest tightened. It wasn't time for Jo to have this baby yet. It was too soon. The tight lines around Florence's eyes told Elaine something was wrong here. Her sister was in danger, and perhaps the child was too.

Would the baby even survive? The only help Jo and the baby had were a Ute woman nearly too ancient to stand, and an ignorant sister with a panic disorder.

She knew nothing about babies, had always avoided children. And with their strenuous history, she was most certain Jo wouldn't want her anywhere near in a time of distress. The two of them had never been close. She was nothing but a frustration to Jo. Yet, there wasn't anything to be done about it.

She rubbed her hands together, over and over, wishing she could wash away the prickle of anxiety that gnawed at her nerves. She blew out a slow breath. Nothing else could be done. Gideon wasn't here. There was no midwife near enough to fetch.

"Come." Florence took Elaine by the hand and pressed her knuckles into Jo's lower back as she bent over, hands pressed down on the bed. "Press hard."

Elaine fisted her hands and pushed her knuckles into Jo's lower back. Her sister's pain-laced moan eased into a shaky sigh.

"Elaine?" Jo's voice wavered, and she breathed out a long sigh. "Stay with me."

"I'm here, Jo." Elaine rotated her fists in circles. *One, two, three. Pause. One, two, three.*

"If I don't make it through this ... help Gideon—help him care for her."

A shiver trickled down Elaine's spine. "What do you mean? Of course, you are going to make it through this."

"Promise me." Jo's words stretched out into a low moan, and all the muscles tightened in her back against Elaine's hands.

"O—Of course I will, Jo, but you are going to make it through this just fine." Elaine's words felt hollow.

Suddenly, Jo dropped into a low crouch beside the bed and wailed an aggressive, guttural cry. Florence's head snapped up, and she locked eyes with Elaine.

"Child will come soon." Florence nodded.

"Oh, dear." Elaine's heart raced and fluttered like a hummingbird's wings, and her shallow breath grew even shakier.

She steadied herself on the footboard Gideon had carved from an aspen tree. "Jo, get up." Elaine knelt beside her sister, hoping to make eye contact.

Jo's face was dark red and freckled with tiny purple markings. She didn't respond, looking beyond Elaine, lost in some internal battle. Elaine put a hand under Jo's elbow and lifted. Jo threw off Elaine's hand and rocked her head back and forth. She clutched the quilt in front of her and the expression of pain turned into a raspy humming as she pressed her forehead against the side of the bed.

Abandoning her effort to lift Jo, Elaine turned back to Florence. "We need to get her into bed, don't we?" Elaine pleaded. Surely the woman would know something she could do to move Jo.

"No." Florence shook her head. "This good." She pressed her hands against the arms of the rocker she sat in and shook in her effort to stand. Elaine helped her rise to her feet.

"What do I do?" Desperation tinged Elaine's words as she pressed a fist against her stomach. She had to push past this sickening feeling of helplessness.

Florence nodded at the box of straw. Elaine blinked at it a moment, not following the woman's intention.

Realization dawned. "Oh." She pressed her lips together and shivered.

This was going to push her far beyond her limits, but Jo needed her. She shook off the fog of fear clouding her judgement. If Jo was going to have this baby on the floor, Elaine needed to give the child a clean, warm entry into the world. She spread out the straw under her sister and rushed to stoke the dwindling fire in the wood stove so the cabin would be warm.

She opened the front door to bring in an armload of wood, and Matthias stumbled toward her on the doorstep, soaked in blood.

Chapter 37

The hummingbird in Elaine's chest stopped its flight. Time stood still for a moment while her excitement to see Matthias faltered at the abrupt realization something was wrong.

He wavered on his feet, clutching a blood-soaked bandanna to his shoulder. Dirt caked his face, and debris clung to his clothes and his hair. In an instant, the hummingbird was back, and she ducked under his good arm and helped him into the house.

"What happened?" Elaine asked as she supported him to her bedroom and deposited him on Mary's bed.

He sucked in a painful breath with a hiss as she helped him lie down, resisting the urge to recoil from the dirt and blood now staining the quilt underneath him.

She swallowed a sour taste in her mouth as she pulled the bandanna away from his shoulder with a sticky, crackling of half dried blood. A gunshot wound.

"McBride's men found us." Matthias forced the words through clenched teeth. "Where's Gideon?"

"He's not here." Elaine's voice fluttered in a breathy whisper. "He went to town ..." Her words dropped away.

Gideon was gone, Matthias was hurt and—

"Clay?" Florence's voice spoke behind her.

Elaine turned back to find Florence gripping the bedroom doorjamb.

"Matthias, where is Clay?" Elaine asked, not sure she wanted to hear the answer. She glanced back to the rifle above door of the cabin. Surely she wouldn't need to use it, would she?

"Clay is alright, ma'am." Matthias directed his answer to Florence rather than Elaine. "He's with the sheep."

He closed his eyes in a grimace of pain, and Jo cried out in the next room, jarring Elaine into action. How was she going to take care of both of them?

She reached for the nearest clean cloth she could find. A handkerchief her grandmother had given her to keep tucked away so she could keep her hands clean. She pressed it against Matthias's wound. Blood soaked through the white fabric, blooming like red roses on the green leaf embroidery.

She pressed Matthias's hand against the handkerchief. "I'm sorry, I have to go. I'll be back as quick as I can." She pressed a kiss to his forehead and darted to the kitchen to scrub Matthias's blood from her shaking fingers. On her way to Jo's bedroom, she lifted her apron from the hook on the wall and tied it tight around her like a knight donning armor.

In the bedroom, Jo remained in the same position. She rested her cheek on the mattress and met Elaine's eyes with an expression of fierce determination mingled with something else—a submission to nature and the battle she was called to do.

Florence gestured to a stool in the corner of the room. Elaine recognized the woman's desire to be an active part of this. Florence would not sit idly in a rocking chair when so much was at stake.

Elaine placed the stool on the opposite side of Jo and helped Florence to sit down. Then Elaine dropped to her knees, unsure precisely what she needed to do now. How could she have ever known she would need to prepare herself for such a task?

Her own breath fell in time with Jo's panting. The room tilted as dizziness assaulted Elaine, and Florence took her hand, squeezing it gently. "Stay with Jo. Jo needs you."

With a smile that came from an inner peace Elaine wished she had, the older woman guided Elaine's hand between her sister's legs and nodded. Elaine's stomach hardened until her fingers grazed the slippery curve of a child's head. The sensation stilled her anxiety and sent a rush of tingling joy throughout her body—bursting to life in a vivid awareness of something far beyond herself. A human life was about to enter the world.

Florence cocked a white eyebrow in question, and Elaine nodded.

"You push soon." Florence's voice took on a strength as she put a hand on Jo's back.

A small sound, nearly a whimper, escaped Jo's lips, and she closed her eyes, leaning her head against the side of the bed.

"I'm here," Elaine whispered to her and brushed the sweat-soaked copper strands from her sister's forehead. "You can—"

Before Elaine could finish speaking, Jo's body tensed again, and her fingers clutched the quilt.

"You push now." Florence commanded loud and clear.

Jo roared with animalistic intensity, and the baby's crown emerged a little further into Elaine's hand. Elation and fear danced across her skin in waves of gooseflesh. But the progress stopped before the baby's face was exposed and the contraction subsided. The tiny head retreated again.

Elaine pressed her lips between her teeth and shook her head at Florence. Jo's face was nearly purple now and her breathing was shallow and rapid.

"Breathe," Florence encouraged.

But the tight line of her lips and the shimmer in her eyes betrayed the dire situation Jo was in. Was this the moment Elaine's life would change forever? Was she destined to live here in the Colorado mountains and care for a child that wasn't her own?

"I can't"—Jo sobbed—"I can't." She heaved a labored breath.

"Josephina." Elaine filled her words with all the steel she could muster. "You're the most stubborn, mule headed, strong-willed woman on God's green earth, and you are far tougher than anyone I know. You can do this. You *will* get through this."

Jo's body convulsed once more.

Florence's eyes closed, and she murmured something in her native tongue. A prayer perhaps?

Elaine whispered her own prayer as she waited for Jo's next contraction. "Please bring this child safe, Lord."

Jo's skin glistened with sweat as she panted in shallow breaths. The scar on her face stood out, stark white against her mottled red face. The swelling had altered her appearance so much she didn't look like herself anymore. Whatever was wrong with her seemed to build pressure, distorting her features.

"Again." Florence's aged voice spoke, more forceful than ever.

An unearthly utterance of strength echoed in the small room, and the baby's head popped free. A tiny nose and lips rested in Elaine's palm.

Elaine gasped. Jo groaned again and her face grew darker as she forced all her strength into the life of her child. Sacrificing her own spirit to give life to another. The baby rushed free in a gush of water and blood. Elaine wrapped the infant in her apron, realizing she'd never stoked the fire.

Joy flooded her chest as she turned the child over in her arms to wrap him—no, her—in the clean cloth they had made ready for this moment. Her features were so perfect, so delicate. Elaine was enraptured.

She held the baby up to show Florence, but the older woman had no attention to spare for the child. Shock was etched in her face as she leaned forward, rubbing Jo's back hard, still muttering in Ute.

Only then did Elaine notice the silence in the room and the odd angle of Jo's body. Her head still lay pressed against the quilt, but she was no longer squatting. She had collapsed on the blood-soaked straw, slumped to one side.

Tears streamed from Elaine's eyes, and she realized, belatedly, the child should cry too. Shouldn't she?

"No," Elaine shouted, her voice full of desperation and anger.

She handed the baby to Florence, grateful the woman's stool was so close to Jo. "Take her."

She ran to the bureau and retrieved the sewing shears and embroidery thread. Glancing briefly to Florence to ensure Elaine was doing the right thing, she tied the thread around the cord and made the cut.

Then she took Jo by the shoulders and laid her down on the floor—running tentative hands over her. Was she truly gone?

She pressed her ear to Jo's chest and listened intently. Waiting for any sign of life was agonizing. This couldn't be it.

There it was. A faint fluttering heartbeat and the slightest rasping of breath.

Relief flooded Elaine. She wasn't gone yet, but something was wrong.

"Jo." Elaine wiped the tears from her eyes to clear her vision.

Florence sat with the infant on her lap. She removed the newborn's tiny feet from her wrappings and ran the turquoise and silver pendant that hung around her neck up the bottom of one foot, then the other. Elaine waited the space of a heartbeat and the mewing wail of new life erupted, filling the cabin.

Elaine let out the breath she held and turned back to Jo. Could she do the same to her sister? She hiccupped a deranged giggle. Her sister's feet were as tough as cowhide. She wouldn't feel a thing. Instead, she untied the ribbon at the neck of Jo's night gown. Bracing her fist against the bones of Jo's chest, she rubbed hard with her knuckles, up and down the length of the bone. Once she started, the compulsion took over, and she rubbed her chest three times.

On the third pass, Jo gasped and clutched her chest, rolling onto her side. "What in Sam Hill was that for?" Jo's voice was raspy and cracked, but it was strong.

Elaine dissolved into tears and laughter. She'd never been so grateful for her sister's temper.

The sound of a throat clearing near the door pulled Elaine from her hysterics.

"Is everything okay, Elaine?" Only the toe of Matthias's boot was visible under the blanket that acted as a door to the bedroom.

"Yes." Elaine sighed. "I think so." If she were honest, she wasn't certain things were fine at all.

Her sister's face was back to its normal shape and complexion, though burst blood vessels ran like spider webs across her eyelids.

"Well then, I'll just leave you to it." His boots disappeared, and the sound of shuffling announced his retreat.

"Wait," Elaine called out, pulling Jo's nightgown over her hip and dragging down an afghan. "I may need your help to get Jo into the bed."

For a moment, he was silent. Finally, he answered, "I think I can do that, yes. Is she decent?"

Elaine checked the nightgown and blanket once more. "Yes, you can come in."

He knelt beside Elaine, his eyes wide. "Is she going to be alright?"

Elaine shrugged and blinked rapidly to dispel the heat prickling her eyes.

The handkerchief he held against his shoulder was soaked through now, dark red. She needed to see to his injury as soon as she got Jo settled.

"I'll live." Jo's voice crackled.

"Will you be able to lift her?" Elaine was doubtful if she should have asked him.

"I think so, yes. But you'll need to help me."

He kept the cloth pressed to his chest with one hand and together, they helped Jo onto the bed. Matthias's expression took on a grimace carved with lines of pain, and he steadied himself on the footboard.

"Let me help you back to bed," Elaine said as she tucked herself under his arm.

"No, I can manage." Matthias pulled away, running a knuckle down the side of her cheek. "You take care of Jo. I'll bide." He winced as he turned and ambled back to the other bedroom.

At least he could walk and speak. Even if his voice held a strained tone that made her uneasy.

She turned back to her other two patients. Florence, who looked truly exhausted, smiled and lifted the bundle of cloth to Elaine. Her heart squeezed as she took her niece in her arms. She was so small, it almost appeared she held nothing but a blanket. Premature. What chance of survival did she have?

Elaine shook off the chill that thought brought and pushed it from her mind. She focused instead on the glowing flame of hope and love that burned inside her now. She had a niece and a sister. She wouldn't take that for granted again.

Chapter 38

Tingles of anxious anticipation thrummed in Mary's chest as she entered the asylum. For three days now, she had visited Charlie, and with each day, he had shown more improvement. Mrs. Slavin peered at Mary over her rounded spectacles.

"Miss Sayer is waiting for you in the rear courtyard." She spoke shortly before returning her intensity back to the ledger in front of her.

"Thank you." Mary hurried down the hall toward the door that led to the grassy space between the main hall and the men's ward.

In the yard, Essie sat with Charlie on a bench, her eyes closed as though peacefully sleeping. Mary approached, and Charlie shifted his attention to her from the bluebird nesting in the tall cottonwood tree.

"Hello, Charlie." Mary greeted him, hoping he wouldn't be shy today.

Essie opened her eyes and smiled, but Charlie dipped his head behind his shoulder to shield his face, putting a hand on Essie's arm.

Essie covered his hand with hers. "It's okay, Charlie. It's Mary, remember?"

Charlie blinked searching Mary's face and frowned. The flutter of excitement in Mary's chest faded. This might be one of the hard days Essie had warned her about. She crossed to Charlie's side and knelt beside the bench, resting her hand on his shoulder.

"Mary's in Kansas," he mumbled and wiped his mouth with the back of his hand.

"I came to see you, remember?" Mary patted his shoulder.

The frown deepened, his lips tightening. "Mary's in Kansas," he repeated. "Boys'r takin' care of her."

Mary's heart squeezed. If he didn't know her right now, at least he remembered her and the boys.

"Yes, the boys have taken good care of me." She nodded and smiled warmly to assure him.

"Where's the boys?" A flicker of recognition brightened in Charlie's eyes, and he glanced around the yard, searching.

"Here," Essie whispered and vacated her seat, gesturing for Mary to take her place. "I'll fetch a blanket for him."

Mary sat next to Charlie. "Gideon owns a sheep ranch now. Here in Colorado. Jimmy will join us soon."

"Sheep?" Charlie shook his head. "No."

Mary sighed. "Yes, he bought a sheep ranch with your silver. It's beautiful. Just a little cabin in the mountains now, but acres and acres of meadows and mountains. You would be so proud of the life he's building." She choked back the crack in her voice.

"Ssilver." His tongue caught on the tricky S sound and slurred the word. "They're coming for the ssilver. We can't let them take it." He looked at Mary with eyes full of panic.

"That'ss for Mary and the boys. We can't let them take it." Charlie's lips glistened with moisture, and he pressed them between his teeth.

Mary's eyes stung, but she blinked back the tears. "It's alright. They can't take the silver now. It's safe."

"It's not safe." Charlie barked at her. "They'll jump us, and we'll lose it all. Put it in the box." His words turned to muttering. "The box in the canyon."

Mary sighed and patted his shoulder. "Alright, Charlie, we'll keep it safe there."

Essie returned with the blanket and offered it to Mary. She arranged it over his lap and squeezed his hand. The tension in him dissipated, and his focus drifted back to the bluebirds.

"Don't be discouraged. He's doing so much better with you around," Essie sat on the bench opposite Mary and Charlie.

"Better? How is this better?" Mary couldn't help the frustration seeping through her tone.

"Today may not seem so," Essie encouraged. "But he's had more good days with you visiting. I think it makes a significant difference. When I first met Charlie, he was irritable and impatient, often with dangerous outbursts. He does better with consistency, which is why I sit with him so often. Your presence these past few days is a gift to him."

Mary heaved a sigh, heavy with mingled satisfaction that she could offer him some comfort and the burden she couldn't stay here long term.

"Tell me about Charlie. Maybe when you are gone, I could talk more about things that are familiar to him." Essie's face brightened. "When we first met, you said he was a play actor in his younger years?"

Mary's laugh fizzled up through her regret. "Well, not a play actor exactly. He was a bit of a swindler, really."

Essie's eyebrows rose. "A swindler? Charlie?"

"Oh, that was a lifetime ago." Mary traced the quilted pattern of the blanket with her finger. "It wasn't his fault, really. He was raised in a traveling carnival. That kind of trickery had been engrained into him from a young age."

Essie sucked in an audible gasp, and a shadow crossed her face that had nothing to do with the clouds overhead. "A–a carnival, you say?"

"Yes, but by the time I met him, he had left that life and was performing a soap scam on the streets of Denver." Mary pressed her lips together. "He regretted his past for years, but by God's grace he—we—were blessed with twelve years of honest work and a happy home after that. Before I lost him—" She faltered and looked up.

Essie sat rigidly on her bench, eyes focused beyond Mary.

"Are you quite well, dear?" Mary pursed her lips, watching Essie.

Essie blinked and focused on Mary again. "Yes, of course. It's just not often you meet someone who has worked in a carnival. Such an unusual upbringing."

"There was—is"—Mary corrected herself—"nothing usual about Charlie Cross." She chuckled. "Never a dull moment."

Charlie coughed and shifted next to her. "Where are the boys?" His hoarse voice sounded like an elderly man's, and the strain of it tightened Mary's own throat.

"Mary, I have a thought." Essie's eyes widened. "Charlie does so much better with you around. Would you ever consider bringing him home?"

A jolt of fear and excitement sent a shock wave through Mary. "Home? Bring him home?"

"It might be a bit of a burden, I know. It's no small thing to consider and—" She stopped short. "Oh, how I would miss my time with him. But he is so much better with you here."

"I—I don't know." Mary's heart raced. "Well, of course I want to have him home, but what if I can't care for him? I know nothing about his condition."

"I don't know. Of course you should talk to Dr. Busey, but it is certainly worth considering." Essie's mouth twisted in a sad smile.

Charlie home. Hope hummed in Mary's veins, and she closed her eyes in a silent prayer. Was it even possible?

Chapter 39

Matthias bit down, his teeth sinking into aspen bark, testing it for a comfortable bite as Elaine prepared to run her first stitch. The bitter tang was sharp, and he spit it out. It would have to do, though. He'd need to be as still as possible if Elaine was going to be the one to stitch him up. The poor woman looked terrified, but more determined than he'd ever seen her.

Elaine had cleaned the wound and asked Florence to do the stitching. But the stress of the day had fatigued the older woman and her hands were shaky. Stitching through a man's flesh wasn't an easy job. The skin was tougher than one might imagine. Matthias would know. He'd stitched up men before when the gang had been too far from a town or lying low.

Elaine opened his shirt and pushed the fabric over his shoulders to reveal the gunshot wound. Her eyes rounded like toffee drops when she saw his scars. She ran light fingertips over the web of thick scarring that covered his chest, then glanced down to his forearm where the rest of the scars were.

"What is this?" she asked in a shaky tone.

Matthias's stomach twisted. "Don't you mind about that. It doesn't hurt anymore." He clasped her fingers and squeezed.

It was true. The marks left behind hadn't caused him physical pain in years. But he wasn't sure the scars on his soul would ever mend. He bit down on the aspen branch again. He would have to tell her his whole truth soon, but now wasn't the time.

The shot had been a clean one, in and out, so luckily no lead needed to be dug from his shoulder. Elaine pressed the tip of the needle to the edge of the bullet hole and hesitated, squeezing her eyes shut.

Matthias took the stick from his mouth. "You can do this, Elaine. Don't be gentle about it—just push through." He managed a half-smile and leaned back on the pillow, biting down hard again.

Elaine drew a deep breath, and the point of the needle sank into his skin with a sharp pain, followed by the unnerving sensation of rope being dragged through his flesh. Of course, it wasn't rope she was using, but the catgut sutures Matthias carried in his saddlebag might as well have been a hemp rope for what it felt like. Another needle stab and Matthias clenched his teeth, blowing out a breath out through his nose and nodding at Elaine to continue.

The cabin door banged open, and Gideon's voice boomed through the small house. "Jo? Elaine?"

"In here, Gideon." Jo's voice called from the other bedroom.

Silence followed as Gideon went to Jo first. Elaine paused, clearly unsure if she should go and explain everything. Matthias shook his head. He removed the stick again.

"Let them have their moment," he whispered low, before replacing the aspen stick once again.

Elaine set back to work, and Matthias focused his thoughts on what must be happening in the next room. What a joyous feeling it would be to see and to hold a life created with the woman you loved. He skimmed Elaine's delicate features with his eyes as she frowned at the task at hand. Would that ever be something he could experience? He certainly didn't deserve it. Had never thought it a possibility before. Yet here was this incredible woman who might love him. Was it unwise to love her in return?

He'd done so much wrong in his life. Too much. Spent years living the life of an outlaw. There was no coming back from that. He swallowed hard and the bittersweet aspen bark nearly gagged him.

A soft knock preceded Gideon's entrance to the room. "What's happened?" Gideon leaned against the doorjamb, holding his daughter in his arms.

Such a contrast, this big, burly man ready to do battle, cradling a newborn and looking down at her with an expression as soft as the wool stuffed mattress Matthias lay on.

Matthias removed the stick and dropped it on the side table. "Ambushed by Jasper and Hank," he said before nodding to Elaine to continue. "They came in on us at dark. Got to a few of the sheep before we could stop 'em. There was a fight, but I think we only lost two ewes."

"And Clay?" Worry darkened Gideon's eyes.

"He's fine," Matthias said, gritting his teeth as Elaine pushed the needle through his skin again. "He saved my life."

Gideon released a huff of air. "And the men?"

"Hank is dead. He came at me from behind and was about to bludgeon me with his nasty club, but Clay shot him."

"And the other?"

"As soon as Hank was down, the fight went out of that white-livered coward. He threw his gun down begged for his life. He tucked tail back to the Lazy M with Hank's body." Matthias's lip curled in disgust. "Hated to let him go like that. I'm sure there will only be more trouble now. But neither Clay nor I felt right shooting an unarmed man."

Gideon nodded, and the bundle in his arms began moving and grunting. Despite the grim conversation, the new father grinned down at his daughter and stuck a finger to her mouth.

"That's alright then. Much as I'm loathed to say it, you did the right thing. Killing Jasper when he'd given up like that would have only made you look worse in the eyes of the law. You're already on a tightrope as it is."

Elaine looked up, twin lines of concern between her brows.

"We've got help now, though." Gideon turned and exposed a man behind him, tall like Gideon, but lean and sharp-edged, with a chiseled jaw.

"Jimmy." Elaine's eyes widened.

The man removed his hat. "Elaine."

"Matthias, this is my brother." Gideon said.

Jimmy nodded to Matthias' wound. "Looks like you folks have run into some trouble after all. I'm glad I came when I did."

"So am I, Jimmy." Gideon gave his brother a somber half-smile. "We'll make sure all is settled here, and Jimmy can go up to stay with Clay. I don't much like the idea of leaving Clay up there by himself. I don't know what other men McBride can rile up against us, but there will be retribution. We can count on that."

The infant in Gideon's arms fussed and groaned more, and a genuine smile twitched under his beard.

"Never mind about that now, though. It will take the McBrides a few days to gather their wits and more men. For now, I have a wife who needs me." With that, he turned back to the other bedroom, humming and cooing.

Matthias pushed down the deep ache of yearning for such a life. A life he had never thought possible. He had always thought of the men he'd killed and the wrong he'd done as a barrier that sealed his fate as an outcast.

Yet tonight, he'd watched Clay kill a man in defense of life and property. A just cause, Matthias supposed, though he didn't feel worthy of such a defense. He'd seen now, a case when it had been necessary to take a life.

Could he say the same about the men he'd killed? What would Elaine say when he told her the whole truth? He watched her as she wound up the suture string and returned it to his saddlebag, then gathered the other tools, dropping them in a metal basin with a clink.

He grimaced and laid his head back on the pillow. He needed to tell her the truth. The whole truth and leave it up to her.

Chapter 40

Elaine turned her face to the sun and pulled in a breath of fresh mountain air laced with young spruce tips and damp earth. She sighed with contented relief.

"You look like a mole coming to the surface." Matthias chuckled next to her.

"I feel like one." Elaine stretched and smiled, shaking her head. "I wouldn't have ever thought I'd be so grateful to be outside."

"Oh?" Matthias's breathing sounded strained as they climbed the slow rise to the hill behind the cabin.

"Do you need to go back?" Elaine stopped and rested a hand on his bandaged arm.

Florence had urged Elaine to take a walk with him, insisting the fresh air would do them both good. She hadn't realized how much she had needed the escape herself.

"Nah, I'll do." His knuckles brushed hers as they followed the path that led to the north pasture. "Why is that? Why does it surprise you to be happy to go outside?"

"I've spent my life finding reasons to stay indoors." Elaine shrugged. "But suppose I've become accustomed to venturing outside since coming here. So, with Jo and the baby, and then your unexpected arrival, I haven't been out to do any chores." She looked back toward the cabin down the hill. "Maybe I shouldn't have left. They might need me."

"They're just fine. Gideon said he would stay close in case there was a need." Matthias stopped, breathing heavily, and sat down on a boulder.

The rope burns on his hands were healing, but the deep purple line across his chest spoke to bruised ribs Florence said would take some time to heal.

He took Elaine's hand and slipped his fingers through hers. His callused skin grazed against her skin and sent a rush of warmth up her arm.

"So, living in the wilderness has changed you, then?" He tugged her hand gently.

"I'm not sure." She responded to his pull and sat next to him on the large boulder, careful not to lean against him. "I suppose it has." Without meaning to, she tapped her thumb against his hand in successions of three. "Maybe not entirely."

Matthias looked down at her tapping thumb. "What is the significance of three?"

A chill settled in Elaine's stomach. Could she tell him this secret that had haunted her since childhood? She never thought she would tell anyone. Grandmama had insisted it wasn't safe. That no one could know. Matthias's solid presence next to her was so comforting, though, and he'd gone to such an extent to help her over the past weeks, he must have had some suspicion already.

"I'm not sure I can—" Elaine chewed the inside of her lower lip. "I'm not sure I can explain it."

"But it helps?"

The ice in her belly swirled uneasily. "You don't understand. I've never spoken of this to anyone. If anyone knew ..." She trailed off.

"You're safe with me, Elaine." Matthias turned and looked into her eyes intently. "I only want to help."

Elaine took a deep breath. "I don't choose the number three." She paused again, gathering strength. "It is a kind of neurosis. A compulsion I can't fight."

At the word neurosis, Matthias's brows knitted together. In for a penny, in for a pound. She might as well tell him all of it.

"My great-grandmother had it. She was eventually sent away. No one else in the family knows about it. Mother may have held suspicions there was something unusual in the family's past, but, of course, no one speaks of those kinds of things, do they?"

"No, they don't." Matthias thought of his own family secret. Had his mother ever told anyone what he'd done? Or had she somehow covered it up?

"As a child, Grandmama was so distraught over her mother being institutionalized, she began telling people her mother was deceased. So, when I started showing signs of something similar as a little girl, Grandmama took it upon herself to make sure I never suffered the same fate as her mother."

Matthias was quiet as he considered what she told him. A woodpecker hammered the tree behind them, startling Elaine. She jerked, and Matthias squeezed her hand in reassurance. She squeezed back, trying to stop at one, but her heart was racing after the sudden jolt, and she gave in to the urge to complete the cycle with two more squeezes.

"I have my own secrets, you know. I would never betray yours," Matthias said.

Elaine released Matthias's hand and stood, pacing—restlessness itching under her skin like ants.

"Grandmama taught me to recognize the things that made me worse and avoid them. Detection meant being put away. If I kept myself from the things that might cause an episode, no one would ever know I had a problem." She pressed a hand to her waist and tapped. "Dirt, filth, unexpected events. They were all things that set me off. So, to avoid being in an environment that would be risky for me, she told me I was to become a fine lady. I must marry a gentleman who could offer me a home in town. A life with servants and schedules would give me the order I needed to keep my secret safe."

"So, is it being exposed to things like dirt and mud that cause the panic, or do you think it is the fear of being sent away that causes it?" Matthias stood now, too, wincing as he did so, and stroked her cheek with the back of his hand.

Elaine blinked. She wasn't sure she even knew anymore. She was so worried about what could happen if she made a scene, she rarely paid attention to the cause. She was stuck in a constant cycle of frustration, panic, and fear. She didn't know how to unravel it all.

"I honestly don't know."

He cupped her face and leaned closer. "You are so much stronger than you give yourself credit for. Look at what you accomplished. You delivered a healthy baby, kept Jo alive, and stitched me back together. And you did it all with no *episode*."

Elaine gripped Matthias's shirtsleeves. He was right. Despite the mess and frightening situations that had occurred, she had gone through it all without falling apart. Maybe Grandmama was wrong. Maybe she didn't need the safety of town if she had Matthias to remind her how strong she was.

"How does your wound feel?" She grazed her free hand over the front of his shirt.

"It bites some, but I assure you, I'll live." Matthias covered her hand with his.

"Why don't you let me check it to see if the stitches are holding?" She arched an eyebrow at him and moved her fingers to the buttons of his shirt.

He nodded and sat back down, allowing her to unbutton the top two buttons of his shirt. Her hands shook, and heat crept up her neck from the high neckline of her blouse. It wasn't as though she hadn't already seen him without his shirt when she stitched him up yesterday, but now that the initial crisis was over, this almost seemed too intimate.

A smile played on his lips as she pulled back his shirt to inspect the wound. A little blood soaked through the bandaging, but not enough for her to be concerned. She bent and kissed the top of his shoulder, then braced her forehead against his.

"You know, Elaine, there is much about me you don't know." His throat bobbed as he swallowed. "So much we need to talk about."

"We have all the time in the world for that now. Thank God he saw fit to spare you."

"I didn't deserve to be spared." Matthias stared at the ground, not wanting to meet her eye.

Elaine buttoned his shirt. "You shouldn't say things like that. You are a good man, and you can't convince me otherwise."

Matthias scoffed. "I've wanted to be good, even tried to be. But it always goes wrong." He stood, and his expression tightened in a grimace.

"You're hurting. We need to get you back to the house."

"It's not that. I—"

Elaine helped him with the last button and rose on her tiptoes to kiss him lightly. She hated to see him hurting. No matter what it was he was so concerned about, it couldn't be anything that would change the way she felt about him.

"We'll talk more later. Okay?" Maybe changing the subject would make him feel better. "We'll change your bandages tonight before you sleep."

The thought of sharing a bedroom with him for another night brought heat to her cheeks and they prickled against the breeze. Last night she'd been so exhausted after a day of cooking, and nursing, she had collapsed into sleep without a moment's pause.

She was pausing now. It was impossible to not notice the man under her hand. But she realized it wasn't fear or indignation of sleeping in the same room as him that had her heart racing. What alarmed her was the fact she didn't mind. Not one bit.

Chapter 41

Matthias walked out onto the porch, stiff from spending too much time in the house, and sat carefully in the rocking chair Gideon had put outside for him. It didn't feel right, staying back while Gideon took Jimmy up the mountain to join Clay, instead of Matthias. Nonetheless, Florence and Elaine both insisted if there was another able-bodied man to go, Matthias should stay behind and heal up a bit more.

"The water barrel is full, and there's not near as many chores to do with the sheep gone. You can still be of use, protecting the women here." Gideon told him, as he loaded his saddle bag with extra food.

"Yes, sir. That I'll do."

Rhythmic thudding announced an approaching rider. "Someone's coming." Matthias's voice tightened as he pushed up out of his chair and stepped inside to grab the rifle from above the door.

"I don't reckon it's trouble, or they wouldn't be coming to the front door." Gideon attempted a relaxed smile but only managed a quick upturn of the lips that disappeared quickly into his beard again.

Matthias attempted to shoulder the rifle anyway but realized that was his injured side. He went back inside and retrieved his gun belt instead. As he buckled the belt, the rider became visible over the rise that led to the house.

It was Sheriff Barlow. This couldn't be good. He'd sent a letter with Gideon the last time Gideon was in town, confirming his freedom contingent on Matthias's assistance in bringing down the Lazy M. But until two nights ago, all had been quiet.

Barlow loped up the drive, his horse dark with sweat. Jimmy came out of the house, a cup of coffee in one hand, the other resting on his pistol grip. He glanced from Gideon to the sheriff eyes trailing over the visitor. He must have noticed the badge then, and he lowered his gun hand.

Elaine and Jo both hovered in the doorway behind him.

"Gentlemen." Barlow nodded to each of them. "I've come to warn you, Gideon. Your sheep are unprotected. You best get a man up there quick as you can."

Matthias's throat constricted, choking him on his words. "Where's Clay?"

Sheriff Barlow leveled a look at Matthias. "Arrested."

"Arrested on what grounds?" Gideon nearly shouted. "And how? He's been up with the sheep for the past week and a half."

"Shane McBride brought him in." He coughed to clear his throat. "They're claiming Clay murdered one of their hands over a dispute on grazing territory."

Elaine gasped, and Gideon muttered something under his breath.

"That sorry, no good, son of a sidewinder," Jo exclaimed.

"Sheriff Barlow, do come in and have some coffee, please," Elaine offered.

The sheriff hesitated. "I need to get back to town as quick as possible."

"You need to rest your horse, at least." Jimmy spoke up. "Why don't you go inside and explain things while I'll brush down and water your horse."

Barlow nodded. "I supposed I'd better do that. Thank you, son."

A muscle in Jimmy's cheek twitched, but he nodded and took hold of the horse's bridle. Matthias was still trying to settle Jimmy in his mind. He was young, but not a kid. Tall, broad chested, and confident, but if Gideon was the older brother Jimmy must not be more than twenty years old.

Matthias followed Gideon and the sheriff into the house, where they all gathered at the table.

Jo sat next to Florence and squeezed her hand. "This is Florence Anderson. Clay is her grandson."

Matthias's stomach felt hollow. The poor woman was liable to be worried sick. Did she have the strength to make it through such an ordeal?

"I'm sorry for the trouble, ma'am." Sheriff Barlow nodded to Florence. "But I need to be honest with you folks. Things aren't looking so good. As I said, McBride is accusing Clay of murdering a cowhand, and they collected Clay themselves and brought him in to be arrested."

Florence shook her head. "Clay does not murder."

"I believe you, ma'am. I'm holding him now, for his protection, while we sort this out. McBride is using his connection to the governor to push through a quick trial on this.

"What do we do?" Gideon asked, his ham-sized fists, clenched.

"I'll take a statement from Matthias here." He turned to address Matthias. "Maybe with the issues we have from earlier this spring, it might be best if you stay back for now until we know what they're going to come forward with."

Matthias's mouth went dry, and he took a sip of coffee. The bitter liquid did nothing to slake his thirst. He didn't need any more explanation. If the McBrides spoke out about Matthias killing that rancher, he would be of no use to Clay's case. In fact, it may only serve to do more damage.

A heavy weight settled on his shoulders, and he leaned forward, elbows on the table, and rubbed his forehead.

"Gideon, I think you ought to come back with me right off. You can be of some comfort to Clay and maybe sort some things out."

"Of course. I'll come as soon as I can, but I need to take my brother up to the sheep before they all wander off or get killed. He's new to the area and wouldn't know the first thing on how to find them."

"Gideon, you go on with the sheriff." Matthias leaned back in his chair. "I'll take Jimmy up to the sheep.

Florence released a breath that wasn't quite a sob. From what Clay had told Matthias, she'd lost her husband, her son, and daughter-in-law, and Clay was all she had left.

"You sure you can handle it?" Gideon raised an eyebrow in question.

"I'll handle it." Matthias set his jaw. Whether or not he thought he was ready, he would do anything for the man that saved his life.

Chapter 42

Elaine poured the pot of boiling water over the raspberry leaves for Jo's tea and added three biscuits to the tray in a tidy row. Standing back, she surveyed the tea service with satisfaction.

She carried the tray to the side table next to Jo's bed. Jo gave Elaine a tired smile of gratitude. The redness had faded from her face, but the scar seemed to pull down on her eye, emphasizing her fatigue.

Baby Grace had surprised them all with her vigor and life despite her small size. Florence had said the child had come "soon, but not too soon." Still, she tended to fuss often and took it in turns sleeping in a crate warmed by the wood stove, or nursing, and Jo's restless nights didn't seem to help her recovery.

"I brought you tea. If you are done nursing her, I can take her for you." Elaine smiled down at her niece, who had fallen back to sleep, slack jawed and drooling milk.

Jo shook her head. "She'll be needing a clean diaper. I wouldn't want you to have to do that." She sighed, resigned to get up.

"Nonsense." Elaine reached for Grace. "I've changed her often enough while you were sleeping these past few days. Don't you realize that?"

A funny look crossed Jo's face, and she hesitated before allowing Elaine to take Grace. Elaine was determined to prove to her sister she wasn't the same frightened field mouse she'd been when she first arrived on the homestead.

Snuggling Grace to her shoulder, she patted her back while she returned to the stove to add a splash of hot water to the bucket of clean, wet cloths they used to wipe Grace's bottom. She swirled her hand in the water to make sure it was a gentle, warm temperature before returning with it to the bedroom.

With one hand, she spread a clean cloth on the foot of the bed and laid Grace down. Then she unwrapped the wet diaper, taking a slow breath, careful not to let Jo see any discomfort register on her face. She wiped the sticky, yellowish smudge from Grace's pink skin with wet cloth then folded the rectangle of cotton flannel between her legs and pinned the edges.

"See? Nothing to it." Elaine swaddled Grace back into a clean blanket and balanced her gingerly as she poured Jo a cup of Florence's raspberry leaf tea.

Grandmama had always warned Elaine that children were unpredictable and would be problematic to her condition—another benefit of an upper-class household. Elaine couldn't say she agreed. All she saw was the precious blessing this child was.

"You seem better." Jo leaned her head back on the pillow.

"Better? You are the one who just delivered a child, not me." Elaine sat in a chair by the bed and snuggled Grace against her chest, rubbing the newborn's back in circles.

Precisely three circles. She tightened her hand into a fist and stifled the groan of frustration that burned in her chest. She had made progress, yes, but it was still there. Might always be there.

Jo waved a hand, dismissing childbirth. "I mean, you seem more comfortable here than you had been. More than I ever expected you to be."

"I am." Elaine nodded and handed Grace back to her sister.

"I'm so glad." Jo ran the back of one finger down the bridge of Grace's nose. "I know you've never liked me much, and I was never the proper lady you thought I should be, but—"

"Oh, Jo. That's not true," Elaine interrupted.

Jo raised a coppery eyebrow, and Elaine sighed. Should she tell Jo the truth? They were sisters, after all. Perhaps all these years it would have been better if her family had known—had understood what she was going through.

"It's not that I didn't like you, Jo." Elaine let a half chuckle escape. "I was envious of you."

Jo's eyes widened, and she blinked. "Of what?"

Elaine leaned back in the rocker and smoothed her hands over the curved arms. "Your freedom." Her voice came out small, like some sheltered part of herself was surfacing for the first time. "You could run wild and free on the farm without a care in the world. I didn't have that luxury."

Jo tilted her head to one side. "I don't understand."

"Do you remember Grandmama ever speaking of her mother? Great-grandmother Forsythe?

"Honestly, I don't. I don't reckon she ever talked about her childhood."

"Well, she did with me. Extensively." She tapped a finger on the arm of the chair. One, two, three. Then bunched her hand into a fist again to stop the cycle. "Grandmother Forsythe was mad."

Jo's mouth fell open.

"Well, I wouldn't say mad. But others did. She had an ailment of the mind. Melancholic panic, some call it, and she was committed to an asylum when Grandmama was a young girl."

"What does that have to do with ..." Jo trailed off, her mouth falling into a silent "Oh."

"I am afflicted with the same condition. It's not that I don't prefer certain things. I'm crippled by them. If I do not carefully control my environment—if I expose myself to any kind of nervous strain—I risk going into a kind of fit."

"Like with butchering the turkey?" Jo asked, her voice hollow.

"Yes. But often much worse." Elaine knotted her fingers together. "Grandmama taught me I was most safe in the house where it was clean and there was little exposure to the things that could cause me distress."

"Oh, Elaine, I am so sorry. I didn't know. All these years I just thought you saw yourself as better than me. Above such things. If I'd known, I never would have pushed you the way I did." Jo sighed. Then her face lit with understanding. "So,

Grandmama told you if anyone knew about it, they would commit you too?"

Elaine nodded, looking down at her hands. "She insisted I must find a husband—a life away from the things that threatened to expose me. Great-grandmother was a farmer's wife, and that life was too harsh. She couldn't escape the constant fear and fight."

"You're certainly not going to find an escape from that here."

She could always count on Jo to be frank.

"I know." Elaine shrugged. "It's why I fought so hard against coming here."

"Why *did* you come?"

Elaine's pulse hummed in her chest, and heat flooded her cheeks. "Jacob Sinclair." No matter how her eyes burned, she refused to cry.

"That snake from back home?"

Elaine nodded. "I was desperate to heed Grandmama's advice. The hysteria was growing worse all the time. I knew if I stayed a cattleman's daughter, I would end up just like our great-grandmother."

She pushed up to stand and walked to the window. The murky glass muted the colors of the summer wildflowers outside. She turned away and leaned back against the log wall.

"Jacob Sinclair's family had money. They had a cook and a housekeeper. It seemed my only option. When Jacob showed interest in me, I thought I'd found my salvation." Elaine squeezed her eyes tight. "It was only a kiss, but"—she cleared her throat—"a rather passionate one. Mrs. Fernsby caught us, and of course, she told everyone within five miles. Jacob—well, he wouldn't marry someone with such a tarnished reputation. The scandal was too much for Mother and Father, so they sent me here."

"Elaine, our folks aren't like that. More likely, they reckoned the scandal was too much for *you* and hoped you might do better somewhere new."

Elaine rubbed her fingertips against her forehead. "Well, I'm here, and I'm trying to make the best of it. Truly, I am."

"I see you are, Elaine. Still, Ma and Pa don't know, do they? About your struggles?"

Elaine shook her head.

"I doubt they would have sent you to me had they known. This is a hard life, Elaine. Even for those of us who truly love it. It is unpredictable, messy, and often dangerous."

"So I've seen." Elaine laughed.

"You are welcome to stay, of course, and I suspect Matthias would like it if you would." Jo winked and Elaine looked down, hoping to hide her pleasure at the thought. "But if you stay, you have to know there is some truth to Grandmama's warnings. Life on a ranch or a homestead will challenge you every day. Are you sure it is what you want?"

Elaine's pride in how far she'd come dwindled. "I think so—I don't know."

"Before you make your decision, I think there are some things I ought to have told you sooner. Things about me, about Matthias"—she chewed her lip thoughtfully—"about the harshness of life out west. I don't want you having any false illusions—"

"Hello?" Gideon's voice carried in from the other room, and Jo's face brightened like an electric light.

"He's back." She sighed with relief and offered Grace to Elaine, tying the neck of her nightgown back into place.

Elaine propped Grace on her shoulder, and the child let out a soft belch.

"Do you need my help?" Elaine asked Jo as she pushed the covers aside to stand.

"No, I'll be fine." Jo waved away Elaine's offered hand and wrapped herself in the blanket before going out to greet her husband with a kiss.

Elaine followed Jo into the front room and handed Grace back to Jo. She should make coffee. Gideon's return from town promised news. Whether good or bad, at least they might have some answers.

While Gideon washed the travel dust from his face and hands outside, Elaine chose several sticks of the good split wood for a quick fire. She had a feeling this meeting might require some strong coffee.

She set the coffee on to boil, then searched the baskets and crates on the shelf for some food to serve with it. There was a charred loaf of sourdough bread Elaine had baked two days before. No. That wouldn't do. It was bone dry and as chewy as a piece of leather. She had no business feeding it to anyone aside from the fact she didn't want it to go to waste. But not now. She would serve it with stew tonight instead, so people could dip it in their bowls before attempting to consume it.

Why had she not yet learned to make a decent batch of bread? She sighed. There were some pickles in the crock, so she arranged some on a plate with sliced sausages.

"I need to be honest, Florence." Gideon began the conversation when everyone had found a seat at the table. "Darby McBride is crooked as a mountain ridge and has more money than any man should. He gives money to powerful men and has a lot of influence." Gideon waited to see that Florence understood.

She looked from Jo to Gideon, and Jo took her shaking hand. Gideon scrubbed a hand over this mouth and smoothed it over his beard. "In any other circumstance, it would be months, maybe a year, before a trial took place, but we don't have that kind of time. I've met the city-dandy lawyer McBride has hired. From what I gather, the man is no slouch. He's moved out here from back East, and he's slick as they come. I hate to say it, but between the pressure from the governor and this Frank Dashel they have working for them, I'm not sure we stand much of a chance."

Elaine dropped the plate of pickles and sausages on the table with a clatter. Little Grace, who had fallen back to sleep in Jo's arms, startled, throwing out her arms and wailing.

Jo gave Elaine a look like a grizzly sow protecting her cub.

"I'm sorry." Elaine straightened the plate and wiped her shaking hands on her apron, giving her sister an apologetic look. "It's only, Frank—Mr. Dashel, that is—I know him. I met him on the train when we came out. He was quite the gentleman. Perhaps it isn't as bad as you fear."

"I've met the man, too, Elaine. He's a snake." Gideon took Grace from Jo and stood, pacing next to the table, bouncing and soothing his daughter.

Elaine stiffened with frustration. Of course Gideon would be on edge about Frank, with Clay's arrest and this bitter dispute between ranches. But perhaps this was the thing they needed. A way to bridge the gap between the two sides.

The enamel pot crackled and popped on the hot stove. Elaine set out cups on the table in preparation for the coffee.

"Either way," Gideon continued. "I was hasty in going down with the sheriff already. I feel it's necessary to go back. Florence should be able to see her grandson. He's in good spirits, as always, but there is much to sort out. I believe they are rushing this trial, so we won't have time to find suitable representation." Gideon spoke softly, bouncing and patting Grace's blanket. "I'd like us to all go back down together. Ma will return in two days on the stage, and I want Jo and Grace to see Doctor Turner."

A brief flicker of hope sparked to life in Elaine's chest. Perhaps she could find Frank and speak to him for the family. He had told her if she ever needed help to send word. Surely, if she explained things to him, he would understand. Perhaps he would defend Clay instead or, at the least, negotiate an agreement between the ranches. She drew a deep breath and relaxed a little, satisfied there was finally something she could do that would benefit the family.

Chapter 43

The wagon jostled down the dirt path with a jerkiness that rattled Elaine's nerves. Although Jo had seemed to recover well enough, a trip to town couldn't be easy for her. She winced with every jerky motion of the wagon. After only giving birth a few days prior, it was no wonder she was uncomfortable.

"Jo, why don't you let me hold Grace for a time and lie down?" Elaine reached out, offering to take the baby.

Jo hesitated only for a moment before surrendering Grace. Fatigue had worn her usual stubborn streak thin. She wrapped her shawl tighter around her shoulders and slid down to lie next to Florence in the wagon bed where Gideon had spread straw and a quilt for the women to have a more comfortable place to rest.

Elaine snuggled Grace close and eyed the tree line. She'd been on edge since leaving the homestead that morning. Though she was hopeful she could aid in finding a resolution, it was clear Darby McBride was a dangerous man. What if McBride had men watching them? They could be ambushed on the road at any time.

A fly buzzed around her head, bumping her ear, and tickling her neck. It only served to further the prickle of unease that moved under her skin. She resisted the urge to tap the brooch. She had grown past this, hadn't she? Breathing in slowly through her nose, she held her breath, hoping to slow her fluttering heart. She would focus on the good things around her rather than the dangerous possibilities that lurked behind every rock and clump of oak brush.

Sunlight gleamed against Copper's shiny coat as Matthias rode a little way behind the wagon. The melody of a tune he was whistling carried faintly over the creaking of the wagon wheels. He was clearly at ease, and Jo and Florence were sleeping. Why couldn't Elaine relax as well?

Determined to distract herself, she ran a finger down the tiny slope of Grace's pink nose. She grunted, opening her mouth wide and nuzzling toward Elaine's finger.

"You are the most beautiful thing in the Rocky Mountains. Do you know that?" She held Grace up in front of her, cooing and whispering.

The fly was back, vexing her. It tickled the side of her neck, and she shrugged her shoulder, hoping to dislodge it, but it wouldn't cease its assault. She bounced one heel on the bottom of the wagon bed, needing somewhere to send the nervous energy building inside. The fly found its way inside the high neckline of her blouse and paced underneath the lace, skittering back and forth.

Finally, the fly pushed her nerves beyond bearing and she could take no more. She laid Grace down on her lap to free one hand and shoo the fly away.

The wagon hit a bone-jarring rut, and Grace fell from Elaine's lap onto the straw bed at her feet. The child screamed, red faced, waving her arms. Elaine scooped her up in an instant. Her shoulders crumpled around the wailing newborn, and she shook, fighting tears. She tried in vain to slow her breathing, but all she could manage were short, empty gulps. She'd dropped her—dropped her newborn niece.

The edges of her vision darkened, and she lost focus on what was happening. Gideon's voice echoed in the distance, commanding the mules. Jo was trying to take Grace from her, but she couldn't let go. Wouldn't let go again. She shook her head violently and clutched Grace to her chest.

"I'm sorry. I'm so sorry." She heard her own voice echoing over and over. Was she speaking aloud or was it only in her head?

"Elaine." Jo was calling her name.

Elaine tried to surface from the thrashing waves of panic, but she couldn't emerge from the drowning chaos. Couldn't focus on what was happening around her. Little pin pricks of light floated against her darkening vision. Her heart raced like the thundering of horse's hooves.

"Elaine, give me Grace." Jo's voice was louder now, and she felt pressure against her skin as someone was tugging at her hands. She was being pulled apart, couldn't hold it together.

A stinging slap across her face shocked her from the storm inside, and she gasped. Finally able to fill her lungs with air, the tension locking her muscles tight released and light burst into her vision.

The rough wood dug into her back as Gideon held her back against the wagon bench. She jerked her eyes around her, trying to gain her bearings. Jo sat in the wagon bed, holding Grace to her chest—eyes wide. Terrified.

"Let her go!" Matthias shouted and pushed Gideon back with one hand. Reaching over the edge of the wagon bed, he scooped Elaine onto the horse with him.

"It's okay, I've got you," Matthias whispered into her hair.

But it wasn't okay. She had shown the true nature and danger of her condition. And now everyone knew the threat she posed to them all.

MATTHIAS KISSED ELAINE'S temple and dismounted in front of the sheriff's office. After her episode on the trail, he had scooted behind the saddle and settled Elaine in front of him where he could keep her calm and safe.

He couldn't blame Jo and Gideon's shocked reaction to Elaine's episode. They were new parents to a fragile, helpless life whose survival depended solely on their care and protection. It had been frightening for everyone involved. However, he was also keenly aware the dismay on their faces would do as much damage to Elaine's state of mind as they had been afraid would happen to their child.

For the rest of the trip, she hadn't spoken a word. She'd only leaned limply against his chest, her head lolling back and forth with the horse's gait. In that moment, he wanted nothing more than to turn Copper's head into the trees, follow a side canyon, and find some cave to hide them both away in.

It was daft. He knew that. Her living rough in a cave certainly wouldn't be better than life on a mountain homestead.

Still, he wanted to take charge—to shelter her from people who might witness her in a moment of distress like that and fear her.

He wasn't sure what had happened with Gideon's pa, but from what he'd gathered with Mary leaving, Gideon had put his father away in one of those dismal places. Would he, as a guardian of Elaine, do the same to her?

Surely not. Jo and Gideon were good people, but he could see now why her grandmother had urged her to find an easier life. If something so small as a bumpy wagon ride could set off such a frightening chain of events and instill fear in the hearts of her own family, she wasn't safe at all. Was she?

He held Copper's rein with one hand and the toe of her boot in the stirrup with the other. "Swing your leg over, now and I'll help you down."

Elaine blinked at him, her fair skin even more pale than usual. He nodded encouragement, and she darted a glance at the others, who were unloading from the wagon a few feet away.

"Everything is alright now, Elaine. It was only an accident. No one blames you." He felt like a hypocrite to say that when his thoughts for the last few hours had spiraled over the same things she must be worried about now.

Taking a deep breath, Elaine dismounted, and he held out an arm to escort her onto the boardwalk. Sheriff Barlow stepped out onto the porch with a solemn greeting.

"Come on in, folks. We've got much to discuss." The sheriff nodded to the door. Inside the sheriff's office was a woman with a cluster of children surrounding her.

Dread seized Matthias's gut and wrung it like a wet dishrag. Was this the family of the man he'd killed? His legs locked up. He couldn't move—couldn't face them.

He trained his eyes on the dusty wooden boardwalk under his feet. The contents of his stomach threatened to make an uprising, and he choked back the bile that rose in his throat.

He darted a look down at Elaine, only then realizing she didn't know. She knew he had a past he was ashamed of, but that differed from coming face to face with the widow of a man he'd killed.

"You see that man there leaving the Riverfront Cafe?" Barlow gestured with his chin to a man in a grey suit and bowler hat across the street.

"Yes," Matthias answered, his mind reeling.

"That's the lawyer Darby has hired."

Elaine whipped around, her eyes locking on the man.

Gideon spoke up from beside the wagon. "Sheriff Barlow, where is the doctor's house? I'd like to make sure my wife and daughter are seen while we're in town."

The sheriff pointed across the street. "Just there, but you might oughta hurry. He makes his rounds on Mondays and is typically gone for the afternoon."

"I'll go now, while you take Florence to see Clay," Jo said, adjusting her hold on Grace.

"I—I'll walk you." Elaine spoke up for the first time in hours. Her voice seemed thin and shaky.

She must dread finding her ease with Jo again, but he was glad she was brave enough to try. Jo pressed her lips together, looking from Gideon to Elaine. "Thank you," she said with a sympathetic smile.

Matthias relaxed his defensive posture. He'd no need to defend Elaine from her own family. Jo would never treat her sister badly, even if their relationship had been strained in the past. The women crossed the street toward the doctor's house, and Gideon held out an arm to steady Florence as she shuffled slowly to the boardwalk.

"We'll be in shortly. You go on ahead," Gideon told Matthias, smiling down at the woman on his arm. It might take them half the day to come inside with her tiny steps.

Inside, Matthias shifted from foot to foot and stared at the floor. He couldn't bring himself to look into the eyes of those children just yet.

Sheriff Barlow sat back on the desk behind him. "Mr. Noble. I would like to introduce you to Mrs. Simon Harris."

Matthias dragged his eyes from the floor and met the woman's. She was young, with a plain, but sweet face and mousy brown curls peeking out from under her hat. Any excuses or justification Matthias had built up for himself drained away as he looked into Mrs. Harris's glassy eyes. She jutted her chin out, not with disdain, but the same way Elaine did when she was trying to be brave.

"Ma'am." Matthias's voice broke on the single word, and he grimaced.

He removed his hat and drew a breath that stabbed in his chest as though his own body knew he didn't deserve to breathe.

Sheriff Barlow cleared his throat. "I'll give you two time to talk in a moment. But first, we need to get to business. I've sent for another lawyer to represent Mr. Anderson, but there won't be much time. As we speak, a trial date is being pushed through. We'll be lucky if Clay's lawyer, Mr. Tanner, arrives in time to greet Clay at the courthouse door, much less take the time to build a defense. That's why I've brought you both here. I need to at least gather all the facts I can about the cattle rustling, what you saw and overheard at McBride's ranch, and what happened the other night. I reckon if I can at least gather the information, Mr. Tanner just might have a chance at defending Clay in court."

The door opened, and Gideon escorted Florence inside.

"Excuse me a moment." Sheriff Barlow stood and guided Florence and Gideon down a short hallway where Clay must be held.

"Mrs. Harris," Matthias choked the words out past the hard lump lodged in his throat. "I'm mighty sorry for"—he faltered, his eyes bouncing between the children—"for what happened."

He was a coward for not being able to say the words aloud. *For murdering your husband.* That was what he'd done, wasn't it?

"Mr. Noble." Her voice shook as she forced herself to speak. "I can't say I've found it easy to forgive you." She smoothed a hand over her little girl's head. "But I have."

The tension between Matthias's shoulders released, and he swayed on his feet, a little lightheaded. He steadied himself with a hand on Sheriff Barlow's desk.

"I'm much obliged, ma'am. It was a grave error in judgment. I don't know that I will ever be able to forgive myself."

"If Shane McBride hadn't stolen our cattle, my husband wouldn't have needed to go after them. We have little. That small herd was everything. We invested our last dollar in purchasing those cows. He had to go after them. But I also know he likely would've been killed trying to get them back anyway. I want the Lazy M held responsible."

"But how? How could you forgive me?" Matthias still couldn't grasp this woman's mercy.

"Plainly put? Because God tells me to. We've all done wrong, Mr. Noble. Every last one of us. My Bible tells me if I don't forgive you, I ought not to be forgiven of my own wrongdoings."

Matthias shook his head and looked out the window. Elaine sat on a bench in front of the doctor's house across the street. Her face was shadowed by the wide brim hat she wore. He longed to see the graceful curve of her cheek. She'd become the bright spot in his life. The sunshine that had broken through the clouds of a dreary and troubled existence. But he didn't deserve her warmth or light. He didn't deserve this woman's forgiveness, either.

What he'd done was no better than when he'd run with Blake robbing stagecoaches. He had robbed this woman and her children of a husband and father.

How could he have grown so complacent as to entertain the hope he could build a life with Elaine? He didn't deserve a family or children when he'd killed another family's husband and father.

It was time he distanced himself from Elaine and the Cross family. He couldn't hide his past and continue this charade from her any longer. It wasn't fair to her. She didn't even know who he was. He didn't want her to know all of who he was—the things he'd done, the men he'd killed.

Knowing his past may be the only way she would let him go. If she knew the entire story, she'd see the path of destruction he'd left behind him from that fateful night he left home until now, and she would realize he was the farthest thing from safe.

Chapter 44

Elaine sat on the wooden bench, waiting for her opportunity to speak to Frank Dashel. He stood outside the Patrick Hotel nearby, speaking with some other gentlemen while watching the river flow by.

She knotted her fingers together in her lap, twisting and working her hands until her knuckles were white with the strain. She noticed belatedly she hadn't donned her gloves today. In fact, she couldn't recall the last time she had. Before moving here, she'd worn gloves faithfully to keep from soiling her hands.

Ironically, on the homestead it seemed every task was something so messy, she couldn't even wear gloves for it—paradoxical as that was. Now, she seemed to have lost the habit. How odd.

It almost gave her the feeling she was overcoming some of her difficulties. But clearly judging by the events of the morning, that wasn't the case. She was just as volatile as she'd always been.

The breeze shifted, carrying the faint scent of rotten eggs in her direction. Her stomach turned, and she pressed her laced fingers to her nose, closing her eyes and willing herself not to be sick. Her nerves were still frayed from the disastrous trip to town, and she still felt weak.

She dropped her newborn niece. Not only had she dropped her, she'd gone into such a panicked state she couldn't surface from the chaos. She could have smothered the child.

Elaine wasn't any better. In fact, if anything, this had only proved not only was she in danger of being sent away, she was putting her family at risk of harm.

She looked across the street to the open door of the sheriff's office. Matthias's form could be made out vaguely inside. She sighed and her heart squeezed in her chest. How could she leave when he had done so much to help her? For the first time in her life, someone saw her for who she was and cared for her, regardless. It wasn't fair to trap him into a life with someone who fell apart at the slightest incident or who might be a danger to their own children.

Footsteps echoed on the boardwalk, and she jerked her eyes up to find Frank Dashel approaching, though he hadn't seen her yet. She stood and smoothed out her skirts, adopting a placid demeanor, though the turmoil inside was anything but calm.

"Mr. Dashel," Elaine said as he neared her.

He looked up and paused his steps, taking a moment to place her in his recollection. "Ah, Miss Bradford. Correct?" He gave a slight bow.

"Elaine, please."

"Do call me Frank, then, as well." He nodded and brandished a charming smile. "How has Pagosa Springs treated you? As I recall, you were moving to the area to help out a family member?"

"My sister, yes," Elaine said, pressing her hand to her stomach. "She's just inside with the doctor at the moment." She gestured to the door behind her.

A look of concern crossed his face. "I hope she isn't unwell."

"Oh, she's well. Just a quick visit for her baby."

"Well, then, I hope the Rocky Mountains have been a pleasant retreat then. It can be a lively place."

Elaine gave a short, humorless laugh. "Lively." She repeated the word to herself. That was rather an understatement. "Actually, I heard you were in town, and hoped I might speak with you."

Frank's brows rose to meet his bowler hat, and his gray eyes twinkled with curiosity.

"You told me on the train I could send word if ever I needed help. Do you still stand by that offer?" Elaine gripped the fabric of her skirt in her fist.

"Of course. I would be a cad not to offer aid to someone in need." His genuine warmth eased her nerves.

She relaxed her grip and breathed a little easier.

"Would you care to take a walk with me? There is a path just beside the river." Frank gestured to steps leading down the small slope.

Sunlight glittered across the ripples of the water gliding under the bridge in the middle of town. It was an inviting scene. The area around the river was open and clearly visible from the main street. She would be quite safe, and this conversation would require some time.

"I'd like that." She stood. Her shaky legs were gaining some strength now. Perhaps a walk would do her some good. "I hear you are in town to represent a Mr. McBride of the Lazy M Ranch in a case against Mr. Clay Anderson."

Frank offered a hand to Elaine and assisted her down the rocky steps that led to the grassy path along the river's edge.

"I am."

"I'm acquainted with Mr. Anderson. He is a friend of my family, and one of my brother-in-law's hired men."

Frank stopped and turned—eyes wide. "Your brother-in-law is Gideon Cross?"

"He is." Elaine stiffened her jaw. "And I'm afraid you've been given some misinformation. You see, Clay—Mr. Anderson—he is no murderer. Those men came and attacked Clay and Matthias. It was self-defense."

"Matthias Noble, you mean?" Frank shook his head and sighed. He met her eyes with a sympathetic turn of the lips. "And was it Matthias Noble who told you this story?"

Elaine nodded.

"Just what do you know about Mr. Noble's character, Elaine? Would you say he was an honest man? Full of integrity and all that?"

"He is." It was the only response she could manage. She didn't like the direction this was going in and her throat was tight and constricting.

"I'm sorry to tell you, Elaine, but I believe it is *you* who has been misinformed."

"What do you mean?"

"Matthias Noble is an outlaw, Elaine. A murderer and a thief. He should be in jail right alongside Mr. Anderson."

All the air escaped Elaine's lungs as though she'd been kicked by a horse. "That's impossible."

"I'm sorry, but it's true. When he first came into the area, he rustled some cattle and killed the rancher in the process. Then he went to work for the Lazy M as a cover. When Shane McBride found out what Matthias had done, he ran."

The iron band of shock around her chest hindered Elaine's breathing. "No. That's not true. Frank, the McBrides are lying. My sister—Gideon—they wouldn't allow someone like that to work for them. Wouldn't allow him in their home." Elaine shook her head definitively.

Frank looked at her sideways, then turned to face her directly. "There's something else you should know. Though I wish I didn't have to tell you this." He paused and rubbed a hand over the back of his neck. "Did you know your sister well before coming here?"

"Did I know her? She's my sister."

"But were you estranged for a time? Forgive me, I shouldn't presume—but someone like you couldn't possibly know—" The corners of his mouth turned down in a pained expression. "Do you know how she came about that scar on her face?"

Elaine's heart hammered, slow and heavy in her chest. She shook her head.

"I have it on good authority that not long ago, she was working in a brothel—a house of ill repute I mean—over in Cripple Creek."

Elaine's stomach churned, and she wavered on her feet. Frank caught her by the elbow, his eyes round and soft with regret. "There was a notorious prostitute who went by the name Copper Kate. She was attacked by some lunatic and scarred so she was no longer … desirable for that vocation." Frank's words traced an icy finger down her spine.

Elaine didn't want to believe him, but how could she not? Her sister had, in fact, been missing for three years, then turned up after living in Cripple Creek with that ragged scar on her face. Why else would she have kept her past a secret?

"How do you know this?" Elaine asked, suddenly concerned with how Frank was privy to this information.

"Not firsthand, I assure you. I was told by a trusted colleague when I began investigating this case."

Elaine backed away, looking for somewhere to sit down. Questions swirled in her head like an angry storm. She was dizzy and about to be sick.

"Here." Frank spoke beside her and guided her to a large rock.

She collapsed onto it—the weight of this new revelation crushing her.

"I'm sorry to upset you, but I thought you should know who you are living with. I assure you, Matthias Noble did kill that rancher. It appears they have all been lying to you. Your sister is a known prostitute, and she and that mountain man of hers are harboring an outlaw. He is a thief and a murderer."

Elaine clutched her arms around her waist and doubled over. She couldn't breathe—couldn't think.

"I fear for your safety, Miss Bradford. You're not safe here with these people. I can't in good conscience leave you here alone with them. Do you have anywhere else you might go?" Frank's words sounded distant. Lost in a fog of uncertainty.

"No." She shook her head. "I have nowhere else."

She couldn't go back to Kansas and face the rumors there. Her reputation had been ruined. But could she return to life in the mountains with people she didn't know as well as she'd thought? People who kept the truth from her. If Matthias was truly an outlaw hoping to hide out in the back-woods, was he just using her for cover?

"Is your party returning tonight or will you be staying?" Frank glanced west, where the sun was beginning its descent.

Elaine's vision swam as she sucked in rapid, shallow breaths. She squeezed her eyes shut and shook her head. "It's too far to return. We're staying at the Patrick hotel tonight."

Frank knelt beside her and squeezed her hand as it rested on her knee. "That's good. I am staying there as well tonight." He rubbed his clean-shaven chin thoughtfully. "I have a proposition for you."

Elaine swallowed, her throat painful and dry. "What is it?"

"My sister Eliza has come out from Philadelphia to join me in Durango. Alas, as it is in most of these backwards western towns, society isn't what it should be. She is often alone as I travel much of the time. She finds herself in need of a companion. I would like you to consider coming back with me to stay with her for a time. She would be delighted to have a friend and we have a fine house with plenty of room. You would be quite comfortable. These people—" He waved a hand toward the main street. "They aren't like us."

Elaine blinked—dumbfounded. This proposition was exactly the situation she'd spent her entire life preparing and planning for. She wasn't sure how long Eliza would be in want of such a companionship, but for now, Elaine would be safe.

She stood, tapping the brooch. Guilt gnawed at her, pushing her to pace. Leaving with this man would be a betrayal against her family—against *Matthias*. But if what Frank said was true, it was her family that had betrayed her by not telling her the truth.

"If you choose to come with me, I will escort you to Durango in the morning. However, I warn you against telling your family. They will only hinder you from going. This should be your decision. What's best for you, not them."

Elaine's arms prickled with unease. It didn't seem right to leave without a word. Did she even know Frank well enough to travel to Durango with him alone?

"I don't know—" Elaine drew a slow, painful breath and pushed down her apprehension.

This was everything Grandmama had guided her toward. Even Jo herself had warned Elaine about the hardships of this life when she found out about her affliction.

"I have hired a young woman as a cook, who will travel with me to Durango. I assure you, it's all quite proper."

What other option did Elaine have? Her condition certainly wasn't getting better. Her last episode could have done true harm to her precious niece. Perhaps it wasn't safe for her to continue living in such an unpredictable place.

She would talk to Matthias—give him a chance to explain. If the accusations were false and she could prove it, maybe she could impress on Frank the need to look further into the matter.

Chapter 45

Matthias pushed the last dumpling around his plate with his fork. He hadn't much appetite tonight. Despite the warm glow of the oil lamps and the homey scent of fresh baked bread and savory spices filling the hotel dining room, none of that penetrated the darkness that shrouded him or the emptiness no amount of food could fill. Meeting Mrs. Harris had shaken him to the core.

The contentment and peace he'd found these past weeks with the Cross family had been a betrayal of the family he had destroyed. He glanced up from his half empty plate to watch Elaine sitting across from him. His heart swelled with the moments of bliss he had with her. He shut them out abruptly. He couldn't allow himself to continue down this path.

He had to distance himself from her—from all of them. He had no business seeking happiness. Besides, all he'd ever brought with him was trouble. What right did he have to think he could offer anything more?

Elaine's plate was nearly untouched as well. She stared out the window, lips straightened in a tight grimace. He nudged her foot under the table. When she looked up at him, he tipped his head in a questioning gesture. She pressed her lips together and shook her head. It was best to leave it alone. He should pull away, but he wanted to be there for her—to comfort her.

It must have been the incident earlier in the morning that was still upsetting her. Baby Grace had been fussy all evening, and with every whimper, Elaine cringed as though reminded of the day's events.

Matthias wanted to help her, but this was a foolish notion. How could he when all he'd ever done was cause harm? No. Now was the time to nail that door shut. He needed to tell her tonight about the rancher he'd killed, about his time as an outlaw, even about Pa.

A knot formed in his chest. He'd never spoken to anyone about Pa, but this might be the only way she would see him for what he was and accept the fact they had no future together.

He laid his napkin across his plate and rose from the table.

"I'd like to stretch my legs for a spell. Elaine, would you care to join me?" He waved a hand toward the door.

Elaine dabbed her napkin to her lips and glanced from Gideon to Jo before nodding. Something in her response felt off. It was more than her usual tentative nature.

She stepped out onto the porch, then hesitated. Matthias offered his arm, and she slid her fingertips into the crook of his elbow. It was nothing like the way she had clung to him that morning as he'd scooped her up into the saddle with him. Now she was stiff, keeping distance between them.

Not wanting to make her any more uncomfortable, he let her take the lead. She glanced up the street in either direction and walked across the street where a bench overlooked the river and the hot springs.

They sat on the wooden bench, and Matthias resisted the urge to pull her into his arms.

"You're not yourself tonight, Elaine." He searched her face for some hint of feeling from her.

She laughed, but there was no humor in it. It was laced with something more like contempt. "I'm not myself, you say?" Her tone was icy. "And just who am I supposed to be?"

Matthias froze. He had never seen this side of her before.

"Perhaps, it is you who's been false, not I?" She scooted farther from him on the bench and crossed her arms around her waist.

Panic shot through him like a rattlesnake bite. How did she already know? Had Jo spoken to her this afternoon? He couldn't blame Jo for doing so. He'd left it far too long. Though, he wished he'd been the one to tell Elaine.

"Actually, that's why I asked you to come out with me tonight."

"Oh?" She didn't appear to believe him, and he couldn't blame her.

"I have much to tell you." He closed his eyes to draw strength. He was compelled, once again, to pray, but why would God help him with this? Matthias had dug his own grave.

"I'm not sure where to start. My life has been a series of failures and poor decisions. Trouble follows me wherever I go." Matthias rubbed the back of his neck.

Elaine clenched the fabric of her skirt tight. He wanted to take her hand and smooth out the tension there. Instead, he would give her the truth and, with it, freedom from any attachment to him.

"I am an outlaw."

A choked breath escaped past her lips, but he pressed on, staring down at the river flowing by.

"My given name is Matthias Noble. That is true. But for years, I went by the name of 'Kit.' My father was drunk and a hard man. I never met his expectations as a son. As a lad, I spent a lot of time with my grandparents, my mother's parents. My grandfather died when I was young, but my grandmother raised me as best as she could in the windows of time I was with her. She had a piano, and I would tinker with it when I was there. She said I had a gift for music and bought me a violin." Matthias scrubbed a hand over his face. "I only played it at her house. Pa hated it—said I was weak and soft, and music was a frivolous time waster. When she died, I brought the violin home."

That had been a mistake. It had only made Pa hate him more. That fateful night came back to him as though it were happening all over again.

"When I was seventeen, he caught me playing in the barn. He took it and dragged me back to the house, threatening to throw it in the fire."

Elaine sucked in a gasp and gripped his hand. He allowed her to take it, but blocked out its intended comfort, continuing the tale woodenly. He needed to get the truth out there. Elaine deserved that much from him.

"He was right. I was soft. I cried like a child and begged him not to burn it." Matthias ducked his head and avoided

Elaine's eyes. "Ma tried to stop him. He hit her with it—hard."

His heart rate picked up pace, and he rubbed his free hand against his chest as the memory came fully to life again. The stove lid askew. The neck of the violin sticking out at an odd angle. The fire roaring. Flames and sparks shooting from the opening. Pa screaming and cursing at Ma how she'd raised a yellow coward.

Pa had knelt on the floor and grabbed the front of her dress. It was a blue dress—Why did Matthias remember that? Pa had picked her up by the dress and balled his big, meaty fist to hit her again. Matthias squeezed his eyes tight, wishing he could blot out the memory.

"I jumped on his back, and he threw me against the stove. The impact knocked the pan of grease Ma was cooking with down and it poured over me." He rubbed the scar on his chest absently. "I didn't think Ma could take much more. She'd stopped crying and just lay there moaning. I grabbed the skillet and jumped up—didn't even notice my hand being burned just then."

Mathias turned his hand over. His palm hadn't scarred nearly as bad as the oil burns on his chest and arm.

"I hit him with that pan as hard as I could. Turns out I wasn't so soft after all."

He swallowed back the bitter anger burning his throat. Pa's head had struck the corner of the stove when he went down. Hard.

"He never got back up."

"Oh, Matthias." Elaine's voice shook, low and breathy.

He looked up to find tears tracing down her cheeks. Several long minutes passed as they watched the river in silence.

Finally, Elaine spoke up. "What happened after that?"

"Ma kicked me out of the house. Said she couldn't bear to look at me—that she had no one to take care of her now." He scrubbed his hand over his face. "I would have taken care of her, but she wouldn't hear it. Said she'd call the marshal on me if I stayed. So, I left. After that, I drifted, tried to pick up work but never found a good place to settle." He shrugged. "One day I met a man who said he and his friends were going to try their luck in Colorado, and I went along with them. Turns out they were outlaws, and before long, so was I."

Elaine choked back a nearly silent sob.

Matthias pulled a handkerchief from his breast pocket and offered it to her. "I was running with them when I met"—he hesitated—"when I met Jo."

Elaine paled even more in the moonlight.

"How—where—"

"That's not my story to tell." Matthias accepted the cloth back from Elaine and crumpled it in his fist. "In the end, we both got free, and Jo and Gideon gave me the chance to start a new life."

Twin lines formed between Elaine's brows as she attempted to put the pieces together in her mind. "How did you come to work for the Lazy M?"

"I was looking for work in the area this spring when I happened on some cattle rustlers and I—I intervened." He heaved a long sigh. "Killed the man I thought was stealing the herd, but turned out he was the rancher. The rightful owner of the cattle." The stabbing pain in his chest eased some, having told her the truth.

Elaine pressed a hand to her stomach, finger tapping, eyes fixed on the river.

"I'm not a good man, Elaine." Matthias pulled his hand free from hers.

She turned and looked up at him with such brokenness, it shamed him. He'd been a fool to think he could ever have someone like her.

"You and I—we don't belong together," he whispered into the dark.

She hesitated, her grip on his hand tightening. "I know." Her voice was so soft he barely heard her.

But there it was, the painful truth he had known all along. In that moment, his heart was torn in half. One half that knew he was no good for her, and the other that couldn't imagine a life without her.

He put a hand over hers on her lap. "When this trial is over, I'm leaving."

She closed her eyes, turning away so her face was in profile against the light of the street lantern.

"You deserve so much more than I can give you," he told her, lifting the tear from her cheek with one finger. "You were destined for more than I can offer. My life will be nothing but this." He waved in the direction of the sheriff's office and jail.

Another tear traced down the side of Elaine's face and her bottom lip trembled.

"There isn't anything else for me." He shuddered a breath that ached in his chest. "Maybe your grandmother was right.

You should find a place in town. Away from all this fighting, and all the unknowns of this kind of life. Promise me when I am gone you will find somewhere safe."

She sniffed and gave him a hard look—one of fear cloaked in a blanket of determination. After several agonizing seconds, she nodded and rose from the bench. Clenching her hands together, she bent to place a kiss on his cheek. Then she walked back across the street to the hotel without another word.

His heart ripped from his chest, dragged along in her wake. It was done. Things between them could never be the same, and he couldn't help but grieve the loss of what might have been.

Chapter 46

Elaine woke to the vibration of the wagon lumbering down a rocky slope. The sky had taken on the pink hue of pre-dawn light and mare's tail wisps of clouds hovered above her.

She frowned and wrapped her shawl tightly around her shoulders, yawning. She hadn't expected to sleep, but exhaustion and heartache had weighed heavily on her, and she had drifted off as the wagon bumped down the road.

When Frank had suggested leaving in the night to avoid any interference with her decision to leave, Elaine had been nearly sick over the idea of running off with a man she hardly knew. However, she took comfort in knowing he'd been nothing but kind to her since their encounter on the train, and she felt better knowing she wouldn't be alone with him on the trip.

She glanced down at Miren, the young woman who had slept next to her in the wagon bed. She was awake now, too. A beautiful young woman, with sad eyes and dark hair, neatly braided into two loops over her ears.

Was Miren as distraught as she appeared to be? Or was Elaine only seeing the reflection of her own grief in the girl's eyes? She wasn't sure.

Elaine had been disappointed to find Miren spoke no English, but it was just as well they couldn't communicate. Elaine wouldn't have been a decent traveling companion if she had.

The empty chasm where her heart belonged ached with a sickening hunger. It seemed a lifetime ago, not a matter of weeks, she had dreaded being sent to her sister's back-country homestead. Though she was every bit as miserable as she'd expected in the beginning, she never expected the satisfaction she found there—even despite the burned bread, savage chickens, and Matthias. He had shown her beauty in the rugged wilderness and made her feel whole and capable in a way she never thought she could be.

She sighed and stuffed down the warmth that crept into her chest at the thought of him. She couldn't afford to allow herself such feelings ever again. It couldn't have lasted, she understood that now. He was an outlaw on the run. The antithesis of safety.

Safety would be found in a place where her abnormality wouldn't endanger those she loved or draw the wrong kind of attention. How could she have allowed herself to wander so far from what she knew she needed?

The wagon slowed, and Elaine sat up from her makeshift mattress to look around. She was eager to see the bustling town of Durango and the fine house Frank had told her about. Instead, they were surrounded by large pinon trees and hills covered in oak brush. This wasn't town. This was a ranch.

Frank pulled the team to a stop in front of a sprawling, one-story house with a porch that stretched across the length of the house. A large barn stood to one side, and horses paced a long pasture, whinnying at the wagon.

Her stomach lurched, and she gripped the side of the wagon. "Where are we?"

"Didn't I say?" Frank wound the reins around a metal fork on the side of the wagon and stepped down. "We will need to stay here at my employer's ranch for a short time."

"Your employer?" Elaine looked back to Miren, who showed no sign if this stop was unexpected for her as well.

"Indeed. Never fear, though, Elaine. You will find it quite comfortable here until we can continue our trip to Durango. I am often obliged to stay here. It makes a welcome respite to break up the trip."

He held out a hand and assisted her from the wagon, and Miren as well. Elaine's pulse quickened, and she tapped the pendant. One, two, three, one, two, three. This wasn't at all the plan.

A tall woman with a bland expression answered the door. Her eyes first fell on Elaine and Miren, and she frowned suspiciously, but she relaxed when she saw Frank.

"Please show Miss Ibarra to the kitchen right away, Mrs. Patton, and please prepare a room for Miss Bradford."

Mrs. Patton hesitated again, glancing from Frank to each of the women. Fatigue still pulled at Elaine's frayed nerves and dulled her wits. She was missing something important. Frank's tone was direct and carried with it a note of something Elaine couldn't quite put a finger on.

"It will be fine, Mrs. Patton. Mr. McBride is expecting Miss Ibarra, and Miss Bradford will be welcome as well, I'm sure."

"McBride?" The name was a stab to the chest that brought her fully awake. "Your employer—your employer is Darby McBride."

It wasn't a question. She was only repeating the facts to herself. She had known it, but in her despair, the obvious had slipped right past her.

The room tilted and she pressed a hand against the wall.

"A room Mrs. Patton. Right away." Frank caught her by the elbow.

"Yes, sir," the woman replied. "Come with me."

Frank urged Elaine forward, one hand still on her arm.

Elaine pulled back. "No, no, no. I—I can't stay here. This isn't where I am supposed to be."

"Don't be silly, Elaine. You will be quite comfortable here until we can continue to my home." He tugged her along, following Mrs. Patton down a long hall and around the corner. She stumbled over her own feet as they came to an abrupt stop. Mrs. Patton fumbled with a large iron ring filled with keys and unlocked the door.

"Get some rest, Elaine. I must go speak with Mr. McBride. I will have your bag brought to your room." Frank escorted her to the bed and deposited her there.

Elaine's shaky legs gave way, and she dropped to the bed, stunned. The door clicked shut, and she pressed a hand over her mouth. What was she going to do?

She certainly couldn't run. They were in the middle of a forest, who knew how far from town. She should demand he take her back. This wasn't what she wanted at all. What was he playing at? Was she to be held captive here as some means of leverage over her family? Or was Frank telling the truth when he told her it was Matthias and Clay who had been the aggressors of the feud, and he was only keeping her safe?

A few days ago, she would never have believed such a thing, but they had all lied to her. Or, if not lied, they had certainly hidden the truth from her.

Her head still swam, and she tucked her feet up onto the feather tick mattress to lie down. She closed her eyes, willing her stomach to settle. She tried to recall all that Matthias had said when she confronted him. He admitted to killing his father, which she had to admit was justified, and also to killing the rancher, which was not.

Who knew what else he had done during his time with the outlaw gang? Could he have lied about the night McBride's man had been killed? They had ended the conversation before she could ask what happened the night he was shot.

Listing all the things she hadn't known about Matthias before the previous night's conversation made her dizzy. How had she been so caught up in being taken care of that she fell for a killer?

She turned her face, burying it in the smooth fabric. Muffling the sound in the pillow, she screamed and kicked and cried. Tears of embarrassment, fear, and most of all, anger, poured from her until she had nothing left.

She rolled over to the dry side of the pillow and faced the wall. Even if she could convince Frank to take her back to her family, what was there for her?

Mary would be back now to step in and take care of everyone. Elaine would be nothing but a burden. Her issues had become a danger, especially to Grace, and clearly no one had cared to tell her the truth about who they were.

She couldn't turn back now. She would have to insist Frank take her to Durango right away. If he were any kind of gentleman, he would have to heed her request.

Chapter 47

Matthias sat alone at a table in the corner of the hotel's dining room, waiting for the Cross family to join him. He drummed his fingers on the table, his knee bouncing under the lace tablecloth.

Sitting here alone had him on a razor's edge. Without the others, without Elaine, to buffer him from the sidelong glances of the other patrons, he felt exposed. He didn't belong in a respectable dining room like this. It didn't feel right.

Nothing felt right after his conversation with Elaine. Having told her the truth, he should be relieved, and on that aspect, he did. Though putting an end to the possibility of their future had gutted him. He wanted a better life for her than he could give, but selfishly, he wanted to keep everything as it had been when they were on the mountain.

He pushed the empty coffee cup away and drummed his fingers on the table. Where was everyone? They should have come down by now. Matthias had slept in the wagon bed at the livery, but the others had rooms here in the hotel.

The coffee churned in his stomach. Something was wrong. He stood from the large table, leaving a coin for his coffee. He ascended the stairs, his boots padding along the carpeted hallway with a hollow thumping that echoed the emptiness in his heart.

The door to Elaine and Florence's room was open, and distressed voices murmured inside.

"It's my fault." Jo's voice shook.

That wasn't something he was used to hearing. In the time he'd known Jo, she'd been unshakable as a mountain.

He crossed the threshold. Jo looked up at him, pale and peaked. Gideon stood beside her, and Florence sat in a straight-back chair near the window—hands folded and head bowed.

"I was too hard on her when she dropped Grace. It was an accident that could've happened to anyone."

Gideon squeezed Jo's shoulder. "Don't blame yourself, Jo. You were scared too."

Jo pressed her lips together and shook her head. "But I didn't reassure her. I should have spoken to her. She told me she suffered from episodes of distress, but I had never realized how serious it could be."

Jo handed Matthias a piece of paper and eased down onto the bed, adjusting Grace in her arms. Matthias stretched the note out in front of him, and his hands shook as he scanned the words.

Jo,

By the time you find this letter, I will be gone. I have taken the stage to Lumberton and will return by train to Kansas. You and I both know I am not cut out for all of this. I would only be a burden to your family, and it is clear you are beset with enough challenges without me. With Mary returning, I will be of no further help to you. I wish you all the best.

Kiss baby Grace for me.

Elaine

Matthias's heart plummeted. She was gone. He'd encouraged her to find a place, but he had thought he would at least have a chance to say goodbye. "This wasn't your doing, Jo. This is my fault."

Gideon straightened, seeming to fill the small room with his daunting presence. "What did you do?"

Matthias held out a hand, forestalling the imminent attack. "Nothing, Gideon. Not that, at least." He waited for Gideon's acceptance.

Gideon released a breath, relaxing slightly, but his arms still bulged across his chest.

"We spoke last night. She knew about me—about everything, I think. She was mighty upset. I told her the truth about Simon Harris, and I told her after the trial I would be headed out of the territory."

"Matthias, no." Jo reached out with one hand and touched his forearm.

He stiffened. "I reckon if I make it through all this alive, it's best if I go. I told Elaine I thought your grandmother had the right of it. That she might ought to look for a situation that would suit her better than the hard life here. But I never meant for her to go and run off like this." Matthias shook his head and pressed stiff fingers against his temples.

Grace fussed in Jo's arms, and Gideon reached down to take her. "What do you reckon we ought to do now?" he asked Jo.

He turned Grace over so she lay on her stomach, her body draped across his forearm, her head nestled in his large hand. He patted her back and her sharp cries subsided into a whimper.

"What *can* we do?" Jo asked.

Matthias didn't think she meant the question earnestly. It was more likely the surrender of being subject to someone else's choice and being left behind with the ramifications.

"Don't you mind about that." Matthias tugged the brim of his hat tight.

He would head straight for the livery to retrieve Copper. He had to find her before something happened to her. He didn't even want to consider what mischief could happen to her on the road with no chaperone or traveling companion.

"I'll take care of it." Matthias nodded to Gideon and spun on his heel to leave.

"You can't." Gideon placed a hand on Matthias's shoulder.

Matthias gritted his teeth and turned back. "Why not?"

"Trial could happen any day. Lumberton is forty-five miles in the wrong direction. You disappear right now, and folks will think you've run off. Clay has no other defense in court without you. It will be him against Darby McBride's deep pockets, and though Sheriff Barlow may be our ally here, we don't know what we'll face if they set the trial in Durango. If you leave the area, we will lose."

Matthias cut an eye in Florence's direction. Clay was all she had. He couldn't risk Clay's freedom, or possibly his life, to chase after Elaine now.

Matthias choked back his own fear. He pulled in a deep breath and crossed his arms. This was his first chance to do the right thing. To make right all his wrongs and earn the forgiveness of Mrs. Harris.

Elaine had made her decision, and though it crushed him to stay behind, Gideon was right. Clay's life depended on Matthias staying put. He had to allow Elaine to choose the path she thought best and stay with those who needed him.

Chapter 48

Mary gripped the open window frame of the stage-coach as it rattled into town. Her chest felt light, and her limbs tingled. She couldn't wait to tell Gideon—both of her sons, in fact—about Charlie and the hope her visit gave her.

No, Charlie was not well. She had seen why Gideon had thought himself incapable to care for him. From what Essie had told her, when Charlie had first arrived, he had been in much worse shape. The chaos in his mind had ruled him, causing angry outbursts and irrational behavior. Gideon would never have been able to take care of him on his own, and without help or guidance, Mary might not have been able to either.

She hadn't wanted to admit it, but a small part of her had been selfishly angry with Gideon for putting his father into an institution. But this trip had done much to give her a glimpse of what Gideon had gone through. After years of carrying the blame of his father's disappearance, and finding the shell of a man he'd become, she could understand the turmoil Gideon had been in.

That was all done now, though. Charlie had recognized her, really recognized her. Though he drifted in and out of a state of awareness, there was some clarity at his core. She would hold on to that hope.

The coach came to a stop and eagerness to see her sons together again hummed inside her. She stepped down onto the dusty street and scanned the faces in front of the stage depot. Gideon was helping the driver unload baggage. She glanced around the crowd for Jimmy. She hoped he would have arrived by now, but there was no sign of him.

Mary waited for Gideon to finish with the bags. When he turned back to her, she hugged him tight.

"We have so much to talk about." Mary beamed.

Gideon's attempted smile was more of a grimace, and her stomach knotted. Something wasn't right.

"What is it?" she asked, though she was afraid to hear the answer. Any number of things could have gone wrong in her absence.

"Let's get out of here, and I'll explain." Gideon led her down the street, carrying her small trunk on one shoulder.

He moved so quickly, she was hard pressed to keep up. Once clear of the busyness, Gideon set her trunk down.

"Sit," he commanded.

She raised an eyebrow at him and cocked her head to one side. "I beg your pardon?"

Gideon sighed, and some of the tension went out of him. "Will you have a seat, please, Ma? You might oughta sit for all this."

The knot in Mary's stomach tightened, and she slid down onto the trunk. "What is it, son?"

Gideon smoothed a hand over his beard and scratched his cheek. "Where do I start?"

"Is Jo alright?" Mary started with the most important item on her mind.

A more genuine smile tugged at one side of her son's mouth. "You have a granddaughter."

Mary pressed a hand to her chest. "Oh my, but that seems early. Are they alright?"

"It was, but they are." He nodded. "Jo got mighty sick there at the last, and baby Grace is just an itty-bitty thing, but it seems all is as well as can be expected. They are back at the hotel now."

"*Grace.*" Mary pushed aside a tear that rose to the edge of her lower lashes.

"Jimmy made it here as well, though I wish you'd have mentioned it to me before you sent for him. I don't know how much he actually wants to be here."

"You need to make things right with your brother, Gideon, and it sure seemed like you could use the extra help when I left."

Gideon chuckled dryly and nodded. "More than you know."

"Well then, what's all this fuss about?" Mary crossed her arms. She'd had about enough of his tiptoeing around.

"Things with McBride came to a head. Matthias was shot, but he's alright. Clay killed one of theirs and has been arrested for murder." Gideon folded his arms across his chest. "Jimmy is up on the mountain with the sheep, and Elaine took off."

Mary's heart thumped slowly, but loudly, in her chest. "Well now, that is a lot to take in. How long has Elaine been gone?"

"Early yesterday morning. When Florence woke up, she was gone."

"Was she taken?"

"No. She left a note. She's going back to Kansas." He shrugged. "But she went alone and told no one what she was planning. She was mighty upset. She had some kind of fit while she was holding Grace a couple days ago, and I reckon it shook her up pretty bad."

"Has anyone gone after her?" Mary's heart squeezed tight for Elaine.

"Can't. McBride is using his pocketbook to push a trial pretty quick. Matthias would be the only one who could go, and he's the key witness to everything. If he leaves, Clay is completely vulnerable in court. Besides, if something were to happen to Matthias, McBride will never be held accountable for all his crimes."

Mary nodded, understanding the predicament. "Well, I have my own news to tell. Though I'm not sure this is the best time."

"There's no rush just yet. We're waiting on word of when the trial will be set."

Mary pressed her hands against her knees and blew out a long breath. "Well, bring me to that granddaughter of mine. I can't wait to meet her."

JO HELD GRACE OUT TO Mary, and her heart warmed at the glow in Mary's face at this first sight of her granddaughter.

"She just couldn't wait to meet you." Jo quirked a wry grin.

"Well, I wish she'd have baked a bit longer. I'd have liked to have been there to help," Mary said with a broad smile.

"Well, I, for one, am glad she came when she did. I think any longer, and I'd have burst like an overripe tomato." She leaned against Gideon, who wrapped an arm around her and kissed the top of her head.

Mary's smile faltered for the first time. "Are you alright now?"

"Good as new. Just a bit tired."

"Well, that's to be expected, now, isn't it?" Mary was speaking to Grace now, as if the child were her confidant.

"Tell us about your trip. Gideon said you have news." Jo moved in front of Gideon and leaned back against him, thumping the back of her head against his barrel chest.

"Well, I met Essie. She took me to your father and—" Mary's eyes shimmered as she locked eyes on her son. "Gideon, he remembered me. Called me by name, even, right off."

Gideon stilled behind Jo.

"I know. I never expected it. He's still infirm, of course. His thoughts wandered, and he seemed to be in the mind you and Jimmy are still young boys. Oh, but Gideon, he was so much better while I visited." She beamed. "Essie seems to think he might be better off at home now that there are more of us to care for him. We will continue writing letters for now, and she will read them to him and keep us apprised on his condition. We hope perhaps hearing from us regularly will spark a fire that will stay lit, rather than the brief flame that flickers to life when he's had a visit that's quickly snuffed out when we leave." The words tumbled from her in an excited rush.

"Ma, are you sure?" Gideon's voice was stiff and reserved behind her.

"Well, no, but we will hope and pray. If he improves after hearing regularly from us, we could. You committed him, Gideon." She brushed a hand along his shoulder. "I understand why you did, but as his immediate family, it would be our choice to bring him home. I also hope to ask Essie to come back here with us. She's so good with him, and I thought we could continue to pay her a nurse's salary from the silver cache."

Jo felt the tension in Gideon release, and he squeezed her tight, kissing the top of her ear. "Whatever you want, Ma. I would like nothing more than to have our family back under one roof again."

"Well, now that is settled"—she hesitated, pressing her lips together—"I think it might be your turn to sit now." She focused her direct gaze on Jo.

Jo's stomach quivered. Gideon laced his fingers into hers and tugged gently, moving to the edge of the bed, and sitting down with her.

"When I was at the asylum, there was a woman." Mary sighed and frowned. "She had red hair, chopped short, and a scar ... Well, a scar exactly like yours."

Jo's heart slowed into heavy thumps that jarred her. Gideon's grip on her hand clenched tight.

"Essie said the woman was attacked in a brothel. She never recovered her wits and was committed."

Grace squirmed and fussed in Mary's arms.

"How long has she been there?" Jo asked woodenly, though she wasn't sure she wanted to know the answer. She stood and reached out for Grace.

"Only a few months," Mary said, handing her child over.

"So, he's still out there." Jo swallowed against the hard lump in her throat.

How many girls like Jo had he harmed? She smoothed a hand over the cinnamon-colored curls of her daughter's head and ran a finger along the soft curve of her cheek. The idea of Grace growing up in a world with men like Mr. Carver chilled Jo to her core.

She turned to face Gideon, with single-minded purpose. "We have to stop him."

Gideon nodded without hesitation and rose to stand by her side. "We will."

Chapter 49

Elaine awoke from a fitful sleep to a tap on the bedroom door. Mrs. Patton backed through the door carrying a tray. Elaine sat up, realizing she hadn't even taken the time to remove her boots when she'd lain down.

"Mr. Dashel asked me to send you up some breakfast." The woman set the tray on the writing desk in the corner and continued speaking over her shoulder as she opened the heavy curtains. "If you need anything while you are here, you can pull that cord and I'll be along shortly." She pointed her chin to a fringed rope dangling next to the bed.

"Thank you." Elaine scrubbed both hands over her face and tried to clear her muggy thoughts.

Mrs. Patton looked down her long nose at Elaine. "I'll draw a bath while you have your breakfast."

Elaine frowned and patted her hair. She must be as rumpled as the bed.

"Wait," Elaine said before the housemaid could leave again. "I need to speak to Mr. Dashel right away. Can you tell me where I can find him?"

"Mr. Dashel is occupied. Eat your breakfast, and I will collect you soon for your bath." The woman's brusque manner caught Elaine off guard. Mary had always been warm and kind, even if pragmatic. Hers had been a presence that added comfort to their home. This woman was stiff and cold.

When the door closed, Elaine crossed the room and picked up a toast corner. She nibbled at the cold, dry bread and took a sip of the strong, black tea that held a bitter edge. The egg was as hard and dry as the toast.

She abandoned the plate. She should be used to terrible food after the past several weeks of eating her own disastrous cooking, but in a house like this, she expected better. Perhaps Miren had been hired to improve the food here, and not at Frank's house.

Her empty stomach ached, but she had no real appetite. What she wanted wasn't food. She wanted to go home, though she wasn't sure where that was now. She'd ruined her prospects in Kansas and abandoned her family back in Pagosa Springs. There was no choice but to move forward now. She needed to find Frank and demand he take her to his sister in Durango.

There was a basin of clean water on the bureau, along with a bar of soap. She couldn't bear to wait until after a bath to talk to Frank, but judging by the disheveled reflection in the murky mirror, she could use some freshening up.

She splashed her face with cold water and did her best to smooth the flyaway hairs that stood out from her chignon. Then did the best she could to brush the bits of travel dirt and straw that clung to her dress.

Clearly, Mrs. Patton was going to be no help. Elaine would simply have to find Frank herself. She peered from her doorway. The house appeared empty. She slipped into the hallway and followed the dim corridor past a formal dining room.

She continued around the corner to the back of the house. A cloud of sweet smoke and the murmur of men's voices rolled from a room at the end of the hall. This must be where Frank was.

"I sent you for the Ibarra girl, Frank. I said nothing about bringing back anyone else." The speaker's voice held a sharp edge.

Elaine paused. She didn't want to barge in on a meeting already fraught with tension.

"Calm yourself, Shane." Frank's cultured voice was much more collected than the first.

"You assured us you would cover up any loose ends that unraveled from our dealings with these mutton busters. All this is going to do is draw more attention."

Elaine's stomach dropped, and her head felt light.

"Ibarra knows we have his daughter. He'll keep quiet. As far as anyone else knows, Miss Bradford simply found better lodgings than that hovel of a homestead. No one will suspect anything different." Frank's tone remained calm and collected.

"Then why take her?"

"I didn't take her. She willingly came." A husky chuckle rumbled through Frank's smooth voice. "Besides, it appears Noble has grown fond of Miss Bradford. If he were to come looking for her, you can kill him and there won't be any witnesses left to stand against you."

"Well played." The scratchy voice of an older man joined the conversation.

A chill swept over Elaine, and her skin prickled with the desire to run. Her breath came short, and the hallway tilted dizzily. She pressed a hand against the wall to steady herself.

She was a fool. She had thought if McBride was guilty, Frank wouldn't know anything about it. She'd even thought she could make him see the truth.

Then the rest of what he'd said snapped into place. Miren. She wasn't a cook. She was a hostage. Elaine's chest tightened, and her breath became strained. She tapped the brooch and looked back down the hallway. What could she do now?

The screech of a chair against the wood plank floor jarred her into motion. She ran down the hallway toward her room. Darting around the corner, she ran straight into Mrs. Patton.

"There you are, girl. What in blazes are you doing down here?" Mrs. Patton's grip on her arm felt like an iron manacle.

Elaine opened and closed her mouth. "I—I was looking for the bath." She stammered an answer, gripping the fabric of her skirt tight on both sides.

"I told you to call for me when you were ready." Mrs. Patton's eyes narrowed, and she turned Elaine toward her room. "Follow me."

Elaine's heart raced so fast, she felt it might take flight. She tried to behave naturally, but behind Mrs. Patton's ramrod form, Elaine pressed a hand against the wall as she walked to keep upright.

In the washroom, steam hovered above her head. She drank in the heavy air, trying to refill her lungs after her distress. She thanked Mrs. Patton for drawing the bath. She could not allow the woman to see her in a panic.

"Your bag is here with all your things. Your room is just across the hall when you are finished."

Relief washed over Elaine. At least the woman wasn't planning to stay and attend her bathing. When the door clicked shut, she collapsed onto the settee in the corner. She bent forward, with her face in her hands. What was she going to do?

She couldn't go to Durango now, not knowing Frank's true nature and intentions. She could demand he take her back to Pagosa, but if he realized she knew the truth, she would doubtless lose her freedom. Then there would be no hope of escape. That wouldn't do.

She stood and undressed. For the time being, she needed to play the part of the naïve woman she had been up to this point and not draw attention to herself. Perhaps if she kept calm and maintained the status of guest, she could move about the house enough to investigate and find some evidence of the McBrides' wicked dealings to take back to the sheriff when she got away from here.

But how would she escape? Matthias couldn't come for her. She had lied in her letter and said she was bound for Kansas. She had no hope of rescue.

Gripping the towel hung on a rod next to her, she fought the urge to scream with frustration at this hopeless situation. She had put up so many barriers to keep herself and others safe that now she was truly alone.

Her hands went limp and dropped from the towel. She looked at the haze of heat rising from the tub and suddenly wished for nothing more than to wash away all her fears.

She stripped her clothes and stepped into the tub. In theory, this was the life she had always wanted. A housemaid to do all the cooking and chores for her, a real bathtub in a room dedicated for the purpose, lavender-scented soap, and tea served whenever she wished.

Frank's home in town would be even finer than this—if his offer had ever even been genuine. But now, none of it held any appeal. Anxious pin pricks skittered through her and she rubbed her feet together restlessly under the water. All she could think about was going back to Matthias and her family.

She had been so wrong. Clearly, there was still much she didn't know about them, but she'd never even given them a chance to explain. She'd run away, afraid both of the threat she was to Grace and of losing her heart to an outlaw. None of that seemed to matter now. Love and family were better than being safe.

Chapter 50

Matthias leaned against the livery corral fence. The desire to saddle Copper and find Elaine pulled at him like the lariat was still around his chest, dragging him away from where he knew he needed to be.

He rubbed a hand across the pain in his chest. Sitting around town waiting for a trial date to be set had him fractious as a badger. Everything in him wanted to do something—go after her.

She was long gone by now, and he likely wouldn't be able to find her. Still, the indecision had him feeling like a man being drawn and quartered. Stretched tight between going after the woman he loved and staying behind to pay penance for what he'd done and save the life of his friend.

"I know you want to look for her." Jo spoke from behind him.

He turned, and she stepped up next to him, bracing her arms on the fence rail.

"Shouldn't you be back at the hotel?" Matthias quirked a wry grin in her direction.

"Grace is sleeping." She glanced over her shoulder toward their lodgings.

"Shouldn't you be resting too?"

"I needed the walk. Whenever my mind is heavy, I'm drawn to the horses too." She rested her chin on her folded hands. "I'm not sure if it's that they love us regardless of our failures or if it's the knowledge they could so quickly carry us far away from our problems."

"Maybe it's both." Matthias chuckled.

Jo nodded and clicked her tongue. Copper trotted over, tossing his head. She bent down to pluck a handful of green grass and held it out to him, scratching underneath his forelock with her other hand.

"You can't go after Elaine. Gideon just got word. The trial has been set for two days from now, in Durango."

Matthias scrubbed a hand over his face, both relieved and anxious about what was ahead.

"What if the judge doesn't trust my word, Jo? I'll stand up for Clay, but you and I both know they will bring up the man I killed. What good will my word be then? We might both hang in the end. I deserve that, but Clay doesn't."

"You hush that talk right now." Her knuckles were white where she gripped the fence rail. "What you did—it was no small thing, but Mrs. Harris has forgiven you for that mistake. It's time you forgive yourself."

"How? How can she forgive me? I owe her a debt I can't otherwise pay. Shouldn't a life be given for a life?"

"Matthias, in a different place and time, you and I talked about God. Do you remember? We were both so buried in our own misery then, we couldn't see our way out yet." She grimaced as the shadow of their mutual past crossed her memory. "You told me your grandmother taught you about God, but you weren't sure you believed it all."

Matthias nodded.

"Do you believe it now—believe the Son of God died to pay your debt?"

"I believe it, but I can't say I understand it."

Jo chuckled and slapped a hand against his arm. "I don't reckon any of us can. Even so, our lack of understanding doesn't change things. God is a god of grace and forgiveness. He paid for your crimes. It isn't up to you or me to balance the scales. It *is*, however, up to us to accept grace and walk away from our old life."

It couldn't be that simple. It was too easy.

"Mrs. Harris said she needed to forgive me, so her sins would be forgiven. I don't s'pose someone like her could have anything as bad as I have that needs forgiving."

"It's not about worse or better. Or being more deserving. Christ died to pay the penalty for Mrs. Harris and for you, alike. The kicker is, He also did the same for men like Kane Blake and Darby McBride. None of us are better than the other—not in God's eyes. If he's willing to forgive us for what we've done, we oughta forgive those who've hurt us as well."

That thought struck home like a bullet to the chest. If he was going to accept forgiveness for what he'd done, he would have to forgive men like McBride, Blake, and even Pa. But how could he? If it wasn't for them, Matthias wouldn't have ended up with the life he had. Maybe he'd have had a better chance at life. Bitterness rose to the surface.

"It's too late," Matthias muttered sullenly. "My pa's been in the ground many a year."

"The forgiving isn't for him." Jo shook her head and looked to the sky as if seeking God's help in getting through to him. "It doesn't matter if he's dead and gone. The forgiving is for you, to soften *your* heart." She jabbed his chest on the word "your."

She may as well have stabbed him straight through the heart. He stepped back, a sick feeling in the pit of his stomach.

"I am not soft." He spat the words and fought to blink back the burning behind his eyelids.

"I didn't say you were soft." Jo's brow wrinkled, and she eyed him for a long moment. "I said your heart *needed* to be soft. We can't go to God with a hard heart. Much as it may pain you." Her cheek twitched. "It sure as shootin' pains me every day to humble myself, confess my wrongdoings, and to forgive those who have done me wrong, but I must. And you must as well. He doesn't want us to be hard-hearted."

Matthias pulled off his hat and smoothed a hand over his hair. To be soft was to be weak. How could he let go of his hard shell he'd worked so hard to develop and forgive the man who had beaten the softness right out of him?

"I just don't know if I can do that, Jo. What kind of man would I be if I chose to be weak?" Matthias huffed and stiffened his neck.

Jo turned back to the corral and leaned against the fence. "What kind of man will you be if you don't?"

Chapter 51

"I'll bring tea shortly. Then you will be called for supper this evening," Mrs. Patton told Elaine after escorting her back to her room. With no further ceremony, she turned on her heel to leave, one hand on the doorknob.

"Wait," Elaine called after her. "I should very much like to pass the afternoon with a book. Might I take my tea in the library?" Elaine strengthened her shoulders and raised her chin. She hoped reminding the housekeeper she was a guest, not a prisoner, would allow her more freedom.

Mrs. Patton hesitated for a moment. "As you wish." She gave Elaine a curt nod before disappearing down the hallway.

Elaine released the breath that had supported her and rubbed her forehead. She wasn't sure how she would go about finding evidence or escaping this place, but she hadn't any other option.

Who knoweth whether thou are come to the kingdom for such a time as this ... The scripture came to mind, giving her strength. She wasn't sure how she'd been so foolish to end up here, but just as Esther had, Elaine would use her situation to protect her people.

She walked down the hall to the library. A grandfather clock, ornately carved with a variety of birds, ticked loudly at one end of the room. It was nearly three o'clock. Tea would be served soon. Funny how this house was everything she had thought she wanted, but now all she needed was to get back *home*.

She walked along the wall of books, tapping the spines as she passed, but not seeing the titles. Reading was the farthest thing from her mind.

She glanced back at the clock again. Where was that tea? In truth, she had no desire for tea and a book. It was only an excuse to not be shut up in her room. But she had to wait for Mrs. Patton to see her settled here, in the library, before she could go on about her search of the house.

She slid a volume off the shelf and forced herself to sit in the high wingback chair near the clock. She turned the pages of a book with disinterest. Seemingly from nowhere, Mrs. Patton appeared in front of her with the tea service. How had she done that? Elaine needed to be more alert if she was going to find anything out today.

She thanked Mrs. Patton and lifted the cup to her lips. The strong tea fortified her for her upcoming expedition. When Mrs. Patton was gone, she snapped the book shut.

She crossed to the door and peeked down the hall, hand pressed against her waist, finger tapping as always.

Mrs. Patton's stiff form disappeared around the corner, and Elaine gripped the door jamb.

"Lord, help me," she whispered the prayer and crept down the dim corridor to the office the men had been in earlier.

She paused outside the door, pressing against the wall, and listened. No voices or shuffling of papers came from inside. She dared a glance around the corner. The room was empty.

She breathed a sigh of relief, and went to the desk, flipping through the stacks of papers. She didn't know what she was looking for, exactly, but surely something would prove the man's sinister business tactics.

She rifled through the desk drawers, but there was nothing. Plopping down on the leather chair, she rubbed a hand over her face. She should set this all back to right before the men returned. She reached down to close the lower drawers and realized one drawer didn't appear as deep as the other.

Her mind latched onto the lack of symmetry of the drawer space and her pulse raced in her throat. She'd read about secret compartments before. The words of Edgar Allen Poe echoed in her mind. *"Any man is a dolt who permits a 'secret' to escape him in a search of this kind ... The thing is so plain. There is a certain amount of bulk space to be accounted for in every cabinet."*

She reached to the back of the drawer and fumbled around for a catch. Her fingers landed on a metal lever, hidden from sight. It gave way, and the drawer slid free, revealing a false bottom.

A black, leather-bound book was tucked inside. Her hands shook as she opened it. It was a journal, or a log book.

A gravelly voice rumbled in the hallway, and Elaine froze with panic. There was no way out of here. She darted a glance around the room. A heavy curtain draped one wall. She hastily replaced the false back and shut the drawers. Her heart had gone from a racing flutter to great, pounding drumbeats. The voices were growing closer. Where was she to go? Having no better idea, she threw herself across the room and ducked behind the heavy drapery.

To her surprise, she wasn't pressed up against a wall as she supposed she would be. The curtain hid a long, narrow corridor. A servant's passageway. Her shoulders sagged with relief and she leaned against the wall, pressing the book to her chest. Safely hidden from sight, she listened to the conversation in the office, praying Mrs. Patton didn't come upon her.

"The trial is set for two days from now." Frank's voice spoke up. "We'll need to leave first thing in the morning."

The morning. Elaine's heart thudded so loudly in her chest she thought surely the men could hear it. Tomorrow. If they were leaving tomorrow, what would that mean for her? How could she stop it?

"And what do you mean to do with the girl?"

"Leave her here for now. It's not like she'll be going anywhere. She's about as strong as a butterfly, that one."

Blood rushed in her ears, and she fisted her skirts at her sides. She was tired of being viewed as weak. Besides, one thing she had learned from this backwoods life was that she was the least affected by her difficulties when she was active rather than idle. It was for the best though, that he thought her helpless. The more he underestimated her, the more likely her success.

She would have to find a way to get the logbook to the trial. It was the only way she would be of any help, though she had no inkling if it would be enough or how she would get there.

She flipped open the book and peered at the pages in the meager light from the high, rectangular windows along the top of the wall. Scanning the entries over the last few months, she prayed she'd find an answer. The notes were vague at best. If only there was more evidence.

One entry caught her eye. A date from the previous month, the notation included there read "Ibarra flock eliminated."

Ibarra. Where had she heard that—Miren? Elaine thought back to the men's conversation earlier. Miren was the daughter of the sheep herder Matthias had spoken of. She shut the logbook and clutched it to her chest. Miren was being held captive to keep her father quiet during the trial.

Where was Miren now? Elaine hadn't seen her since their arrival when Frank had played her off to be a new cook. She turned and looked down the servant's passage. Had Frank been forthright when he'd told Mrs. Patton to take her to the kitchen?

She had to find Miren. She glided down the hall, hoping and praying she didn't meet Mrs. Patton along her way. Just as she had expected, the hall opened into a large kitchen. She stayed back, listening for any sign of the housekeeper.

All was quiet. If she were to hide someone, where would she put them? She tucked the logbook into the pocket of her skirt and inspected the kitchen as quickly as possible for another hidden room or passage.

A cellar would be the perfect place to hide a captive. She had seen no stairs to show a lower level or stairway, though. She leaned against the wall and let her head thump back. Smoothing loosened hairs off her brow, she slowed her breathing and her spiraling thoughts.

What would she do if she found the girl? Tension thrummed through her veins, begging for an outlet. It moved through her fingertips as she tapped the brooch and up her arms, spreading throughout her body. Her breath quickened and heart pounded.

She pressed her hands against the wall behind her. Now was not the time to go into a fit. The brooch wasn't helping this time. This was all too much.

Desperate for additional relief, she tapped the toe of her right foot. One, two, three. One, two, three. The boards beneath her feet made a hollow sound. She looked down at her feet and found a handle bolted to the floor underneath her.

The cellar. It was right here. Excitement replaced her anxiety as she gripped the handle and lifted. The door came open, revealing steps that led down to the dark space below the kitchen floor. Miren sat huddled at the bottom of the steps, arms wrapped around her knees, eyes wide.

Footsteps echoed down the hallway as Mrs. Patton approached the kitchen and Elaine scrambled down the steps, closing the door above her head.

The musty scent of earth and over-ripe apples filled her senses. She balanced, crouching on the steps, one hand pressed against the damp rock wall. She pressed a finger over her lips with her other hand, signaling silence from Miren.

Miren nodded.

"I don't care what you think your job is," Mrs. Patton said to someone. "The men are going to need food packed for the road tomorrow and it's gettin' nigh on time for supper. You go on out to the tack shed and fetch the panniers so I can pack them some food for the road."

Dust floated down through the cracks in the plank floor as someone walked overhead. Elaine shivered as the dust trickled down the back of her blouse. The grit of it scraped across her skin, and she scratched ferociously at the maddening itch creeping up her neck.

Miren gave her a wary side-eye, and Elaine prayed for composure. If Miren didn't speak English, Elaine would have to work extra hard to maintain an air of confidence to encourage the girl's trust. She rubbed the dirt off the back of her neck and clenched her fist to still the shaking.

She had to make a plan to steal away with Miren, but how would they escape without being caught? Surely Mr. McBride had men who would track them down in no time.

Elaine waited in silence, seated next to Miren, until Mrs. Patton's footsteps retreated from the kitchen. She grasped Miren's hand and squeezed. "I will come back for you."

How Elaine wished the girl could understand her. She pointed at Miren and folded her hands, pillowing her head on them in a sign for sleep, then held up one finger. One sleep. Then she pressed a hand to her chest, then gripped Miren's hand and pointed toward the cellar steps. Miren nodded slowly, but uncertainty shadowed her features. Elaine prayed God would impress on Miren the need to trust Elaine when she returned.

Chapter 52

Elaine lay on her bed tapping her waist. She was equally exhausted and jittery. It had taken every ounce of strength she'd had to get through the evening meal last night with some sense of decorum.

She had smiled placidly as the men spoke of mundane business, acting as though they didn't have a captive in the cellar and weren't leaving the next day to convince a judge to hang an innocent man.

Instead, Frank had claimed there was urgent business back in Pagosa he and Darby needed attend to before he could take her to Durango. He must think her entirely dimwitted to believe she wouldn't see the situation for what it was now. Knowing now how she'd been duped, though, maybe she had been dimwitted to have trusted a word the man had said.

Morning light streamed in through a gap in the curtain, painting the wall with a broad stroke of orange. The jingle of harness and the thudding of hooves faded from her hearing as the men left for the trial.

How long should she wait? She had claimed a headache this morning when Mrs. Patton come around that morning, and asked to be left alone to rest. She hoped that would buy her some time before her disappearance was discovered.

She tapped her shaky fingers again. She didn't know how she would do what needed done, but she hadn't any choice. She had what may be the only proof of the Lazy M's crimes, and she couldn't sit back and allow the worst to happen.

She rose from the bed and pulled the curtain back. A young ranch hand pushed a cart of hay out to the corral and tossed it over the fence. As far as she could tell, he was the only man left at the ranch just now.

At dinner the previous night, she had gleaned enough from the men's conversation to know the cowboys had taken the cattle to higher ground.

The time to act had come. If she had any hope of avoiding pursuit, she needed to disappear before Mrs. Patton came to check on her.

She made her way silently down the hallway to the office and slipped into the servant's passage. With the McBrides gone, there would be no need for Mrs. Patton to use the passage to and from the office.

When she neared the kitchen, she pressed flat against one wall and listened. All was quiet. Earlier she had caught a glimpse of Mrs. Patton dusting in the parlor, but she didn't know how much time she would have before the housekeeper moved on.

Crossing to the cellar door, she lifted the handle. Miren blinked at the light introduced into the dark cellar.

Elaine extended a hand. "I'm a friend," she whispered.

Miren looked up, straining her neck to peer as far into the kitchen as she could from her corner. Clearly too frightened to trust anyone, she shook her head and hunched her shoulders around her ears.

Elaine pressed a hand against her own chest. "Friend." She held out a hand, resisting the temptation to drag Miren out against her will. "Please, we have to go."

Miren locked her hands together around her knees, squeezing even tighter into herself.

Elaine pressed her lips together. What could she do? She breathed deep and held out a flat palm, walking across it with two fingers in a running motion.

Miren's eyes widened, and the lines of her face softened. Elaine waved a hand toward herself. "Come. We must go."

"Go." Miren repeated the word in an unsure tone. "Utzi?"

She looked past Elaine, and an itch crept up her spine at the thought of Mrs. Patton coming up behind her. She darted a glance over her shoulder. No one was there.

Elaine wasn't sure what "utzi" meant, but by the hope gleaming in Miren's eyes, she thought they had reached an understanding.

Elaine nodded and beckoned again. Miren stood on shaky legs and gripped Elaine's hand. The tremor in Miren's fingers made Elaine wonder if they had fed her at all.

She took a few apples from the counter and handed one to Miren, tucking a few more into the large pocket of her dress. Miren filled her pockets as well.

They exited the back kitchen door and crept to the front of the house, shuffling along the wall, and keeping to the shade. The barn wasn't far. Just across the drive. She was tempted to flee on foot, but Durango was over twenty miles away. They needed horses.

The young ranch hand had gone back into the barn. Elaine scanned the area. How would they take horses without being caught? An axe leaned beside the barn door. It was their only hope. She turned to Miren and pressed a finger over her lips.

Drawing a deep breath, Elaine steadied herself. She pushed away from the house and ran to the barn. She grabbed the barn door and pushed it firmly shut.

"Hey." The ranch hand's muffled voice sounded indignant and confused from inside the barn.

Miren reached the door and leaned against it as well, just in time for the lad's blow against the door from the inside. Both women were knocked forward, but they pushed back, digging their heels into the soft dirt. Elaine reached down with one hand and wrapped her fingers around the axe handle. Quickly, she spun and slid it through the large handles of the barn door, locking it.

The door rattled as he slammed into it again. They needed to get out of here before he managed to break the door down. A few horses milled around the corral, lipping bits of hay from the dirt.

Elaine reached into her pocket and withdrew an apple. Miren nodded, retrieving her own. Shock registered as Elaine remembered the need for a saddle and bridle. She looked back to the rattling door of the barn. Young as the lad was, there was no way they could subdue him. If they opened those doors again, he would come flying out like a wildcat bent on murder.

Miren followed Elaine's gaze and looked back to the horses. She pressed her lips together and shook her head. They would have to ride bareback.

On the front wall of the barn, several ropes for wagon rigging were coiled and hung on pegs. Elaine took a rope for each of them and climbed between the wooden rails of the corral fence. She knotted the rope, as Matthias taught her.

Banging on the barn door and shouting echoed in the clearing. Her hands shook on the rope, but she focused her mind on the task at hand.

She completed the first halter and held the apple out, whistling. Would there be a few cooperative horses they could catch?

A white horse with kind eyes walked forward and took the apple from Elaine's hand. "Thank you, friend." Elaine pressed her face against the horse's neck. She slipped the rope halter over his head and looped the rein over his neck.

She made another halter for Miren, doing her best to block out the racket the boy was making in the barn. Then she girded up her skirt the way Matthias had taught her. Miren raised a dark eyebrow and watched as Elaine stepped back toward the horse's head, gripping its mane, and swung up on its back.

A thrill of exhilaration flooded Elaine's chest. She'd done it. Just as Matthias had taught her. Maybe they would make it away from here after all. After witnessing Elaine's freedom of movement with her make-shift pantaloons, Miren followed suit and tucked her dress up as well.

Then she opened the corral gate, and Elaine rode out. "Leave it open." Elaine reached down to stop Miren from closing the gate.

Perhaps if the other horses escaped the corral, there would be even less chance anyone could pursue them. Miren gave Elaine an understanding smile. She swung up onto her horse and rode a wide arc around the other horses in the corral, driving them all out of the pen. Elaine reined her horse out of the way as the ranch horses scattered into the trees.

Miren rode up next to Elaine and nodded. Elaine nudged her horse with a tap of her heel, and it lunged forward. The sudden motion caught Elaine off guard, and she slipped backward on the horse's sleek coat. She had little control of her horse without a bridle. She grasped at its mane, weaving her fingers into the coarse hair, and gripped tight with her thighs to keep from falling.

Miren rode ahead and pulled her horse to a stop, blocking Elaine's path.

Frustration burned in Elaine's chest. "What are you doing?"

Asking was senseless. How would she communicate her need to get on the road to Durango? Forced to ride bareback, they wouldn't have any chance of overtaking Frank and the McBrides, but she couldn't risk not making it to the trial.

As memory served her, the way they had come from—the road to Durango—was south. She pointed to the road that led south, but Miren shook her head. She sat straight and tall on the chestnut's sleek back and Elaine realized she had underestimated the woman. Miren was no silent partner in this ordeal. Rather, she was quietly confident and, to Elaine's dismay, obstinate. She reached out and turned Elaine's horse by the halter.

Pointing up the hill in the opposite direction, Miren urged her horse forward, leaving Elaine to follow if she would. Her arms prickled, and she gripped the rope tightly in her hand. Should she follow, not knowing where Miren was going? It seemed she had a plan, but Elaine needed to get to Durango.

She hesitated, uncertainty gnawing at her belly. Miren's horse crested the hill behind the ranch house. The time had come to decide. Would she trust this stranger or go off on her own? Miren disappeared over the ridge, and Elaine's mouth went dry with panic.

Praying it was the right decision, she tightened her legs on her horse's sides and followed Miren deeper into the backcountry.

For hours, they weaved through juniper and pinon trees, branches scraping Elaine's cheeks and snagging her hair. The invisible trail Miren followed continued farther and higher into the mountains until the trees changed into aspens and spruce. Her muscles cramped with the effort of clinging to the horse's back. Sweat mingled with dirt and horsehair on her thighs, and the skin on her legs burned with an itchy rash.

The sun had crested its peak and was well into its descent toward the horizon when Miren pulled her horse to a stop at the edge of a ridge. Elaine rode up next to her. Sprawling across a large meadow was a ranch.

Was this Miren's home? Her relief was contagious as she sat tall on her horse, beaming. She nodded toward the house and rode forward. Elaine took a deep breath and followed her down the steep slope toward the house.

Chapter 53

Matthias leaned against a column in front of the General Palmer hotel, waiting for Gideon to arrive with the wagon. He pulled the brim of his hat low to block the rays from the rising sun that crested the hill in front of him.

He hadn't slept at all, and the bright summer morning assaulted him with its demanding presence. This was the day that had haunted him for weeks. The day of reckoning. Despite Mrs. Harris's assurance she'd stand behind him, he couldn't be sure a jury would be as forgiving. It was likely he would be no help at all. What kind of witness could he be when he was a murderer himself?

It was time he made things right with God because this may well be the last sunrise he would see. But if settling things with his Maker meant forgiving his Pa, that was something he couldn't do.

"I can't do it," he muttered to himself, rubbing his brow.

Jo adjusted her hold on Grace and handed her to Mary. Then rising from the bench, she walked over to stand next to him, her back to the other women.

"No one is making you do this, Matthias." Jo wrapped her arms around her waist and eyed him directly. "But if you don't, Clay will likely hang." She mouthed the last words in

336

a whisper, darting a quick glance over her shoulder in Florence's direction.

Matthias sighed and turned his back to the sun before removing his hat and smoothing a hand over his hair.

"You are a good man." Jo emphasized the words with a finger to his chest.

Hadn't he had this conversation with Elaine once? He wasn't a good man. Though he'd tried to be. No matter how hard he tried, he always failed.

"I need to stretch my legs." Matthias pushed away from the railing. I think I'll go walk for a spell down by the river.

Jo's troubled eyes narrowed.

"I'll catch up," he assured her. "You all go on without me. I'll get Copper from the livery when I'm done and meet you at the courthouse."

Jo gripped his sleeve. "You want company?"

"No. I need to be on my own just now. Thanks." He pulled his hat down tight onto his brow and turned west, crossing the railroad tracks and walking down the gradual slope that led to the Animas River.

Pain radiated in his shoulder from the bullet wound, and he rubbed the heel of his hand against the spot. Though he was ashamed to admit it, a small part of him wasn't sure he wanted to go through with this.

It was the right thing, he knew that. Clay had been one of the few friends he had in all his years of wandering. But why did this lot fall to Matthias? Why risk his life to help when no good had ever come from anything he'd ever tried to do?

He picked up a rock at the edge of the swiftly flowing river and ran a thumb over the smooth surface.

He would testify. Of course, he would.

The real battle in his mind was whether he could bring himself to forgive the man who caused him to be here in the first place. How could he bring himself to not hold the man responsible who had beaten him near daily, hated him for being weak—who forced his hand into killing his own pa to protect his mother's life?

It wasn't Matthias's fault he ended up with the Blake Gang; it wasn't his fault he'd gotten mixed up with the McBrides even. At the bottom of it all was the man who should have loved him—should have protected him.

He gripped the rock tight in his fist and hurled it into the churning water. He'd hoped coming to here would calm his mind, but the river was still high from runoff and the roiling, muddy water mirrored the turmoil in his soul.

"Well, look who it is." A nasal voice spoke over Matthias's shoulder, and a chill ripped through him.

He spun around just in time to glimpse Jasper wielding a tree branch behind him. He shied to one side, but the branch connected and pain exploded his vision with white before he was plunged into the frigid water.

He surfaced briefly and gasped for air before an unseen force tugged at his boots and dragged him under. The swift undercurrent held him beneath the water tumbling him this way and that. It swept him down the river, slamming him into rocks under the surface as the rapids tossed him around like a rag doll. The force of the violent torrent disoriented him entirely. He had no bearings to guide him to resurface.

His lungs burned, screaming for air. Panic squeezed his chest tight as the desire to gasp for air battled reason. Heeding the driving need to inhale would fill his lungs with water.

His heel struck bottom, and he shoved against the gravel with his bare foot. The momentum brought him to the surface. He gasped for air, sucking in a greedy breath before being pulled back down again.

He fought to find the base again, but the current rolled him, and his head slammed into a rock. His vision shattered into bright white stars—pinpoints of pain—before closing in with darkness.

Chapter 54

Elaine fisted her skirt in her hands as the wagon rumbled down the street, approaching the courthouse. Her nerves were on fire from the anticipation of getting to the courthouse in time for the trial. Miren reached out and grasped her hand, squeezing.

Mr. Ibarra looked over with a sympathetic smile. "Do not worry." He nodded confidently.

Elaine was exceedingly grateful Miren's father spoke some English. After many tears and hugs, Miren had introduced Elaine to her parents. Then a flurry of a language like nothing Elaine had heard before ensued as Miren explained the circumstances of their escape. The language was Euskara, Miren's father had explained to Elaine. The family were Basque immigrants.

Mrs. Ibarra had fed the girls lamb stew and crusty bread spread with sheep's cheese, while Mr. Ibarra asked Elaine questions about the McBrides and what her connection had been to them.

While they spoke, Mr. Ibarra sent Miren's brother out to hitch the wagon. Elaine hadn't known exactly when the trial was supposed to take place. She only knew the men said it would be the following day. After the meal, Mr. Ibarra,

Elaine, and Miren had loaded up in the wagon and set out for Durango, traveling through the night.

Now, he pulled the wagon to a stop in front of a large courthouse with a towering clock, and Elaine's stomach twisted. Had they made it in time?

Mr. Ibarra dismounted and held out his hand to assist them down, speaking rapidly in the native tongue to his daughter, and then turned to Elaine.

"You go inside. I follow."

Elaine's effort to draw a deep breath failed, and the clock tower seemed to tilt in front of her. She gripped the wagon bed for support. Would she even be of any help? She hoped so but couldn't be sure. The ledger tucked into her pocket only had vague notes that *might* support the Ibarra's account of their dealings with the Lazy M. It wasn't a detailed journal or confessional by any means.

She reached for the pin, but Miren took Elaine's hand and tugged. Miren's firm grip absorbed Elaine's compulsion, and together, they turned to face the unknown. She may not know if what she had was enough to be of help, but what she did know was Matthias would be inside. No matter the precarious circumstances, having him nearby would give her the strength she so desperately needed.

She straightened to her full height and raised her chin. She would not let fear control her any longer. Too much was at stake.

They mounted the courthouse steps as the tower clock chimed nine o'clock. Inside, the tension was palpable. Frank and the McBrides conversed at a table at the front of the courtroom. Gideon, Jo, and Florence were in the front row of chairs behind the partition.

Elaine scanned the room again. Matthias wasn't with them. Upon Elaine's entrance, Jo froze, blinking back at her.

"Elaine?" Jo's voice carried across the courtroom.

Frank's head whipped around, and his face drained of all color. Darby McBride, whose face, in contrast, turned a mottled red and purple color, gripped Frank's arm and jerked him close, whispering in Frank's ear.

Jo passed Grace off to Florence and came to meet Elaine in the back of the room.

"What in the Sam Hill are you doing here?" Jo clutched Elaine in a bear hug that brought tears to the surface.

"It's a long story—I—I came to help." Elaine's heart pounded, and she gripped her skirt as she strove to ignore the attention of Frank and the McBrides.

"Where is Matthias?" She searched the room again.

Jo's shoulders sagged. "We don't know."

"What do you mean you don't know? Didn't he come with you?"

"He did, but he's been right agitated these past couple of days. I think he may have left," Jo said, wrapping her arms around her waist.

"He wouldn't do that." Elaine's voice came out hollow and shaky.

She had been wrong to distrust him despite the doubt Frank had stirred up in her. She refused to doubt him any longer. He wasn't the man Frank had said he was. He wouldn't abandon Clay at this moment.

"Well, this morning he said he wasn't sure he could go through with it, and he left for a walk. He was supposed to meet us here, but we haven't seen hide nor hair of him since." Strain tightened Jo's mouth.

A sinking feeling dragged at Elaine's heart. It couldn't be. Could it? Had she shaken his resolve, leaving the way she did?

The door to the courtroom opened, and Elaine whipped around, holding in a hopeful breath. The air fizzled out of her when she saw it was only Mr. Ibarra, not Matthias.

She sighed. Matthias may be missing, but Mr. Ibarra's presence reinforced her resolve for optimism. Even if Clay didn't have a witness, she and Mr. Ibarra could stand against Mr. McBride.

"Wait," Jo looked from Miren at Elaine's side to Mr. Ibarra. "You said you came to help? What is it?"

The sharp rap of the gavel snapped everyone's attention to the front of the room.

"Order." The judge's voice boomed across the large room. "Take your seats."

A bailiff escorted Clay to a table, hands bound in front of him, and Gideon moved up to sit next to him.

"Clay's lawyer never made it either. We have no one to speak for him," Jo whispered as they sat down.

"Quiet." The bailiff raised his voice to be heard above the din. "Judge Spencer wishes to address the court before we proceed."

Silence settled over the room, blanketing the underlying hum of tension.

"Before we bring a jury out here, I have a few things to say." The judge was younger than Elaine had expected, perhaps in his forties, with a groomed, handlebar mustache and neatly combed hair.

He sat straight and tall behind the bench and possessed a stern look that made the knot in Elaine's stomach tighten. She hadn't spoken to anyone about the information she and the Ibarras had brought. How would she go about bringing it forward?

Elaine glanced around their party. They were a motley crew compared to Frank and the McBrides, who all wore respectable suits and ties.

Gideon, a mountain man, who had never looked civilized a day in his life, sat next to Clay—clearly part Ute, with the dark complexion of his grandmother showing through his sun-baked skin. Florence's even darker coloring also stood out, contrasting boldly with her silvery hair. Jo's ragged scar split her face, which presently held an expression of fury on the brink of breaking over.

Matthias, who would have been the one respectable-looking man in their party—even if a cowboy—was nowhere to be found. It was up to Elaine, a mere woman, and the Ibarras, Basque migrants who barely spoke English, to interrupt the court proceedings as witnesses.

If Judge Spencer was as closed-minded as some, prejudice could easily hinder any attempt they had at proving the truth.

The judge continued his speech, "This hearing is unorthodox, to say the least, and frankly an insult to my office. For whatever reason, the governor's office has declared this case urgent and has pushed it ahead of my others. That being said, before we even begin these proceedings, I expect to get down to business and see no one is wasting mine or this jury's time."

Elaine breathed a small sigh of relief. Clearly, this judge was none too pleased to have his court manipulated. Perhaps he would see this for the ruse it was.

"It is my understanding your witness has decided not to bother showing up." Judge Spencer scowled down at Clay from his bench.

Clay cleared his throat and pushed the hair back from his face. "No, sir."

Elaine knew she should speak up, but the tall, grim judge looking down from his bench and the baleful glare Frank shot her, froze her in place.

She reached to her waist, but the brooch wasn't there. She ran her hand over the front of her dress, frantic. She must have lost the brooch somewhere in her escape from the ranch. Pain radiated through her arm, an electric current pulsing through her with the need to satisfy the compulsion. Her hand shook, and she breathed in shallow panting breaths, spots forming in her vision.

For such a time as this. The words came to mind like a gentle whisper. She shook her head and closed her eyes. *Speak.* The whisper grew firmer. Clear and distinct. But how could she?

Without the brooch, or Matthias, how could she face this crowd and the intimidation of the judge, glaring down at them?

The shaking in her hands became more pronounced. She wasn't even sure she could form coherent words, much less address a judge in court without proving herself to be a hysteric.

Gideon shifted to rise, but something unexpected came over Elaine. A confidence settled in her bones. With Matthias gone, she was Clay's only hope.

"Your honor." Elaine stood and raised her voice. Her hands still shook violently, but she pressed on. "Mr. Anderson's witness is not here, but I am here with proof the accusations about him are false. Mr. Darby McBride is the criminal here." She relaxed a little and drew a full breath.

"As am I." Another woman spoke up from behind Elaine.

She spun around to see who had spoken. She didn't recognize the mousy, brown haired woman at the back of the room.

"And who, might I ask, are you?" Judge Spencer asked, pulling Elaine's attention back to him.

Elaine realized his leveled stare was directed at her.

"My name is Miss Elaine Bradford, and this is Mr. Jon Ibarra." She motioned beside her.

The judge nodded once, then turned his gaze to the back of the room.

"Mrs. Simon Harris, Your Honor." Mrs. Harris bobbed a curtsy, and Elaine smiled at the woman's confidence. "Mr. McBride stole our cattle."

Frank jumped to his feet and slammed a hand on the table. "This is preposterous. Mr. McBride is not the accused here. Mr. Anderson is."

Judge Spencer tugged at his mustache and leaned back in his chair, the wooden frame squeaking under his muscular weight. "And where is your husband, Mrs. Harris?"

Mrs. Harris bit her lip and darted a glance at Gideon. "He was killed, your honor, while attempting to retrieve the stolen cattle."

"As a matter of fact," Frank straightened his tie, "Mrs. Harris's husband was killed by the witness *this* rabble planned to bring to your court today."

"The witness who isn't here?"

"Well, no, your honor, he isn't, but—"

Mr. Ibarra stood then, leaning his weight on the polished brass head of his cane. "I also speak against Mr. McBride. He sent his men to slaughter my sheep."

The judge's bushy eyebrows rose.

"I object." Frank shouted.

"Pipe down, Mr. Dashel." Judge Spencer's voice boomed across the courtroom. "We're not in session yet. I have my own suspicions about what's going on here, and I'll get to the bottom of it. As I understand it, Mr. Anderson is accused of murdering one of your men, Mr. McBride. Is this correct?"

"It is." McBride's gritty tone was filled with hate.

"Over a matter of grazing?"

"That's right. Gideon Cross's men attacked my hands for simply scouting out new grazing territory."

"We did no such thing." Clay jumped up, and Gideon put a hand on his arm. Clay tempered his tone. "They attacked us."

"They poisoned our sheep, Your Honor." Gideon stood next to Clay. "And when we tried to move the sheep to higher ground and fresh water, they attacked my men. It was nothing more than self-defense."

The judge leaned forward and muttered to his bailiff, "This isn't a court hearing, it's a schoolyard squabble." He narrowed an eye at Frank and the McBrides. "A matter of sheep, was it?"

"A matter of grazing, Your Honor." Frank strove for self-possession.

Judge Spencer turned back to Mr. Ibarra then, and relief washed over Elaine. The judge saw it, the pattern of violence. "Mr. Ibarra, you claim Mr. McBride killed your sheep?"

"His men did. They killed one of my shepherds and threatened to kill my daughter if I told anyone what they had done." His voice wavered, and he put a hand on his daughter's shoulder. "He took her to keep me quiet."

"And yet you are here ... as is she?"

"Yes. Miss Bradford—she set my daughter free."

Judge Spencer looked from Miren to Elaine, and then back at Mrs. Harris. He sighed and rubbed his forehead. "Does anyone have evidence of this, or are we going to be basing this trial solely on accusations and circumstantial evidence?"

"I have something, Your Honor." Elaine stepped forward, the ledger clutched in her hand.

Fury darkened Darby McBride's face, and Frank blinked stupidly. The judge waved Elaine forward and held out his hand for the book. She had already marked the pages referencing the Ibarra flock and the Harris cattle that had been "acquired" and sold a week prior to the incident with the Ibarra's.

He scanned the ledger and then looked up—his heated gaze bouncing between the parties gathered. Slamming the book shut, he leaned forward, forearms braced against the bench. He directed his attention to the McBrides' table.

"Frankly, Mr. Dashel, I don't see that your client has a leg to stand on."

A collective release of tension filtered through the Cross party and witnesses.

"By the looks of it, your client is the only criminal here." He tapped the black book. "However, I refuse to operate my courtroom like a backwoods barbershop. We've got to have some order."

At that moment, the courthouse door opened, and light poured into the aisle. A man was silhouetted against the morning sun, hunched over and shoulders heaving. He stumbled forward into view.

Elaine's breath caught. It was Matthias—hatless and soaking wet. His dark hair was plastered to his forehead and blood ran down his face from an open wound on his head.

Elaine's heart nearly exploded with the relief and excitement. What on earth had happened to him? She ran to him and tucked herself under his arm, supporting him as he wavered on his feet.

"What now?" The judge groaned.

Matthias limped forward, and Elaine looked down, noticing he was missing his boots in addition to his hat.

"And just who are you?" Judge Spencer looked as though he was afraid to ask.

"My name is Matthias Noble, Your Honor. I'm here to stand witness against Shane and Darby McBride.

"Neither Mr. McBride, nor his son, is on trial." The judge sounded exasperated.

"Then to stand witness for Mr. Anderson." Matthias heaved a breath, holding his side.

"And what, might I ask, happened to you?" A muscle twitched beside the judge's eye.

"One of McBride's men"—he pointed a finger at the lanky cowboy sitting behind Frank—"clubbed me on the head and tossed me in the Animas." Matthias wavered on his feet.

He was pale as a ghost and looked as though he may be sick at any moment.

The judge leaned to the side and spoke privately to his bailiff, who exited the courtroom at a brisk walk.

"Is this your witness?" the judge asked Clay.

Clay blinked. "Yes sir, it is."

Judge Spencer shook his head before bringing the gavel down with a crack that Elaine thought may well have splintered the wooden bench.

He thundered, "I'm declaring this circus a mistrial." Then he leaned forward, directing the next statement to Darby McBride. "The next time you want to bribe your way into my courtroom, think again."

Chapter 55

Matthias sagged with relief, and Elaine strained under his bulk. He forced himself to stand straight again.

"I'm sorry," he whispered into the top of her hair.

Her soft brown curls tickled his lips, and he wished he could pillow his weary head against her and sleep.

"Nonsense," she said as she helped him over to a chair that creaked as he sat down. She took his hands in hers and squeezed. He closed his eyes, absorbing the warmth of her.

Across the courtroom, McBride slapped his son on the back of his head. "Get the horses, you idiot."

Shane cowed and rubbed the spot his father hit. "Pa, I tried. I sent Jasper—"

"I oughta drown both of you in the river. Useless fools." McBride's hoarse voice grated over Matthias's nerves.

Shane and Jasper stomped from the courtroom, muttering blame at one another and eyeing Matthias with malevolence as they passed.

Elaine ran soft fingertips over Matthias's forehead. "You're bleeding badly. We should find a doctor." She grimaced but raised her chin in a show of strength.

"You don't want to stitch me up again?" he asked, raising an eyebrow and wincing at the motion.

"I'd rather not." She sighed and kissed his knuckles. "I may be capable, but I'd prefer to leave it to someone else in future."

"Let's get on the move." Gideon clapped Matthias on the shoulder and bent down to speak in a low tone. "The judge may have dropped the charges against Clay, but it ain't over for *them*." He nodded toward McBride and Frank in a heated debate.

Matthias nodded and immediately regretted the gesture. His head throbbed with sharp pain and his stomach rolled. Thankfully, he'd had no appetite that morning and had nothing to retch.

He leaned heavily on the chair in front of him as he stood, then hobbled to the door and down the courthouse steps. Elaine kept close to his side. None of the pain mattered with her beside him.

Outside, the Cross family gathered in front of the courthouse, discussing arrangements for returning to the homestead. Elaine stepped away for a moment to speak to an older man and dark-haired young woman Matthias didn't recognize. Clay wrapped his arms around his grandmother, who clung to his waist and murmured something to him in Ute, shaking.

Was it truly over? How had it been so easy? It was barely ten o'clock. He wasn't sure what had happened in that courtroom. He'd have a lot of questions when his head didn't feel like a blacksmith's anvil.

Elaine looked over the shoulder of the young woman she spoke to, and met Matthias's eye. Pink blush bloomed on her fair cheeks, and one corner of her mouth lifted. His pulse quickened, and his knees weakened.

Then an odd expression replaced the coy smile. Her eyes snapped wide, and she opened her mouth, but no sound escaped. The cold barrel of a pistol pressed against the back of Matthias's neck.

"I will not be made a fool of again." A gravelly voice spoke over his shoulder, and the overpowering stench of cigar smoke filled Matthias's senses. "I'm sick a you mutton busters overrunning my territory."

Matthias's stomach dropped to his wet socks. He had no pistol, no means of defense. He was utterly helpless.

Darby's voice rasped over Matthias's shoulder. "You come with us quietly, or the lady will be the next one to take a swim."

Matthias's focus shifted to Elaine. Shane stood behind her, a vacant expression on his face as though he had no mind of his own. Matthias recognized the dangerous subservience. Shane would do whatever his father commanded, without thought for himself or anyone else.

Panic gripped Matthias like a noose. No one else seemed to notice what was happening yet. Shane hovered menacingly behind Elaine, as a warning. All Matthias had to do was step away quietly with the old man, and Elaine would be spared.

"Darby McBride." Another voice boomed from the courthouse steps.

McBride clutched Matthias's arm, jerking him around to face the direction the voice had come from.

A man wearing a marshal's badge stepped forward, pistol aimed over Matthias's shoulder. "You are under arrest," the man finished coolly.

To Matthias's surprise, the cold steel against his skin dropped away as Darby lowered his weapon. Typical of men like him who sent others to do their bidding, he was a coward. The marshal lowered his weapon and stepped forward to put McBride into manacles.

"Do something, you cowards." McBride spat the words in Shane and Jasper's direction.

Jasper pulled a pistol, and the crack of a gunshot rang out. He dropped to his knees, then crumpled to the ground. Another marshal holding a smoking pistol walked over and stood guard next to the first.

"Shane!" McBride rasped.

Shane grabbed Elaine with an arm against her throat and dragged her back, pointing a gun at the marshals. A woman in the crowd screamed and people scattered.

"Put the gun down, son," the marshal shouted at Shane.

"Not until you let my pa go." Shane turned the gun on Elaine and pressed the barrel to her temple.

Tears welled on her lashes, and her whimper tore through Matthias. Had he come this far just to lose her for good?

Matthias looked down at his empty hands. He had nothing to fight with, but he wouldn't stand idly by while this sniveling wretch threatened to take everything from him. He stepped forward, sensing Gideon's bulk at his flank.

"Stay back." Shane's voice cracked, and his pistol shook violently.

God, help her, Matthias prayed in desperation. Matthias held out a hand behind him, motioning Gideon to be still. Shane was completely unhinged. If his trembling finger even twitched, he could kill Elaine without even meaning to.

"You weakling. Shoot the woman and show them you mean business." McBride's words to his son seared Matthias's conscience like a hot iron. It was what Pa would have said to him.

That was when he finally saw it. The deranged look in Shane's eyes—it was desperation—fear. Fear of his father.

The old man's bitterness had poisoned and paralyzed his son. He had been raised by an evil man. No doubt Darby had beaten Shane down until blind obedience was all he knew. It was no wonder he ended up who he was. What example had he been raised with?

At that moment, Matthias wanted nothing more than for Shane to be free of the cruelty he had known all his life. Matthias stepped forward again, this time with hands raised.

"Don't do this." He kept his voice low and calm, finding a careful, soothing tone. "I can help you."

"I don't need your help," Shane sneered and his voice took on the same grating tone of his father's.

"Put the gun down before you hurt her. Don't let him drag you down with him." Matthias took another step, moving to block Shane's line of sight to his father.

Shane's hand relaxed slightly, and his throat bobbed as he swallowed hard.

"I'll speak up for you, if you just let her go." Matthias held out an upturned hand. "I'll do my best to talk to the marshals for you, Shane, but you have to choose to let her go.

Prove to them—prove to yourself that you don't want this kind of life anymore." He took another step and Shane stiffened, tightening his grip on the gun.

Matthias stopped and waited.

"Don't you listen to him, you twit," McBride hissed behind Matthias.

Shane's eyes bounced frantically between Matthias and the marshals. Matthias bent his fingers in a silent entreaty for him to give up the pistol. He kept eye contact with Shane, refusing to allow himself to look at Elaine. He couldn't afford to break the connection.

Shane blew out a hard breath and dropped the gun into Matthias's waiting hand. He released Elaine, and she crossed to Matthias's side, burying her face into his shoulder. The marshals swooped in to put Shane in irons.

Matthias pitied the man. He had likely never been shown anything other than violence. Why wouldn't he have followed the same path?

As the sheriff's deputies put Shane into manacles, Matthias wrapped both arms around Elaine and held her tight. Jo passed Grace off to Gideon and rushed over to her sister.

Matthias relinquished his hold on Elaine and allowed Jo to take his place. He heaved a heavy breath as he watched as father and son were led down the street toward the Marshal's office. Matthias would keep his word and do what he could for Shane. He'd been conditioned and threatened into the criminal he'd become.

Matthias turned and watched as Gideon cradled Grace in his bearlike arms and crooned sweet endearments to her.

She was blessed with a good father. Shane hadn't been so lucky.

What about his own pa? Had he learned his cruel ways from a father who beat and belittled him as well?

If Matthias could find forgiveness for Shane, maybe it was time he forgave his own pa too. He couldn't hold on to the hate and bitterness any longer. It was time to make a difference, to change the pattern for future generations. He wanted to hold his own child in his arms and love his wife the way a woman should be loved.

Jo and Elaine stepped apart, wiping their eyes, and Jo squeezed Elaine's hand before holding it out to Matthias. He squeezed her hand tight. He had no plans of ever letting go again.

So much had happened, and the blow he'd taken to the head left him nauseated. The noise and press of people around them only added to the discomfort.

He closed his eyes. "Walk with me?"

Elaine nodded, falling into step with him as they stepped away from the bustle of the crowded street. They found a shady spot around the side of the building away from the throng. He had some things to say to Elaine, and he didn't want the distraction of onlookers.

She brushed light fingertips across his forehead near the aching wound. "Does it hurt much?"

Matthias shrugged. "Not as much as losing you again would." He pressed a hand to her back and pulled her closer. "Don't leave," he whispered. "Don't go back to Kansas. I'll do whatever you need to feel safe. I'll find a job in town. I'll build you the finest house, and you'll never have to gather eggs again. Just don't go."

She snorted a laugh and leaned in. "I don't want any of that." She moved her face back and forth, nuzzling his nose with hers. "I only want you."

His heart soared, and he bent, capturing her lips with his own. Her mouth was warm and welcoming, and she relaxed into his arms. He took his time, relishing the moment. Her smooth fingertips grazed his neck and sent a shiver up his spine.

He pulled back and brushed her cheek with his hand. "Marry me, Elaine. Marry me, and I will always keep you safe." His voice came out husky and hollow.

"I don't need to be safe." She looked up at him with more confidence and peace than he'd ever seen from her. "I only need you."

Her hands slid down to his shoulders then and gripped his arms tight. She leaned closer and lifted on her tiptoes. She kissed him again—firm and sure—and he fed off her steadiness. After a long moment, she pulled away again.

"Now," she said, pressing her cheek against his chest and wrapping her arms behind his back. "Take me home."

Chapter 56

J o grinned at her sister through their combined reflection in the mirror as she pinned the last of Elaine's hair into place. "Are you ready for this?"

Elaine pressed a hand to her stomach and took a deep breath. "I've never been more ready for anything." She blushed prettily. "Do I look ready?"

"You look radiant, sister." Jo beamed, thinking of a moment like this they had shared half a lifetime ago, before a barn dance.

Jo hadn't understood Elaine back then. If only she had known what her sister had gone through—the fear that had shadowed her for all those years. It was no wonder there had been a rift between them.

Elaine had been jealous of Jo's freedom and, whether or not Jo had wanted to admit it, Elaine's seemingly effortless femininity was something Jo would never have, so she had mocked and shunned it.

"Elaine, I'm so sorry." Jo propped her hands on her hips and stared at the floor. "I'm sorry for all the years we spent at odds. And I'm sorry I kept my past from you. I always saw you as the perfect one and, frankly, I feared you would turn your back on me."

Elaine rose from her seat then and brushed Jo's cheek with a gloved hand. "I'm sorry too. I suppose I did judge you at first, but not for the brothel—the life you were forced into. It was more that I was hurt you didn't trust me enough to tell me. That you saw me as an outsider."

"I suppose it was *me* that judged *you*." Jo shrugged one shoulder.

"I'm sorry too. I just envied you so much."

Jo swiped a hand under her nose. "We were a pair of fools, weren't we?"

"I suppose we were." Elaine pressed her lips together and shrugged.

"Well, I reckon I ought to make it clear here and now I'm glad you are staying. You aren't an outsider, and I'm grateful you've found your place here with us and not in some stuffy sitting room, sipping tea."

Elaine chuckled. "Well, I'm not sure I wouldn't mind an afternoon teatime."

"Well, maybe that's a habit we can adapt to. Though if you want the menfolk to join in, you might have to compromise with coffee instead."

Raindrops pattered on the tin roof, and Elaine sighed, moving to the window. "It's bad luck to have rain on your wedding day." She pressed her lips together and lifted the curtain to peer outside.

"Phooey." Jo waved a hand, dismissing the old adage. "If it's raining today, it must be good luck, not bad. Because nothing could dampen this moment."

There was a soft knock at the door, and Jo gripped Elaine's hand, squeezing tight. Mary poked her head through the door. "Are you ready? I think if you don't hurry, Matthias is liable to wear a rut through the boards of Pastor Tom's porch."

ELAINE STEPPED OUT onto the covered deck of the pastor's house. She had no bouquet to carry, but climbing purple clematis covered the lattice that stretched the length of the porch. Soft summer rain drizzled behind the curtain of blooms, and the cool air was damp and fragrant with the floral essence surrounding her. This June bride may not have sunshine on her wedding day, but at least she had flowers.

Jo kissed Elaine's cheek and disappeared around the corner of the wraparound decking. Elaine clutched her skirt, and the rough texture of the lace grounded her into the here and now.

She drew a deep breath through her nose and stepped around the corner of the house where Matthias waited with the pastor. He was clean shaven and wore a crisp, white shirt under a silver vest. His dark hair was neatly combed, and he clasped his hands in front of him, knuckles white. He raised his eyes from his knotted fingers, and the smile that lit his face pushed all the clouds away.

She floated to his side without taking much notice of her family and friends clustered on the porch or the drizzling of rain that found its way through the tin on the porch roof and soaked the puffed sleeves of her wedding gown.

Matthias took her hand, tucking it into the crook of his arm. His presence beside her was strong and reassuring. Her life would be far from what she had planned. She wasn't going to spend her days sipping tea on an overstuffed sofa and making polite conversation. Life would be hard, and she would have to get her hands dirty. But she could do hard things. She knew that now.

They faced one another, and he took both her hands while the pastor spoke of two people becoming one flesh. Elaine looked down at their fingers, intertwined so they were nearly indistinguishable. Her burdens would become his, and his would become hers. They would bear them together, through sickness and health, through the good and the bad, forsaking all others, until death parted them.

Her cold fingers trembled at the thought of being parted from him, and a tear dropped onto their joined hands. Matthias reached up without letting go and lifted a tear from her cheek. His own eyes shone with emotion.

She no longer feared what others would do if they found out about her infirmity. Because he would be with her through it all. They would share their trials, grief, pain, joy, and blessings, because it was the two of them now. And what God had brought together, no man could tear apart.

"You may kiss your bride now, son." The pastor leaned forward and nudged Matthias's arm.

Matthias's mouth tucked up in a small smile. He held her gaze as he moved in slowly and embraced her. His kiss was soft but firm, and his hands tightened on her waist. The pressure of his lips against hers promised his protection and faithfulness.

She didn't care who was looking on. She circled his neck with her arms and leaned into him with promises of her own. To love him unconditionally and trust him.

Love wasn't blind. She wouldn't be able to forget what she knew of his past, but neither would she hold it against him. It was part of who he was, and she would love all of him, even the parts he wasn't proud of.

Chapter 57

Matthias helped his new bride out of the shepherd's wagon. Her bare leg peeked out from under her dressing gown, sending his heart racing. She hesitated as she set her slipper clad foot down on the grass.

He tugged on her fingertips. "Come on, you have to trust me."

"I certainly don't *have* to do anything." She slipped her fingers from his grasp and crossed her arms.

"I reckon you're right about that." He leaned close. "*Please* trust me, then?" He whispered the last words against her neck in that spot he knew would make her putty in his hands.

She sighed and moved forward with ginger steps. "I don't understand. Why am I outdoors in my dressing gown? And without proper shoes no less?"

"You'll see, Love." He took his time guiding her to the stream's edge, matching her tentative pace.

It had been a miracle she'd even agreed to this unorthodox honeymoon in the mountains. This next surprise, though, might take her too far from her area of comfort. He needed to go slow.

"I want to share something with you." He unbuttoned his union suit and dropped it to the ground.

She made a small squeaking noise and jerked her eyes to the sky. A pink flush filled her cheeks.

"Now, take off that frilly thing you're wearing, and come join me."

"What?" Her voice came out shrill, sounding both affronted and amused.

She stepped back, and Matthias grasped her gown by the tie, lifting his eyebrow in a playful challenge. She was caught now. If she tried to run away, she could be stripped to her skin, anyway. Of course, he wouldn't go through with the teasing threat if she truly bolted.

He rubbed a hand over his mouth to cover the laugh that threatened to erupt. "El, you've seen it all before. There isn't anything to be shocked by. Besides, we are only going to enjoy a blissful soak in these hot springs and watch the sunset."

"But out here? In the open?" She pressed a hand over her chest, eyes wide and fixed on his.

"There isn't a soul within ten miles except your husband." He leaned in and grazed her lips with a tender kiss. "I'll get in first, if that will make you feel better." He let go of her gown's tie and lowered into the water.

She bunched her lips. "But, isn't it dirty?"

"The rocks are smooth. Not gritty at all, and the water is fresh from a spring, see?" He dipped his hands under the surface and came up with crystal clear water pooled between his palms. "This will be the finest bathing experience you've had in months. I promise."

She hesitated, hand pressed against her stomach, and tapped. Even with her talisman lost, the habit was still there.

"Will you try it? If it's too much for you, we'll get right out and go back to our cocoon in the wagon." He winked, and she flushed again.

She sighed and pressed her lips together. Slowly, she dipped a toe, jerking it back quickly. "It's hot!"

"Well, yes. That'd be why they call it a hot spring. But it won't hurt you; it's no hotter than fresh bathwater."

She tested it out again, then submerged her whole foot. A contented sigh escaped her lips. She stepped into the shallow edge and paused, her hands on the tie of her dressing gown. The heavy, damp air rising from the pool stilled in Matthias's chest.

She chewed the corner of her bottom lip, finger tapping on the tie of her wrap.

"I'll close my eyes while you get in." Matthias winked and gave her a reassuring smile.

He covered his eyes with one hand, resisting the temptation to peek. The water rippled around him as she lowered herself into the pool.

She gasped and breathed out a quiet, "Oh."

Matthias lowered his hand. Lazy heat trails rose between them, and sunlight flickered over the surface of the water. Elaine was submerged to her collarbones, and her soft brown hair floated in the water around her.

A cedar branch hung low, creating a screen between them. He wanted to swim around the separation and take her in his arms, but he didn't want to push her. It was best to give her time. They had only been married a few days, after all.

She stretched her legs out, sliding her toes over his, and he sucked in a breath of hazy air. A grin tugged at the corner of her lips, and she swam closer, sitting on the rock next to him.

He wrapped his arms around her waist and pulled her closer. "Are you happy, wife?"

A pink flush crept up her neck and into her face. She dipped warm water into her hands and splashed it over her face.

"Very." She wrapped her arms around his neck, nestling her face into the bare skin of his chest.

"I know this isn't the life you planned on. Certainly not the honeymoon I reckon you thought you'd have one day. A shepherd's wagon in the high country and hot springs for a bath isn't exactly high society."

She pulled back and searched his face, running her fingers through his hair. "Society was never what I wanted—well, not what I needed, anyway. What I really wanted was to feel safe. And I've never felt safer in my life than when I'm in your arms." She pressed her lips to his. They tasted like sweat and the mineral-rich water from the pool.

"If I had found a place to live in town, I never would have known the beauty you've shown me. I never would have experienced what it's like to sit under the stars and listen to beautiful music or to wake to the sound of birds singing outside the canvas wagon cover. I lived my life hidden away from the wonder of God's creation and the freedom trusting Him could give. You did that for me. You gave me that gift in a way no one else ever could have." Her fingers curled against his neck, and she pressed her lips together.

The muscles of her back tightened under his hand, despite the soft smile stretched across her lips.

He touched her cheek with the back of his fingers. "You want to get out, don't you?"

She released a hard breath and nodded vigorously. "I tried, but I can't. I just can't."

Matthias laughed and took her by the hand, helping her up. She stepped out of the water onto her dressing gown, protecting her feet from the grass.

"Here," he said, drying her toes with the soft fabric. "We'll wash this later. Let me help you with these things." He reached for her slippers and slid them on her feet.

Once her shoes were on, he stepped out of the pool and pulled his union suit on while she shook out her own garment and wrapped it around herself.

"I'm so proud of you." He gathered her into his arms and kissed her temple. "Thank you for trying it."

"You're welcome to enjoy your bath in the ground all you like, but I think I still prefer my bath water from a kettle." She sighed a long breath, clearly satisfied to be out of the water.

He closed his eyes and pressed his forehead against hers. "I don't deserve you," he whispered against her lips and kissed her tenderly.

He never thought he could be so happy. He certainly didn't have any right to it. But now he understood letting go of the anger he'd harbored against his father had set him free. Free to accept forgiveness for his own failures and free to love and to be loved in a way he'd never known before.

EPILOGUE

Elaine carved her knife through the pristine ball of sheep's butter on the table. It was a shame to disturb the smooth surface, but the creamy reward would be worth the sacrifice. She spread the butter over her roll and marveled that it wasn't burnt.

Anxiousness had plagued her for days that she would ruin Thanksgiving dinner by burning her offering of fresh rolls for the family meal. She'd watched her Franklin stove like a hawk on a mouse, counting down the minutes, and miraculously they hadn't burned.

The stove had been a late wedding gift from Gideon and Jo to christen Elaine and Matthias's new cabin they had just dried-in last month. She was grateful they had completed the small home before the crisp bite of winter chill had set in. Their shepherd's wagon cocoon wouldn't have been enough to keep them warm much longer.

She took a bite of the roll and was rewarded with a symphony of sweet, creamy butter and soft, salty bread.

Matthias nudged her arm, and a smile played on his lips. "I told you they would be good."

"I just can't believe they're edible at all." Elaine shook her head.

"They're superb," Mary encouraged from across the table. "I'm so proud of you."

Warmth glowed in Elaine's chest. Grace squealed from Jo's lap, echoing Elaine's excitement.

"It was a mighty fine meal." Jimmy leaned back in his chair. "You ladies outdid yourself. I'm ashamed you did all this work, and all us men did was show up in time for dinner."

"You spent all summer in the high country watching the sheep. I'd say that was contributing plenty to the meal." Jo pointed a lamb chop bone in Jimmy's direction. "We're so grateful we had you this summer. I don't know what we'd have done without you."

"Just think." Mary piped up. "By Christmas my Charlie will be here with us. The whole family—" She faltered, brushing away a tear.

Elaine blinked back moisture from her own eyes. She was so happy for Mary, and Charlie too. Though none of them knew what life would look like once they brought him home.

Mary rose from the table and piled up dishes to carry to the washbasin. Jimmy jumped up quickly to help.

"I can help here, Jimmy. Why don't you fetch some water to heat so we can wash up?" Elaine patted his arm.

Jimmy bobbed his head in gratitude and took the pail from the counter before heading outside. Mary's gaze lingered on the door where Jimmy had just exited.

Elaine gave her a reassuring smile. "He's such a help."

Mary nodded and chuckled, though concern wavered behind the laugh. "He doesn't know how to be anything else."

The women worked together to gather dishes and put food away in the cellar. As Elaine cleared the last dish from the table and brought it to the dish tub, a tingle of excitement trailed its way up her spine, and she shivered.

Tonight was the night. It had just about driven her to madness to keep the secret she had wrapped in brown paper and hidden under Mary's bed. She had meant to wait until Christmas, but the excitement had been too much for her to bear.

Jimmy filled a large pot with water on the stove. Dishes would wait until the water was warm. Everyone had gathered in the sitting room, sharing stories of the summer's adventures. This was the perfect time for her surprise.

She went to the bedroom and retrieved the package, cradling it gently against her chest. When she returned to the sitting room, anxious prickles danced under her skin. She tapped a finger against the brown paper and took a deep breath.

Standing tall, she cleared her throat and Matthias's curious blue eyes twinkled in the lamplight as he crossed the room to stand by her side.

"I want to say ... how very grateful I am for you all. I know I may not be the easiest person to live with." She darted a glance at her sister, and Jo blinked innocently before her lips quirked into a crooked smile. "But you all have helped me learn to live a full life, no matter how hard it can be."

Matthias pressed a steadying hand to her lower back, and she turned to him. "I'm grateful most of all for you." Her voice wavered, and she pressed her lips together as he kissed her forehead. "I bought this for you as a Christmas gift, but I simply can't wait to give it to you." She held it out to him. "Thank you, Matthias. Thank you for giving me your heart and teaching me that love and family are better than being safe."

Matthias took the package and weighed it in his hands. Then, realization flashed in his eyes. The paper crinkled in his hands, and he blinked rapidly.

"Open it already before you give me heart palpitations." Elaine's voice cracked.

He untied the twine and peeled back the layers to reveal the shiny, black leather case. He sniffed and tucked it against his chest, closing his eyes.

"Will you play for us? Please?" Elaine couldn't stop her tears now.

"I—I don't know. It's been so long," Matthias whispered.

"I even bought rosin and a pitch-pipe to go along with it." Elaine beamed proudly and put a gentle hand on his wrist.

Matthias played a tone on the pitch-pipe and plucked the correlating string on the violin, adjusting the knob until the sound matched.

After only a few moments of tuning the violin, Matthias raised the instrument to rest under his chin. Elaine sat next to Jo, who squeezed her hand.

Matthias took a slow breath and closed his eyes. The bow glided over the strings in a note that peeled a clear tone and silenced the room. Giddy bubbles of delight rippled through Elaine as Matthias moved his arm, and ribbons of joyful melody filled the cabin.

She would never forget this Thanksgiving. She had more to be grateful for than her heart could hold. This wasn't the life she had always wanted. It was so much more.

Continue the adventure of the Cross Family Saga in Redeeming the Shackled[1], coming in 2023.

FREE BONUS BOOKS!
Read Mary and Charlie's love story in Redeeming the Swindler[2] for free by subscribing to Jodi's newsletter.
(https://BookHip.com/BNACPVS)

Get a glimpse at the Cross Creek Ranch series (following Jo and Gideon's descendants) by reading the prequel, Morgan[3], for free also by subscribing to Jodi's newsletter.
(https://BookHip.com/FTPZJXR)

I hope you enjoyed Matthias and Elaine's story of love and redemption.
Would you take a quick minute to leave a review?
It can be as long or as short as you'd like—just a little something about why you liked the story.
(I only ask that you try not to give away any spoilers! I like to keep my readers in complete suspense.)
Thanks for being a reader!

---

1. *https://shop.jodibasye.com/products/redeeming-the-shackled-pre-order*

2. https://BookHip.com/BNACPVS

3. https://BookHip.com/KLFVZZW

Read more by Jodi Basye
<u>Cross Family Saga</u>
Redeeming the Swindler[4]
Redeeming the Prodigal[5]
<u>Redeeming the Outlaw</u>[6]
<u>Cross Creek Ranch</u>
Morgan[7]
Brant[8]
<u>Maddie Jo</u>[9]

———— ⌘ ————

Connect with Jodi
Instagram:
<u>Jodi Basye (@jodibasyeauthor) • Instagram photos and videos</u>[10]
Facebook:
<u>Jodi Basye - Author | Facebook</u>[11]
Goodreads:
<u>Jodi Basye (Author of Redeeming the Prodigal) | Goodreads</u>[12]
Website:
www.jodibasye.com[13]
Jodi's Cowboys & Coffee Online Book Club[14] *(Facebook)*

---

4. *https://dl.bookfunnel.com/bh3ewyytok*

5. *https://books2read.com/u/bwaX0y*

6. *https://books2read.com/u/mgjwNx*

7. *https://dl.bookfunnel.com/94611zqpab*

8. *https://books2read.com/u/mdd7XX*

9. *https://books2read.com/u/mBw7GM*

10. https://www.instagram.com/jodibasyeauthor/

11. https://www.facebook.com/profile.php?id=100068389219890

12. https://www.goodreads.com/author/show/21711469.Jodi_Basye

13. *http://www.jodibasye.com*

Acknowledgments

AS ALWAYS, A HUGE THANK you to Ranee and Kaylee at Sweetly Yours Press for helping me fine-tune a messy manuscript into what it is now. You take the heart of my story and help me polish it so the message can shine, even through my own imperfections as a writer.

To Sara Blackard, thank you for the initial inspiration for this book. Your story idea was the springboard that set this concept into motion. Your vision is a gift, and I am so grateful for your generosity, friendship, and support.

About the Author

Jodi Basye is an author of inspirational romances and family sagas that span the centuries. Her passion is writing authentic westerns full of heart-pounding adventure and happily ever after. She is also a born and bred country girl with a western heritage and a love for stories that stay true to her cowgirl boots and ranching roots. She's been writing all hours of the night since she was sixteen years old. Old habits die hard. Now, she is the blessed wife to a rugged mountain man, a homeschooling mama, and living her dream of writing books by her wood cook-stove in the wilds of Alaska.

Read more at https://www.jodibasye.com/.